5/26/89

To Dad

Happy Birthday!

Love,
Your Son!
John

THE RUB

OF THE

GREEN

THE RUB

OF THE

GREEN

William Hallberg

Doubleday

NEW YORK

Library of Congress Cataloging-in-Publication Data

Hallberg, William.
The rub of the green / William Hallberg.
p. cm.
I. Title.
PS3558.A3784R8   1988
813'.54—dc19   87-32035

ISBN 0-385-24568-8

BG

Published by Doubleday, a division of
Bantam Doubleday Dell Publishing Group, Inc.,
666 Fifth Avenue, New York, New York 10103

Doubleday and the portrayal of anchor with a dolphin
are trademarks of Doubleday, a division of
Bantam Doubleday Dell Publishing Group, Inc.

For my wife, Vicki,
and my children, Garth and Rachel

I would like to acknowledge the following people, all of whom, in one way or another, conspired to make this book possible: Barney Karpfinger, my agent, for his faith and kindness; Gordon Fulp, PGA Professional, for his technical expertise; my mom and dad for their love and forbearance; James Gordon Bennett for his unfailing friendship; Jack Nicklaus and Arnold Palmer for their inspiration; and David Gernert, my editor, for taking the plunge.

R is the rub that
   may lay us up dead . . .
Or leave us in sand . . .
   buried over the head.

  —A Golfer's Alphabet
    H. G. VANTASSEL SUTPHEN
    1898

One

At first golf was only a green shade protecting me from the gathering white heat of my mother's death.

Stan, my dad, wouldn't admit she was going to die and refused to make any plans for her cremation. Instead he spent the last weeks of her hospital stay rearranging all our furniture in ways that would please her when she came home. Of course, she never made it home. He wanted the sofa where she could see the boiling yellows and reds of the maples lining Fairway Avenue. The painting of fish and cheese and apples above the mantel gave way to an abstract print she'd bought at an auction in Toledo. Stan's obsession seized him and held him; finally it got to be more than I could take. One Saturday, while he was alphabetizing books in the den, I escaped to the garage, where the previous week's chaos had been brought, in a couple of furious mornings, to an almost military order. Thin rolls of chicken-wire fence, bicycles, a wicker birdcage, a tent, a bamboo rake—all of it hung neatly from spikes. In the corner above the hot-water heater was a corroded set of golf clubs, which I yanked from the wall and kicked so the contents of the plaid bag spilled across the floor. I picked up an iron, stood in the center of the garage and swung the club as hard as I could over and over again. The sole clicked against the cement, making a trail of sparks. My follow-through barely missed the bug light suspended from a wooden beam. Somehow by swinging the club I seemed to cool down by degrees until the process was organic and regular like the beating of my own heart. Uptake, downswing and follow-through together made a wide circle like an invisible lariat.

That night I slept without dreaming of my mother in her orange robe and blue slippers being fed into a furnace. I could never bear to think of her brown hair on fire. For once my dream found me standing in a patch of sunlight amidst tall pines, halfway up a narrow green fairway.

Stan and I walked to see Mom twice every day. I'd come home from school and we would walk past the country club, through the brown leaves scattered on the sidewalk. "Your mother's quite a gal," he'd say. The leaves came in and out of focus for me. There were thirty-six telephone poles between our house and the Wood County Hospital. After pole number twenty came a small shopping center where we stopped occasionally. Lucille's Cafe was flanked by a flower shop and DiBenedetto's Grocery. On the way to see Mom we'd have a cup of coffee (Lucille had convinced Stan I was plenty tall and that he didn't need to worry about my growth being stunted) and a cinnamon roll at the cafe, after which Stan would buy some cut flowers, hoping he could convince Mom they were from the garden. But an early frost had wiped ours out, and I doubt she ever really thought those red chrysanthemums were from the garden. She wanted him to think he was fooling her, though. Her voice was low, like a man's almost, and halting. She'd say, "Oh . . . aren't they nice," and touch the stems. Then Stan would hold a plastic mirror for her while I brushed her hair.

Coming home we'd buy some frozen dinners and Coca-Colas and potato chips at DiBenedetto's. Then we'd cut across the golf course, provided it wasn't too wet. Stan would put his hand on my shoulder. "You like the turkey pies or the beef? I like the beef. Your mother likes the beef, too . . ." The weather had turned the golf greens the color of straw and the flags were gone from the metal poles. Sometimes it was possible to hear the greenskeeper filing the mower blades or banging at a piece of machinery inside the aluminum quonset.

We always ate the pies from their tin containers. Then I'd go upstairs to do my homework while Stan sat motionless in front of the picture window and looked at the last golfers of the season in their fall windbreakers and heavy sweaters, pulling their carts in the last hour of gray light. Or maybe he was just watching a sluggish October fly crawl across the glass and the golfers were only blurred figures moving in the distance. From my desk in the bedroom I'd look out at the same scene. The golf course looked bleak to me. The golfers themselves seemed desperate, as if each shot were their last. It wasn't right that the swings were so choppy and clumsy or that the color was gone from the course. I'd go down to the garage and swing a golf club, imagining a white ball flying off toward a beautifully manicured green. I could feel banks of grass folding around me like a blanket. When the garage windows went black I'd go inside and watch television with Stan.

My mother finally died on the fourth of November; Stan allowed her body to be cremated and we scattered her ashes in the garden behind the house as she'd requested.

After her death I devoted even more of my time to golf. I used the snowless November to practice. Stan was working late at the insurance office, so I'd race home from school, take the clubs out from under my bed where they were hidden and sail out the front door to the golf course. A copy of Ben Hogan's *Power Golf* always went with me. The seventeenth tee was hidden from view of the clubhouse by an enormous barren forsythia hedge. In my cold hands I'd grip the club exactly as Ben Hogan suggested. I imitated all the diagrams of proper backswing, downswing and follow-through—hitting five or six shots off the tee, then retrieving the balls and hitting them again. Stan never returned home from work in time to discover what I was up to.

He had a bad reputation among the golfers who played the country club course across the street. Living on Fairway Avenue had poisoned him. Those windows that looked onto number seventeen had short life spans. Fortunately, Dexter's Glass Works had a stockpile of windowpanes precut to fit our house perfectly. They were quick at repairs and Stan was probably the best customer Dexter ever had, and no doubt the most irate. Almost every week a hacker would slice his drive off number seventeen tee. The ball would land on the asphalt road, make a grandiose leap and, as if guided by radar, home in on one of our windows. There was the crash, and a Maxfli or Titleist would dribble across the carpet, sometimes coming to rest at Stan's feet. When that happened his round face would contract slightly like a grape in the early stages of becoming a raisin and he'd lift the ball to his eyes. He'd glare at the thing, then storm to the front door for a face-off with the culprit.

Every now and then he'd find a golfer, spindly legs dangling from slack Bermuda shorts, preparing to ring the doorbell. Not to apologize or offer payment for the damages, but to recover the ball. On one occasion Stan found someone worming beneath our station wagon. The man was yanked by his ankles onto the grass, and when he stood up he was greeted with an awkward punch that caused a bloody lip. There was supposed to be a lawsuit, but it never came about.

Enough was enough, though. Soon the house had shutters, and the stockade fence that had merely framed the lawn before was closed in on the fourth side so that the front yard became a kind of fort. Stan bought a Doberman pinscher that answered to exactly nobody, him included. To feed the dog he'd hurl a shank bone across the yard, and when Fritz ran snarling after it Stan would slide a bowl of Ken-L-Ration through a crack in the door. It wasn't long before the Doberman was sold to an adult bookstore owner from Toledo, and replaced with an epileptic dachshund named Sally. The fence was plastered with signs, some of

4

them handmade, others orange and black from the K mart. BE-WARE OF DOG. TRESPASSERS WILL BE PROSECUTED. WE ARE ARMED. LOST BALLS ACCRUE TO PROPERTY OWNER.

Vandals retaliated by painting the words FUCK YOU in two-foot-high red letters on the cedar fence boards. Stan called Garlington's Lumber Company, and they sent a young man to replace these boards. The next morning a new message for Stan appeared: EAT A RUBBER.

Mom was sure Stan had gone overboard. She argued against his crusading until the day she went into the hospital. One morning about a week after her admittance he was sitting at the breakfast table. "What sort of people live on this planet?" he asked me.

"Apes," I said, my mouth brimming with shredded wheat.

"Apes mind their own business. They eat their bananas and bamboo and do their crapping off . . . well, way off somewhere. These punks do their crapping all over everything and everybody. When I was a kid playing golf things were different, I'll tell you *that*."

Even several months later it was pretty clear to me that he'd never favor my taking up the game of golf. But practicing filled long vacant stretches of time when I would otherwise think about Mom. I read Ben Hogan's book from cover to cover maybe twenty times that winter after she died, and practiced on the sly.

When spring came my friends from school rode their bicycles past our yard. I could see their baseball hats skimming above the fence. They were flocking to the golf course, which was open to them on weekdays after school let out. I wanted to join them but I didn't think there was much point in asking permission from a man who considered golf one of the great American diseases.

There was no choice but to pull myself out of bed when the sky had barely turned pink over the smokestacks of the Heinz 57 ketchup factory, visible from the bathroom window when I stood at the toilet. I'd hoist the golf bag over my shoulder, holding the cold steel clubs so they wouldn't rattle and wake Stan,

5

and sneak down the stairs. I prayed they wouldn't creak. Sally had to be given some bologna from the refrigerator so she wouldn't whine or have one of her seizures when I went outside.

The mornings were cool and ketchup-smelling. Listening for the first birds, I would cross the street and walk up number seventeen fairway, then eighteen until I got to the clubhouse, where the Miller High Life sign glowed through the curtains of the bar. From there the first tee was only twenty-five or thirty yards. But it was important to work at the practice green before heading to number one. When I putted, a little rooster tail was thrown up by the rotation of the ball on the wet grass. I'd take ten short putts, ten mediums and ten long putts. Then it was time to go to the first tee.

In the quiet of the morning I could hear Arnold Palmer breathing as he waited on the bench. The course spread out before me was Augusta without azaleas. Bobby Jones had seen to it that the greens were cut to a slick thirteenth of an inch. Ben Hogan, "the Hawk," watched me from where he stood off to the left. I hit my drive pretty well. It was a dark speck in the morning light.

I heard Arnie tell Ben, "The kid's going places."

"Great tempo," said the Hawk. "A human pendulum."

I followed through the wet grass after a new Titleist, my only one. Dew soaked my sneakers and water trickled out of the metal shoe eyelets. When I turned to look back at the clubhouse, my footsteps were emerald green in the gray moisture that had settled during the night.

Sometimes starlings would be gathered at number one green, eating ungerminated seed. My approach shot would land in their midst and they would scatter in a noisy swarming cloud, finally blackening the branches of the big Dutch elm.

If the club went back just right the weight of the steel clubhead would shift at the top of the swing, just like Ben Hogan said it should, and I was really throwing the blade down into the ball. The impact of clubface against the ball came just before the leading edge of the club cut through the soft turf and tossed it into the air. When everything happened just right I'd drop the club and applaud. The morning was so still that my clapping would echo inside the tunnel of elms that darkened the fairway.

I returned from the golf course one morning and found Stan already up. He looked startled when I came through the door with my clubs. "So you're a golfer, eh?" he asked me. His voice had a hard ring to it, and there was a queer pitch to his bushy eyebrows. The chair he pulled out from the table for me squeaked against the linoleum, causing Sally to bolt from the dinette into the living room.

By that time my clubs were on the floor by the hat rack. I scratched an imaginary itch behind my ear.

"Can't you say something?"

"I was afraid to tell you," I said, "the fence and all . . ."

"Well, there's no need to be a damned sneak. I just don't like this damned sneaking-around-behind-my-back business." He waited for my apology, and once it was given he motioned for me to come through the wide arch to where he sat. I slid onto the seat and looked at the spoon Stan was aiming like a sword at my nose. He had a habit of pointing with anything handy—a pipe stem, a pencil, a spoon—when he was feeling emphatic. It was an authoritative technique he'd picked up from selling insurance policies to unwilling buyers. I took a slice of Wonder bread from a loaf he'd brought to the table, folded the bread and took a bite from it. "You know what?" he asked, stirring his coffee. "I knew all along what you were up to."

I asked him how he knew, and he said that Sally would stand broadside to the front door after I left in the morning and would whack the wood with that noodle tail of hers until he got up to let her out. My footsteps in the grass of the front yard had given me away. "Teddy, I don't care if you play golf. God knows, I used to play a little bit myself. You could've told me. Just don't be one of those jerks out there with half their damn clothes off, cussing and throwing their clubs and pissing on trees." I saw him digging for the spoon again. He was on the brink of a big point. "If I ever catch you being anything but a gentleman, I'll put those clubs up in the attic with the exercycle and the stuffed wolverine, and that'll be *that*. Hear?"

So Stan was setting me free. From then on I gave up the early morning skulking, all that tiptoeing down the stairs. Spring and summer opened up like a broad fairway inviting endless golf shots. I emptied my savings account in favor of a junior country club membership.

Throughout the month of June I spent my days practicing. Shadows would swim back and forth across the grass as the sun drew from east to west. I mashed shot after shot through the mottled branches of a sycamore in the rough of number fifteen. Trees are theoretically ninety percent air, a supposition I put to the test. Twigs and leaves rained down when my ball clattered through or ricocheted off the wood. The tree was impenetrable, and the theory proved a vast exaggeration.

Only darkness or throbbing hunger could drive me from the golf course, and even then I'd pore over golf magazines and instruction books and biographies of the game's greats—Guldahl, Zaharias, Travis, Nelson, Ouimet, Demaret, Berg, Snead . . .

On weekends when the country club was overrun with duffers, I'd drag a bushel basket of golf balls, the spoils collected over the years from bushes and flower beds, to the side of the yard nearest the driveway. I overturned the basket, then placed it empty at the other side of the lawn. My game was to chip the balls from where they were spilled into the basket sixty feet away. When he could, Stan would sit on the porch with Sally and watch me. My club bit into the lawn and there would be divot after divot, but he didn't seem to care, because he had a burlap bag of seed in the garage. Anyway, a temptation would sweep over him every now and then, and he'd grab the club from me and take a few shots himself. Usually he'd blade the ball so it flew over the stockade fence into the neighbor's yard, or he'd scuff it so it would dribble only a few feet. When by some miracle one of the balls happened to rattle into the basket for him, he'd look at me and say, "See, it's a piece of cake if you do it right."

In the summertime, when dusk had chased the golfers off the course, Stan and I crossed the street and I practiced short irons, moving up from seven, to eight, to nine, to a full wedge . . . arcing the ball up into the pink sky where martins bored through the atmosphere in search of mosquitoes. The ball would be a black dot falling near a particular tree or sand trap. Stan lurked just out of range, a hulking silhouette, shagging balls for me. I imagined strange penalties for every bad shot—loss of thumb, wilted ear, a life of ugly pointed shoes like Stan wore when he raked leaves. I was working for perfection, that flawless contact of clubface on ball . . . drawing the iron back with the left hand to the top of the swing, pulling it down and through exactly as Hogan would, so the wrists broke into the ball, exploding it skyward and down, toward the dim figure who scurried back and forth through the twilight.

Without Mom, our days together became ritualized that way. We continued to have supper once every week at Lucille's. She made pies from the sour cherries of her private orchard, and often she insisted on Stan's taking a freshly baked one home with him. Every time we ate at the cafe, he'd leave a dollar bill under his plate for her. Lucille called my dad Stan, which seemed peculiar since even his clients called him Mr. Kendall, although he called *them* by their first names. Somehow she knew about my golf obsession. Maybe it was because my left hand was pale white from wearing a glove, or it might have been that she overheard Stan and me talking.

Jimmy, the club pro across the street, couldn't help noticing the hours I spent on the driving range or the putting green, deliberating over every swing as if the Masters were riding on it. He was an old shrunken Scotsman who'd more or less landed at the country club for what he called his "semi-retirement." Sometimes he'd come out of the clubhouse to watch me. He'd spit out his toothpick and grab the club away. "You've got to come to the inside with your uptake." His swing was slow and graceful. "Now let's see what you can do with it. Remember, inside. *Inside.*" I aimed at a pin oak three hundred yards out, took my swing and watched the ball land halfway there and roll another sixty yards across the baked ground.

He would ride an electric cart alongside me when I played, occasionally jumping out to kick a perfect drive into the rough or nudge the ball into a brown divot. "Now play the bleeding thing," he'd say. "You have to make the tough shots if you're to be any good." On the next hole he might roll the front tire of the cart over my ball, squashing it into the overwatered turf up by the green where the sprinklers had run overnight. "How're you going to play this shot, Teddy boy?"

Rather than ask Stan to pay for lessons, I accepted Jimmy's offer of a summer job at the clubhouse. That meant getting out of bed at four-thirty, feeding Sally, then trotting in the dark to work. My job was to clean up the locker room, mop the floors, wash the golf clubs belonging to the members and scrape accumulated grass and mud from golf shoes. Every now and then I would stand between rows of benches and swing a borrowed persimmon driver, grazing the rubber spike mat with the sole of the club. Or I would use someone's putter to roll golf balls from over by the urinals, through the corridor of lockers, down a concrete straightaway and into the shower, where the ball would orbit the drain grate seven or eight times before it spun dead center. There would be hysterics from the gallery, pats on the back from wonderful-smelling women . . . and I'd push aside the microphones in search of Stan or Jimmy.

At the first sign of light outside, I'd lock up and head for Lucille's. She liked me and let me drink all the coffee I wanted. "There's the golfer," she'd say when I came inside. Lucille ate a lot of her own food, and as a result she was too fat for her yellow uniform. I'd sit at the counter and she'd talk to me. "Your dad says you're getting to be a good player." She always leaned across the counter in such a way that I could see between her big breasts. There was a white hankie down there. I wolfed my breakfast so I could get back to the course before the early golfers. That way I could play unimpeded.

I always hit two drives at every hole. The first ball was in competition with the second one. The Titleist was Palmer, the Maxfli was Nicklaus. I always rooted for Palmer to win, through I tried my hardest on every shot. Somehow Nicklaus won.

When the fairways were overrun with bright pants and pastel shirts, I practiced on the putting green, making targets of tees and matchsticks. In the afternoons, as usual, I headed for the driving range for my hour's worth of instruction. Often Jimmy chewed me out for "cupping my wrist" on the backswing, or "picking up the club" on the takeaway instead of drawing it smoothly back. He was fond of yelling or throwing grass in exasperation. But I didn't mind.

"How's that?" I'd ask after bouncing a shot off the two-hundred-yard marker.

"It'll do for now," he would say. "You've still got a lot to learn, Teddy boy."

One evening in late June when I was washing up the supper dishes, Stan called me out into the living room and told me to sit down on the couch. "Wait right there," he said after I'd settled onto a cushion. He went to the closet and fished around behind some of Mom's coats and winter dresses until he found what he was looking for. It was a hickory-shafted putter with a brass blade. "This is from Lucille," he said. "Before her husband passed away it was his. She wanted me to give it to you. What do you think? Is it any good?"

The putter had a new leather grip, and when I examined the sole of the brass blade I saw the word "Schenectady" imprinted there. I'd read about Jerome Travers using such a putter throughout his golfing career at the turn of the century. He'd won the U.S. Open at Baltusrol with one just like it. My fingers trailed over the tiny nicks and dents. "It's a beautiful putter," I said. "Probably it's seventy or eighty years old." I imagined

Travis rolling a gutta-percha ball over severely undulating greens.

Through the front window I could see that Jimmy had already taken in the rental carts. He'd closed up and gone home for the day. Still, I carried the putter across the street and trotted through the waning light to number seventeen green, where I practiced until it was too dark to see.

Jimmy weighed the putter in his hands when I showed it to him the next day. "It's very valuable," he said. "I wouldn't use it except when you can be sure it won't be lost or stolen."

"Don't worry," I said.

I had the putter with me when I pushed into Lucille's cafe that morning. She was serving old Mr. Farliss another cup of coffee. "Well, I see Stan gave you my present," she said.

"It's a great gift, Lucille," I said, and thanked her for it.

"I'm glad for someone to have it. It's been in my attic for fifteen years, ever since Ernie died, God rest his loving soul."

"Travers won the U.S. Open with a putter like this," I said, swiping at an invisible golf ball on the cork floor.

"Is that so," she replied. Her eyebrows floated up under her bleached-blond bangs.

"He was one of the greatest players of all time," I said.

"Is that so," she said again, wiping the counter with a gray rag, the fat of her arm bouncing as she did so. She could whistle like a bird when she felt like it, and this was apparently one of those times. She quit her whistling and looked at me in a friendly way. "I'm happy that you like that old club so much."

During the following week I nearly wore out the putting green. Every putt was to win the Open. Sportscasters were buzzing about the thirteen-year-old *phe*nom who had taken the pro tour by storm.

On the Fourth of July the country club always held its bingo bango bongo tournament, and then at dusk the fire department shot off fireworks. Club members began drinking beer in the morning and didn't stop until nightfall. They littered the fairways with Budweiser cans. Electric carts rolled off bridges into water hazards. Naturally, Stan wouldn't allow me on the course while the festivities were taking place, but from my window I could see the red, white and blue pennants and the long tables set up in front of the pro shop.

Late that afternoon, Lucille, who had closed up her cafe for the holiday, drove her pickup truck into our driveway. I saw Stan go out to meet her. She looked like a big yellow flounder from my high vantage point. Lucille gave Stan a bucket of sour cherries from her orchard. He carried the bucket to our front porch and set it on the top step. They chatted for a long time after that. When she finally got back inside the truck, I watched them laugh over some joke Stan had made. It was probably an insurance man's joke—maybe the one about the divorcée who wanted to insure her pet monkey. That was one of his favorites. Lucille's hefty arm came out of the rolled-down window and touched Stan on the cheek.

I lay on my bed, found a green page inside a golf magazine and pushed my face against it. Sporadic firecracker explosions sounded in the distance. I remembered my mother sitting on the front-porch steps, a few weeks before the stockade fence went up, the lap of her skirt overflowing with green beans from the garden, her snapping them into pieces which she dropped into a metal pail like the one Lucille had delivered to Stan.

When Stan knocked on the door of my room I sat up on the bed and told him to come in. "Lucille's coming with us to the fireworks tonight," he said. "How does that sound?"

I told him it was fine with me if that's what he wanted. He shut the door, and I listened to his footsteps on the stairs.

That night at about eight o'clock Lucille showed up at the front door with a grocery bag, grease-spotted from the popcorn inside. I showed her into the living room and said that Stan would be down in a second. He was still upstairs smoothing his unruly eyebrows with candle wax, or at least that's what I thought.

"Well," said Lucille, groaning into a wing chair my mom had

reupholstered a few months before she got sick. "How's that putter working out?"

"Fine," I said, and excused myself to see about Stan. He was in his bedroom, sliding a belt through the loops of his trousers.

"All set," he said. He sucked in his belly and checked himself in the mirror one last time before leading the way down to the living room. He handed Lucille a big army blanket from the hall closet. She smelled like cherries. Stan administered one of Sally's anti-seizure tablets, stroking the dog's throat so she would swallow it. "She's terrified of loud noises," he explained. Then the three of us went outside. We crossed the street, found a good spot halfway up number eighteen and spread out the blanket. Lucille and Stan sat there smiling and waving at everybody.

"Don't you want some popcorn?" Lucille asked, tilting the grocery bag toward me.

I told her I didn't want any, and of course Stan never ate popcorn because the husks bothered his dentures. While Stan chatted about humidity and mortality tables, she ate every kernel. I watched kids wave sparklers in the gathering darkness.

When the light was gone from the sky the fireworks began with an explosion of red and green on the horizon. Lucille howled with delight after every burst, as if she were witnessing all this for the first time. She patted Stan's knee. "Aren't they *beautiful?*" she'd say, and Stan would nod his agreement.

I coaxed Sally into bed with me after Lucille had gone home and Stan had locked up the house. I heard him humming across the hallway. It was impossible for me to sleep.

Instead of going to work at the clubhouse when the alarm went off, I took the putter from my bag and plodded down the stairs.

The eastern sky was tinged with color as I crossed the street and walked through the damp grass of number seventeen. The golf course was littered with the wreckage from the day before —paper bags, beer cans, unexploded firecrackers, candy wrappers. That the Boy Scouts would arrive shortly to clean up the mess was no consolation to me. The fairways seemed corrupt and strange as I made my way toward the pond situated deep inside the back nine. I could see Stan's window, still dark, when I paused to look back. I wondered what he was dreaming about.

I walked farther into the golf course, across number eleven fairway to the edge of the pond, which was secluded by trees from the street, where only occasional headlights gleamed through the branches. The weak morning sun threw the distant swales of the doglegged water hole into relief. I'd played number eleven more times that I could count. I knew every roll from every part of that green.

I stood at the rocky eastern edge of the pond for a few minutes. Finally, without really thinking much about it, I threw the Schenectady putter out into the mist hovering over the water.

I didn't feel much like going to work that morning. I performed my various clubhouse chores in a complete perfunctory way, wrote Jimmy a note that said, "Thanks for everything but I have to quit," placed the note and my key on the counter and headed home.

Stan would be at his insurance office until late afternoon. So I took my bicycle from the garage and rode up to the Anthony Wayne Pike—something Stan had forbidden me to do—and pedaled west. Lucille's orchard was five miles outside of town. I hadn't exactly decided what I wanted to do once I got there.

When her two-story white house was in sight, I got off my bike and walked it the rest of the way. Lucille's yard was surrounded by cherry trees whose branches drooped under the weight of the fruit. I lay my Schwinn Corvette in a patch of long grass, longer than any rough at the country club, and sat down.

The house was much larger than ours. Across the road were grazing cows and black oil derricks whose heads bobbed up and down like enormous mechanical birds. The farmland was too rocky and flat for a golf course, and the black ugliness of the oil pumps was a blight, and of course there were no sources of water for the creation of ponds and creeks, and except for the cherry trees the land was razed clean by the farmers and oil drillers. I imagined living in the farmhouse, eating Lucille's food, feeding chickens so we could eat them. I pulled myself up onto one of the gnarled tree branches and stayed there for a long time. What would happen to Mom's ashes in our garden? Would we leave them behind for the new tenants of our house on Fairway Avenue?

I picked ripe cherries and lobbed them against the side of Lucille's house, leaving stains that looked like blood.

Dark clouds were huddling over the clothesline behind Lucille's, so I decided to ride back home. Wind was coming from the east, which always meant rain. I pedaled hard for over an hour before the first heavy drops plummeted down on me, stinging my face. Cars splashed past me in both directions, honked their horns and flicked their lights on and off.

The station wagon was in front of the garage when I turned onto the concrete driveway. Sally was standing in the wing chair at the picture window, her black nose pressed against the glass. Her breath made fog circles that appeared and disappeared.

As quietly as I could I opened the front door and went inside, leaving my wet shoes in the entryway. There was no sign of Stan. I presumed he was in the kitchen fixing hamburgers, except that I couldn't smell them cooking if he was. I tiptoed up the stairs, past Stan's bedroom. He was sitting at the foot of his bed, staring across the room toward his bureau, where there was a framed picture of Mom. "Where in the hell have you been?" he asked when he noticed me.

"I went for a bike ride," I said. I realized that my T-shirt was cherry-stained.

"You might have left some message to that effect," he said.

I told him I was sorry, and he said I'd better get cleaned up.

I sat in a tub of hot water for a long time, until Stan rapped on the bathroom door. I told him to come in.

He sat down on the needlepoint toilet-seat cover, grabbed the plunger from beside the sink and bounced the rubber end on the toe of his shoe for a while. "You could have been a little nicer to

Lucille last night," he said. "She's awfully fond of you and it hurt her that you were so . . ." Stan didn't finish the sentence. He carefully put the plunger in the niche between the toilet and the vanity. "Anyway, you might want to give the matter some thought." He got up and walked out of the bathroom.

We ate our beans and hamburgers in silence. I fed Sally chunks of meat under the table. When we were preparing to gather dishes from the table, Stan picked up a butter knife and peered at his reflection in the stainless-steel blade. "You're worried about something, aren't you?"

"I don't know," I said.

"Well, I know . . . and I can tell you what it is."

But I wouldn't let him say. Before he could tell me I ran up the stairs to my room, dropped onto my bed and stared at the ceiling. After a while I heard the phone ringing. Stan, who had been watching a ball game on the TV, yelled up that it was Jimmy.

I picked up the receiver of the kitchen phone and held it against my ear. "I tore up that note of yours, Teddy boy," the voice said. "You can't quit without two weeks' notice. I'm expecting you to be at work by five o'clock in the morning."

Before I could get back up to my room, Stan had filled the only avenue of escape, which was the arched kitchen doorway. When I tried to push by he grabbed my shirt sleeve. I yanked free from his grasp, ripping my shirt in the process, but he pushed me against the refrigerator and held me there. His voice was shaking when he spoke. "Listen, Teddy. You have everything upside down. I'm not leaving this house, not with your mother's remains in the flower garden. And Lucille's not giving up her farm either. Anything else you can figure out for yourself." He took his hand from my chest and let me go. My eyes were wet and my jaws ached.

It was long after the last house lights had been turned off when I finally fell into a dark sleep. There were dreams, probably deep symbolic ones, but my mind was clean when I woke up.

17

I didn't go to work first thing that morning. I walked out the front door toward the golf course and the distant pond. With me I had my swimming mask and a yellow towel. The air felt cool in my lungs. I found a wrinkled golf glove in the rough of number five. The little finger of the glove had been sheared off by the big four-reel mower.

At the western edge of the pond the water was shallow, with cattails spiking through the surface. I took off my clothes on the tee at number eleven and waded in. Mud oozed between my toes. I secured the mask, then glided headfirst into the water, where I came face to face with minnows, swam through them, then surfaced near the middle of the pond. I took a deep breath so I could dive through the barely illuminated water to the murky bottom. Within a few minutes I'd located several dozen golf balls duffed into the drink by some of the club's worst golfers. However, the Schenectady putter was bound to be several yards farther out, in deeper water. So I swam toward a dark, bowl-shaped hollow at the middle of the pond, fearful of snapping turtles and other unknown dangers. In the dim light I saw bluegills schooled around an old corroded refrigerator, squat on the mud bottom like a sunken frigate. For fifteen minutes I searched the murk for the Schenectady, but there wasn't much hope of finding it among the tires and bottles. I resurfaced one more time, swam a few yards farther out and went down again. I'd just about used up my lungful of air when I saw it, its shaft vertical like a reed. Although my chest was near bursting, I clutched the putter and swam toward the pale expanse of light above me.

I sidestroked to the shallows and climbed up the bank, where I dried off. Without bothering to put my clothes on, I grabbed an immaculate Titleist from the pocket of my jeans and walked toward number fourteen green. On the way I clipped the heads off some stagweeds with my putter.

I placed the ball at the fringe of the green, leaving myself a difficult fifty-footer to win the Open. I analyzed the putting surface to detect its personality. The ball would travel over a mound, through a shallow valley and gradually down. I rubbed my hand over the grass, feeling its texture in the morning dampness.

Anchoring my bare feet firmly, I stroked the ball. I could read the print as my putt moved with the rise and fall of the green. It followed the path I'd planned for it, accelerating on the downslope of a small hillock, taking a harsh inward break, gathering momentum to climb up the opposing rise, in the middle of which was the cup.

As the ball painted its dark green trail on the dew-covered putting surface, the gallery came to life. Their voices formed a chorus. "Get going." "Get legs, baby." "Go." "Roll." The putt had been struck perfectly. The line was absolutely correct, and the speed was just right. The ball was destined to fall for me, dead center.

TWO

Dear Stan,

    I'm sitting on my cot in this urine-colored cell, listening to the calliope of the Mississippi Queen *moored on the other side of the river. The wind brings in smells from New Orleans: fish, beer exhaust from the Jax brewery, exhaust from the barges. On the ceiling directly overhead is a handsome chestnut-colored roach the size of my big toe, and for the last half hour or so he's crawled back and forth between two Freudian water stains. Named him Bubba after Bubba LeDoux, my cellmate. This guy actually tried to steal a mobile home, a feat worthy of the* Guinness Book of Records. *His case is still pending, but he can't make bail.*

    Sorry, Stan, no energy for transition from above paragraph. I can barely push the pen across this page. Not that I've gone totally down the dumper. But to tell you the truth, I haven't been sleeping very well lately. I rack out on this wicked cot with no pillow and Bubba over there sawing hardwood logs with a dull blade. Got a nice pair of gray bags under my eyes. Could easily be mistaken for a creature from Village of the Damned. *Anyway, I'm writing mostly to let you know I'm okay and to say I miss you. Give my regards to Sally the wiener dog. Snap. Snap.*

Take a guess who came to see me yesterday. Janice the contrite. Every other word was "sorry." She was sorry she couldn't testify in my behalf, sorry I have to spend time in the slammer . . . &c. You ought to have seen her. Fingers all tobacco-stained. Bags (worse than mine) under her eyes. Blouse buttoned so crookedly I could see she wasn't wearing a bra. She might have cut her own hair the way it looked. I told her I forgave her, that I understood her predicament. Blood is thicker than scotch on the rocks. Stand by your man, and all that.

Trayn was something to see during the trial. He was beautiful. Wrapped in gauze and plaster up to his gill slits, looking for all the world like a pharmaceutical salesman's dummy. An extra from The Mummy's Curse. *Unfortunately, it made for an effective show. The judge was moved to tears. Janice sat a couple of rows back of Trayn, and she was sobbing into a Kleenex. Pretty woeful scenario.*

I pleaded guilty to a reduced charge: assault with intent to do serious hurt to a wife-beating turd bucket. According to my attorney, the resplendent Hoot Boudreau, things could have been much worse. Attempted murder, for instance. Ted Kendall the assassin. Hoot plea-bargained. I got 1st degree Vehicular Assault. I have to accept that as a fair verdict, really. I don't know what I intended to do on that night. My brain was swimming with every emotion ever invented. And I was a little drunk, too.

The judge never heard the whole story. She only heard how Ted Kendall deliberately and with malice aforethought tried to maim and mangle the plaintiff by "running him down" in the parking lot of an economy motel at two o'clock in the morning, and how yours truly succeeded in inflicting injuries sufficient to jeopardize a promising career on the professional golf circuit.

Anyway, she finally retired to her chambers, where I suppose she applied another coat of lipstick, maybe sprayed her hair again, stared at a picture of her kids, ate a Cert, then came back to the courtroom. She allowed that since I was a first offender, and that because there was a stack of character references, and that since there were mitigating circumstances up the wazoo, she would go easy on me. She said, "Step forward, young man." I obeyed. She was a fairly attractive middle-aged woman with an ample bosom beneath her judicial robe. You would have liked her, Stan. "You have committed a very serious crime, as you are obviously aware. The fact is, Mr. Kendall, that by all rights you could spend a very long time in prison for what you have done. However, I doubt you would be served by prolonged incarceration, nor would anyone else." (Stan, I'm making some of this up, but it's close.) "Well, as you may know, there's presently a court-ordered freeze on the inmate population of the state of Louisiana, so in accordance with our temporary reciprocity with the state of Mississippi, I am sentencing you to two years at Moss Point Minimum Security Prison, of which sentence you must serve a minimum of thirteen months, and two years' probation thereafter. I hope that during your imprisonment you will evaluate your behavior, and change it! Bailiff! Remand the prisoner to somebody or other."

I was in a sort of stupor through most of the sentencing. All the time I was watching translucent amoebas squirm beneath a bank of fluorescent lights. Then the bailiff latched on to my elbow. As he was leading me away, I rattled my handcuffs at Trayn and said "Boo!" He almost jumped out of his plaster cast. I wanted him to know that if I ever got word of his manhandling Janice again I'd eat the bars off my window and come after him.

So, here I am in the beautiful Plaquemines Parish House of Detention. In a day or two I'm to be transferred to Moss Point, down in the nether region of the netherest state in the U.S. of A. Prevailing sentiment is that there are worse places to be; still, I'm pretty scared, Stan. I don't have any idea of what to expect, and I doubt my golf game will be improved by the layoff.

It's a blessing your phlebitis kept you in the hospital during the trial. I know you would have been here if you hadn't been under the weather. I don't want you to worry about me. I'll be fine. In thirteen months (I'll be good) you'll see me out on the links, duck-hooking again.

I've told you just about all I can for today. I'll keep in touch with you on a weekly basis, and probably more often than that. I've already decided on something to fill my time in the prison: it's a pretty egocentric project, I guess. Call it taking stock or something like that. Maybe I'll let you read it in a few years.

Anyway, in a few months you can come down for a visit, okay? When you're better. But until then, would you do me one big favor? Send me some old photographs of you and Mom and even Sally if you've got some. I'm a lonely mother, that's for sure. And make me a cake with a hacksaw in it, too, would you?

The wind has just shifted, Stan. I can smell diesel exhaust from the big semis that come in and out of the warehouse district in which the PPHD is located. Bubba LaRoach has disappeared out the window. The other Bubba is still snoring to beat hell.

Take good care of yourself. Hug Lucille and pet Sally.

Your son the convict

Three

It puzzled me that so many great golfers emerged from the Midwest, where golf is a seasonal thing like cornhusking or spitting watermelon seeds.

I was standing next to Jimmy in the clubhouse on the first Saturday in March. "It's been a long damned winter, hasn't it, Teddy boy?" he said. We were watching the last dirty crests of snow melt on the fairways. Mudley's beagle was out there taking a crap by the number one tee. We always talked golf for an hour or two after I'd mopped the floor in the country club bar and scrubbed the gang shower in the men's locker room. He told me that the liquid inside a golf ball was latex, and he could cite the rule that came into play if Mudley's beagle stole your ball from the middle of the fairway.

There was a picture of Jimmy, flanked by Harry Vardon and Walter Travis, up on the wall behind the display case. In the background of the photo was a putting green ringed with spectators, among them Katherine, who at the moment the camera shutter clicked didn't know that in a few minutes this stranger would buy her tea at the Cormorant Tavern overlooking the Royal Troon golf club.

After their wedding he went to war. A piece of shrapnel shaped like a small boomerang severed the triceps of his left arm, and that was the end of his career as a soldier and as a golfer. So, despite having finished second in the British Amateur at the age of nineteen, and leading the British Open at Troon for two days a year later, he was done with competition at the age of twenty-three. In 1925, he and Katherine said goodbye to Scotland and headed for America on board the HMS *Windermere*.

Jimmy seemed taller in that black-and-white photograph than he was standing next to me at the big plate-glass window behind the display counter.

Between those early spring snowfalls there would be occasional thaws, revealing wide yellow swatches of dormant grass. And this was one of those blue-skied days when I ached to get out on the course for a quick round of golf, but fearing the wrath of Ernsthausen, the Nazi greenskeeper, I could only hope this one sunny day would be followed by another until the fairways dried sufficiently for the course to open.

But on Sunday morning it was snowing again, slowly at first, then heavily until the benches and ball washers and forsythia bushes were cocooned in white. "I hate Ohio. I hate damned snow," I said, watching big wet flakes swirl against my bedroom window. When Sally jumped against me with her paws I pushed her down, then felt bad and patted her head. I put on my jeans and went down to the garage, where an old canvas wrestling mat was hanging on the cinder-block wall. I'd salvaged the mat from a trash bin behind the junior high school, and I dragged the thing home one foot at a time. On its dirty belly I'd painted a red bull's-eye. For an hour I stood in the garage, slugging practice shots at that target until the pile was gone from my green indoor/outdoor carpet fairway and cotton batting coughed out from the buttoned tufts of the mat.

I went to school on Monday, sat at my abysmal desk in Mr.

Dugan's earth science class and watched melting snow drip from the roof onto the bushes outside. I did a few isometric exercises to occupy myself. I tried to lift the desk from where it was anchored by thick bolts to the floor, and succeeded only in ripping loose an oak slat just as he was demonstrating Bernoulli's Principle. He spilled half a quart of red water onto the lab table. He gave me a don't-do-that-again look, so I pulled a tennis ball from my book bag and squeezed it until my hand was a sore claw.

I rode the bus home, with the sun floating above a bank of clouds gathered on the western horizon.

As soon as I'd shut the front door behind me, I hustled into the garage. All winter I'd been working on my strength. Stan thought his boy had gone narcissistic and said so. He caught me once or twice flexing in front of the mirror, so I started locking the bathroom door.

Anyway, I had an exercise ritual designed to transform my pencil arms and twig legs into industrial-strength tensile steel. I had the process memorized.

1. Take the five-foot length of hemp rope (tied to a cement block on one end and a sawed-off broom handle on the other). With palms facing up, grasp the broom handle at either end. Reel cement block up to eye level, 25 times.
2. Turn palms over and repeat the process, 25 times.
3. Grind out 50 push-ups and 50 sit-ups.
4. Proceed to where the one-inch-thick rope hangs down from a crossbeam. Grasp the rope and haul yourself hand over hand to the top, 10 times.
5. Put a 50-pound bag of manure on each shoulder. Perform 50 hip swivels until your trunk is limber enough to rotate 360 degrees like an owl.

That afternoon was the beginning of an unbroken string of crisp sunny days. On Friday of that week, Manny Robeski summoned the golf team to room 214 immediately after the last bell. He erased the diagram of the human reproductive cycle from the blackboard and wrote the words GOLFER = GENTLEMAN in yellow chalk. "Gentlemen," he said. "Meet you at the country club in half an hour."

Manny taught Latin and Spanish, but the principal gave him a few hundred extra dollars to inhabit the putting green for a couple of hours after school while a dozen adolescents knocked their way around the course. He wasn't much bigger than me, and he knew almost nothing about golf. However, he had a reasonably good nose for talent and a station wagon and a very pretty pregnant wife. Sometimes Peggy, a soft little mound of belly barely pushing out the front of her jumper, would bring a shoe box filled with brownies out to practice, and we'd Hoover them down to the last molecule. We wondered why Manny looked so underfed. "Okay, boys," he would say, "wipe the crumbs off your faces and hit the first tee." Clipboard in hand, he would sit next to Peggy on the green bench and read the names of the threesomes that were to play together on that particular day. She was always plucking grass blades from his trousers or fiddling with his hair.

Peggy was there for the first practice, right next to Manny on the bench, watching groups tee off. Nobody wanted to hit a bad drive in front of her, but there was a tendency on the part of me and everybody else to impress her with our masculinity. I watched Huey Blaine completely whiff one right in front of her. "It's okay, Huey," she said. "I still love you."

And when a month later she had a miscarriage, I sat in my bedroom for two days, turning pages of magazines or bouncing a tennis ball off my wall. The death of Peggy's baby and my mother's death flowed together and grew in that corner of my mind where I stored my grief.

Stan knew I was feeling bad, so he went over to the clubhouse and spent three hundred dollars on a new set of Hogan woods and irons (Jimmy's suggestion). He brought them up the stairs in their cardboard boxes and knocked on my door. "I've got something for you," he said. He stood at the threshold, framed by the white doorjamb, smiling. "Sally chewed on the corner of one of the boxes, but she didn't hurt the clubs."

"Come here, dog," I said. Sally jumped up next to me, leaking a little trail of pee on the bedspread.

Manny took that week off to be with Peggy, during which time Stan supervised the practices. Mostly he sat in front of the clubhouse with Manny's scorebook in his lap. In high school golf, you can shoot a 95 and outscore the opponent who shoots an 80. This can happen if you make lots of birdies and triple bogeys while your opponent is cruising along with pars and bogeys. Scoring goes like this: 1 point for the match play winner of the front side; 1 point for match play on the back nine; 1 more for match play overall; and 1 point for medal play overall. The scorecard for the front nine might look like this:

Me	3	6	4	8	3	8	3	7	3
Other guy	4	3	5	4	4	5	4	4	4

My consistent opponent shoots 37 while I shoot 45. I beat him 5 holes to 4, so he goes out to the parking lot and bites the tires off his father's car. To prepare us for this queer scoring system, Manny worked out an ingenious scheme of his own to help him figure who would comprise the top six players. We always played nine holes after school. He awarded 2 points for each birdie we made, 1 point for a par, and 1/2 point for a bogey. After two weeks he added up our total points and divided by the number of rounds we played. That was a major factor in deciding who would make the playing squad and who wouldn't. The top eight point getters would compete on the Saturday before the first match to decide the six golfers who played on the team.

Manny came back on the Friday before the play-off, looking frail and bedraggled. His clothes hung on him like they belonged to somebody about the size of Stan.

After practice he called us together out in the parking lot, where his Country Squire was parked under a big oak tree. He sat on the hood, pulled his knees up under his chin and gazed off toward a foursome hiking up number eighteen. His eyes looked tired and his tie was crooked. "I want to thank you guys for the flowers. That meant a lot to Peggy, it really did." It occurred to me that it was Stan who had sent the flowers. I'd seen them in the back seat of our car, but thought they must have been for Lucille. "Gentlemen, I want everybody here at eight o'clock sharp tomorrow morning. Eight of you will be playing for spots on the team. The rest of you will be playing to improve your games." He read a list of names, including mine. He didn't read them in any particular order, so I didn't know exactly where I stood, not that it mattered.

Since I was only a freshman, Manny didn't know quite what to expect from me. We had two seniors, Spengle Wilson and Bobby Summiteer, who were the top players. The coach was just trying to find a respectable quartet to back them up. He probably thought I might make fifth or sixth man if I was lucky.

I slept maybe two hours on Friday night. I spent the rest of the time snaking in imaginary thirty-foot putts, popping nine irons within inches of the cup, blasting high arcing drives into the center of the fairway. At six in the morning I was doing sit-ups in my bedroom, my feet wedged under the footboard of my bed, when I heard Stan flush the toilet across the hall. I got my clothes and went downstairs to let Sally out and make some cereal. I knew I'd need some fuel for the morning's round of golf.

Usually Stan lounged around in his pajamas and robe until about noon on weekends, but on that morning he was wearing an orange Ban-Lon shirt and khaki pants. I didn't have the heart to tell my gallery of one to stay home. "How you feeling, Teddy?" he asked. "Ready to bust par?"

"Sure," I said. "I'll put on a real show for you." I watched him disappear from the dinette into the hallway. When he returned he was loading a film cartridge into a Kodak Instamatic.

"For posterity," he said.

Before we even crossed the street he'd taken three snapshots. In one I was to freeze at the top of my backswing. In another I was to pretend I was putting a golf ball across the lawn. He made me take all the clubs out of the bag for the third picture. I had to arrange them in ascending order on either side of me while Sally and I sat on the front porch. I grinned like a possum for that one. "Now, will you leave the camera here?"

"Nonsense," he said. I was trying to melt a glacier with a kitchen match.

The temperature was forty-five degrees when we walked across the street a half hour before tee-off time. We went to the driving range and Stan shagged balls for me until a few minutes before eight, when we moseyed over to the practice green, where Manny and the rest of the team were gathered. Peggy was there, too, and I was glad to see her. She waved to me, and I waved back. She had her hair in a ponytail, which made her look about fifteen. "Take ten minutes or so on the putting green," Manny said, "and then get your hindquarters over to number one tee."

I dropped three Wilson Staff golf balls on the fringe of the putting surface. My eyes were watering from the cold, and my hands looked blue. But when I stroked the first ball, it curled nicely toward its target and fell in. The sound of a new golf ball clattering inside the hole is the most beautiful sound imaginable. When the second putt rolled perfectly into the cup, I felt something almost mystical take hold of me. I had total control of each putt I made. If the ball didn't go in, it was because I didn't want it to. My eyes stopped watering, and my hands felt warm and sensitive to the touch of the club.

Jimmy came out of the clubhouse to watch us tee off. He seemed to know from the look on my face that I was going to do well. Maybe he'd had the same euphoric feeling when he was a kid, that loose-jointed, goofy, king-of-the-mountain feeling . . .

It was early enough in the year and frigid enough so that there was no one on the course but the high school team. I was to play with Spengle Wilson and Louie MacBeth, the asthmatic. "Remember, Teddy boy, stay inside your game." I didn't know

30

if that was Jimmy talking to me or whether it was the echo of something he'd told me a million times before. But I looked over at him and nodded, almost fearful that the up-and-down motion of my head might dislodge me from the mystical plateau where I'd been roosting for the last fifteen minutes.

Stan told me to "go get 'em" after I'd won the coin toss and teed up my ball. I imagined my golf swing, a perfect arc, tilted at just the right angle. I thought of Beethoven's Fifth, the opening four notes, pum-pum-pum-PUMMM! That was the rhythm Jimmy had taught me. Take the club up, pum-pum-pum . . . fluid like the shoulders are oiled ball bearings . . . then PUMMM! down into and through the ball so its liquid center goes flat as a tiddlywink. Kiss your right shoulder on the follow-through. I drew the club back along that invisible track until my chin touched my shirt sleeve. I pulled the clubhead down through that same plane until its screwheads met the ball and sent it rocketing dead center down the fairway. "Awesome," Stan said behind me. The drive was not awesome, but it was well past the sand trip two hundred ten yards out. An excellent drive. Once I'd hit it, I raced to a urinal in the clubhouse, where I challenged known records for duration and velocity. When I returned, MacBeth was out about one fifty, but in the rough, and Wilson was in the trap. Stan helped me get the strap of my golf bag over my shoulder, and I jogged down the center of the fairway after my ball.

MacBeth's breath came out of his nostrils like quick bursts of smoke—he was still nervous. He'd made a mess of his first drive, and he was buried in the wet winter grass that hadn't been mowed since October. He shanked his four iron into the City Park, out of bounds, then looked over at me like there might be something I could do. I shrugged and yelled for him to hang in there. He dinked his next shot onto the fairway and trudged after it. He was still twenty yards short of where my ball lay. Wilson hit a nice clean shot out of the sand but came up forty yards short of the green. MacBeth's face was bright red as he stood over his ball, a four iron death-gripped in his meaty hands.

He took a fierce swipe at the ball, and once again shanked it out of bounds. He calmly picked up his plaid golf bag and walked back toward the clubhouse. I think he was crying. Manny didn't even try to turn him around. Louis stomped past the bench en route to his dad's Chrysler Newport.

I parred the first hole and Wilson bogeyed it. I bogeyed number two, three-putting from only twenty feet, but parred the next several holes. On number seven, a mean doglegged par four, I snap-hooked my drive into a maple and dropped straight down into a tangle of roots at the base of the tree. The only way I could advance the ball was to bring the blade of the wedge down and into the equator of the ball, imparting a trajectory so low it could dodge the overhanging limbs. If I didn't hit it exactly right, it might go nowhere, or it might go backward, or it might kick up and nail me in the chops. Stan had that facial expression reserved for when he lost a sale. My testicles started to hurt, and my hands were shaking as I waggled the club. I did not hit the ball perfectly. In fact, it clipped a limb on its way out of danger but took a lucky hop through the rough and back onto the fairway. I drilled my next shot, a four-iron, onto the fringe of the green, forty feet from the flag stick. Wilson's second shot had nestled into the center of the green, only a couple of yards from the hole.

I lined up my putt from three different directions, plumb-bobbed it to check the angle of the green and then stood over the ball for a few minutes. I knew even before I struck the putt that it would go in the hole. There was nothing to consider but the meandering route my ball would follow, through a swale, up the side of a small hummock, down through a shallow valley and up a slight rise into the cup. I sent my putt rolling across the damp, newly mown green. It traveled in slow motion in one direction, then another, until it approached the cup and neatly disappeared. Stan was dancing around beyond a deep greenside sand trap, hooting and clapping his hands. This seemed to unhinge Spengle, who proceeded to three-put, close in as he was to the hole.

We finished our round at about noon. When I told Manny I'd shot a 76, he seemed skeptical at first. He probably suspected me of altering the scorecard. "Is this legit?" he asked.

Spengle put his arm around my shoulder. "He's a god, Manny. A god pure and simple." He'd shot an 81 himself, which placed him second behind me in the qualifying round. That meant we'd be partners in our foursome when we played our first match on Thursday of that week.

Stan made Manny and Spengle and Peggy and me pose for a picture. We sat on the green wooden bench at number one tee.

Four

It's a ninety-mile ride from Plaquemines to Moss Point Minimum Security Prison, home, sweet home for the next thirteen months. (It was all I could do to convince Stan not to rent a trailer outside the MPMSP grounds. He's very, very worried about his boy.) Anyway, we've just rolled across the Honey Island Swamp Bridge, the halfway point between my immediate past and my temporary future. Every now and then I catch a glimpse of myself in the patrol car's rearview mirror. My face is red and puffy, eyeballs sunken from lack of sleep, hair a variety of seaweed. The handcuffs pinch the skin around my wrists, but there's no point in complaining.

Billboards, utility poles, jack pines and scruffy palmettos wash past me. I wonder how on God's green earth I managed to flounder onto this sidetrack when only six months ago my future was laid out before me, clear and full of promise like blue highways on a map: golf was a euphoric obsession (an art form, almost); money was an extravagance; and loving Janice was a painful frustration I could live with.

"My cuffs are too tight," I tell my chauffeur, Deputy Fussell (rhymes with "muscle").

"We're almost there," he says, but I know we've got more than an hour ahead of us.

"Okay, then, no problem," I tell him, then lean against the back of the seat and try to doze. Instead of dreaming, I witness something like a slide show taking place on the insides of my eyelids. Photographic images of Janice making bread, of my mom ironing one of Stan's shirts, of Jimmy making change for a dollar bill. A train of non-sequiturs. They're not what I'm after at all.

It's noon when we arrive at Moss Point. We speed through a concrete arch guarded by a man nearly as thin as the rifle he carries. My driver skids around a beige brick quadrangle and angles off toward a small outbuilding, this one red brick. He hops out of the car, opens my door and orders me to get out. If I weren't handcuffed, I'd salute him. "Get on out," he says. From the way he gestures, I can tell he used to be a traffic cop. Deputy checks me in at the admissions desk, manned by a fat guy in a khaki uniform. His name tag, kind of like the ones gas station attendants wear, says AMES, but I don't know if that's his last name or his first. Deputy Fussell leans my golf clubs and suitcase against a Naugahyde chair and empties my PP (personal possessions) bag onto the countertop. Ames examines one by one my Pinehurst cigarette lighter, my combination spike wrench/divot fork/bottle opener (which Jimmy gave me when I graduated from high school), a photograph of Janice in a bikini, a few dimes, three packages of golf tees, a left-hand golf glove wrinkled like a scrotum, an empty money clip . . . all sediment from my day-to-day life on the pro golf tour.

My first impression of Ames (Mafia leg breaker) changes as soon as he grins and winks at me. "I guess you don't have a stiletto or a grenade in this mess, so you can take it all up to your room," he says. Deputy unlocks my handcuffs, signs a few forms, nods to Ames and swaggers toward the door, his holster squeaking against his thigh. "Hey," I yell, just as his fingers touch the doorknob, "thanks for the ride." Air whistles through the hair inside his nose; he shakes his policeman-of-the-month head and muscles his way outside. Ames's sad-looking eyes bulge out from that heavy face of his. "It really ain't that bad here, unless'n you make it that way." He biffs me on the shoulder. "You a pro golfer, ain't you? I heard. Warden says he's got a special job for you."

"I wonder what that might be," I say. "Any idea?"

"I don't know and I ain't sayin'. You just have to ask the warden when you see him tomorrow morning at eight o'clock."

"He comes in on Sunday?"

"He always comes in for about an hour on Sunday mornin'. I can't explain it myself. He just always done it for about the last year or so. But anyhow, you're supposed to see him first thing tomorrow."

I imagine a gray-haired grump in a blue suit, mulling over the particulars of my case: Ted Kendall, the obvious man to whip weeds along the fence. Practice his golf swing. Yessiree bob! Ames and I carry my things over to building 2-C, one of the four buildings that comprise the prison quadrangle. Inmates are stretched out on their bunks in almost every room up and down the hall. I'm surprised at how many of these guys are white. When we pass the doorless shower room, however, I hear what sounds like the Four Tops singing "Can't Help Myself." Ames tells me that two members of the quartet are in for counterfeiting. It dawns on me that I'm in with people who have committed real crimes; my harebrained vehicular assault seems puny by comparison.

Ames unlocks the door to 253 and hands me the key. "Don't lose this," he says. "Tie it to your pecker if you have to. If it comes up missing you'll have to work extra time. Okay?" I tell him I'll submit to Turkish torture before I lose track of my room key. "Now," he says, "there are a few policies you ought to know. First, you can spend your free time just about any way you please, and you can have your belongings with you in your room. But that's your risk, not ours. The only exceptions to this

36

is anything too dangerous or too big. Some goof wanted a Low-rey Genie Organ in his room. Warden nixed that in a hurry," Ames informs me. "One last thing. Everybody works eight hours a day, five days per week. That's the rule." He pushes the door wide open and I finally see the room I'll be inhabiting for the next year or so. Two metal beds at opposite sides of the small cinder-block room, two steel bureaus, a steel double desk with a steel lamp bolted to the wall above it and one small window with a view of the prison grounds and the swamp looming beyond the chain link fence. On either side of the door are small alcoves. My roommate has made what appears to be a grotto in one of these two niches. On a low shelf is an aquarium full of tropical fish, while on the next shelf up is a plaster of paris Virgin Mary painted pastel blue. She's surrounded by dime-store plants in little plastic cups. Illuminating both statue and plants is a neon Gro-Lite. On the top shelf is an array of burned-down candles in varying colors. "Your roommate is a real corn-flake, Kendall. Keeps his clothes in a box under his bunk to make space for all this shit. He's a queer one."

"Each to his own," I say, but I'm beginning to worry.

"Tell you what," Ames says. "Soon as you get parked here you can walk around the grounds. You know, get familiar with the place."

I ask Ames where my roommate is. I've been wondering about that.

"He's probably off somewhere praying. He prays a lot. He's got some healthy damn plants, though, ain't he?" Ames reaches in his shirt pocket and pulls out a folded diagram of the prison grounds: tennis court, library, warden's office, rec room. "Well . . . you take care," he says, and gently closes the door behind him. I'm alone for the first time all day.

It takes me over an hour to stash all my belongings in the various drawers and shelves. I've finally hung my last pair of irrelevant Sta-Prest trousers on a permanent hanger attached to a tamperproof clothes bar, and now I'm wondering exactly what I want to do with the rest of the day. I sit on my bunk for a while, feeling immensely sorry for myself. Well, Teddy boy, I say, Here you are . . . trapped again, only in a different cage, with no possible escape. One minute, Janice is within your grasp, and the next thing, well . . . I've been saving her last letters, all those she wrote after the assault, but unwilling to read them once again, fearful of coming nose to nose with reality. But now seems as good a time as any to face facts. I pull the rumpled letters from their envelopes and smooth them on the gray blanket. These latest letters are without stick figures dancing in the margins. Her usually immaculate print now falls in clumsy loops across the page. She suspects I've turned inward (I haven't written her back, after all), and that I've become opaque. Opaque? Now what can that mean? She could probably go for somebody more *translucent*. I want a definition of terms here. She worries that I'll fall into a deep emotional basin now that our little un-fling is finito.

I take fingernail scissors from my dop kit and cut the letters into thin strips so that the sentences and paragraphs come apart like pieces of a watch. I shuffle the parts and rearrange them. I line up her salutations side by side. "Dearest, Dear Ted." "Ted, Dearest." "Ted, Ted." I can't decide which combination I like the best. But somehow it's satisfying to imagine Janice writing these words, her slim fingers grasping the fountain pen, saying each word as she writes it, pushing at her soft lips as she mulls over every sentence. It's dark in her room, except, of course, for the lamp glowing next to her, and there is a breeze blowing through her hotel room, washing the air with the smell of her cologne. She wears a cotton nightgown with nothing on underneath, because the air is warm and humid.

I use the slivers of paper to create the letter she might have intended to write, but couldn't:

[*I wake up sometimes at night forgiving you. I make myself tea and I stare out at the lights of the Shamrock Motel down the street and they remind me of you.*] [*I mean, I do forgive you.*] [*But I want you to understand that you were providing me with something I needed at that stage of my marriage.*] [*I'm surprised so little happened between us. I would like to have tried out my life in a different context, to see if it was real.*] [*Just once!*] [*I still love Trayn, although we are ending our marriage.*] [*So now I don't have either one of you.*]

The letter fragments become a blur. The parts I carelessly arranged fit together a little too well. I gather all the shreds and pitch them into the wastebasket, then wander over to the small window to look out. In the distance, grass waves like wheat in the southerly breeze.

According to the little map Ames has given me, any tour of the prison grounds will be a fairly dismal undertaking. I settle for the library, where I might at least have some privacy. I choose to decompress there, over in I-B. On my way down the stairs I pass a pulpy-looking creature, his navel visible through a gap in his denim prison shirt. He aims the corner of his Bible at me, as if he's about to utter my name. He instinctively recognizes me, and I recognize him. It's my roommate, Chapman, stalled like a big truck on a steep hill, groping for some phrase. I say hello, and descend the stairs two at a time.

I know I'll have to cope with Chapman sooner or later, but the prospect bothers me more than it should. I don't look forward to a year of fending off somebody else's misshapen notions of faith and salvation.

Buildings B and C are connected by a thirty- or forty-foot breezeway, paved with concrete, so unevenly poured that I'm forced to slalom my way around the puddles of standing water. The inmates I encounter march straight into the wet as if it didn't exist. One of them says, "How're you doing?"

I tell him I'm doing fine, and shove my way through the heavy steel door of I-B. My destination is straight ahead. At the end of this garishly painted corridor, a green and orange yellow nightmare, is the library.

I flick on the overhead light. This is not so much a library as a storeroom for books nobody in his right mind would want to read, most of them donated by benevolent ladies' organizations.

Power Through Faith. Prayers for All Occasions. (Lord deliver me from my roommate . . .) *How to Raise and Train a Budgie. Compendium of Medical Terminology.* Fortunately, there are a few popular magazines on a rack beneath the only window in the room. I pick up an old *Sports Illustrated*, select a soft fake-leather chair in a corner and leaf through the pages. It doesn't take long before I find an article on the top five rookies of the pro golf tour. Right there in the middle of the page is Trayn, standing up to his ankles in a sand trap. His lips are pursed like he's unhappy with his misfortune. I'm about to rip the magazine to shreds when I see something that stops me; in the blurry background of the photograph; almost hidden behind a spectator's straw hat, is Janice, looking for all the world like she's been lobotomized. Poor thing was never cut out to be a tour wife. Her husband is getting his picture taken for a national magazine, touted for greatness, and already she's scrambling for a high safe place where she can escape the flood of publicity. If she'd stuck with yours truly, there wouldn't be any such problem, unless she had a similar aversion to obscurity.

I'm ready to hit the next stop on my tour when a little guy with sideburns and eyebrows like my dad's comes in with a tube of paper clutched in his hand like a baton. He looks at me, wiggles those caterpillar eyebrows up and down and walks in my direction.

"I've got some pitchers of the warden. Odenfinger did 'em up for me in the darkroom." This fellow is strange. He clears his throat and moves his face close to mine. He coughs once to make sure I'm paying attention. "He's with a lady and they're both nekkid as new pigs. Want to see?"

When I tell him I'm not especially interested, a heartbroken look sweeps momentarily across his face. Then his features brighten. He straightens up, marches to the bulletin board, pries a thumbtack out of the cork, trots over to the wooden door and fastens the photograph to its inside surface. "Lookee, lookee. Warden's got some nookee," he says.

Even from where I'm sitting I can see that a nude woman is

sitting in the lap of a shirtless man who could, for all I know, be none other than the warden. "Just out of curiosity, how did you get your hands on that picture?"

"Took it myself. Right through his office window. Every Sunday morning Gladden's sister comes to visit her brother over in 4-A, but not until she does the old wham-bam with the warden. Everybody knows about it, even Gladden."

"The warden will hang you if he sees this," I say. The little guy plops into the other soft chair and looks up at a water stain on the acoustical ceiling. It's an enormous rust-colored Rorschach: a vampire bat, a tattered kite, a dilapidated stingray. His expression looks so mystical I ask him if something is wrong.

"Naw," he said. "It's how I think. Some people put their hands like this to think" (he does a perfect imitation of the Rodin statue) "and some people, if they got beards, rub them. I look up because that's where my thoughts are. It's like they're written in the air."

He's a poetic little drone. "I hope you've thought about burning your X-rated photos of the warden."

"Well . . . maybe I'll sell 'em," he grumps. It takes him a while to pry the thumbtack out of the door. "Hey," he says, "I seen you come in today. Whaddya in for? The name's Drago, by the way."

"Mass murder," I tell him. "Bunch of nuns. Killed them with a machete and a blowtorch."

He says, "Naw . . . you ditten," but I notice one of his eyebrows bouncing up and down like it's on a string. "Nawwww!" Quick as a cat he's out the door. I hear his sneakers slapping on the tile floor of the hallway.

There's only an hour or so before evening chow, not quite enough time to circumnavigate Moss Point. Instead, I wander out to the asphalt basketball court, where a couple of uncoordinated Ivy Leaguers take old-fashioned Bob Cousy set shots from twenty feet out. Nothing is going in; somehow I don't think they're too surprised by this. The basketball net is made of chain, and there's a bull's-eye painted on the backboard. Just a few paces beyond this pair of anachronisms is the shuffleboard lane, overrun with weeds and faded so badly the numbers are all but invisible. However, the nearby tennis court is in surprisingly good condition. The white-collar-crimers have probably chipped in some of their embezzled money to have it resurfaced, because it looks almost immaculate. Two men volley a yellow ball back and forth. A cooler squats next to the chain net. One of the tennis players touches his visor and nods to me as I walk by.

The supper horn sounds from atop the main building, where the mess hall is located. As I understand it, Saturday meals are on a catch-as-catch-can basis. I head back toward 2-C, wondering if I'll survive more than a year of this charade.

I manage to avoid Chapman at evening chow, though I see him eyeballing the various tables, trying to spot me. He sits in one corner of the room, and fortunately I'm at a table as far away as I can manage, even if that means rubbing elbows with Drago, who chews with his mouth wide open. Occasionally, Chapman stands up and looks around like somebody who has lost his seat at a baseball game.

Drago says, "You're hiding from him, aren't you?" Or at least I think that's what he's said. It's hard to tell exactly because his mouth is full of macaroni.

"How do you know that?" I ask.

"Well, I never seen a guy so interested in what's under his table as you."

Finally, Chapman finishes his meal and carries his tray to the conveyor belt. He surveys the mess hall one more time, shakes his head in disappointment, then hulks out the door.

I realize I haven't touched my food: Spam with a pineapple slice, overbaked yam, cole slaw, Jell-O and a brownie. I eat a little of the Spam and all of the brownie, a dried-out insipid thing. Drago lights up a cigarette and waits for me to get up from the table. When I do, he crushes his butt into the macaroni and follows me. When I ask if he doesn't have someplace to go, he rolls his eyes, one of those you've-got-to-be-kidding looks. "There's a movie tonight, right here in the mess hall, but it don't start until eight o'clock," he says. "Don't know what it is, though."

We hike together over to the rec room in 3-A, where there's a TV, some plastic chairs, a Ping-Pong table and a disreputable sofa with tufts of cotton blooming from the cushions. The smoke alarm must be broken; there's a thick gray pall hanging just below the recessed overhead lights. With all the profanity going back and forth between the Ping-Pong players, and the smoke and general corruption here, I feel quite safe from Chapman. On one side of an imaginary line, the white inmates play bridge or watch the CBS news. On the other side of the room most of the black inmates watch a dead-serious Ping-Pong game that rages beneath the only unprotected lighting fixture in the prison. An old gray-haired man, very black, clutches a fistful of dollars. Apparently gambling is big sport at Moss Point, because a few paces behind the Ping-Pongers, another group pitches nickels at a crack in the floor. Somebody among them has brought down his ghetto blaster, big as a suitcase. The music is Mississippi Fred McDowell, pained and lonesome.

Drago and I occupy a couple of the plastic chairs lined up against the wall on the black side of the room. We watch the white ball zip back and forth. One of the players is pretty good, the one with a black cat tattooed on his coffee-colored triceps. He hits a wicked spinning serve, which his opponent clumsily returns in my general direction. Drago hops up, grabs the ball, pops it in his mouth like it's a marshmallow, puffs out his cheeks and makes a bullfrog face. "Give it over, motherfucker," says the player who isn't so good, but who eats nails for breakfast. I'm fearful for Drago's life, twerp that he is. Drago waits until the guy is on the verge of throttling him, and then whacks his own cheeks and spits the ball almost up to the ceiling. "You goddamn slobbered on it, you fucking lunatic."

Drago sits down and smiles a goofy smile. "Jesus Christ, you're lucky you're not dead," I whisper. "You're *nuts*, you know that?"

Even when people here seem to be having fun, they're not

really very happy. They're only trying to get through. If they could, the Ping-Pong players would be glad to hit the ball back and forth a billion times until Ames or someone else came along and told them they could go home. The game is just a time killer for them, like everything else that goes on around here; it's all just another way of obscuring reality, the same way the smoke makes the lights all but invisible.

At eight o'clock sharp, Drago (my date for the evening) and I push through the swinging doors of the mess hall. The tables are shoved out of the way to make room for the rows of chairs arranged in front of a portable screen. A black guy with a shaved head (every prison has at least one guy who looks this way) is threading film through the projector. I overhear somebody call him Grayson. I make a mental note to steer clear of him.

An inmate flicks off the lights. The projector aims a luminous beam at the screen, and pretty soon Gene Pitney is singing the theme song: "Well, it isn't very pretty what a town without pity . . . caaaaaan dooooo!" The movie is in black and white, apparently set in Germany.

"Whaddya think?" Drago whispers.

"About what?"

"The movie. Whaddya think?" He's no longer whispering.

"It only just started. Why don't you settle down and watch."

Then Drago yells, "Too loud. Turn it down. Too loud." In the dim light I can see his hands clapped over his ears like Quasimodo. Everybody boos. Several moviegoers holler for him to "shut the hell up."

The movie is about a teenaged German girl who may or may not have been raped by an American GI, played by Johnny Horton. Kirk Douglas plays the military attorney in charge of defending the GI from the townspeople who want to hang the kid. I get up and leave before the movie is even halfway over. I don't feel much empathy for either the Americans or the Germans, except for maybe the confused girl who thinks she was raped.

44

By now I'm resigned to meeting my peculiar roommate; after all, it's inevitable. But when I unlock the door to 253 and step inside, nobody's home. The aquarium hood and the Gro-Lite cast a strange light inside the otherwise dark room. Chapman's bed is neatly made; there's no evidence that he's come in yet. Maybe he's at the movie, although I didn't see him there.

I undress, put on some pajamas, shut off the Gro-Lite. A pair of kissing gouramis are giving one of Chapman's zebra fish a ferocious chase. I wonder if the little fellow is going to make it through the night. I shot off the aquarium light, hoping that might help his plight. I stumble over to my cot, pull down the cotton blanket, thump my pillow and slide in. If I'm lucky, maybe I'll fall asleep before Chapman arrives. I roll over and face the wall.

The sound of the fish pump almost drowns out the miscellaneous noises coming from up and down the hall. However, my distance from that prison activity only gives me a queer sense of isolation. I draw in a huge breath of air. Just the smell of fish food and humus takes me back to the time when Stan took me to the pet store where we bought Sally, who was no bigger than a rat groveling around in a box full of cedar chips. Although Sally is now an arthritic blimp of a dog, grouchy and almost toothless, I can't help missing her. And I miss Stan, especially knowing how tough all this felony business has been on him.

I feel crazy and helpless lying in this room. There's a parade of jailhouse visitors lined up in the back of my brain, where I've managed to hold them at bay until now. Janice, Jimmy, Stan, Trayn . . . all ready to invade the hours between now and day-light.

Five

Stan was still at the office when my letter from Coach Forbes arrived. I carried it back and forth across the living-room carpet for a while, held it up to the light of the picture window, weighed it in the palm of my hand, sniffed it, studied the bold red OSU on the upper left corner of the envelope. OHIO STATE UNIVERSITY. Nicklaus had played his college golf at Ohio State. Weiskopf had followed on his heels. *Nicklaus, Weiskopf and Kendall. The holy trinity of Buckeye golf.*

I shooed Sally off the couch and sat down to open the letter, which I nervously unfolded and began to read.

Dear Ted,

I'm sorry to say there is no scholarship for you at this time. Our graduating class from last year is very small, so we had only a few to give out. I think I can guarantee you a 100% grant-in-aid by your sophomore season, if you choose to join us, which I hope you will. There is one possibility you might consider. Every year we hold back one scholarship, which goes to the winner of a 54-hole qualifier. This means you would have to compete with approximately fifty walk-ons who would like to try out. However, with your talent, I think you have an excellent chance of coming out on top. (That would certainly solve our problem, wouldn't it?) If you want to go that route, just come down a few days early. I hope to see you at Ohio State in the fall.

Yours truly,
BEN FORBES

Although I had been offered athletic scholarships to a few other Big Ten schools, and some of the other universities in Ohio, my mind was made up. I wanted to play golf for the Buckeyes. I'd competed in the state high school championships at the Scarlet and Gray courses during my sophomore and junior years. The trophy case in the clubhouse there was full of Nicklaus memorabilia: letter sweaters, golf clubs, trophies, old photographs of "Fat Jack" looking like a hefty farm boy. I made a private vow to donate my old J. C. Higgins woods and irons to Ohio State if I ever became famous, particularly since I wasn't using them anymore.

When I was a high school senior, the golf team, except for Ned Scaffington and me, was a total embarrassment. I always came in at one or two over par, with Ned a few strokes behind. Our other four men could barely break ninety, particularly Amory Wilcox, a voracious overeater who had undergone stomach stapling in January. He'd lost eighty-five pounds by golf season, but his skin fit him like a half-filled laundry bag. And we had "Twerp" Waterson, whose dad was a big lawyer in town. Twerp was always dressed like somebody from the cover of *Golf Digest*. Houndstooth pants, white monogrammed shirt, Don January headgear. His swing was a puny classic, technically sound, but gutless and weak. Jimmy told me his stroke would look great in slow motion, except that it already *was* in slow motion! Twerp always wanted me to give him a few strokes so we could bet on our practice rounds. My principles back then were fairly ill-formed, but I drew the line at scarfing easy money from such a weakling.

The mighty Bobcat golfers competed in the regional play-offs, held at Findlay Country Club, about thirty miles south of Bowling Green. Our team's performance was a very sad thing to behold. Wilcox shot a 112 on the first day. Manny had a heart-to-heart talk with him just to prevent his quitting before the second day of competition. Amory was blubbering next to a ball washer, with Manny patting the slack skin of his shoulder blades and his father bribing him with french fries. We were so far behind everybody else that Scaffington and I were playing for our own glory. If we scored in the top four, we could compete for medalist honors in the state championship held the following week.

Stan drove down to watch the Saturday and Sunday rounds. He'd absorbed enough TV golf to know when to clap or groan, although he occasionally embarrassed me by baying like a lonely wolf if I sank a long putt or punched a nice drive off the tee. He'd say things like "That's my boy there. Way to go, Teddy boy." Fortunately, Jimmy decided to ride down with him for Saturday's competition, and he seemed to have a calming effect on Stan.

On the sixth hole, I pushed my drive toward a line of trees and nailed somebody's green-clad mother squarely on the hip just as she galloped from behind a sycamore. Although she had no business racing across the fairway like that, I felt bad when she flopped onto the rough like a wounded goose, squawking for first aid. I sprinted off the tee to see if she was okay. (I couldn't help noticing that my ball had taken a nasty kick into the deep rough.) Her iridescent dress was hiked up to her thighs, and the contents of her purse were strewn between her ankles. "My hip is broken," she moaned. Stan and Jimmy came laboring up the fairway. I could see Stan mentally reviewing the provisions of his liability insurance. "My God," she moaned. "Oh . . . my God!"

"Sorry, ma'am," I said. "I really didn't see you hiding in the trees."

She huffed once or twice, then Jimmy and I hoisted her into a standing position. Stan picked up the rumpled Kleenexes and combs and lipstick tubes, dropped them into her purse and gave it to her. "You should have yelled 'Fore!'" she snapped, and hobbled across the fairway toward a Port-o-Let.

I caught Stan's eye just as he was about to hurl an insult in her direction.

From that point on, my concentration was nil. Jimmy exhorted me to put the incident out of mind, to stay inside my game. "You'll never make a pro if something like that stops you. It was *her* fault, not yours."

But my game had left me. The best I could do was shrug and take my lumps.

At the seventeenth hole my tee shot hit the down-hanging limb of a maple tree and boomeranged directly backward. It rolled just past my left shoe, trickled down the back of the tee and into a muddy creek. "The rub of the green, Teddy boy." It was Jimmy again, with one of his innumerable clichés.

Neither Scaffington nor I earned the right to play in the state tournament that spring. In fact, for a week or so I lost interest in the game. That is, until the letter from Coach Forbes arrived.

I tried on several occasions to approach Stan with the subject of Ohio State, but he seemed to sense it and immediately changed the topic. Finally, I found him in the yard, raking up some twigs knocked down by a recent windstorm. "How about playing a round of golf with me?" I asked. "Tomorrow morning. What do you think? We've never played eighteen holes together before." I theorized that I might be persuasive on comfortable turf.

"That wouldn't be much fun for you, would it?" He picked up an armful of debris and carried the mess out to the curb. "Don't think I can do it, Teddy," he said over his shoulder. "Got to get the car into Sears for some new tires tomorrow morning."

"Come on. It's a once-in-a-lifetime opportunity," I told him. "Besides, tomorrow's Sunday. Stores are closed."

"Let me think about it," he said. "Ask me again at supper."

I spent the afternoon at the high school gym pushing tufts of pink toilet paper into a chicken-wire mold of a giant flamingo. The prom was a week away and I was taking Tammy Listerman, the daughter of Stan's best insurance client. The previous summer, Ned Scaffington and I had swum naked in the golf course quarry with Tammy and her cousin from Toledo. In the July moonlight I was able to discern the dark silhouette of her slim adolescent figure, a vision that sent a sudden wave of heat racing through my veins. Tammy caught me gaping and made me turn my back while she and her cousin stood on the rocks and dried off. Later that night, on the deep slope behind number five green, she and I came close, but not quite close enough, to being lovers. I'd had what might be called a sexual accident, the outcome of which had caused my madras shirt to bleed onto the front of my khaki shorts. Afterward, I walked her home, shirttail untucked to cover myself, then ran grass-stained and dew-soaked up Fairway Avenue. Anyway, she was my date for the senior prom, an event Stan was genuinely looking forward to, as much for what it might do for his sagging insurance trade as for my rudimentary social life. "You can't marry golf," Stan used to grumble.

That Saturday evening, after I'd come home from the gymnasium, I was helping Stan set the table. "Have you thought about golf tomorrow?" I asked.

"Teddy, I just don't know," he said. "I really don't know."

The next morning we were up early enough to beat the nine o'clock glut of golfers onto the first tee. Stan didn't own golf cleats, and he was wearing his ridiculous pointed shoes, which I think he liked because I hated them. He worried that his feet would slip on the wet grass, but he refused to change into sneakers, I'm sure because they didn't fit the image he had of himself. He never wore Levi's either. All his trousers had a crease. He carried the plaid golf bag laden with J. C. Higgins woods and irons, while I carried my pristine Hogan golf clubs in a new Naugahyde bag.

Stan insisted on playing with new balls, fresh ones he bought at the pro shop. "How about a package of Orbits," he told

Jimmy. With his nose for bargains, he insisted on purchasing a low-compression brand that, on impact with the clubface, made a sound like fudge dropping on a sidewalk.

"They're *cheap*," I said. I saw Jimmy winking at me.

"Nonsense. They're nearly two dollars." End of argument. They were shiny and he could make a big show of biting open the packet and spilling the balls onto the grass at the first tee. That was his main concern.

Al Waterson, Twerp's dad, was waiting with a pair of his law partners behind us at number one tee. "Good to see you out, Stan. Nice day for it, wouldn't you say?"

"Beautiful," Stan said, warming up by hoisting the club over his head as if it were a slim barbell, and then repeatedly rotating his trunk. I saw one of the lawyers roll his eyes when he glimpsed Stan's practice swing, an outlandish motion with wild flourishes on the backswing and follow-through. He finally stepped up to his new gleaming Made-in-Japan Orbit, waggled over the ball for what seemed like a minute or more, then sliced a wild shot that drifted high and right toward the picnic tables of the public park. Out of bounds. "You're stiff from raking the lawn," I said. He wouldn't have any part of that theory. He shook his head no. Next, he clouted what country club players call a worm burner, a shot that incinerates everything in its grassy path. The ball skittered out approximately one hundred yards, but dead center. "That'll play," I told him. He slammed his dilapidated three wood into the bag and gestured for me to hit away.

I knocked a gem of a drive slightly right of center, two hundred fifty yards out. Stan fired a that's-my-boy glance toward Twerp's dad, and picked up the golf bag like a suitcase.

On the fifth hole the lawyers lost patience with Stan's slow play. He was gauging the complexities of a shot requiring that he chop his way out of a dense rough when a ball trickled within a few feet of where he stood. Four iron in hand, Stan marched to where the ball had come to rest, took aim in their direction and hit his nicest shot of the day, a low screamer that sent them ducking behind their pull carts.

The fourteenth hole was a par three, requiring a short iron over the pond. Stan had just splashed his last Orbit into the drink and was digging in his bag for a reject he could clobber across the water. "Go ahead," he muttered. "Hit away." I punched a clean eight-iron shot that floated on a beautiful parabolic line toward the flag. My ball landed on the fringe at the back of the green, bit into the turf and began to trickle toward the hole. I leaned on my club and watched. "Will you look at that thing?" Stan said. "It's going in. I think the son of a bitch might just go in the hole." The ball curled across one side of a swale, gathering enough steam to climb a small opposing rise, then once again funneled toward the pin, situated in the middle of the shallow trough.

"Roll," I said. "Get legs."

"The bastard's coming up short," Stan said.

"No. Watch it now. It's still moving." The ball crept toward the edge of the cup and seemed to hang there in defiance of gravity. Stan slung the clubs over his shoulder and trotted around the rim of the pond, his irons clicking together at every footfall. I followed at a walk, never taking my eye from the ball that hovered on the brink of the cup.

Stan was already on hands and knees, his nose only inches from the ball, when I arrived at the green. A foursome on the nearby eleventh tee paused to watch this peculiar sight. The ball seemed frozen on the lip of the hole, its round shadow darkening the yellow cylindrical liner. Stan stood up to let his wide shadow fall over the focus of his frustration. (There is a theory —and how Stan had come to know it was beyond me—that shade causes an imperceptible wilting of grass.) Maybe he figured his porky penumbra would spill the ball into the hole. No luck. He jumped up and down, leaving size-eleven footprints on the soft green. "It's not going in," I said.

"It's *got* to fall," Stan insisted. He resumed his all-fours posture on the green and pushed his eyeball close to the recalcitrant, dimpled "son-of-a-bitching" sphere. "You bastard," he whispered to the Titleist.

Although the trio of lawyers had quit an hour before, another group was waiting at the tee. "I'm going to tap it in," I said.

"Like hell," Stan muttered. He filled his lungs and fiercely blew air, like Buddha inventing wind. The ball teetered, then tumbled into the cup.

"What did you do that for?" I asked.

"It was a great shot," he said. "It should have gone in."

After Stan had added up our scores on the eighteenth green, he shook my hand and said, "You won."

We walked across Fairway Avenue. When we had entered the gate at the front of the yard, I broke the news to Stan. "I want to go to Ohio State."

"I knew it all the time," he told me. "That's fine. You should go where you want to go."

There was no predicting this man, who had accumulated 144 strokes during his morning's round of golf.

Six

Standing behind the stainless-steel food bins are four black guys with hairnets; they're harmonizing to "Boardwalk" by the Drifters, and doing a decent job of it, knocking out the rhythm with slatted spoons. "Whatchew wont, brother?" says the one who sings bass. "Dese grits is good." He's wearing a gold loop in one ear.

"Are they really good?" I ask.

"Nah. Nothin' any good. I'd skip it all and go get a Twinkie out'n a machine." Floating in a trough of heated water are the food bins: overcooked eggs, undercooked bacon, grits, something resembling hash browns, toast soaked in oleo . . . I slide my tray past the hot food to the melon bin. I reach through a cloud of fruit flies for a wedge of cantaloupe to go with my coffee.

The mess hall is illuminated by neon tubes protected by metal grates. Everything breakable—windows, lights, clocks—is protected by metal webwork, just in case minorities and white-collar-crimers start heaving anthracite potatoes back and forth over the middle zone where neutrals like me sit. I pull a molded plastic chair up to a Formica table and sit alone, watching steam swirl from my coffee. (For a minute I half believe I'm back at my college dorm, sitting across from Janice in the cafeteria. Her hands, beautiful, swirling a spoon through her coffee. Something so ridiculously everyday as that could give me goose bumps.) I take a sip of my prison brew and it's industrial runoff. The cantaloupe, however, is surprisingly tasty. With my plastic fork I dig off a nice-sized piece, lift it to my mouth and chew. I've decided to spend my upcoming year this way—benignly chewing my food, blotto like a cow. I'll get up early every morning so I can eat alone, thereby steering clear of Chapman, amble off to my menial job, keep my nose clean, write letters at night and work on my book. Think about Janice every now and then. Or maybe try not to think about her. (I haven't decided.) In other words, wade as best as I can through this nonsense.

I'm nearly midway through my second cup of coffee when about a dozen inmates appear in the chow line. It's the born-agains, scrubbed and upright, ready for the early worship service. Chapman waddles at the end of the line, but nobody is talking to him. They fill their trays and sit together at a table beneath the big Seth Thomas clock, so they look like a Salvador Dali painting of the last supper. Chapman leads them in an intensely devout prayer. Then they dig in.

I don't want my roommate to see me, but I've got nowhere to hide. Inevitably he spots me and scoots his chair back. He's on his way over to convert me when I stand up with my tray and carry it to the conveyor belt and hurry out the door.

Connecting the four main buildings at Moss Point is a breezeway which enables inmates and guards to stay dry on rainy days. In the middle of the quadrangle stands a large bronze statue of the governor responsible for building this prison. There are no shrubs in the courtyard, and only a few stunted geraniums around the base of the statue. Even this early in the morning the air feels damp and hot. The khaki shirt of the guard who stalks in my direction is sweat-soaked. "Where do you think you're going?" he asks, holding his billy club out horizontally like a roadblock. He's right out of *Cool Hand Luke*. Nice pair of mirror sunglasses, acne pits on his face, a handsome revolver holstered on his hip. I hand him my note from the warden, but he doesn't bother to read it.

"I'm supposed to see the warden this morning."

"Well, he ain't here yet."

"If you don't mind, I'll just mosey over and wait for him." I gesture toward a small brick building situated near the enormous concrete front gate. Somebody has spray-painted the words ARBEIT MACHT FREI across the lintel, fifteen feet up. This strikes me as astonishing, both logistically and intellectually. I wonder who did it.

"You go ahead on, but he ain't here yet."

I hike down the hot sidewalk and knock on the door of the office building. Ames opens up. "Kendall," he says. "Come on in. How's about some coffee?" There's a Bunn Coffeematic centered on a wallside table. Before I can refuse, Ames hands me a Styrofoam cup of steaming brew that smells like the real things. His hands are shaking so ferociously that he slops java all over the cement floor.

"You got the DTs this morning?"

"My ass is in a sling. Somehow I lost the warden's newspaper. I swear I put it in his pigeonhole first thing . . ."

"It'll turn up," I say. "When will the warden be in?"

"Oh, he's in there already, eating breakfast. Go ahead and rap on his door." When I do so, I'm greeted by a redheaded pauncher with doughnut frosting clinging to his lips. "So you're Kendall. I expected somebody bigger." He grabs a twice-bitten doughnut from a greasy bag.

"Mug shots make me look taller than I am."

"Well, come on in." He returns to the chair behind his desk, brushes some crumbs off his blotter, fluffs some papers, pretends to read one of them and finally motions for me to sit down. "Well," he says finally. "You've probably already seen that cow pasture that used to be a golf course." He looks out his window toward the broad field where weeds are beginning to stir in the freshening Gulf breeze. "It sure would be nice if we could do something about that mess. The former warden let the course go to hell in a hand bucket, and I'd sort of like to bring it back to life." One of his eyes closes. The other one aims at me. "You seem like the right man for the job."

I wonder if I've heard him right. Was that abominable weed patch I saw yesterday actually a perverted species of golf course? Even an unfortunate specimen like that one was better than nothing. Could the founders of Moss Point have been an enlightened race, capable of including a links as part of their regimen for rehabilitation? Maybe there is some acreage I haven't been told about. Could I have overlooked it yesterday? "You've really got a golf course? Seriously?"

"Well, it's not but two holes, so don't get overly excited."

"Two holes are better than one," I tell him. "And you want a greenskeeper, right?"

"That's about the size of it. Unfortunately, we don't have exactly the right equipment to do a proper job. But we'll certainly do the best job we can. I think we've got a mower for the greens, but from what I hear, the thing's busted."

"Do I get some help? I'll need some help if you want a decent job of it."

"Well . . . we've got a couple inmates in the laundry who haven't quite worked out. Nobody likes them much, me included. Maybe the open air will be just the thing for them."

"Who are they?"

"One's named Drago. And the other is a fellow named Chapman. I might even give you a black guy named Grayson if you think you need more help. Anyway, you'll see Drago and Chapman out there at eight o'clock sharp tomorrow morning." Warden Maples fishes a key out of his desk drawer and tosses it to me. "It goes to the equipment shed."

"Is there somebody else besides Drago and Chapman?" I ask. "I'd prefer somebody else, if possible. And I'd like to know about my budget."

"Budget? Son, there isn't any budget. Your budget is your own sweat. And your crew for right now is Chapman and Drago."

"If you want the job done properly, you'll have to give me a budget for some trees and sand and plants. I might even need some heavy equipment."

He leans across the desk toward me. I focus on the sugar around the perimeter of his mouth. "Son," he says. "I'm not asking for goddamn St. Andrews. I'm just interested in a two-hole golf course, period. And frankly, I was looking out for you. I thought it would be a situation you might enjoy. But if you want to work in the laundry . . . well, that's fine with me."

I tell him "Okay, I understand," but that I'll need the services of Grayson. The prospect of working with Chapman and Drago is almost chilling. I figure maybe Grayson will kill them sooner or later, and then we can get something done out there. I shake hands with the warden and suggest he do something about that white stuff on his face. I step out of the building and draw in a huge lungful of swamp air.

So I'm to be greenskeeper and zookeeper at the same time. I stand on the sidewalk for a long time considering this truth. It's almost impossible to comprehend how completely jumbled and absurd my life has become in two months. Ted Kendall, amiable chap, frustrated lover, professional golfer, decent son to a strange father, Midwesterner, agnostic, relatively bright guy (all things considered) . . . finds himself playing the leading role in a play written by a lunatic: *Kendall is first of all depressed. He's lost all hope of recapturing his former lover, Janice Thompson Traynham, after having attempted to murder her husband, not with a gun, but with a disreputable-looking yellow car; Kendall is convicted and sentenced to a thirteen-month prison term in the groin area of Mississippi; he finds himself bunking with a three-hundred-pound born-again Christian with evangelical leanings; and so on . . .* But the final ironic touch, the stroke of twisted genius actually, is to place neophyte convict Ted Kendall in charge of the most ludicrous links in the annals of golfdom. Unfortunately, these circumstances are so totally bizarre that the playwright can only toss the characters together like the ingredients of some weird soup and let the play fend for itself. So the stage is set before me and I only have to walk onto it and let the drama unfold. It's a lark, I tell myself. Have fun with it, Teddy boy. Keep breathing for thirteen months and it will all be over. I take my first few steps into the unknown. My Adidas scuff on the dusty sidewalk.

A deep tractor rut leads out toward the lovely Moss Point Golf and Country Club, home to fire ants, quail, tunneling rodents and a variety of iguana thought to be extinct. This unmowed pastureland, beneath which lies my golf course, is overgrown with calf-deep, dew-soaked Bermuda grass. Kudzu is rampant in the two sizable oak trees; it has swallowed long sections of the chain link fence and spilled over into the algae-covered drainage ditch. By the time I get to the rough bordering the first fairway (I can only suppose it's the rough) my Levi's are soaked clear up to the zipper. From this spot it's about two hundred yards back to the quadrangle. I consider inserting a pair of tricky little par threes in this no-man's-land, maybe a putting green, and possibly a humble clubhouse. There's enough room, it seems to me.

I prowl toward a mound of grass, no bigger than a bedspread, fifty yards away. The "putting surface" is a riotous snarl of Bermuda grass a foot or more deep in places. A crescent-shaped trench, filled with leaves folds around the tiny green. Of course there's no flag, and at first glance no hole. Only when I get on hands and knees and grope do I discover a shallow depression camouflaged by roots and mud. With my fingers I scoop dirt until the hollow becomes more like a golf hole, four inches deep.

"What a disaster," I say, and try to take in the task confronting me.

Off to my right, at the tail end of number one fairway, is the dejected wooden equipment shed. I wade through the thick grass. A hefty quail flies up in front of me and flaps out toward the swamp. The morning sun muddles the already vague contours of the course, so I can easily reinvent it in my mind: *A beautiful kidney-shaped pond folds around number two green; deep sand traps guard the right side of the fairway, mowed so close now that the subtle swales and hillocks are apparent; thousands of spectators clutch the chain link fence, waiting for Ted Kendall to march forth, his caddy, Lawrence, in tow, Janice a little bit farther back (wearing her now famous pastels); applause builds as the young pro from Ohio strides toward the beautifully manicured green. "Thank you," he says. "Thank you." His putter is held aloft in triumph. He tips his hat to Kendall's Caravan. They go crazy. Women faint. Grown men cry. This fellow has done so much for the game of golf . . .*

I'm immobilized by this vision. Moisture beads up on my forehead, clings to my eyebrows, then drops onto my shirtfront. I realize that I'm crying, perhaps from squinting into the sun. No, I'm crying for real. Maybe, like Kendall's Caravan, I love that man out there on the fairway, the man who has given so much back to the game. I know suddenly that I will do my best to resurrect this little two-hole track.

Brakes screech out on Highway 447. It's a gawker leaned over the steering wheel of his '79 Camaro. I haven't mooned anybody since high school, but I'm tempted to let him have it. Unfortunately, he's probably the warden's nephew, the guy would feel obligated to tell Maples about that "prevert" on the prison grounds. So I keep my pants buckled.

The shed has a heavy sliding door, warped and off its track, like me and all my buddies here. The padlock is on the ground near the door. This seems odd, though not surprising. Prison security leans toward ultraliberal. Anybody who wanted to could drag a stepladder across the golf course to the hurricane fence, climb over and fox-trot to freedom. It would be lights-out before Ames inventoried the prison population, and then maybe morning before he did anything about the missing inmate. It takes all my strength to shoulder the door open. The sun flings a rectangle of light onto the dirt floor, and when I step inside I'm illuminated like St. Francis of Assisi. Scattered about the shed are scythes, rakes, shovels, seed bags and a few other unidentifiable tools. Stan would have an infarction if he saw this mess.

Near the back wall is a barricade composed of hundred-pound bags of 8-8-8 fertilizer. Parked at odd angles are a variety of mowers. There's an apparently healthy Yazoo mower that will be fine for the roughs, but the Cub Cadet Rider, new though it is, will have to go. You need something with reels, not rotary blades, for the fairways. I check out the greens mower and discover that the cutting edges are nicked and bent, as if somebody has been mowing gravel with it. I'm pondering the possibilities of all this machinery when I hear rats scurrying behind the mountain of fertilizer bags. No, it's something bigger than rats. A mutant armadillo or a swamp wolf. With a fractured rake handle in my hands, I approach the spot where the noise is coming from. I whomp the top bag a good one; white dust coughs from the seams. Almost instantly a human head appears from behind the stack, a slightly bald, very perturbed human head belonging to none other than Drago.

"What the hell are you doing here?" I ask. "I might have killed you."

"Could I ask you to give me about five minutes of privacy?"

"Tell me you're not jacking off. You're not, are you?"

"Please? Five minutes. Tops."

"Goddamn, Drago. You're a real sicko." I do a one-eighty and hike out of the shed so my Yugoslavian friend can finish himself off. Maybe the shed is the official jacking-off place for all Moss Point. There could be a mattress behind the fertilizer bags, and porno magazines. Drago acted like I had no right to intrude like that; he was entitled to his privacy, and I'd just have to wait my turn, thank you very much.

I stand there in the wet grass, casting a shadow that makes me look like the Colossus of Rhodes, rolling all this craziness over and over again in my mind. The warden is a raised glazed bureaucrat; Ames is a pleasantly crazed buffoon; my roommate is a born-again zeppelin; my greenskeeping assistant is a beat-off freak and a klepto. I'm expecting a crew from *60 Minutes* to show up anytime. "You mean to tell me, Warden, that your prison actually has a masturbatorium?" "Well, Mike, we've found that it keeps the prisoners happy, and it has actually cut down on the number of sexual assaults here at Moss Point . . ."

I'm almost ready to get the stepladder and make my escape when two things happen. First, a blue heron, big as a pterodactyl, glides beautifully above the swamp with its long legs straight out behind. It banks slightly to the right and makes a complete circle over the cypress swamp. In my college English textbook there was a story about the young slave Frederick Douglass standing on the shore of the Chesapeake, watching sailboats, their sails taut in the wind, the absolute metaphor of freedom. I feel that way about the bird, sailing out there midway between the low-hanging sun and the misty horizon.

The second thing that happens, almost simultaneously, but fortunately not quite, is that Drago hollers to let me know he's finished. I think this is what my English professor called *juxtaposition.*

"You want to use the shed?" Drago asks, casual as anything.

I tell him I want to check out the mowers and tractors, to see if they're in working order. He looks worried, as if I've jeopardized a way of life. "Incidentally, where did you get the key?" I ask.

"Warden's desk. No problem, there were two of them," he says.

"Well, I'm putting on a new lock tomorrow, so you'll have to find a new place to pound your pud."

"You're not giving me a key? How am I going to be your helper with no key of my own?"

"I just don't want you whacking off in there. Do it in bed."

"Come on. It ain't no church. It's a dirt-floor shed. A man's gotta do what a man's gotta do. An' you telling me you don't jerk off yourself? Hell, everybody here does it, even old Chapman. I haven't seen my girlfriend in six months, so I get my jollies where I can. You don't need to be uppity righteous about it." He seems on the verge of tears. "You want all that sperm to back up to my brain and kill me? Then how would you feel?"

"Drago . . . ?" He cocks his head like a terrier. "You see that

62

pasture behind me? By the time I leave here, that's going to be fairways and greens and white sand bunkers. This shed is where I keep the tools for the job. It's not a pleasure palace, it's a shelter for keeping my mowers and fertilizer dry. If I catch you in here doing anything like what you did this morning, I'll snap your little neck, hear me? I'm a violent man."

Drago's face goes pale and he seems on the threshold of a seizure. "Okay, boss. You just tell me what I got to do, and I'll do it."

"I'll keep you so busy you'll forget where your zipper is," I say.

"Okay, boss. You just tell me what to do."

"Right now . . . get lost." Off he goes, my Sancho Panza. I notice he has a newspaper tucked under his arm. I have a strong hunch it's the warden's.

The Yazoo's tank is almost empty, so I drain a few quarts of gasoline from a three-gallon can into the tank, screw the cap back on and hop aboard. To my dismay, the mower cranks right up when I push the electric start button. Getting the machine through the doorway without destroying mower, shed and rider will be no mean feat, especially considering the temperamental throttle: the engine howls like a banshee when I give it a twist. Ominous black exhaust has filled the shed so completely that I can barely see daylight. Fumes have apparently aggravated a colony of wasps, because I hear them strafing through the smoke. I'm not interested in sacrificing myself to any stinging insects, so I jam the shifter into first gear. The mower lurches forward, knocking both door panels off their tracks. One panel flops on the dusty ground in front of the shed, while the other knocks yours truly off the mower, then lands on top of me so the two parts of the door form upper and lower halves of a giant hoagie sandwich with me laminated in the middle. From my vantage point, squashed and prone, I watch the Yazoo make dangerous circles just to my right. Each revolution brings it slightly closer, and I know if I don't clear out immediately I'll be in serious trouble. One of the wasps stings me on the ankle; I scream and do an adrenaline-induced superhuman push-up, lifting the heavy door panel in the process. I then struggle into an all-fours crouch, which slowly evolves into a sort of sumo squat, with the door panel resting on my back. My ankle burns like hell, and another wasp is only inches from my right ear. The little bastard is sharpening his stinger on a metal hinge. I use my strong thighs to push into a standing position, and in the process heave off approximately two hundred pounds of lumber. Miraculously, the Yazoo is no longer making circles and has actually begun carving a drunken swath toward the chain link fence. It might just knock the fence down and mow a path from here to Biloxi. I don't have much time to consider this idea, though, because the wasps, a dozen of them, are making ever smaller orbits around my head; it's time to make tracks. I run hunched over like a fullback in the general direction of the basketball courts. All but one of the wasps give up the chase. Twice I swat him out of the air, but he always comes back, meaner than ever. He finally nails me on the right kidney, a stab wound, a hot poker. I howl and slap him dead. There are no more wasps. I'm wounded, but home free. A quartet of black guys, the mess-hall crew, interrupt their basketball game to stare in wonderment at the spectacle I present. "Man," says the thin guy with the high-top sneakers, "you a fleet sombitch. You a track man or what?"

"Wasps," I gasp, my hands on my thighs.

When one of them starts to laugh, the others are helpless. This is the happiest moment of their lives. Their laughter is all but drowned out by the sound of the Yazoo grinding away against the fence, spinning its wheels.

I'm having a lovely day.

Seven

Stan took his week of vacation in August so he could spend a few days with me before I left for Columbus. As long as I could remember, he and I had never been much good at meaningful conversation. His talent was for small talk, especially the softening up of potential clients. But even then his amiable chatter was carefully rehearsed. Over the years of my childhood I'd practically memorized those phrases he kept stored in the loops of his salesman's brain. He would pick up the telephone and pull out a little mental stopper; everything spilled out of him like pills from a bottle. "And the kids, how are they?" "Oh . . . I thought you had kids. Well, how's the wife?"

On the Tuesday before my departure, we drove up to Detroit for a Tigers game. Ball games always gave Stan the chance to scream insults without fear of reprisal. He delighted in taunting the home-plate ump from the safety of his upper-deck perch. "Who paid you off?" he'd yell.

Stan was in a rare mood to talk as we drove up I-75 toward Mo-town; maybe he felt it was a now-or-never situation. As we were rolling across the state line into Michigan late on Tuesday afternoon, he started fiddling with the rearview mirror until he got it right. Then he glanced toward the big green Lambertville exit sign. Out of the clear blue he said, "I know it's been tough on you, not having your mother around these last few years."

I told him it hadn't been so bad. I noticed those tiny dimples forming on the nub of his chin, as they always did when he got emotional. "The corn is late this year," I said, pointing through the windshield at the endlessly green horizon.

"It was a dry spring," he told me, and adjusted his pipe in the ashtray.

"Hey, Stan," I said, trying to steer him away from what was bound to be a fairly maudlin spell. "Remember when Mom burned that Hawaiian shirt of yours? And what did you do? Went in her closet and found that purple blouse of hers and threw it in the burn barrel."

"It wasn't a flattering garment. Made her look like an eggplant." He tried to accelerate around a slow-moving Belaire, but every time he made an attempt the other car would speed up; to Stan other drivers were adversaries to be vanquished and humiliated. He honked his horn, shook his fist at the bald-headed driver of the Belaire, then tromped the gas pedal and sped out front. "That'll show the son of a bitch," he said.

Anyway, I guess it was my fault for heading off his chance at a major philosophical statement. But I knew what he wanted to say.

On August 17 we were cruising down High Street with its bars and Burger Boys and T-shirt emporiums, until we came to the university district. It took us half an hour to sort out the one-way streets and dead-end drives that led us nowhere. We finally got some competent directions from a green-clad medical student.

After picking up my key from the Chadwick Hall resident adviser's office, we carried my suitcases and cardboard boxes up the stairs, pausing at every landing so Stan could catch his breath. Coach Forbes had arranged for me to live among the behemoths who were going through pre-season football drills. Between the third and fourth floors, a big kid on crutches maneuvered down the steps past Stan and me. He looked scornfully at me as if I were one of those imported field-goal kickers; what else could I be at 155 pounds?

On the fourth floor, I looked into an open room and saw a nice-looking black kid who didn't seem big enough to be a football player. He glanced up from his *Playboy* magazine and gave us a friendly wave.

The door to 414 was unlocked. The air inside the room smelled of fresh paint and Pine-Sol and floor wax. I unfolded the doubled-up mattress of the bunk nearest the window and lay my boxes on top. "Not too bad," Stan said, gazing out the window toward the practice fields and Buckeye Stadium beyond. "You've got a view at least." He ran his index finger the length of the windowsill, scrutinized the result and nodded approvingly. I suggested we get the golf clubs and my other belongings from the car.

Only after I had situated the stuffed wolverine on a shelf above my bunk did it occur to me that this creature was mascot to the University of Michigan, OSU's hated archrival. Considering the clientele of this dorm, I decided to let Stan take the thing back to Bowling Green.

We walked together out to the parking lot for our goodbye. He groaned into the driver's seat, leaving the door open, and grasped the steering wheel as if it might guide him through what he had to say. "Listen, Teddy. You call me anytime you need more money, or anything else you can't get here. Okay?"

I said, "Sure. I appreciate the offer. I've got just about everything I need, though."

There was a long awkward pause, during which Stan cleared his throat. "Work hard in school. That's just as important as golf. *More* important!"

I promised I'd do my best, and gently closed the car door, knowing that if Stan went on with his speech he was bound to get weepy. At that moment, I felt selfish for not accepting the scholarship to Bowling Green State; I was concerned about how Stan was going to get along without me. "Good luck, son," he said in a thick, quavering voice. I shook his hand through the rolled-down window, thanked him for everything, made a weak joke about Sally peeing on the bedspread. "You know, I wish your mother were here now. She'd be very emotional."

I told him to take care of Lucille and Sally, and he promised he would. Then he started the engine and guided the Pontiac wagon slowly between a row of cars. A minute later, I could hear horns honking. Stan, no doubt, was cruising the wrong way down a one-way street. It wasn't hard to guess what he was hollering through his windshield.

I spent all day Wednesday on the Scarlet and Gray courses, trying to acclimate myself to the long, tight fairways and demonic bent-grass greens. I drove three balls from every tee, picking up the best one and playing the other two. With school out of session there were few players on the course. This was when golf became an almost mystical game for me. The crack of the ball against the driver's epoxy faceplate reverberated inside a pocket of oaks surrounding the tee. With no one behind me I could linger over every fairway shot, envision the club sliding perfectly beneath the ball and lofting it like a comet toward a green target far beyond a sleek pond. A golf course was an art form, good for inhaling, or if you wanted, for lying down on. It was something you sponged off the toes of your shoes at night. You could slice its fairways with a wedge, dent its green with a high arcing nine-iron shot, throw heaps of white sand out of its traps. And the golf course seemed to have parts like a human body: hillocks and valleys and dark forbidden parts that could break your heart.

By noon I'd played thirty-six holes, and I intended to play another thirty-six before I returned to the dorm. I was eating a Stewart sandwich in the clubhouse when a rangy kid walked in. The clubhouse attendant shook his hand across the counter and asked, "How're you hittin' em, Trayn?"

I knew immediately that this guy was no hacker. His glove

hand looked as if it had never been exposed to sunlight. And although his golf shoes were ready for the dumpster, his cleats were brand-new. Details. Signs. Dead giveaways. He had Popeye forearms; the old flexor digitoriums were unmistakably those of a golfer.

He noticed me over in a corner, munching on my rubbery cheeseburger, and asked if I wanted to play a round of golf. "What say?" Somehow he looked familiar to me; I was certain I'd seen him at one of the junior tournaments held through that summer. He walked across the green carpet and offered his sun-tanned right hand. I shook it and introduced myself.

"Dave Traynham," he said. And then I knew. He had won the medalist championship of the high school tournament two years in a row. I wondered why he wasn't attending Houston or Wake Forest, one of those schools that mass-produce golf professionals.

"I know all about you," he told me. "Coach Forbes said you were coming down to OSU." He ran his fingers through his tight-cropped curly hair. "He's high on you. Thinks you might be a real sleeper."

"I wonder about that," I said.

"Instead of making you play in that goofy qualifier, I can't understand why he doesn't just give you the scholarship and save himself some trouble. You can have an off day and waltz away with it, believe me. The whole thing is just tradition, *stupid* tradition at that."

On the way out to the first tee, we talked a little bit about the team and the next day's tournament. Trayn told me that he and the other scholarship players were required to play, too. "It's a pisser," he said. After Trayn had warmed up for a few minutes, I told him to tee off. It was clear from the enormous arc of his practice swing that he had excellent flexibility and power, so I wasn't surprised when he creamed his drive two hundred ninety yards almost dead center. He nonchalantly picked up his tee and lodged it behind his ear. "That's an incredible poke," I said, and he replied that he wasn't hitting very many like that one, unfortunately.

A temporary ego deficiency caused me to overswing my driver. That happened sometimes when I forgot I wasn't six feet four. I snap-hooked my drive into a row of pine trees guarding the left side of the fairway. "Want a mulligan?" Trayn laughed.

"I'll play it," I said. "Damn it."

Almost every freshman who owned a set of clubs was allowed to try out for the team. On Thursday morning, the putting green was swarming with golfers, some of whom were dressed in sneakers and cutoff Levi's. One wild-haired guy actually intended to play barefoot. Several others were pulling carts like the weekend golfers from the country club back home. A serious golfer would rather eat sod than be caught pulling a cart.

Coach Forbes blew a whistle and stood, clipboard in hand, just to the left of the putting green. He read a list of names, then assigned threesomes and tee-off times. Luckily, I was paired with one kid from the golf team and another freshman who was at least dressed for the occasion. It's difficult to concentrate on your own game when you're playing with a duffer who makes nines and twelves, shanks balls out of bounds and four-putts every other hole.

Some of the players on hand for the tryout managed only a few miserable holes before they marched like angry lemmings across Olentangy River Road to the parking lot.

All that practice from the day before had sharpened my game, and I felt very confident from the moment my yellow tee punctured the turf at number one. Trayn came by to wish me luck as I stood behind my ball and looked down the narrow first fairway. "Hit 'em straight," he said, and gave me a thumbs-up signal. My drive was a low fade that gained altitude until it lost steam and landed dead center of the fairway, two hundred fifty yards out. "You got it knocked, Teddy," he said. "Nice and easy all the way around."

I holed a miraculous bunker shot on the fifth hole, more than an hour later. Bill Garvey, the kid from the golf team, stood on the green and clapped for me. One nice thing about good golfers is that they appreciate a nice shot, and I *did* intend to land the ball high of the flag and let it run down to the hole. The shot simply overreached my expectations. I blew sand off the face of my wedge, slid the club into my bag and held up three fingers. I'd scored an eagle.

Because I was only an average driver, par fives didn't usually afford me the same advantage they did for the long hitters like Trayn. But on the last hole of the front side, I banged a low screaming fairway wood up toward the hole. The ball caromed off a sprinkler head and rolled to within twenty feet of the cup. I had to wait at the green while my playing partners knocked soft wedge shots onto the putting surface, slightly inside where I'd placed my marker. Garvey and the other player, whose name I never quite caught, watched me rim my putt one hundred eighty degrees around the hole. I dropped my putter and moaned, lamenting my inability to cash in on my eagle putt. Still, I'd carded a wonderful 33 on the front side of Scarlet, a score Nicklaus would have taken without complaint.

"How in the hell did you do that?" Coach Forbes asked me at the turn. He was sitting in an electric cart, eyeing me skeptically from beneath the bill of his Buckeye cap.

"Putter is carrying me," I told him. "It's magic. What else can I say?" In fact, my old Schenectady had been on fire all morning long. I was programmed to sink even the most mysterious putts, long meandering snakes that followed the contours of the green.

He had *known* I would be one of the favorites to win the floating scholarship, but he couldn't believe that I'd partially dismantled one of the tougher courses in the state. I was two shots ahead of Buzz Williams, the number one man on the team. But there wasn't much riding on it for him, just a foregone slot on the fall team, for which Trayn and I were ineligible. For me, this was life or death.

A kid from Sandusky was already twenty shots behind me after only nine holes. Back at the first tee he appeared to be a good golfer. But there he was, throwing his sticks into the back of a VW. He looked so disgusted, peeling out of the parking lot, that I wondered if he would ever play the game again.

The coach asked if I'd mind his driving the cart along with us on the back side. Maybe he thought I was bribing Garvey, paying him to shave strokes off my score. When I bogeyed number ten (I mashed a long three iron into the face of a greenside bunker) I felt some air leaking out of my ego. I tried to look cool as a julep at the eleventh tee, but my testicles had fled up behind my pancreas. Sweat ran into my eyes, my belly churned. And my concentration had floated off like a vapor trail. Instead of golf, I was thinking of money. Stan's money going into tuition, food, books . . . I shouldn't have gambled that my skills would save the day. It was a bad bet. I should have taken the scholarship to Bowling Green. I was a stupid ass for not doing it. On number eleven I came within one foot of a row of white out-of-bounds stakes. If Jimmy had seen me out there, stiff as a stork, he would have told me to pull myself together. "Relax, Teddy boy. Play your game," I said, strangling the rubber grip of my five iron. I slashed my ball toward the green. According to all laws of physics, it should have landed on the backslope and rolled all the way to downtown Columbus. Miraculously, my shot hit a sand-trap rake and stopped dead on the high side of the putting surface.

"You're one lucky bird," the coach said.

"Lucky? I was *playing* it to carom into the hole. Look at this rotten bounce I got." Garvey and the other guy had to watch while I rolled my putt to within four inches of the cup. The tap-in gave me par, and I knew I was back on track.

That Sunday night I phoned Stan to tell him I had won the scholarship. "No, I didn't come in first," I said.

"Oh?" He sounded surprised.

"I came in third, actually, but I beat all the other walk-ons. So I get free room, board and tuition and a private masseuse."

"Wonderful, Teddy, I'm very proud. A masseuse?"

"Just kidding, Stan."

For two weeks, I basked in my own glory. I attended my classes sporadically, golfed in the afternoons and played pinball with Garvey in the student union after supper. Although I'd purchased a collection of writing utensils and study aids at the bookstore, most of them were still in their packages. Then, when frowning Dr. Yashevsky handed back my first biology quiz, a horrendous 25 out of 100, I realized my plight; I could relate suddenly to numbers. I had offered practically nothing in the way of assistance to Ozzie, my zoology lab partner. He was always pointing at some pink gut, and I could only shrug. "Ozzie, I've been goofing off. I'm sorry," I told him. "From now on, you can count on me."

He said, "Yeah, sure," and rolled his eyes.

On a Friday night one of the jocks from down the hall knuckled my door and told me I had a phone call. I trotted down to the pay phone and said, "Stan?"

"Nah, it's Trayn. What're you doing?"

"Waxing my three wood," I said.

I heard him repeat what I'd said to somebody in the room with him. There was some giggling, which I vaguely resented. "We're going bar hopping. You and me and Janice and Candy."

"Who are Janice and Candy?" I asked.

"Janice is my girlfriend." Once again I heard him speaking to someone else: "Who are you, Candy?" Then he was talking to me again. "She's Janice's bosom buddy."

I told Trayn I'd meet them at the reflecting pond in half an hour, and hung up the phone. I was mentally selecting my attire as I padded barefoot down the hallway to my room.

Because it was a cool September evening, I wore a sweater with my Levi's, but pushed up my sleeves to show off my muscular forearms, a physical attribute I was proud of. They were standing there under a lamppost, Trayn's cigarette smoke obscuring their faces.

"Teddy, how's it going?" he shouted, and flicked his cigarette butt into the pond.

"Pretty well," I said, and smiled at the prettier of the two girls, hoping that one was Candy.

"This beauty here is Candy, and this little stump to my right is Janice." Bad luck. Candy *might be* passable in the smoky darkness of a downtown pub. Janice, on the other hand, had a beautiful mouth, and eyebrows that girls with less sense would take tweezers to. She had her hair in pigtails that should have looked foolish, but didn't. It was crazy for me to let my hormones riot through my system, as they were doing then. Maybe it was her mouth that undid me. Fitzgerald wrote a golf story called "Winter Dreams" about a beautiful girl that a hopelessly infatuated guy named Dexter saw on the links. Her name was Judy Jones, and F. Scott said that Judy's mouth "wanted to be kissed." I'd always thought of that as one of the silliest phrases he'd ever come up with—until I saw Janice's beautiful lower lip. "Hi," she said, and smiled her squinty, heartbreaking smile.

We walked in a foursome to Trayn's Malibu. He held hands with Janice, while Candy and I made absurd small talk behind them. My date for the evening was a very tall girl, with her Taiwanese shoes a bit taller than yours truly. When I made the obligatory move to hold her hand, I felt a monkey's fingers engulfing my own. I wondered if she could dance, and what I would look like in the dusky light, bumping hips with this Nordic giant. I made up my mind to imbibe as much beer as I could in as short a time as possible. Janice was Trayn's girl anyway, and Candy was pleasant enough and not really ugly. I might have a good time with her, and with a few beers in both of us who could tell what might happen later on. Tammy Listerman wasn't exactly the Mona Lisa either. She'd been good practice for situations like the one I was now involved in.

We went to the Rathskeller on High Street. Candy proved to be a remarkably good drinker, who seemed to stay sober until a stuporous tidal wave washed over her all at once. It was at that point that she and I ceased chatting about freshman English and wove out to the dance floor, where Trayn and Janice had been for almost an hour. "Hey. Is Candy a good time or what!" said

Trayn. "What did I *tell* you, buddy." He reached out and pulled Candy close enough to kiss her on the mouth.

Janice jabbed her elbow into his ribs and started dancing to the music, "Get Off of my Cloud," by the Rolling Stones. I liked the way she moved; nothing about her dancing seemed rehearsed or exaggerated. Instead, she was merely reacting to whatever music was coming through the speakers, or maybe it was the other way around. Meanwhile, Candy was a determined dancer with grandiose moves, so calculatingly seductive that I couldn't wait to get back to our table for another beer. She was such a big girl.

I'd gulped two quick ones and was about to put away a third when Janice put her hand on my shoulder. "Trayn won't slow-dance. I'm looking for a surrogate," she said. I saw her wink at Candy, a clear signal that this was purely platonic activity. Trayn stood in line outside the men's room.

It was a terrible song we were dancing to, a jukebox oldie some sadist had chosen. "Blue Velvet" by Bobby Vinton. Janice put her arms around my neck and leaned her damp forehead on my clavicle. I could feel her breasts, small but amazingly firm, against my rib cage. I felt something happening that I didn't want to happen, an eighth grade phenomenon I thought I'd outgrown. She knew exactly what was going on, drew her head back, squinted and smiled. "I love you too," she teased. I thought of Judy Jones and Dexter, what a forlorn case he was. I was sure I loved this girl just as much as Dexter loved Judy.

Trayn drove the smoke-filled car cautiously through the maze of one-way streets until we arrived at the parking lot. Candy pushed her door open, raced around the perimeter of the reflecting pond and disappeared behind a small bush. I could hear her throwing up over there, and then the laughing of the couples lying on their blankets under the stars. "God," Janice said.

"Don't kiss her good night," Trayn said.

Ever the polite gentlemen, Trayn and I walked the girls back to their dorm. I shook hands with Candy, who looked washed out and crazy-eyed, then waited awkwardly beneath an apple tree while Trayn and Janice embraced on the portico of her dormitory.

Trayn was laughing as he walked toward my outpost. "Sorry about that, buddy," he said. "Janice said to thank you for being so nice to that turkey."

"She wasn't that bad," I said.

Trayn slapped me on the shoulder and laughed so hard I thought he might lose his balance and fall down among the rotted apples. He made a sound like a hyena baying at the moon, and then we walked toward the men's dorms.

Eight

At dawn a bell clangs like misery in the hallway. I recoil under the blanket, then bolt upright, thinking that I'm thirteen, back at home, and I'm going to be late for school unless Stan has already cooked the oatmeal.

Only when the bell rings again five minutes later do I realize fully where I am. Instead of fending off nightmares for eight hours, I've slept in a dark dreamless void that seemed so much like death I'm just glad to be breathing.

My roommate is within seconds of emerging from an apparently pleasant dream; maybe he's been playing a harp or something up on cloud nine. He smacks his lips, groans a few times and rolls over, eyes wide open, a rotund zombie. He looks at me as if I'm a holy apparition, shakes his jowls a few times and sits up with his bare feet on the cement floor. "I certainly don't appreciate that bell," he says, more to himself than to me. "Not one bit." I believe he says those same words every morning. He looks over in my direction again, only this time with a sort of

77

hungry evangelical expression on his face. "So . . . you're Kendall. I was wondering if our paths would ever cross. But here you are." He whacks at his gut for no apparent reason. Then I hear the reason: he lets go with a low moaning fart, not quite muffled by the blanket bunched up behind him. "I beg your pardon for that little indiscretion. I'm afraid it's a cross the Lord has asked me to bear. My bowels are in rebellion against the prison food."

I'm already rehearsing my request for a change of rooms. I could probably outlast him on the born-again front. But his farting problem is hard to take. The room stinks from Chapman's all-night blasts of gastric wind. "No problem," I tell him. "The prison food will get us all sooner or later."

"Well," he says, "you're far more tolerant than my last roommate. Why, he threatened to kill me if he so much as detected the faintest . . . Well, I told the warden about it. And he moved me to this room, which I had all to myself until your arrival."

"Do you suppose we could open the window?" I ask.

"Of course. Of course." He ambles over to crank the window open himself. "I do appreciate your patience. Large people like me are so often stereotyped as somehow repugnant in all respects, and I'm afraid I don't do much to counteract that misjudgment."

I'm embarrassed that his pajamas are so much like my own, gray with red piping around cuffs and collar, except that mine fit and his seem to have been made for somebody about the size of Drago. "Thanks, thanks very much. That's better."

"I imagine you're rather curious about my little shrine over there in the corner. Worried, I suppose, that I'm one of those nuisances whose only purpose in life is to save lost souls." He sits down on his cot again. "Not to worry. If the Lord wants you, he'll find you, just as he found me."

"True," I say.

"The warden has informed me that I'm to be your greenskeeping assistant. I'm not unhappy about that, but I feel I *should* tell you; I'm prone to sunburn, although you won't hear me

78

complaining. I've invested in a straw hat, which should help somewhat." He looks on the verge of cutting loose another boomer, but it's merely the strain of elevating his body from the sunken mattress. He pads across the room and offers me his hand. "Let me say that I'm pleased to meet you, although I can't help believing you purposefully avoided me all day yesterday."

I shake hands with him. "I was just getting myself acclimated. You know how that is." For a while neither one of us can think of anything else to say. Finally, I ask the inevitable question. "What are you in for?"

"Nothing especially interesting. I embezzled funds from my brother's potato-chip business. At the time, the lure of money was more than I could resist."

"Ah," I say. He doesn't ask me why I'm here. Maybe he already knows.

While Chapman stands barefoot at his dresser, leafing through an open Bible, I snatch my dop kit and a Ramada Inn towel from a shelf and head for the shower. I want to get there before the other inmates do. It's an embarrassing thing to admit, but I've never been a big fan of gang showers. Even on the tour, I always waited until I got back to the motel before I showered off. Maybe I just didn't want to know what the Golden Bear looks like in the buff. Or vice versa.

About the time I get my hair wet, Grayson stalks into the shower clutching a bar of green soap. I suddenly don't exist. He's focused on two stainless-steel faucets, which he twists simultaneously, as if it doesn't matter if he boils or freezes. "How're you doing this morning?" I ask.

He lets a stream of hot water land on his pink tongue, rinses his mouth and spits the water out. He grabs the green soap from a metal dish, lathers his scalp, armpits, chest, balls and finally his feet. I realize I'm staring, which could be hazardous to my health. I rinse off, grab my towel off a hook above one of the porcelain sinks and wrap it around my waist. "See you later," I chirp, and trot like a wimp albino back to my room.

I put on my dirty Levi's, a crisp denim shirt and my Adidas.

Chapman, I presume, has already dressed and gone down to breakfast with his Christian friends.

My guess proves correct. When I walk into the mess hall, they're sitting around their usual table beneath the clock. For breakfast this morning there is an enormous shallow box full of doughnuts and jelly rolls. "You can take three," says one of the Drifters. (He doesn't recognize me.) I take two vanilla cremes and a blueberry. I'm still a little groggy from having slept so well, and I fill a Styrofoam cup with coffee so strong it spews black as death from the machine.

At 7:55 I return my tray and head for the exit.

In the distance, out by the shed, I see Drago hurling a bamboo rake like a javelin. He gets a Babe Zaharias running start, then launches the tool in a high arc. The rake end seems to work like a huge fin, and he gets surprising distance with his throw. The handle actually sticks into the muddy ground alongside the dirt road.

"Did you see that?" he asks when I approach. "A hundred yards or more, I'll bet."

"You're nuts, Drago," I say. He gets a hurt look on his face, retrieves the rake and plods back like a shamed spaniel. "Have you seen Chapman?"

"Not yet. He'll be along. Don't worry."

While Drago stands with his rake at present-arms position, I step inside the doorless shed so I can figure out what's at hand. The wasps are quiet in their nest. I make a mental note to fumigate them before the day is over.

Warden Maples was right. The greens mower is broken. I pull the thing by its rubberized handle out into the daylight. It stutters and coughs when I yank the starter cord. The second attempt yields the same results. I unclamp the blade housing and set it aside. The reel is badly damaged. It will probably need to be replaced; that will cost money, which I apparently won't get from the warden. There's still eighteen thousand dollars left in my account; it's probably wise to spend some of the cash before

Trayn files the inevitable personal damage suit against me. "I can fix that," says Drago, whose shadow now squats next to mine. "I'm a trained mechanic."

"Are you really?" I ask.

"U.S. Army trained me. Used to fix whirlybirds. You got the tools, I got the talent."

"Can you really do something about this damned mower?"

He disappears into the shed and reemerges seconds later with an adjustable wrench he's obviously hidden God knows where. His hands work like a frantic surgeon's. He loosens a couple of setscrews, removes a cotter pin, disengages the gears, twists out a few bolts (which he carefully places in the upturned blade housing) and with the heel of his hand knocks the reel from a pair of lateral brackets. "Easy as shoofly pie," he crows. I'm astounded, dumbfounded and incredulous. The little bugger actually knows what he's doing. "What we need to do," he says, "is file the blades down about a quarter of an inch, all three of them, then straighten the suckers out with a rubber hammer and then put the whole kit and caboodle back on the rig. If we set the brackets down a quarter inch to make up for what we shaved off, we're in business. Might have to carve 'em down a bit, though. Not sure they're deep enough the way they are now." I feel like clapping for him.

"You can do all that?"

"Naw . . . ain't got no file."

"I'll get you one." My brain is swimming in a euphoric cloud when I notice a khaki apparition trudging slowly in our direction. Chapman is wearing a straw hat big as a birdbath.

"Oh *my*," he says upon arrival. "You mean to tell me that the third member of our crew is this . . . creature?"

"Hey, fuck you," Drago says. He's still got the wrench in his hand and means to make a martyr out of my roommate.

"Cool it, Drago," I say. I tell Chapman he's not being a good Christian, figuring that might be the best approach.

"That man is the devil incarnate. The demon seed."

81

"I'm gonna kill that fat turd," says Drago, who strains against the hand I've planted firmly on his sternum.

"I'm going back to the laundry. This is not, decidedly *not*, for me!" Chapman pouts.

"Both of you, sit down!"

Chapman reluctantly sits down, a hostile Buddha, on the wet grass. Drago squats, still clutching his weapon.

"Chapman, do you mind telling me what's going on here?"

He blows out an explosion of breath, hauls in a lungful and looks at me. "He desecrated my statue of the Virgin Mary. I had to have her professionally repainted."

"Naw, I ditten. It was somebody else. Hell, boss, he's not even a *mackerel snapper.*"

"Drago, did you damage Chapman's property?"

"I only painted a little mustache on it. That's all. Big deal."

In this case, I've got to side with my roommate. But there's not much I can do to placate him. I try anyway. "Chapman, is there something Drago might do to make things right with you?"

"I rather doubt it."

"You want to go back to the laundry, then?"

"I'd prefer to work with *kneegrows* than with this heathen." Drago hurls the wrench end over end at Chapman, who instinctively tosses up his beefy arm and deflects the tool. He knocks his hat off in the process. "I rest my case," he hisses.

He struggles to his feet, picks up his enormous chapeau and waddles angrily toward the warden's office building.

"That's *that*," I say. "Let's get back to work."

"Just tell me what you want me to do, boss."

"Think you can ride the Yazoo without killing yourself?"

"A piece of cake," he says, his shirt-cardboard ears actually wiggling with anticipation.

"Okay. Take the empty gas can over to the big tank at the gate, fill her up, and we'll start mowing."

Remembering the wasps from yesterday, I put the Yazoo in neutral and roll it out of the shed and onto the dirt road well out of harm's way. I do the same with the Cub, which is practically new, and set the blades up a couple of inches.

Drago looks almost gleeful scurrying through the wet grass with the five-gallon can of fuel. What a strange bird he is. I can't help wondering what's his crime. Probably showed his wienie to a troop of Brownies.

We gas up the mowers and climb aboard. My assistant greens-keeper looks like he was born on the seat of a Yazoo. He starts the engine, adjusts the choke so the dark billow of exhaust clarifies, pops the machine into gear and roars away. He cuts an almost perfectly straight line toward the chain link fence. That first swath will be the dividing line between his half of the acreage and mine.

The Cub is slower, less powerful and less maneuverable than the Yazoo, but it hums nicely when I turn the key. I overlap the newly mowed strip and make my first pass along the fence. The grass is so thick that my mower keeps stalling out. My one regret is that I'm probably destroying the nesting ground of hundreds of wild game birds. I flush a bevy of quail before I've even completed one loop around my portion of the links. Every time we pass each other in the middle zone, Drago salutes me. He's having the time of his life.

I'm lucky to have begun my mowing in late May, before the ferocious summer heat arrives. Not that it isn't already hot; it is. But the Bermuda grass hasn't fully returned from winter dormancy, meaning that it can be mowed back almost to its roots, which ordinarily sprawl just beneath the surface of the soil. But this field of grass is unused to being mowed; the root system hasn't been trained to stay underground. Instead, it has cheated its way up the tiny shoots, making itself vulnerable to a mower blade set too low.

It will be a gradual process, coaxing the roots back to where they belong, a matter of mowing frequently, and a little closer every time out. Before anything else can be done with the golf course, the Bermuda grass must be carefully retrained. Drago and I will need to rake up the clippings after each mowing to let the grass breathe. I suppose I should be frustrated by the tediousness of what lies ahead, but I've got thirteen months to kill, plenty of time to do the job right.

Drago and I knock off for lunch—hamburgers and fries—then return to our mowing. At three o'clock we finally finish. It's easy to tell where we were when the dew evaporated because the grass cut after midmorning is overlaid with an even blanket of clippings, while the early morning harvest lies in clumps, some the size of basketballs. Drago has cut more than twice as much as I have, and I'm determined to talk the warden into trading the rotary Cub mower for a good set of reels suitable for mowing fairways.

We park our machines just outside the shed, then wheel them silently into the dark interior. "You did a good job, Drago. Honest. I didn't think you had it in you." He's sweaty, and grass clippings cling to his eyebrows. Our sneakers are stained green.

"Did I really do a good job?"

"You did a good job," I tell him. He flashes a gnomish grin. "Tomorrow we rake."

Nine

In January of my freshman year, the OSU golf team headed south for the winter tournaments held in Florida and Georgia. I had hoped to make the trip as our sixth man, but when Coach Forbes called me into his stadium office the news was bad. Mitch Hazeltine, a senior, would make the trip. "Sorry, Kendall. This is his last year. All things being equal, I have to give him the nod." I gazed at the puny trophies on the coach's bookshelf.

All things were *not* equal. Throughout the fall I'd been playing with either Trayn or Hazeltine or Williams nearly every day. While Mitch occasionally put together a nice score, he was just as likely to blow his engine on the first hole. I wanted to argue the point, but all those years living with Stan had conditioned me to smile politely and accept illogic as a fact of life. "I understand," I said. "I know it will mean a lot to him."

If a howling westerly wind hadn't been blowing me toward my dorm, I might not have had the energy to make it home. I trudged up the stairs, realizing how laborious this climb must have been for my heavy, out-of-shape father, a man who inhaled pipe smoke and ate pork for a hobby. I didn't even speak to Kip, my new roommate (the insane Ned Byers had flunked out after one semester), but sat on the bed, pulled off my chukka boots and hurled them into the closet. I lay back on my mattress and stared at the plaster ceiling. I was suddenly fed up with golf, tired of Ohio State, sick of women who didn't look and act like Janice, and maybe even homesick. Stan, while affecting a sham euphoria during my Christmas vacation, wasn't doing well. The garage was a mess for the first time in my recent memory. If he was watching a football game on television, he could never tell me the score. More than once, he failed to answer the ringing phone, although it sat on the table right next to his La-Z-Boy. Maybe it was a client he simply didn't want to talk with, but I doubted it. My first-semester grades were adequate, but I didn't hear Stan bragging about Teddy the scholar over at Lucille's. Instead he rambled about my composition grade, a very generous B given me by a graduate student who put up with a series of essays on golf.

I decided to put on my winter garb and let the wind blow me toward one of the High Street saloons this time; I wanted to give my self-pity something to float in. As I was rounding the corner of Kirby Infirmary, Trayn's Malibu eased up behind me, its engine so beautifully tuned that I didn't notice the car until he leaned on the horn and spooked me out of my funereal trance. He angled his head out the window, and with gray billows of frost issuing from his mouth he said, "Hop in, buddy. I'll give you a ride." A huge gust caught the passenger door when he shoved it open, almost blowing it off its hinges. I climbed into the passenger seat, and was subjected to about three Gs as Trayn popped the clutch and peeled onto High Street. "I *do* love speed," he whooped, power-shifting from second to third. He had already barreled through two yellow lights before he got around to asking me where I was headed.

"Pinelli's," I said. "Got to have a few Saturday-afternoon beers."

"Mind if I join you?" He was drumming out the beat of a Fleetwood Mac song on his steering wheel.

"No, I don't mind," I said. "So . . . when are you heading south?"

"Tuesday, buddy." Trayn slowed down suddenly as if he actually foresaw the patrol car hiding behind a dumpster near a 7-Eleven. "You crafty *dog,*" he said to the cop who sat behind the wheel. Then, in that straight-in-the-eye way of his, he looked at me and said, "Wish you were going. Goddamnit, you *ought* to be going instead of that fag Hazeltine."

"He's not a fag."

"Nah, I guess not. He might have buggered old Forbes to make this trip, though. If you want to know the truth, Hazeltine is just a pussywhipped dick."

"And you're a damned caveman, right?"

"Don't *have* to be."

I sincerely hoped Janice would haul off and poke him in the chops someday. Once at the Rathskeller I'd seen him shove his hand inside the front of her sweater, then look over at me with his tongue hanging out and a lunatic gleam in his eye. I laughed then, probably because I was drunk. If I'd been her brother instead of just another of his golfing pals I might have slugged him. Trayn had embarrassed her and she was furious at him. She stomped toward an exit, but he grabbed her shoulders and wouldn't let her leave. He might have been apologizing to her; I couldn't hear what they were saying to each other. But he kissed Janice on the forehead and that, he supposed, made everything okay. Trayn winked over at me: *he* was in control. Despite incidents like this one, I was fond of Trayn. Part of his likability hinged on that dangerous line he insisted on walking. He was the same way off the golf course as he was on, with a reckless kind of power that no one, including him, could alter. If you liked Trayn, you just hopped aboard and rode along.

Trayn and I sat at the bar in Pinelli's, draining pitchers, alternately gaping at the fish tanks set beneath the rows of liquor bottles or commiserating about my failure to make the traveling team. We engaged in some idle speculation over how we might disable Hazeltine without drawing attention to ourselves. "Wait until the SOB is hiking up an adjoining fairway. I'll drill a liner right up his butt hole."

Trayn dropped me off at Chadwick dorm shortly after darkness had swallowed the football stadium. He had a date with Janice later that evening. Meanwhile, I spent my Saturday night in the downstairs TV room watching an Atlanta Hawks basketball game with the other dorm rats who didn't have dates. I ate a Baby Ruth and some cheese crackers, called that dinner and was sound asleep in a Naugahyde chair before the game ended.

I awoke at three in the morning with a roaring hangover that had collapsed my skull like a popcorn box. I groped toward the staircase and stumbled up the steps to my room. Without bothering to get out of my tobacco-smoke clothes, I flopped on the bed and lapsed into a morbid dream state which found Janice in variously dangerous situations. The outcome always featured Ted Kendall dashing onto the scene like an idiot knight, slugging it out against some clod strangely reminiscent of Trayn. At dawn I fumbled through my dresser drawers, then Kip's, in search of Alka-Seltzer. My quest yielded only a smashed Rolaid, whose particles I nudged onto a Shell credit card as if they were high-grade cocaine. I licked them off the card, then fell again onto the mattress, where I lay in agony until approximately noon.

Later, wearing only a T-shirt and blue jeans, I was standing in the dorm parking lot, letting the crisp January air heal me, when Janice and Candy appeared from behind a Bonneville station wagon. "Good Lord, Teddy, what on earth are you doing?" Janice asked.

"Worshipping Ra!" I said. I knew my eyeballs would reveal whatever secret I wanted to hide.

"Well, you look like death's first cousin," she said.

I said hello to Candy, but the sight of her reminded me of the last minutes of our first and only date. I was immediately so nauseous that I had to sit down on the bumper of an old Volvo.

88

"Do you think you'll feel well enough to drop by my dorm tonight? I need to talk with you."

I said I'd be fine by then, and that she could expect me at around eight o'clock. She put her cold bare hand on my neck and gave me a squeeze. *"Ciao,"* she said. I watched the two of them cross Cannon Road, then walk into the Holloway Pharmacy.

One of the favorite sports among the residents of Chadwick Hall was long-distance window gazing. It was common to find guys crouched among the shrubs that bordered the reflecting pond, their binoculars trained on the windows of Medford Tower, the tallest building on campus. One of those windows belonged to Janice. I was feeling fairly well restored by 7:45 on that Sunday night, so when I saw Maury Benson skulking among the forsythia bushes I asked him if I might have a peek. "Sure," he said, and handed me his Bausch & Lomb binoculars. I skipped them like a dead turtle into the center of the barely frozen pond.

"Sorry," I said, and walked heroically toward Medford for my chat with Janice.

I heard Maury yelling at me from the bushes. "You fucker!"

I used the desk phone to call Janice's room. "Be right down," she said. I waited by the elevator for her.

I wondered why Janice would want to see me on a Sunday night. Did she want me to give Candy one more chance at love? I guessed that was probably it. No doubt they'd gone over to Holloway's Pharmacy to buy condoms for me.

The elevator door wheezed open and there she was, wearing one of Trayn's red OSU golf shirts like a smock over her faded corduroy jeans. Janice's new short haircut suited her perfectly; it made her look smart and a little bit impish at the same time. "Hi, Teddy. Feeling better?"

"Yeah. Thanks," I said.

She grabbed my hand and wordlessly led me to the carpeted guest room with its old Kimball spinet and fake Van Gogh paintings. We sat together on a tufted sofa far away from a girl and her parents who were having a heated argument about money. Janice folded and unfolded a fresh Kleenex for a minute, then looked at me. "Trayn thinks the *world* of you," she said. "And so do I, Teddy. In fact, I probably love you, although it may be a different kind of love than what I feel for him." She was trying to read the asymmetrical expression on my face. "See what I'm driving at?"

"Not quite."

"Well," she said. "I can trust you. Have faith in you."

"Good," I said. Never in my life had I been more in doubt about the destination of a friendly chat.

"Teddy, I think I'm pregnant. That's what I'm driving at. And I'm not sure what I want to do about it." So there it was. A nuclear bomb blast.

"And you want my advice?" I asked. It was pure reflex. Instead of sitting there acting logical, I wanted to tip over the piano and rip out its wires.

"Maybe you can tell me what Trayn would do if I told him." She pressed the Kleenex to her eyes, then blew her nose. "I'm at kind of a loss."

"Weren't you taking the pill? You're not Catholic. I know that!"

"I can't take them . . . female reasons. So we were counting days, and we sort of miscounted."

"You could have an abortion," I said, almost coldly.

"I probably will. I just don't know if I should tell Trayn. He's got this Florida trip coming up."

"The *hell* with that," I said, so loudly that the father of the spendthrift looked angrily in my direction. "Why don't you make sure you're pregnant first? Maybe you're not."

"Well, I'm two weeks late for my period. God. This sounds just like one of those *troubled-teen* movies. 'I'm two weeks late!' The boyfriend always gets scared and joins the Army. Think Trayn will join the Army?"

I groped for an ejection button on the arm of the sofa. All those impossible fantasies I'd had about her and me were sink-ing like granite into the pit of my stomach. I held her hand for a minute, trying to think of something sage I might contribute. Trayn was a bastard for putting her in this situation. And she was just stupid for allowing it.

"Listen, go to the infirmary tomorrow. Find out for sure. Then tell Trayn," I said. "He's got to know. He's the father, after all."

"All right," Janice said. She seemed disappointed by my pragmatism. But what else could she expect? I wasn't a guru and I wasn't a guidance counselor, either. I certainly didn't understand Trayn any better than she did. "I'll call you tomorrow. Okay?"

"Sure. As soon as you hear anything." We stood up. I put my arm around her and guided her to the elevator. I could feel her trembling as we walked. *Is this an act?* I wondered. Before she stepped through the opened doors, she kissed me briefly on the cheek, stepped back momentarily, then pressed her lips heavily against my mouth. Finally, she retreated into the brightly lighted cubicle. It was very theatrical.

Still, she looked very small, miles away, standing there. The doors closed and she was gone.

On Monday night Janice phoned to say she wasn't pregnant after all. "False alarm," she said. Everything was fine again and Trayn could play his golf and I could reinflate my ludicrous notions about life with Janice.

Ten

Drago and I watch the sky every day, and listen to the radio for the weather forecasts. If showers are predicted, we broadcast fertilizer over the entire golf course so the rain can dissolve it and drive the nutrients deep into the soil. This entices the roots of the Bermuda downward, so we can mow closer and closer every time out. The stack of 8-8-8 in the shed is almost depleted, and soon we'll need to replenish.

It has taken three weeks of almost constant mowing to bring the turf back to where it should always have been. Although he's a bona fide loony, Drago cuts the straightest line I've ever seen. Sometimes he gets bored going back and forth all day on the Yazoo; I've seen him out there standing one-legged on the seat, steering with his other foot like Buffalo Bill Cody. I know he's ready to do something besides mow and rake for a change. And I have my plans.

Warden Maples has come out a few times to check on our progress. "This looks mighty nice, boys. Mighty nice." He thinks we're only a week or two away from planting a couple of flag sticks in the middle of the two mounds and accepting that as the finished product. Today I have to tell him the facts of the matter.

Ames has been scarce lately; he took a week of vacation to visit his son over in Mobile, and he just returned yesterday. He seems genuinely glad to see me when he opens the office door and let's me in.

"Coffee?" he asks. I wonder how many cups of the stuff he drinks every day. He reveres the percolating machine the way Chapman does his statue of the Virgin.

"Sure, thanks," I say. He hands me a Styrofoam cup brimming with perfect brew.

"How're you getting along with Chapman?" he wonders. "Any troubles? Has he stunk you out yet?"

"Let's just say we sleep with the windows open," I tell him. "He's a peculiar one, that's for sure, but he keeps pretty much to himself."

"Well, that's good. Everybody in the laundry hates his guts. He rubs people the wrong way, I guess."

"You might say so," I reply. We don't get any further than that in our conversation because the warden's door opens and he tells me to come on into the office.

"Have a seat," he says. This morning he's already eaten something from McDonald's. The empty bag is crumpled in the trash can to my right. "What can I do for you?"

"Warden, it's about the golf course. I need your help," I say.

He cuts me off before I can finish. "You know I'll help you in any way I can, Kendall, because I really appreciate the job you're doing out there. I wouldn't have believed it could look so good."

"Thanks very much. It means a lot to hear that from you. Makes it easier to ask a favor."

"Oh? What sort of favor?" His eyebrows become unparallel. He sniffs trouble.

"We can't mow the fairways properly unless we have a reel assembly we can pull behind the little Jacobsen tractor."

"Why, I was out there yesterday. The fairways looked perfect to me."

"We have to mow them closer, and we can't do that with the Yazoo. If we drop the blade even another quarter inch we get bald spots wherever the ground is uneven."

"Son, you're just going to have to make do with what you have. Wish I could help you, but I have to account for every nickel I spend on maintenance and equipment. It would never wash with the higher-ups."

"I know that, sir. So I was thinking we could trade in the Cub rotary," I say. "If you could spare just another two or three hundred dollars for a set of reels, I think you'd be happy with the results."

"Out of the question," he almost shouts. "Can't justify it. I'm only a bureaucrat, son. I don't own the purse strings any more than I own this mower you want to trade. Everything comes down from the capitol."

"What if I can get some used equipment? How about that?" I don't think I've ever seen a classified ad for a used reel assembly. Maybe in a greenskeeper magazine, if there is such a thing. Who knows? I'm desperate.

"Sorry. Can't be done."

I don't know if I really expected any help from Maples, but I'm frozen in my chair, unable to respond to this it's-out-of-my-hands logic. I can see the golf course through the window above his left shoulder. From here it looks like a beautiful green field you might admire from the window of an airplane.

He leans across the desk toward me. The red tint dissolves from his face. "I'd like to help you, but I can't spend more money than I already have. Hell, Kendall, that fertilizer you've been using costs nine dollars per bag." He coughs nervously. "Let me ask you something. What do you suppose would happen if one of those task forces from the State Senate dropped in for a little visit? And they see this goddamn showplace of a golf course. They'd figure it's about time they find better ways to spend their money, don't you think?"

"So you're telling me I can't make any more improvements on the course? You're telling me my job is complete, that from now on I'm just a mower jockey?"

"Not at all. You can make any improvements you want, so long as they don't cost us any more money. That's what I'm telling you."

"I just want a set of reels to pull behind the tractor. That's all I want. You could justify that lots of ways. There's other grass in this prison. And I want some white sand for the traps. I need some good white beach sand. Like the stuff you find over at Pensacola."

"Sorry, no can do. That's dollars. It costs money to buy and transport sand."

"Shit!" I say, and I pound out of the office, right past Ames and through the front door.

Drago is asleep on the seat of the Yazoo when I arrive at the shed. "Hey," I shout. He springs from his perch and assumes a Tai Kwan Do stance. He comes quickly to his senses, shoves his hands in his pockets. "We're screwed," I tell him. "Warden won't shell out a dime, not even for sand. Can you believe that?"

"Man, I knew he was a asshole. Maybe I should talk to him, boss."

I believe Drago is serious. If he ever found his way into the warden's office, both of us would be folding denim shirts for a year. "Forget it."

I lead my goofy little Friday out to number one green. We stand on the brink of what looks like a crescent-shaped, leaf-filled latrine. "Guess what we're going to do."

"I can't tell you, boss. Got some big plans?"

"We're going to expand the greens. The first thing we'll do is pull up sod about two-thirds of the way around both of them. Then we'll enlarge the bunkers on the course, saving all that sod and reusing the dirt to broaden the slopes of both the greens. Then we use all the grass we set aside, plus whatever we can dig up around the fence, to complete the job."

"Sounds good to me," Drago says. I can tell he's glad we won't be mowing for a few days. "When do we start?"

"Go get the wheelbarrow and two shovels," I tell him. He trots back to get the tools, pausing every so often to do a wild-looking pirouette.

We spend all day Friday carving long strips of grass away from the banks of the greens. We roll them into bundles and barrow them to an area where the south and east fences converge. This is a good spot because it's near one of the spigots distributed at approximately one-hundred-yard intervals throughout the prison grounds. The sod needs a thorough soaking in order to survive the next several weeks.

At the end of our workday, Drago looks like the loser in a mud-wrestling competition. His teeth gleam through the grime like piano keys. "We did pretty good work today, didn't we?"

"Yes, Drago," I say. "We really did."

When I return from the shower that afternoon, Chapman is sprawled on his bed, groaning, an ice pack pressed against his face. I don some clean clothes, comb my hair and roll on some pine deodorant. He's apparently not talking, so I ask what on earth happened to him.

"The *kneegrows,*" he sniffs. "In the laundry. They tried to kill me. I should have known better than to go back there. Ham's race. God's outcasts. I made one innocent statement about genetics and intelligence. Before I knew it I was swarmed." He pulls the ice pack away from his eye, which is, even in the context of his already blubbery face, swollen and red.

"So now what. Did you get the situation resolved?"

"Far from it. If it hadn't been for Grayson, black though he is, I would either be dead or in an iron lung even as we speak. He was magnificent. I'm certain that if you bother to check their rooms, you'll find that some of the attackers are in far worse shape than I."

"What happens on Monday when you go back to the laundry?"

"You must be joking," he snarls from a sitting position. "I'll never go back there. Grayson and I have been exiled, as it were, to the golf course for the indefinite future."

I'm not quite sure how I feel about this bit of news. Certainly, I can use some help with the newest phase of the project, but I'm not sure Grayson and Chapman will be anything but an obstacle to progress. I envision a state of constant warfare between Drago and my roommate. Grayson is an enigma. He may be a good worker for all I know. But I suspect he'll wreak havoc on the esprit de corps, assuming I can neutralize the hostility between Chapman and the mad Yugoslavian.

I'm so tired from having shoveled sod all day Friday that I'm still sleeping at eight o'clock when Ames knocks on my door. I push myself into a sitting position and ask him what's the problem. "Warden wants to see you right away," he says. "He's mighty pissed off about something."

Feeling like the tin woodsman from *The Wizard of Oz*, I push my stiff limbs through shirt sleeves and pant legs. I follow Ames down the stairs, a man en route to his own execution, and walk with him to the office building. "Do you know what this is all about?" I ask.

"I ain't saying. But I think it's about the golf course."

This morning the warden is in the outer office before I even get a chance at the coffee. "Get in there," he snaps, and points at his desk inside. He face matches his red tie.

I sit down in the chair, waiting for him to move to his side of the desk. "Stand up, you won't be here that long," he says. I scramble to my feet and look at his squinted eyes. He has a crushed Styrofoam cup in the fist he shakes in my face. "I don't know what the hell you think you're doing out there, but I don't like it one bit. By Monday night I want all that sod right back where it was on Friday morning. If it's not, you'll be on the shit detail for as long as you're here."

"I beg your pardon, Warden. You said I could make any improvements . . ."

97

"I didn't say you could tear the course apart. Now get the hell out of here."

My ear tips feel hot, my limbs are rubbery and weak. I can barely walk back to 2-C. In fact, I make a detour past the dormitory to the dirt road leading out to the golf course.

I stand on the rough of number one fairway, studying the black scars left by yesterday's excavation. I sit down on the wet grass. The dew soaks through my jeans, all the way to my skin. There's an empty feeling in my stomach. This is the first time since I arrived here that I've seen this golf course as literally as I see it now. It's grass and dirt and dead leaves and a couple of kudzu-infested oak trees. Nothing more. Not a damn thing more. It's okay with me if we spend all day Monday resodding. Then on Tuesday we can strip it all off again so we can put it back on Wednesday. That's what it's all about anyway, killing time. Like Ping-Pong and Soul Train and bridge and poker and basketball and writing a book or letters to Stan. The golf course is nothing. Just an excuse to make the time go.

Saturday afternoon a letter appears in my mailbox. It takes three tries for me to get the combination lock to work, but finally the little door opens and I pull out the envelope. Stan's handwriting it still slightly wobbly, but noticeably better than three weeks ago.

I walk down to the library with it and sit next to the window. Included with the letter is the picture of me sitting on the bench with Manny and Peggy and Spengle. There is also a snapshot of my mother holding Sally like a loaf of bread under her arm. Mom looks healthy and beautiful in the photo, although I know she's only a few days from going into the hospital. My vision is so blurry that it takes me a minute or so to focus on the last of the three pictures Stan enclosed. It's one I took myself. Stan is with Jimmy in front of the clubhouse. There's nothing very interesting about the photograph, except that it's the only one I recall in which the two of them are together. My jaws start to hurt and my throat thickens. I know if I start reading now I'll be a mess. I walk around a bookcase to compose myself before somebody, like Drago for instance, comes through the door. But it doesn't work. I'm sobbing away, wiping my eyes on my shirt sleeve, taking deep breaths in hopes that when I exhale all the amorphous misery will float away. Finally, the technique works. and I return to the chair, where I read the letter. It says:

Dear Ted,

I found these photographs in a shoe box in the hall closet. I hope they fit the bill. The one of your mother, I think, is particularly good. Don't lose it, because it's one of my favorites.

Dr. Jamison is very pleased with my recovery so far. Phlebitis. Sounds like something Sally would get, doesn't it?

You sounded depressed in your last letter. I hope that feeling lifts. Just ride it out, Teddy. Tempus fugit. Remember that. Time flies.

Tammy Listerman works in the pharmacy now. She asked about you. I think she's a nice girl. You should look her up when you get out. I think the sooner you put Janice behind you, the better off you'll be.

I'm sorry to tell you that Sally is going downhill. Her seizures are a frequent occurrence now. She's very slow and I don't think she feels too well. I may take her to the vet tomorrow to see what he thinks about her chances of coming out of this thing.

Not much other news here. Nobody to replace Jimmy yet at the club. Lucille is fine and sends her love. She's been a wonderful help to me.

Keep your golf game sharp. You've got a nice future ahead of you as a professional golfer if you can stay sharp.

It's hard for me to write nowadays. Stay well and happy, son.

Love,
STAN

I spend a while longer looking at the pictures and rereading Stan's letter. Than I go to my room, lie on the bed and try to sleep.

Eleven

Trayn's relationship with Janice was, in a strange sort of way, like a round of golf. But everything else in life is, too, if you work at the metaphor, so why bother with useless comparisons? Trayn loved her, she loved him, and that was that. I was always in the background, though, the courtly eunuch, ready to offer Janice advice or platonic affection when they had one of their rows, which was often. If they were having a bad time of it, Janice would call me on the phone like a high school girl. "Is Trayn still mad at me?" she'd ask. Usually, I'd say something like "How could he be mad at you?" but other times I'd tell her I had no idea, and why didn't she ask him. "Now *you're* mad at me," she'd say, and I'd say no, I wasn't, but I had some homework to take care of. It felt good, frustrating her that way. However, when I put the receiver in its cradle I invariably felt like hell. There was something under the surface of her phone calls; I knew what it was, but could never manage to draw it into daylight: she *loved* me, although it was a screwed-up kind of love, full of contradictions. Trayn treated her badly most of the time. He borrowed money from her without paying it back, used her meal coupons as if he didn't have his own, things any civilized male just wouldn't do. She called him once from the Laundromat because she was stranded in a rainstorm. But he was watching a basketball game on television and couldn't be bothered with picking her up. If she wasn't writing his freshman compositions for him, she was up in his dorm room giving him a back rub or making love if that was necessary for his ego. I wanted to grab her by the shoulders, shake her, pry her eyes open, give her the real picture. But I never did, because I think she already knew it. I even began to wonder whether that strange pregnancy episode was some kind of test calculated to measure my level of commitment.

On a Saturday afternoon Trayn returned, the conquering hero, from the Florida trip. Janice and I met the shuttle bus in the parking lot behind the student union. It was a mild January day, maybe mid-forties and sunny, the kind of day a diehard might sneak onto the course for a desperate round of golf. When he stepped out of the chartered Greyhound, he was wearing his red OSU blazer and a garish yellow tam. Janice ran to him, threw her arms around his neck and kissed him; the scene resembled a lovers' reunion from a forties movie, except that Trayn hadn't returned from war. He'd been medalist in the Miami Intercollegiate Golf Tournament. He saw me leaning on a hydrant, strode over and hugged me, too. "I heard you shot the lights out down there," I said.

"Teddy, you'd have eaten that course up. Short par fives, left-to-right fairways, fast greens . . . right up your alley." He took off his tam, plopped it on Janice's head and whispered, "Hazeltine played like a fucking goose. Shot 82, 84, 81 and 79. Except for some guy from a Baptist college, he was the caboose." I watched Hazeltine step out of the bus, his head lowered like a sex criminal's, and walk over to his wife, who gave him a consolation kiss and a pat on the back. She appeared to be at least six months pregnant, puffy-faced and awkward when she walked, like the ground beneath her was uneven. I felt kind of sorry for him.

It was hard not to like somebody who pulled for me the way Trayn did. He would gladly have stayed in Columbus so I could make the trip in his place. I spent a lot of time trying to figure out why Trayn had adopted me as his bosom buddy, but I couldn't come up with an answer, except that our personalities intertwined in a complementary way. He was the amiable rogue, I was the acquiescent toad. Or maybe it was even simpler than that. Trayn was the only person I knew besides Jimmy who loved golf, in all its dimensions, as much as I did. So, in spite of the jealousy I felt, I knew Trayn genuinely cared for me and I couldn't help liking the guy. I *almost* understood why Janice wouldn't let go of him.

The driver finally opened the bay containing luggage and equipment. I shouldered Trayn's golf bag and he carried the suitcase so he could hold Janice's hand as we walked to his car. "Janice and I will poison Hazeltine if necessary. Right, kiddo?"

We walked through the brittle sycamore leaves blown onto the parking lot by the westerly wind. The sun gleamed beneath a bank of gray clouds huddled above Buckeye Stadium. A cold front was moving in. The forecast was for snow, which, except for a light dusting in November, would be the first of the winter. That would put an end to those illicit rounds of golf I'd been sneaking in after my twelve o'clock comp class.

Cold weather tends to decompress a golf ball, reducing the length of an average drive by twenty yards or more. If golf were a cold-weather sport I would be a hopeless loser, because I couldn't possibly reach the longer par fours in two. So playing in January forced me to focus on the crucial approach shots, a part of the game I'd neglected in the past. My philosophy had always been to hit it down the middle and go from there, a brainless and shortsighted way to play the game. Meanwhile, I'd discovered something on the frosty Ohio links that might serve me better.

In March, the team was scheduled to play a series of triangular matches in North Carolina. Of course, I wasn't making the trip. The first of these matches was to be held on Pinehurst, a magnificent course designed by Donald Ross, who probably understood golf the way Michelangelo understood human anatomy. One of my high school teachers, maybe Mrs. Hodges, who ran senior English as a kind of retribution for the sins we had committed during the previous three years, said that Michelangelo used to wander out into the Tuscany hills in search of a nice chunk of marble for a statue he might have been mulling over for a while. Then he would find a wonderful specimen, but in finding it he had to rethink his creation because the marble had dictated its own artistic form. Sometimes anecdotes like that stayed with me for reasons I couldn't put my finger on.

Ross was a Scotsman, familiar with sand hills like the ones he found at Pinehurst. And I wondered if, when he walked onto that terrain, he sniffed the fresh wind, sized up the trees and the roll of the land, then let the topography dictate the contours of the golf course. Almost every great player considers the No. 2 course at Pinehurst to be a genuine work of art, brilliantly harmonious with its natural environment. I'd read about Ross and Tillinghast and the Fazio brothers, and Robert Trent Jones, the patriarchs of American golf architecture. I wondered where they found their insights. I'd played the Inverness Club in Toledo once while I was in high school. It's a Donald Ross course, tight and tortuous, with small, lightning-fast undulating greens. As I walked up one fairway and down the next, I felt as if I'd been absorbed into a magnificent landscape one might admire on a museum wall. Punishment for a bad shot was as predictable as twilight, while a good shot was nearly always rewarded with some clear advantage. To combine that kind of honesty with natural beauty was as clean an artistic statement as any man could make.

I was eating a pizza in my dorm room on a Thursday night when someone down the hallway yelled, "Kendall, horn!" I'd spoken with Stan on Wednesday, so I doubted it was him. I guessed it was Janice, upset again because Trayn had hung up on her, or maybe he'd thrown away her Christmas present to him. The traumatic possibilities were endless. When I put the phone to my ear it was Coach Forbes.

"Kendall, how are your grades? Can you miss a week of classes?" I put my hand over the mouthpiece and whooped so loudly that Paul Drake, a nose guard for the Buckeyes, ran naked out of the shower to catch the action. I was going to make the trip to Pinehurst. "Dave Traynham says he's got two tests and a term paper next week," Forces said. "Claims his grades are bad and he can't make the trip, so I've penciled you in as sixth man. How does that sound?"

"Coach, can I call you back?" I asked. I knew what Trayn was up to. He was fulfilling his potential as a martyr on my behalf, and I didn't want to be indebted to him.

Residents of Folger dorm, where he lived, had phones in their rooms, but when I dialed his number there was no answer. So I called Janice, knowing he would probably be there. Medford Tower was a new dorm, and it also had phones in every room. In fact, Chadwick, my own dorm, was the lone anachronism on the west campus.

Candy picked up the receiver. "Hello, Teddy," she said. I wasted a few seconds trying to think of something pleasant I might say to her without getting her hopes up. I asked her how her Christmas vacation was, and she told me she'd had the flu throughout most of the break.

I told her I was very sorry to hear that. "Listen, Candy, is Trayn there?" I asked.

Trayn came on the line, laughing over some goings on there in Janice's room. "Hey, buddy, what's new?"

"Forbes just called me. He says you can't make the trip to Pinehurst."

"That's right, pal. I'm going to flunk out if I don't book it this week."

"That's crap, Trayn," I said. "I know exactly why you're not going. It's noble as hell, but if you don't go, neither of us goes, because I'm not taking your place."

"Well, Teddy boy, listen to what I have to say, okay? Forbes was going to take Hazeltine down to Carolina instead of you. And that's bullshit. He's going to keep pulling that nonsense unless you get in the lineup and kick some ass. If you do that, and I know you will, we can travel together all spring. So don't let me down. I'm queer for you Teddy. Ask Janice. The links is nothing without you."

"You're a jerk, Trayn," I said.

"I know," he answered, almost incidentally. "Make Forbes sit up and take notice, will you?"

"I guess I owe you one now, don't I?"

"You owe me some good golf, that's all."

After sixteen hours on the bus, we finally arrived at the Econo Lodge in Sanford, North Carolina, one hour away from the golf course. (A motel in Pinehurst or nearby Southern Pines, even in the off-season, would have been beyond the bounds of OSU's athletic budget.) Garvey and I shared a room as far away from Forbes as we could get, knowing that the sound of a beer can opening could wake him out of a dead sleep. After we'd had our team supper at a Morrison's cafeteria, I scuttled off to a Fast Fare and bought a six-pack of Budweiser. Garvey and I guzzled two cans apiece, knowing that three would dull our competitive edge, and one might not be sufficient to knock us out. "I can't believe Trayn didn't make the trip," Garvey said after we'd turned out the lights at around midnight.

"There's no predicting what that guy's going to do," I said.

I awoke at about 4 A.M. with Janice in bed beside me. I rested my hand on the small of her back, realized it was only the extra pillow and got up to go to the toilet.

Because it was a triangular match, I would be playing with one golfer from each of the other two teams. The three coaches were standing on the clubhouse patio, swapping locker-room stories, no doubt, while we warmed up for the day's competition. The clubhouse at Pinehurst is a Tudor-style dowager that looms over the old courses. In the early morning it casts its huge shadow over the putting green. I was going to play in a threesome with the number six men from Clemson and Wake Forest. The kid from Wake Forest was black, a rarity in collegiate golf. He was about my size, except that he had the physique of an Olympic weight lifter. The other player was one of those scowlers, angry with God for making him five feet five inches tall. I didn't much care who I was playing with, because this was Pinehurst. The more awesome the golf course, the less important your company becomes. That was my thinking at the time, anyway.

Since we were the tail-enders, we were required to tee off first. If the number six men hit first, the number one golfers can hump their way up the eighteenth fairway with the glorious weight of victory or defeat on their shoulders. When Henry Kale, the black player from Wake Forest, hit his first tee shot, I knew he was either a sandbagger or the best sixth man in the United States. His swing was right out of a textbook, but effortlessly powerful. He made a remarkable rotation, brought the club well beyond parallel at the top of the swing, then hurled the club forward with so much thrust that the ball made a sound I'd never heard a ball make before, something like the explosion of an M-80 firecracker. "Did you drive the green, Henry?" I asked. He smiled as if this was nothing new.

Martin, the golfer from Clemson, kept a wad of Skoal in his cheek. He's been spitting juice like a grasshopper, up and down the most beautiful fairways in America. Once when we were waiting for Henry to hit his drive, he leaned his lopsided face toward me and said, "Where I come from, niggers can't even get on the course."

I told him that was probably to their credit, and walked away before I cracked his skull with my driver. I was embarrassed that this redneck dwarf had somehow taken up golf, a game I happened to love.

On the fourteenth hole of that morning round, a peculiar thing happened. Henry had laced a two-iron tee shot onto the heart of the green, no more than twenty feet from the cup. And for the first time all day, Martin had hit a beautiful shot himself, just inside Kale's ball. I had hit my usual fade onto the fringe, maybe thirty feet below the hole. We were all surveying the topography of the green, trying to figure what it would do with our putts. Henry Kale and I were tied at one over par; the Clemson player was at about plus ten. His putt was pretty irrelevant, whereas ours were crucial. As Martin was marking his ball, he casually dropped some brown spit directly onto Henry's Maxfli. Before I could stop him, a black bull was charging across the green. He flew shoulder first into Martin, knocking him off the putting surface and into a sand trap. Kale leaped on top of him, and force-fed him about three handfuls of beautiful white sand. Then he stood over his victim, so his foreshortened shadow fell perfectly over Martin's prone figure. I watched a curious, close-mouthed smile appear briefly on Kale's face. Then he reached down and helped Martin up. Embedded in the sand was a human imprint like the ones I used to make in snowbanks. "Go clean the spit off my ball," he said.

I watched the third member of our threesome skulk across the green, place a dime behind his opponent's ball, wipe the tobacco juice off on the grass, then replace the ball in its original position.

Kale calmly sank his putt, I got up and down in two, and Martin three-putted for a bogey.

When the round was finished, we'd trounced poor Martin, but neutralized each other by shooting identical 74s. Coach Forbes slapped me on the back when I told him the outcome. It turned out that Kale was Wake Forest's number two man. They *had* sandbagged him after all, hoping to deflate my ego by pairing me with a hotshot. But the strategy had backfired and I was beatified by my mentor as a variety of golfing immortal.

When our bus pulled into Columbus on Friday night, Trayn and Janice were there to greet me. He threw his arms around me and hugged me so tight I could feel the beer can he had concealed in his coat pocket (it was for me). Janice kissed me on the cheek, but when Trayn saw that, he said, "Go ahead, kiss him on the lips. He deserves it."

Except for Buzz Williams, I had played the best golf of anyone on the team. Trayn had gotten his wish. And I owed him one.

Twelve

We're waiting for Drago, who hasn't shown up for work this morning. Chapman is sitting on a five-gallon paint can next to the shed. Grayson has just arrived, wearing a paisley do-rag over his hairless skull, a black calypso shirt unbuttoned to the navel and chinos. He reluctantly shakes my hand when I offer it, but says nothing. I finally provoke a grudging "yeah" when I ask if he's ready to work. It's hard to know what to make of Grayson. Ames told me he's in the slammer for his part in an illegal dog-fighting racket, and that he only has a few months left to serve. I know nothing else about him. Right now he's gazing off toward the highway, dreaming of the day when his girlfriend or his brother picks him up at the prison gate and they drive into the wilderness of billboards and mobile homes and other assorted squalor visible only if you stand close to the fence and look east. Since there seems to be so little at stake anymore, I don't much care if he works or doesn't work, so long as he can tolerate everybody else. The golf course is as good a place as any to kill time.

Chapman can apparently tell I'm down this morning. I'm not much encouraged by his reminder that God works in mysterious ways. A stack of platitudes fifty feet high isn't going to help my mood today. I watch Grayson spit every so often through the gap in his front teeth. "I heard you saved Chapman's neck," I say, always the bright conversationalist.

The whites of Grayson's eyes aren't white at all. They're yellow. He glowers at me for a long time. "What's it to you?" he asks, and we're off to a lovely start.

"Nothing." I give him a big Caucasian smile.

"Let me tell you something, man. Ain't no whitey's ass worth saving. Three of those niggers beatin' on the fat dude are the reason I'm here. That's all. Dig? So let's drop it." I'm more than happy to drop it.

Drago is fifteen minutes late. I've decided to get Chapman and Grayson started on resodding the greens while I look for him. My roomie whines, "If someone had told me a few years ago that I would be a day laborer on a prison golf course I would have hanged myself." He carries his shovel like one of the Seven Dwarfs. "Then again, the Lord forbids self-slaughter . . ."

"Why don't you shut the fuck up!" says Grayson.

"Where is levity? *Dead* alongside conviviality, I suppose," Chapman laments, at least until he senses that his life is in peril.

Chapman and Grayson only half listen as I explain the technique of replacing the sod. I'm sure that Chapman is fairly safe from Grayson, who probably doesn't want to risk a longer sentence just for the satisfaction of demolishing this plump honky. It would be impossible to prove self-defense. Grayson puts a cigarette between his lips, lights the thing and blows a plume of smoke toward Chapman, who coughs and fans the air frantically with both hands.

I leave the two of them out there by the fence, loading rolls of sod into the wheelbarrow. Grayson lifts them like they're weightless. Chapman can barely lift them at all. But to my amazement, he's actually trying. Maybe he's afraid Grayson will make pudding of him if he doesn't do his share.

I'm almost to the basketball court when I see Drago running toward me from the warden's office. I can see his teeth, big as Scrabble tiles, even this far away. "Boss," he yells. "The trucks are on the way." He's leaping through the air like Baryshnikov. "We got sand coming. Two trucks." He stands breathless in front of me. He grabs my biceps. "Warden changed his mind. He's going to give us whatever we need."

"Are you serious, Drago? What the hell happened to turn him around?"

A funny look crosses his face. His eyebrows drop down from beneath a greasy lock of hair. He raises an invisible camera to his eye, squints and clicks the shutter. "Drago!" I shout. "Tell me you didn't. That's blackmail. Jesus Christ, Drago. You're an idiot!" A certain part of me wants to pick him up by his ears and kiss him square on the mouth. "How about some reels for the tractor?"

"Think seven hundred bucks will do the trick?"

"Drago, you're crazed. A crazed genius," I tell him. He starts rubbing against me like a lonely cat. I shove him away. "I can't believe you really did that."

"You've got to fight fire with fire. That's what I always say."

When I tell Chapman and Grayson to take all the sod back where they got it, one of them says, "It's no small wonder so many people find life meaningless." Grayson wordlessly chunks bundles of sod into the wheelbarrow. It's all the same to him.

At about eleven o'clock in the morning, the prison gates open and two large dump trucks roll in, overfilled with white sand. "Drago, look at that," I say.

He tosses one more shovelful of wet dirt into the wheelbarrow, drops the tool and says, "God a'mighty. What're we going to do with all that stuff?"

Ames climbs onto the running board of the first truck, signs something trapped in a clipboard, points toward the golf course and hops down. I hear the transmission clunk into gear, and the driver aims his vehicle in our direction.

"Where you want this stuff, buddy?" the lead driver asks. I

tell him to dump it along the fence, beyond number two green. This is far more sand than we will need for the traps, but I can use it as foundation for some mounds I've just now planned for the fairways.

We follow the trucks so we can watch the show. The sand makes two formidable heaps, the tallest about ten feet high. Drago gets a running start and scampers up the bigger pile. "Mount Kendall," he bellows, flinging handfuls of sand skyward.

"Fools love simple pleasures," Chapman clucks.

"Shut up," says Grayson.

Chapman and I spend the rest of the day carving out the bunkers guarding number one. Drago and Grayson pack soil around the shoulders of the green. I'm enjoying the simplicity of this equation: as the bunkers grow wider and deeper, the green expands proportionately.

I have a glimmer of what it must have been like for the great golf-course architects—Ross or Tillinghast or Travis—as they watched their visions take shape before their eyes.

Thirteen

I spent the summer in Bowling Green readjusting to Stan's eccentricities. During my nine-month absence he seemed to have refined a variety of new peculiarities, including the habit of waking up at five o'clock in the morning, rattling through the house in the semi-darkness and finally walking Sally around the block. Sometimes I would watch him through a gap in the Venetian blinds as he plodded into the morning fog, southward down Fairway Avenue. The sight of him walking with his arthritic dog toward the invisible corner made me sad. His feisty nature, which fit him like a well-worn hat, had dissolved into a resolute grumpiness that sagged his features and made him seem older than he was. And the garage, his pride and joy, was no longer immaculately neat, and he'd allowed Sally's brown turds to accumulate in the front yard. I spent most of one afternoon shoveling them into the lime pit.

There were two things, however, that could perk him up. One was a visit from Lucille, who, judging from her tolerance to Stan's idiosyncrasies, had probably survived a very interesting first marriage. Occasionally she would talk him into coming out to her orchard to help her with pruning. Something about the act of amputating three branches agreed with him; he even bought a pair of leather gloves for the task. At least once every week Stan and I ate dinner at the cafe, at which time Lucille would deviate from her predictably Germanic menu in favor of something to please him, like lasagna or seafood gumbo. It wasn't always prize-winning fare, but it was a kindness that endeared her to my father. I hoped he would pop the big question some day soon, and they would marry. Maybe he'd already asked, and she couldn't find her way to say yes.

The other joy of his life was watching me play golf. During the months of July and August, he drove with me to a couple of tournaments, including the Ohio Amateur held in Cleveland at Willow Creek. On the outskirts of Cuyahoga Falls he found a Cricket Inn, suitably cheap, and only fifteen minutes from the course. He was determined to stay in Cleveland as long as I kept winning my matches. The Ohio Amateur, like most tournaments of its type, was a match play event, which meant that the competition was head to head. After a round was complete, the player who had won the most holes also won the match, unless one of them so thoroughly trounced the other that victory was assured before the round was finished—a situation called a dormie. (I'd always wanted to dormie someone.) I waltzed through my first few matches until there were eight players remaining. If Trayn had been entered, he would have had an easy time of it, too. He was almost unbeatable one on one. Some of the best players weren't much younger than Stan. They could still make all the shots, but their nerves just couldn't seem to withstand the strain. For example, I was two holes down with six to play in my match with a dentist from Elyria when he four-putted number thirteen, then hit his drive out of bounds at number fourteen tee. (I had to quietly remind Stan that it was poor etiquette to cheer when a golfer runs amok. He said he forgot.) That little streak of bad luck was enough to undo the mental armature that kept the dentist's game on track. When I shook hands with him on the seventeenth green, his hand was like half-melted Jell-O. I don't know how he'd managed to hang on to the club.

In my quarterfinal match, I was paired with an excellent college player from Miami of Ohio. Like me, he wasn't a long hitter, but he played the chip and putt game like he invented it. The enormous greens at Willow Creek were slick and tilted, so everything but a short uphiller was a potential disaster.

My play had been crisp all summer, but there was a significant difference between playing a leisurely eighteen at the local club and a tournament round on a demanding course. Even so, that winter golf in Columbus had taught me to position my drives for the optimum approach to the green. So, while my opponent saved par after par with miraculous bunker shots and floating wedges, I was hitting every green in two and making enough birdies to offset the occasional bogey. At the turn, I was up by one hole. Stan told everybody he saw that there was a wonderful match underway between me and some kid who was playing "over his head." It was then that he met the father of my opponent. The man was very polite, and so patronizing of Stan that I wanted to knock him in the shins with my brassie. "Oh, really?" he said. "You don't say. One of the best in the state? Pro career?"

I was so bothered by Stan's boasting that I lost my concentration on the twelfth hole and knocked my drive into a gaping fairway bunker. The half-buried ball resembled a poached egg. I could only hope to punch it thirty yards up the fairway with an open-faced eight iron. If I used a sand wedge, I risked dumping my ball into the next trap just a few paces ahead. The breeze was blowing directly toward me, so that when I tossed a few grass blades into the air they flew briskly over my shoulder. I anchored my shoes in the soft sand, a particularly grainy type that demanded a slightly deeper penetration of the club than some of the more powdery varieties. The Miami kid was standing in the nearby rough, waiting for me to make my shot. When I plunged my clubhead into the sand, a great cloud of the stuff hovered for a few seconds before my eyes, then engulfed me so thoroughly that I had it in my ears and eyes, down the front of my shirt. I tasted sand and tried to spit it out. Meanwhile, my ball had gone nowhere; in fact, it was behind me. *Beached.* A lost cause. I picked up my ball, a concession of defeat, then pointed toward the next tee.

I managed to win the next three holes, creating a dormie situation for my opponent, with whom I politely shook hands. Stan buttonholed the kid's gray-haired father and politely informed him that his son might have a better chance in a few years, after I turned pro.

The sand had by then worked its way into my underwear. I could feel it with every step I took as we walked to the parking lot.

Unfortunately, I was annihilated in the tournament's penultimate match by a banker from Toledo. He was having the day of his life, ricocheting approach shots off of hot-dog wagons and onto the green, drilling in ten-footers as if they were tap-ins and generally stomping me into the ground. I really wasn't in the right frame of mind to play well; my brash one-man gallery had finally worn me down.

During the three-hour drive back to Bowling Green, Stan told me he was sure his following me around had contributed to my downfall. "You were probably nervous," he said.

I didn't want to hurt his feelings by agreeing with him, so I mentioned that I'd developed some problems with keeping my head down over the ball, and of course Stan agreed that maybe I *was* looking up.

On the last day of July, Stan's payday, Lucille dropped by in her truck to take Stan off somewhere. I was so glad to see him get out of the house that I didn't even ask where he was going. An hour later he pulled into our driveway, behind the wheel of a canary-yellow Pacer, a vehicle designed by men with a sense of humor. "What do you think, Teddy? A beauty, isn't it?" I said that it really was, and asked what on earth he was up to. "It's yours. Part of an insurance settlement. Quid pro quo." His favorite phrase.

He climbed out of the car and tossed me the keys. It was an amazingly well-cared-for automobile, with a hint of that new smell most cars abandon after the first thousand miles. "Where's the money coming from?" I asked.

"Never mind that," he scolded. "You need a car if you're going to play in these tournaments." If Lucille hadn't rumbled into our driveway just then, I might have hugged him.

For the balance of the afternoon I cruised the main streets of Bowling Green. I gave Spengle Wilson's dad a ride home from the hardware store. I ordered a cheeseburger at the Sambo's drive-in, then drove away without stopping at the window to pick it up. I fantasized a little back-seat tryst with Tammy Listerman, who was also home for the summer.

Trayn called me long-distance a few days later to ask if I would be interested in sharing an apartment with him at Columbus. This wasn't the first time he'd asked the question, but I'd always fended him off. I figured it would be unhealthy for all of us if I invited that confusion into my life, and I didn't see how I could remain sane with Trayn and Janice carrying on right under my nose. Then, almost against my will, I heard myself saying that I'd talk to Stan about the matter. By the time I hung up, I had all but agreed that he could count me in.

I drove myself down to Columbus on the twentieth of August. The stuffed wolverine, packed in among the lamps and the beanbag chair and the reject black-and-white TV, glared out the bulbous side window.

Trayn was watching a Braves game on his color TV when I opened the door to my new apartment. "Hey, pal, good to see you. I like the rodent. Nice touch," he said. We shook hands and he helped me carry my golf clubs and suitcase into my room. "What do you say? Is this nice, or is this nice?"

In fact, it was pretty nice, and not terribly expensive either. The bedroom carpet had been recently shampooed, and the walls repainted a serviceable beige. "I like it. It's pretty nice," I said.

Trayn, new gold chain around his neck, opened the acetate curtains and pointed toward a sorority house a half block away. It had a flat-roofed sun deck, served by a double French door opening from the second floor of the building. "Teddy, wait until the women come back to campus. Vikings! All of them."

Alpha Chi Omegas. I thought of poor Benson, who had to lasso his binoculars and reel them in from the ice in the middle of the reflecting pond. It had been a mean-spirited thing to do, slinging them out there.

Because Trayn and I were on campus early for the obligatory intrasquad tournament, Janice's arrival was a week or so away. Oddly enough, with Janice out of the picture, I really enjoyed him. We played a lot of golf together. He had a phenomenal imagination on the course, an ability to manufacture golf shots to accommodate any situation. If his ball was hunkered among some roots, he found some means of propelling it at least a hundred yards down the fairway. Temperament was his only real problem. He expected nothing less than perfection every time he struck the ball, and if the shot didn't measure up to his impossible expectations, he lost his temper, which tended to disable him for several holes at a time. He wasn't the kind to throw clubs or kick his golf bag, but if you looked closely you could almost see the steam coming out of his ears.

Trayn and I finished one-two in the intrasquad match, with the third-place finisher seven shots behind me.

Janice had joined the Delta Gamma sorority at the end of her freshman year, so when her parents drove her up from Cincinnati, they went directly to the brick house only a block from the Alpha Chi Omegas. I was beginning to understand why Trayn had picked this particular apartment. Candy had gotten only one bid, that from the Tri Gammas, a friendly but horsey group, half of whom played on the women's softball team. As soon as her parents had departed, Janice came over to see our new habitat with its cheap furnishings and sparse decor. She hugged and kissed both of us. The kiss she gave Trayn was one of those lingering types that I interpreted as a gentle signal: over the summer things had resolved themselves, and Trayn was *her* man. Rather than escape the apartment, which was what I felt like doing, I grinned while she sized up our new quarters. "This is terrible," she said. "You need some paintings and lamps. And plants! There are no plants! What's this thing?" She thumped the wolverine so hard that dust puffed from its mouth. We sat in the living room for a while, drinking beer from sweating cans. Trayn was in rare form; I suppose because he was glad to see her. He told her a couple of jokes he'd heard over the summer, both of them pretty seedy. One of them was about a snapping turtle and a Marine Corps drill sergeant. The other was about a harelipped toothbrush salesman. She laughed hard at his jokes. "Listen," she said. "I've got to get back to the house. My stuff is still in boxes." She walked halfway across the living room, paused for a moment and said, "I'll bring you some plants." She did one of those finger-wiggle waves that sorority girls do and told us *"Ciao."*

I'd slugged down five or six beers by the time Janice returned, this time with a flourishing spider plant, a small bag of groceries and her new roommate, Ginny, who said, "Hi," and reached out to shake hands with me. I asked her how she was getting along so far. "Well, I *love* my new roomie," she said, and winked at Janice. Trayn took the plant and set it on a card table.

"I'm making spaghetti," Janice announced. "I have Chianti, and French bread, too. You and Teddy get acquainted while Trayn and I get things started in the kitchen." He put his arm around her shoulder. I noticed how perfectly she fit under his big wing.

I asked Ginny if she'd like a beer. When she nodded in the affirmative and smiled, I told her she had beautiful teeth. A stupid thing to have said. She laughed in a friendly way and asked if I needed any help carrying the can. Candy never had that sort of humor in her arsenal. This girl was *okay*. Not quite in the same league with Janice. But in the enormous span of ten minutes I'd convinced myself that I liked her. The beer cans were now hidden behind a gallon of milk and a liter of wine. As I was shifting things around in the refrigerator, Janice put her hand on the small of my back. She leaned down and turned her face upward toward mine. "How're you doing?" she asked. I knew what she meant. How are you doing now that you know the score?

I told her *fine*, meaning I wasn't blotto yet. It was almost fun pretending I didn't understand. Janice patted my spine and said, "Good." I could smell her herbal shampoo. "She's nice, isn't she?"

"Sure," I said. "She's nice. And thirsty."

I placed the beers on the coffee table, which was actually a surfboard mounted on cement blocks, and sat on the couch next to Ginny. She was leafing through my high school yearbook, pausing every now and then to look closely at one of the photographs. "I read what this Tammy wrote. She must have really liked you." It felt good sitting close to someone who apparently didn't belong to anybody else and who was looking with interest at one of my personal artifacts. "Was she your girlfriend?"

"Not really. Just a pal. You know." She nodded, apparently not quite convinced.

After a while, Janice and Trayn and began arranging plates and silverware on the card table. "You don't own any candles, do you?" Janice asked.

I told her I had a flashlight. Ginny laughed, but I could tell she was being polite.

We ate spaghetti in light filtered through one of Trayn's beach towels, which Janice draped over our window. "Not bad," Trayn said with his mouth full. "Could use a little more garlic."

"Thanks," Janice said. She had a quality of motion that gave something as simple as lifting a wineglass a kind of elegance. Meanwhile, Trayn was crushing his cigarette into an uneaten crust of bread on his plate.

Ginny and I washed the dishes while Trayn and Janice fiddled with the TV set. There was an old movie Janice was intent on watching, a Bogart-Bacall classic called *Key Largo*. The western sunlight was finally subsiding by the time the movie came on. "I pay four hundred bucks for a color TV so we can watch a damned black-and-white movie," Trayn said.

As the movie was coming to the end I began to wonder whether Ginny planned on spending the night. She'd been leaning against me all evening, patting my thigh when Bogart did something admirable. But it was all pretty fuzzy. I tried to sort out my motives. To use Ginny that way exceeded even *my* flimsy moral limitations. I wanted to be certain that any action on my part would be as clean and uncomplicated as I could make it. "I'm about ready to crash," Trayn said. He crossed the room and snapped off the TV. Ginny and I sat on the couch in the semi-darkness, watching the white circle dwindle in the middle of the screen. "I'm a little tired myself," Janice said. She followed Trayn into his bedroom and shut the door behind her.

Ginny started to laugh. "The moment of truth has arrived," she said in a Transylvanian accent. I had sobered up enough during the previous few hours to know that I was being presented with an option. She kissed me on the cheek and said, "Come on." I let her pull me up from the couch, and went with her into the other bedroom.

We undressed in the dark. That was a relief to me. She wasn't a vamp who wanted to make a Broadway production of the whole thing. We slid under the sheet almost in unison. I pulled her close, feeling her thighs against mine, and her small breasts. My hands were shaking when I touched her. I felt a little bit self-conscious about that, until I noticed that hers were shaking, too. Rather than make some ridiculous comment about her having beautiful skin, or flaxen hair, I snuggled against her warm body for a while, a little bit scared, and maybe too analytical of her response to my touch.

Then something happened. There had been nights when I'd lain awake, waiting for the exact moment when sleep came. And on some nights it never came. But when I did fall asleep I was totally unaware. Something similar happened with our love-making. Suddenly I was just floating in a sort of mindless cloud filled with wonderful sensations that didn't need any interpretations. Ginny's body seemed very small, while mine seemed enormous. And then it was the other way around. Astounding. I could hear her breath, and a dog barking somewhere, and the backfire of a car, while pure physical sensation expanded inside my brain like a swarm of bees. They poured through me and into Ginny, and I wanted right then to say I loved her, but was afraid I didn't really love her at all, which would make it a cruel thing to say. We held on to each other for a long time in the dark room without saying a word. For some curious reason I was thinking about her mom and dad, and how odd it was that their daughter was in my bed. I had never met her parents.

The last words she said to me before we went to sleep were "You're a very nice person."

I was glad I hadn't told her I loved her. But I liked her quite a lot and thought that sleeping together had probably been good for both of us.

Ginny was still asleep when I woke up the next morning. I put on some blue jeans and padded through the living room to the kitchen. Janice was sitting at the Formica kitchen table with a fresh cup of coffee. "Good morning," she said, and gave me a wistful little smile. I noticed that her eyes were watery. If she said another word she would start to cry.

"Java," I said. "I must have java." She laughed, and shook her head. Things were every bit as muddled then as they had ever been. I poured some coffee into a mug, blew some air across its surface and took a sip.

Fourteen

After eight weeks of nurturing, the minuscule Bermuda grass seeds we sowed on the new greens have begun to produce shoots, not much bigger than whiskers. Drago and I go out to the course every night after dinner, when the day's heat has subsided, and we soak the sprouts of grass thoroughly, making sure the moisture penetrates deep enough in the soil so that the immature roots chase it down. Right now the black soil is covered with a soft green fuzz which, if you peer at it from an almost horizontal angle, looks like you could putt on it tomorrow. But like lots of other things around here, that's an illusion which vanishes the minute you try a different angle.

Tonight, we see something very curious. I don't know quite what it means, and I may never know. Drago and I have just finished our gourmet dinner of meat loaf and canned green beans and blanched pears. We're on our way out to the golf course to water the grass, with the sun hanging low in the southwest, hurling tall swamp cypress shadows halfway across the fairways. A battalion of doves occupies the barbed wire strung above the chain link fence.

With the twilight sifting through the trees behind them, their feathers are iridescent gold. In the foreground of this scene, the newly mowed fairways are astonishingly vivid. I try very hard to freeze this sight in some cerebral archive where I can call it back whenever I want. Even Drago is amazed at how the golf course has progressed in so short a time.

Maybe we're too awestruck by the birds and the emerald fairways to immediately notice something we never expected to see. Grayson is out there by himself, spraying a fine mist over the new Bermuda grass shoots of number one green. He's being very methodical about it, guiding the nozzle slowly back and forth to assure even distribution of moisture. Every now and then he twists the flow valve off, squats at greenside and presses his index finger into the soil to gauge the degree of saturation. He spot-checks the entire green, then resumes his watering. Drago and I stand still, partially obscured by the tennis net, almost reluctant to intrude. Finally, Grayson walks over to the spigot and shuts the water off. Instead of heading back to the quadrangle, he wanders slowly up number one fairway, glancing every so often at the doves perched on the fence. He stands dead still for a moment, turns left and tiptoes very slowly toward them. He comes within a few feet of the birds when one of them spooks. The rest of them swirl above the swamp in a feathery ruckus. I can hear him out there there laughing.

Right now I find it very difficult to believe what Ames told me about Grayson. I can't see this man leaning over the wooden walls of a pen while two dogs fight to the death.

Drago wants to go out to the golf course so we can make sure he's soaked the greens properly. "I think Grayson did a good job of it," I tell him. So the two of us head back to 1-A for some television.

I'm lying on my cot at about nine-thirty, an hour before lights-out, reading *Golf in the Kingdom* by Michael Murphy. It's a wonderful book about the mystical aspects of the game. Most of the novel is set in Scotland, on an imaginary links course, which, if it were real, would be the one I'd want to play above all others. I'm on page 145 when Farley, one of the country-clubbers from down the hall, knocks on my door to tell me I have a telephone call. My heart immediately starts hammering inside my chest. I'm afraid something has happened to Stan. But Farley gauges the panic on my face and tells me it's a young woman. This is the first bit of consideration I've ever seen coming from Farley. I make a mental note to return the favor as soon as possible.

The phone call, I'm certain, is from Janice, unless Stan has convinced poor Tammy Listerman to fan the dead flames of our short-lived high school romance. When I press the receiver of the hall phone to my ear and say hello, I hear the operator tell whoever it is at the other end to deposit some coins. Bells ring for approximately thirty seconds. Then I hear Janice's voice. "Ted?"

"Hello, Janice." I purposely don't ask how she's doing. I don't want her to know exactly how curious I am about that.

"Gee. It's nice to hear your voice. How are you?"

"Fine. I'm in charge of the prison golf course. Can you imagine that?"

She tells me that sounds very interesting, but I can tell she has something else on her mind. Every predictable question brings her one step closer. "I want to come and see you," she says at last.

"Why would you want to do that?" I ask.

My matter-of-fact tone is not the one she wanted to hear. Her voice begins to quiver at the other end of the line. "I love you and I want to see you. That's all. I *care* about you."

"Janice, I don't know if I'm quite up to a visit from you right now," I say, but if she presses it at all, I'm done for.

"We need to talk, Ted. Believe me."

"What do we need to talk about? Would you like to marry me tomorrow in a double-ring prison ceremony?" What a son of a bitch I am. "Look, Janice, I'm still mulling everything over. I'd like to figure some things out before I talk with you. Can you understand that?"

"Trayn and I are getting divorced," she says. She can't hear it, but I'm having some trouble getting my breath. My mouth is very dry.

"I'm sorry," I tell her. I know I'm not sorry; it's the best thing for both of them. I just don't know how I fit in.

"Please let me come to see you. It won't be for two weeks."

I tell her, "Okay." She asks me how Stan is doing, if I'm getting enough to eat and all the other perfunctory questions she's been storing up for the past couple of months. I give her the stock answers, and finally say goodbye to her.

After I hang up, I walk back to my room, spend a few minutes watching Chapman's fish eat the food I've sprinkled in the tank for them and pick up the book I abandoned to take the phone call. But I can't read it anymore. My mind is too crowded with other things. All I really want to think about for the present is my golf course and my book, the one I've been laboring over every night, my explanation for why I'm here. But then Janice finds her way into the scene, and everything else simply vanishes. I don't even want to know how I feel about her right now. I wish I had somebody to talk to about this mess. It occurs to me that Janice is the only person on the planet I *can* talk to about it.

Fifteen

Janice refused to learn much about the game of golf. She would sit politely in the living room of our apartment while Trayn and I discussed "weak grips" and "fluffy lies" or the perils of kikuyu grass, a wicked and increasingly popular fairway turf with the consistency of Brillo. Our conversations were so much babble to her. This stubborn ignorance was one of her foremost charms in my estimation, but it didn't sit too well with Trayn, who probably whispered golf clichés in her ear when they made love. For her birthday, and against my advice, he bought her a set of secondhand woods and irons, which I knew would disappoint her. She was probably expecting perfume or a ring, at least some flowers.

To celebrate the occasion, Ginny and I bought a chocolate birthday cake and a large pizza, of which Trayn and I ate all but a few slices. Then I went into the kitchen for the double-layered beauty that had set me back eight dollars and fifty cents. I lighted twenty-one candles and carried the cake into the living room. We sang "Happy Birthday," then wrestled her to the carpet and spanked her. When she threatened to wet her pants, we let her up so she could blow out the candles. Then Trayn presented her with his gift. This I wanted to see.

She laughed when he leaned the golf bag against the sofa where she sat. "They're nice, Trayn," she said. I think she was waiting for some punch line that wasn't coming. I knew then how my mom must have felt when Stan bought her a Veg-O-Matic for their twentieth anniversary. She used it for just a few days; after that, the thing went into an obscure cupboard, where it remained until I salvaged it for my life in the Kings Arms Village Apartments. Stan at least had the good sense to see his error and set it right with a pair of pearl earrings and an assortment of tulip bulbs.

Trayn took Janice and her golf clubs to the driving range that April afternoon during our junior year. I imagined him leaning over her shoulder, explaining the subtleties of proper grip and stance, and her getting it all screwed up and Trayn losing patience with her. "It's simple if you listen, goddamnit." "Keep your eye on the ball." "Now look what's happened to your grip." I wasn't a bit surprised when less than an hour later Trayn stomped in carrying Janice's birthday present. He opened the door to his bedroom and hurled the clubs inside. "Tell me something, Teddy. How can she get straight A's and be unable grasp the simplest technique of a golf swing?"

"Maybe she just doesn't think it's essential to her life on this planet," I said. "By the way, where is she?"

"Bitch is walking home. Couldn't reason with her. What a waste of my damn time." He went to the refrigerator, pulled out a can of Busch and collapsed onto the sofa. "Damn," he said, and glared out the window. "Guess I'll have to buy her a necklace or something."

I didn't see Janice for a few days after that. Then, as I was coming from my art appreciation class in Ragsdale Hall, I saw her waiting for me in the corridor. She looked as if she hadn't slept in a few days, and she wasn't wearing any jewelry or makeup. "How're you doing? You okay?" I asked. She and Trayn had these little bouts once every couple of months; I always did my part to set things straight between them. It wasn't that I had stopped loving Janice. She could wag me any way she pleased, but Trayn could not be manipulated (maybe he'd evolved from a resistant strain). In fact, he often manipulated *her*. She and Trayn were only days away from their foregone reconciliation, and I didn't really mind being the go-between.

"I need to talk with you," she said.

"What about?" I asked, holding the outside door of the building open for her.

"I'm a mess. Look at me. I'm not sleeping, my hands won't stop shaking . . ."

"All this because you can't hit a straight drive, right?"

"I wish that was it. I just can't seem to please Trayn anymore, and I know I ought to just break off the relationship. But I love him. I wish I could figure out why I do, but I can't." I saw the inevitable tears welling up in her eyes. She had a way of producing just the right number of tear molecules. One more and there would be a flood. (Trayn would have told her to stop the blubbering; he was *waterproof* on top of everything else.)

"I don't really see how you can love somebody who treats you so badly," I said. It occurred to me in a hazy sort of way that this patronizing phrase applied to me as much as it did to her.

She was miffed by my seeming so objective. "What's it to you? You don't care!" The last couple of words seemed to catch in her throat. There she was, leaning on me as if I were a $60-an-hour shrink, but she wasn't the least bit interested in sound advice. She just wanted to share her miseries. To lead me on. And I was, for once, trying hard not to be led on.

Now she was really crying. Her nose was running and she didn't have a Kleenex. Students were loitering between classes, and we were a nice spectacle for them. "C'mon, let me buy you a Coke," I said, and she said that would be nice.

I bought her a medium Pepsi and a small package of Kleenex at the SBX, and we circumnavigated the softball fields for a while, trying to burn off some of the tension by talking about things other than her and Trayn. We speculated on whether the albino squirrel that roamed the West Quad was lonely for another of his ilk, or whether it was okay with him to screw any of the grays that were so abundant. I theorized that he wasn't particular, while Janice held to the opposite point of view. We finally found a bench near the reflecting pond. The weather was warm, but not so warm as to lure sunbathers into the arboretum.

She wanted to hold my hand, so I let her do it. In spite of myself, I felt sensation ripple through me. No logical reason existed for my feeling about her as I did. There were lots of very beautiful girls on campus, and I liked looking at them, but I had no real need to love them. Ginny was much more levelheaded than Janice, and perfectly happy to take things as she found them, including me. We had a nice arrangement, based completely on *like*, not love. But there I was, holding this weeping girl's hand and wishing I could kiss her. Unfortunately, she knew that as well as I did.

She took a big breath and said, "I'm okay now, really. I just need to get Trayn out of my life. And I really don't know how." I noticed her fingering the little blue cellophane package of Kleenex. "He's really a good person, and I love him. I do." Her voice was cracking now, and I knew she was seconds away from coming apart again. "But he just . . . hurts me. I don't know why he does it." She blew her nose, then scrutinized the Kleenex as if it were emblazoned with a picture of Trayn himself.

"So are you going to break up with him?"

"I'm not sure."

"Do you want me to talk you into it? Or out of it?"

To my amazement, she started crying again, and then, in a funny hicupping way, laughing, too. I'd never seen anyone do such a thing—like bright sunshine in the middle of a howling rainstorm. it was one of her really genuine moments, and it made me halfway hope she wouldn't call it quits with Trayn. If she did, when would I see her? I imagined a whole year of only accidental meetings—maybe bumping into her at the library or in the lobby of her sorority house when I came to pick up Ginny. I felt a sick ache at the thought of not having her within the confines of my fouled-up world.

Janice had settled herself, dried the tears and bitten her lips until the paleness was gone. Her jaw was set now; at least I thought so. "Okay," she declared, stuffing wads of soggy tissue into her too small handbag. "It's over. Officially, completely over. Dave Traynham and I are quits."

"Are you sure?"

She nodded emphatically. "*Sure.*" Janice then looked around us as if she'd suddenly come awake in the middle of a strange island. "Thanks," she said hoarsely. Then she brought her face up to mine and kissed me on the mouth. We kissed longer than friendship required and I halfway expected her to say, "*See?* It's really over with me and Trayn." But she didn't. She just quietly detached herself, walked around the edge of the pond, ducked beneath the green tentacles of a willow tree and melted into the busy landscape.

I almost felt sorry for Trayn during the next week or so. He didn't like losing, and he had lost Janice. She refused to answer her phone, though he called her every half hour or so. So he wrote her long incoherent letters full of clichés and impossible promises. He stayed in bed late in the mornings, cut his classes, played halfhearted golf in the afternoons, then drank beer for supper. His drinking continued until midnight, at which time he would stagger into his bedroom and sleep fully clothed.

He tried waiting outside her speech class, the only one that didn't conflict with practice. She emerged latched on to the arm of a linebacker on the Buckeye football team. Trayn apparently tried to pull Janice away, but the guy punched him so hard in the rib cage that he could barely swing the golf club for several days.

By the weekend he had started to pull himself back to normal. He was sitting at the breakfast table early on a Saturday morning. We had a home match at nine o'clock. Trayn and I were slated to play in the number one and number two slots. "You look better, pal," I said. "Dereliction seems to suit you."

"I still feel like a truck ran over me," he said. "This thing with Janice was no good. Didn't think it would matter as much as it did. Curious how things work on the old psyche. I treated her like shit and she dumped me. That's fair enough, isn't it?"

"My dad would call that quid pro quo."

"Yeah, it was something like that."

"For what it's worth, I'm sorry," I said.

"Me, too, Teddy boy." He took a couple of sips from his coffee, then got up from the table, leaving behind a nearly filled cup.

On Wednesday of the next week the team was scheduled to play a match in Bowling Green, and another one on Friday in Ann Arbor, which meant that Stan could watch me play, and Jimmy, too, if he was up to it. His health had declined over the previous few years. He was working only half days at the clubhouse now and cutting way back on his lessons. Still, I was sure he'd enjoy driving an electric cart around the university course with Stan riding shotgun.

The gray van arrived at the Bowling Green University Union late on Tuesday night. Stan was there with Sally to greet me. The dog was straining so hard at her collar that she made a strange choking sound, like a candidate for exorcism. I gave Stan a big hug and introduced Trayn, who shook hands, smiled and said, "Nice-looking dog. A show animal, I'll bet."

"Champion bloodlines," Stan replied. That was the first I'd ever heard of it. Trayn had managed, within a thirty-second span, to charm him so thoroughly that my dad invited Trayn the dog lover to spend the night at our house. Unfortunately, we were required to stay at the motel with the team.

Coach Forbes wandered over to meet Stan, whose effusiveness seemed to embarrass him. "Teddy says you've been a splendid coach."

"Well, the boys do all the work. I just keep them in line and on time." Coach coughed once or twice, then said, "Well . . . nice meeting you." He turned toward Trayn and me and told us we needed to check into our rooms by nine. I told him we would be eating at my house, but that we would be at the motel on time. I saw Stan's features sag at this bit of news. I told him it was a matter of insurance liability, which wasn't true at all. But that was something he could understand. "Well, why didn't you say so?" he said.

Lucille hand-delivered some homemade Stroganoff and cherry pies that afternoon. When she saw me she put the food containers on the porch steps and threw her fleshy arms around my neck so she could kiss me on the cheek. I told her that the tall guy standing next to me was my roommate. She embraced him in the same fashion. "It's so *good* to see you," she said, and patted my wrist. Stan pushed through the screen door, and she gave him a noisy kiss on the forehead. "Wish I could stay, but I'm breaking in new help. God knows they'll burn down the cafe if I leave them alone," she said, laughing. We watched her scurry back to her truck. She climbed behind the wheel, screeched out of the driveway and roared north on Fairway Avenue.

All through supper, Trayn was very nice to Stan, patient with his plodding sense of humor, careful to appear attentive when my dad was resurrecting one of his insurance salesman's tales: "This awful, ugly boy answers the door, see, and the salesman steps back, the boy is so ugly, but he says to the boy, 'Where's your daddy?' and the boy leads him around back where the daddy is screwing a sheep. Salesman says to the boy, 'Isn't that the most disgusting thing you've ever seen?' and the boy says 'Na-a-a-a-a!' " Trayn laughed as hard as I'd ever seen him laugh, when actually I was expecting him to roll his eyes or kick me under the table. I guessed that his dad was probably just as crazy as mine, so he understood. Stan, whose face was red from howling at his own joke, patted him on the back. "Wasn't that a good one?" he said. I liked seeing Stan enjoy himself, and I don't think I ever liked Trayn as much as I did at that moment.

I know Stan was disappointed that we couldn't spend the night away from the team, but when we said we had to be going, he accepted the news with a shrug. A few minutes later he was driving us to the Falcon Plaza Inn. "I guess I'll see you tomorrow afternoon, then," he said when we arrived at the motel parking lot. Trayn shook Stan's hand. "You would think . . . ," Stan started to say, but caught himself before he went any further with his complaint. I told Stan I was sorry we couldn't stay the night at the house. "It's okay," he said.

Trayn and I were to tee off with the number one and number two men on the Bowling Green team. I'd golfed with Ed Harvey before. He was from De Vilbiss High School in Toledo. He weighed in at around 230 pounds, but he wasn't what anybody would call fat. He was more like a bag of gravel with incongruously thin arms and legs. Ed's strong suit was consistency. He was programmed to hit the fairways and greens in regulation, and get his putts down in two. He was absolutely no fun to play with, because his personality was almost as interesting as his game. The other kid was a freshman, probably a schoolboy hotshot who might be a world beater in a few years. But now I could tell he was nervous.

We were loosening up at the first tee. Stan hadn't arrived at the course yet. I guessed he was picking up Jimmy or dickering over the rental of a cart. (The match was being played on the university course, crosstown from the country club.) Coach Forbes was inside the clubhouse attending to some business.

"Let's have a little fun with these dildos," Trayn whispered. He did a double cartwheel up to the blue markers, dropped to his knees on the grass, then gave a quick rendering of the mantra: *Ommm Mane Padme Ommm.*

I winked at Ed. "Part of his flight plan."

Ed was so befuddled after Trayn's little show that he cranked his drive into an algae-covered ditch that paralleled the first fairway. Trayn said, "Oops!" By the time the two coaches came out of the clubhouse, Trayn and I were slouching toward number one green while our opponents were over in the drop zone, lying three. I doubted they would be able to pull themselves together before the round was over. "That's called *gamesman-ship*," Trayn said.

"Forbes would throw you off the team if he found out," I said.

"Naw. He's a Christian."

Our opponents weren't speaking to us. After four holes we were three up on them, respectively, and way ahead on strokes. It was right about then that I saw the electric cart weaving up the center of the fairway, oblivious to the cart paths that skirted both roughs. No one had to tell me that Stan was driving.

When the cart hummed up to greenside, I saw that Jimmy was pale and very thin. He smiled at me and gave a feeble wave. I scrambled down the slope to greet him. "How're you doing, Jimmy?" I asked.

"I'm feeling good," he said, but his voice was shaky and his smile was weak. "Are you winning?"

"Sure," I told him. "But I knew you were coming, so I saved a few birdies." I waved to Trayn, who trotted over to say hello.

"I've heard you're good," Jimmy said to him.

"Just rumor," Trayn said.

Stan jumped in. "Teddy says Trayn's going to be a great pro."

"Well, I wish you luck," Jimmy said. His eyes seemed milky and far away. "Are you winning, too?"

"At the moment," Trayn answered.

"Well, good luck."

I told Jimmy I had to line up my thirty-foot putt. It was a left-to-right uphiller, totally makable if I could get it rolling. I wanted to knock it in. But I made poor contact, and the Titleist stopped more than two feet short of the hole. "Nice putt, you wimp," Trayn said.

Trayn halved the hole with his opponent, while I went to four up on my Ed. We moved to the next hole, an easy par four with a fairway wide as a football field. This was a good chance for

Trayn to let loose. He teed his ball a good two and a half inches high, stepped back, took a few practice swings and crunched his drive more than 320 down the right-center of the baked fairway. Jimmy shook his head in disbelief. I overheard what he said to Stan. "My God. Never did anyone hit the ball like that in my day."

I was aware that this might be one of the last times Jimmy would ever watch me play golf. My focus drifted from the task at hand to that feeble old Scotsman sitting next to Stan. I wanted to play the way he'd taught me, rhythmic and steady, but I was more nervous than I had ever been. I bogeyed several holes in a row, and my opponent was cashing in. Finally, Jimmy had seen enough. He stepped out of the cart as I was gazing back and forth from my ball, which was buried in the rough, toward the green two hundred yards ahead. "Forget that I'm here and play your bleeding game," he scolded. He tapped me on the elbow, then climbed back into the cart. I closed my eyes for a minute, visualizing my club cutting through the tall grass and lofting the ball onto the front edge of the green, where it skipped once, then trickled down beyond the hole. I took my stance, drew the club back almost without thinking, and down, into and through the ball, so an explosion of grass made it impossible for me to see the outcome. Then I heard Trayn clapping on the other side of the fairway.

"Hell of a shot, Teddy boy. Two feet past the hole."

I glanced over at Jimmy, who was nodding his head. He looked happy, finally, and so did Stan.

Sixteen

Every night the lather I rinse down the shower drain is green, as if the golf course has become a part of me. It's under my fingernails, between my toes, behind my ears . . .

After my shower I go to bed, but for several weeks my sleep has been erratic, not that I haven't adapted to Chapman's incessant snoring and his gastric problems. The fact is, I've gotten used to Chapman, and in a totally unexplainable way I sort of like him. Furthermore, his gaseous nature has been much improved by daily physical exertion on the golf course. My wakefulness is caused by other things. One of them is the impending visit of Janice, who will undoubtedly stir up some embers I've been smothering since the day I arrived. For the past months I've tried very hard not to feel badly about what I did to Trayn, although for some reason the image of a thoroughbred like him hobbling around on crutches is a difficult one for me to accept. He wasn't meant to marry anybody, particularly Janice; and now without his sport and without her, his life must be very dismal. And I've only just gotten around to accepting the fact that I was fond of him in spite of my jealousy. Once of twice I've imagined myself bumping into him at a bar somewhere, and our talking things out, shaking hands, laughing the whole thing off . . . just like those days at Ohio State. And tomorrow, Janice will make her visit. She'll probably inform me of her tender reconciliation with Trayn, and how she has tried her best to talk him out of the inevitable million-dollar personal damages suit. Of course, I have only $18,000 in my account nowadays, give or take some pending attorney's fees. I'd gladly forfeit that sum if it would buy me a clear conscience.

The other thing troubling my sleep is a recurrent vision of the Moss Point golf course with a beautiful meandering stream and a deep, fish-filled oxbow pond enfolding number two green. I've grown a little bit tired of mowing and raking day after day. I'd like to add contour to the fairways . . . swales and shallows, uphill and downhill lies. I want trees, grandiose cypresses and water oaks and pines, not ten-dollar saplings.

In the yellow 6 A.M. light, Chapman and I sit on our beds across the room from each other. "Another day," I tell him.

"Indeed," he sighs.

"Isn't God taking care of you?" I ask, realizing immediately that I've triggered something even more irrepressible than the flatulence with which he greets each new morning.

"God is providing a stern test, Kendall. Perhaps this travail is more than just a state-imposed expiation for my sins. It could be that in this case the judicial system is an agent of Almighty God."

"Pretty heavy concept, God working hand in glove with the bureaucracy," I say, hurrying to get dressed before he begins quoting Scripture. "How does he feel about *golf?*"

"I beg your pardon?"

"Let me tell you what I've been thinking," I say from the threshold of our door. "I see this beautiful meandering creek running through our golf course like a silver vein, and a deep pond wrapping itself around number two green . . ."

"Enchanting," he sniffs. "But impossible. Warden Maples is more than irate over our latest attempts at landscaping."

"That's right, Chapman. We're screwed." His eyebrows fly up. "Excuse me. We're at an *impasse.*"

"However, God *will* provide," he says. "Of that we can be certain."

Later in the morning, while Drago and Chapman follow behind us with hand-held clippers, Grayson and I circle the saplings with our push mowers. The roughs are so astonishingly lush that I can't help wondering if we've overfertilized. It would be a sorry golfer whose drive strayed from the narrows of our immaculate fairways. "Break time," I say at exactly ten o'clock. For the past five minutes Chapman, partially obscured by a meek *Ligustrum,* has been standing stock-still in anticipation of this moment. No sooner have I finished the phrase than he is waddling at a high rate of speed toward the water spigot. To avoid exposure to the "dreaded Bojangles virus," carried (he is certain) by all Americans of African descent, he has his own tin cup, which is clipped to his belt. It is while we four are standing around the spigot that Chapman lets the others in on my little fantasy. ". . . but of course Maples would have a conniption . . ."

"Shit, Kendall," Grayson interrupts, "why don't you jus' forget what the *man* say and go ahead on and and start digging. The motherfucker comes out here and give us lip . . . we got the hole to bury him in." Chapman is too busy choking with moral outrage at Grayson's choice of words to react, but Drago is already on his way to the shed for the shovels. "Hold on," I yell. "We want to get *out* of this joint eventually."

"Maples a *pussy,*" Grayson says in his gravelly monotone. "He ain't gonna do nothin' to keep four big pains in the asses around, now is he?"

"Go get the shovels, Drago," I say.

"*Yavol!*" he shouts, and trots toward the shed.

"Drudgery is my middle name," says Chapman.

"God is working through Grayson," I tell him. "His mysteries are unknowable."

Chapman does a classic "Hrrrrmph!" and folds his corpulent arms across his chest. His smooth, pale freckled face looks womanish beneath the straw hat.

The rationale of my plan is wasted on three men who have never touched a golf club in their lives. The most I can hope for is that they will follow directions and work hard. We squat around a smoothed patch of sand between the depleted remains of the original piles. With a stick, I draw a diagram for them. "My plan is to bring a tentacle across number one fairway, right at the two-fifty marker; that way the golfer who plays the hole will be challenged to either lay up or go for broke. Then I'll channel the water down the center of the rough, toward the rear of number two green, where it will broaden into an oxbow pond that fits snugly around the backslope . . . right *here*. The water will return to the swamp through a deep slow-moving creek that will brush the tee box of number one. See, the pond needs access to the swamp to avoid stagnation, or flooding if we get heavy rains. We'll use the soil we collect to add contour to the fairways, uphill and downhill lies, maybe a couple of elevated tees."

"A piece of cake!" says Drago. "But the time old Maples gets wind of it, we'll be half done."

"You *crazy*, man!" Grayson says. "It's a damn lot o' work is what it is. An' you can be damn sure Maples is gonna find out someways. We gotta go fast and get so far wit' the project he cain't do nothin' but cuss."

What Grayson says is true, and Chapman's willingness to cooperate is a question mark. It's one thing to putter around the course like a Japanese gardener, and it's another to grunt and sweat and heave dirt like a coolie. At least he's got the hat for it.

Fortunately, Maples' route from home to Moss Point is to the west. Unless he happens to wander out to the golf course, or unless one of the guards mentions the strange goings-on, it may be weeks before the warden gets wind of our activity.

I mark the beginning point of our shovel work near the fence bordering the ditch, which is fed by the swamp via a series of gigantic cement culverts that pass beneath the highway.

Chapman sits behind the wheel of the tractor while the three of us toss the first scoops of dirt into the wooden equipment trailer. When it's full, he rumbles off to a spot behind the shed where he presumably uses a hoe to drag it onto a pile. Grayson and Drago were born to shovel just as surely as Trayn was born to play golf. By quitting time, we've dug a trench nine feet wide, five feet deep and thirty feet long. The dirt pile behind the shed has proven to be a bad idea. In one day, it's become a conspicuous gray mountain, and a dead giveaway. I know we will have to do our fairway landscaping as we go along.

We all look very much like Grayson at the end of the day. Our flesh is black from soil darkened by sweat. When I take my shower in the evening, the suds are black.

I know that I won't sleep tonight, but of course neither will Janice. She'll read magazines until 3:30, at which time she'll drive across the Ohio River to the Greater Cincinnati Airport, where at around 4:45 she'll board her plane. She'll have a stopover in Atlanta, long enough to fend off some early morning Moonies, then fly out at 6:18 to Mobile. Then one half hour, minimum, to rent a car, another hour to drive from Mobile to Moss Point. By ten o'clock in the morning she should be here. This is all according to what she has scratched on a postcard which arrived two days ago.

Maybe it's the exertion of hard labor that does the trick, but on Friday night I sleep as I haven't slept in months. I'm almost groggy in the morning, and Chapman is long gone. To my amazement, the bureau clock says 9:15. Unless I hurry downstairs I won't even get coffee, and the doughnuts will be so thoroughly picked over I'll have to settle for whole wheat.

Although I'm a little too nervous to be hungry, I know I'll have to keep up my carbohydrate level if I'm to be a good ditchdigger. I'm masticating one of these reject doughnuts when Ames jangles into the mess hall, spots me at my private table and waves me over. Janice has arrived.

"She your girlfriend?" he asks.

"Nope. Wife of my victim."

"Come on. Are you serious?"

"I'm afraid so."

When he lets me into the visiting room, he pauses momentarily to take another look at Janice, who manages a very awkward smile. The door shuts, and we're alone. "Oh, Teddy. You don't belong here," she says, and hugs me for a good thirty seconds, during which time I'm only halfheartedly returning her affections. Then she gives me a brief kiss on the lips, steps back and looks at me. "God, you're so brown."

"I'm a day laborer, just like always."

"Ah . . . ," she says.

"How are you doing?" I ask. "You look nice."

"I'm getting by somehow. Living at home for the present time. You can imagine what that's like." In fact, I can only begin to imagine what it might be like living with a three-pack-a-day bridge club president.

"What do you hear from Trayn? How are his legs?"

"I guess he's coming along fine. The doctors say he'll make a fairly good recovery, except for some minor muscle damage. He intends to golf again, but I guess you suspected that."

"That's good. That's good. I'm glad."

"I've filed for divorce, Teddy." There's a long pause here. I don't know quite what to say, since I've rehearsed only my retort to a reconciliation speech. And I'm not certain why, but I'm neither displeased nor especially pleased by her news.

"Is that what you want to do? Divorce him? On the night I assaulted him I thought . . ."

"Wait a minute, Teddy. He was hurt. It didn't matter to me that you were responsible. He was *hurt*." Her hands are trembling now, so I guide her to the card table where we sit in folding chairs opposite one another. "I don't hate him . . . you know?"

"But you don't love him either, is that it?"

"Yes, that's it, I'm afraid. I still love *you*." She fumbles inside

142

her purse for a few seconds, trying to pull a Winston from a plastic case. She has brought the cigarette partway to her mouth when she changes her mind and drops it absently into her purse. "God, I don't know why I smoke. When my mother does it I hate her. Now look at me!"

"I have been," I say. "It's good to see you. I mean that. Seeing you makes me suddenly want to get out of here. Goddamn, I really want to get out of here. Know where I want to go?"

"Where, Teddy?"

"Scotland. I'd really like to go there. I'd like to play St. Andrews someday. Then hike up the road a few miles to where Jimmy was born. That would be nice."

"Would you go alone? Or would you want a traveling companion?"

"That's the funny part. I've always thought, in the back of my mind anyway, that I'd like you to come along. But now . . . I think I'd just like to go alone."

For maybe the last time in my life I'm watching Janice cry. She knows now what I've been afraid to admit, even to myself. I put my arms around her and hold her until she's cried out. She stands up, looking very beautiful for someone red-eyed and sniffling. "Trayn wanted me to tell you he had it coming, what you did to him. And that he isn't going to file suit against you, if you're worried about that. He says maybe someday you and he will be paired together in the Masters."

"Is that what he said?"

"Yes. That's it."

"Will you tell him I'm sorry?"

"Sure," she says. "I'll tell him."

"Well . . . I'm glad you came down."

"Thanks," she says, brushing a strand of hair away from her eyes. We look at each other for a moment, trying to freeze something in our memories, I suppose. And then I watch her open the thick wooden door. "Bye," she almost whispers.

"Bye, Janice," I say. And then she's gone.

I sit for a moment in the quiet of the room, with my eyes closed. I'm imagining a Scottish moor, a North Sea wind folding color into the long grass. Carved into the moor a serpentine golf hole greener than green.

Seventeen

Somewhere in an otherwise vacant portion of my brain, I probably knew that when Mom died she'd left behind some insurance money. Actually, I remember the Sunday night when she'd endured Stan's long-winded discussion of cost-benefit ratios and lump-sum refundabilities. Through the crack of my bedroom door I saw the coffee table drowning beneath his Byzantine charts and cryptic tables, with Stan using a pocket flashlight to literally illuminate the many virtues of his particular favorite—THE WHOLE LIFE POLICY. Customers who chose the less profitable *term insurance* policy he classified as "*term*ites." I remember Mom saying over and over, "Anything you want is fine with me," and Stan insisting that she get the entire picture so she could make an "informed decision." They had a big fight that night, the only real shouting match I ever saw her participate in. "Give me anything that covers suicide," she screamed. "You spend *your whole life* haranguing people to buy whole life policies. *I'm* easy. Just get me a pen."

As I was helping Stan wash the aluminum siding of our house

during the July before my senior year at Ohio State, he turned off the hose and told me to join him at the picnic table in the back yard. "Go get yourself a beer," he said. "I have something I need to talk to you about."

I went into the house and returned with a Stroh's for myself and a glass of iced tea for Stan. "What's on your mind?" I asked. Sally was under the table with her head resting on my sneaker.

He seemed a little bit alarmed by the dirt under his fingernails, but composed himself by taking a long swig of tea. "When your mother died," he said, tossing his head slightly toward the garden, where we'd scattered her ashes, "she left behind a small inheritance. God knows I tried to convince her to buy a bigger policy, but you remember how thrifty she was. Anyway, Teddy, she left behind about forty thousand dollars, half of which was to go to you when you turned twenty-one." I had a mouthful of beer when he told me how much money he was talking about. I was barely able to swallow it. "With the interest accumulated over the last eight years, you have a little bit more than thirty-two thousand dollars."

"This is unbelievable," I said. "Why didn't you ever tell me?"

"Well," he said, "I always got the impression from her that you weren't to know about it until it happened. Maybe she felt it would worry you, or that you would be preoccupied by it in some way. I can't quite explain . . ."

"I don't think I really know what to do with that kind of money. I guess I'll just leave it where it is. Is that a good idea?"

"I thought you were going to take a crack at the pro tour when you graduate."

"Well," I said, "I'm not going to gamble all my money on it. The odds of surviving on the tour are pretty grim, unless you're somebody like Trayn. But he's a phenomenon."

"Well, you're an All-American. That's a good sign, isn't it?

"*Trayn* is an All-American. I'm just Honorable Mention. You know, faint praise. Anyway," I said between sips of beer, "I've got another year to see what develops." The beer felt cold going down my throat. "God, Stan, this is all pretty amazing . . . thirty-two thousand smackers."

On my birthday the following Thursday, Stan met me at the Midwest Bank, where we transferred the money from a trust fund to my individual account. My hands were shaking so ferociously that I could barely sign my name. "It's all yours," Stan said. "Save it, or spend it if you want. I have faith that you'll use good judgment." He shook my hand as if we'd just completed a big business deal.

Stan had to get back to his office, so I drove over to the country club to practice. Trayn used to tease me for practicing as often as I did. He believed that bad habits could become ingrained; if you had a good fundamental swing, you were better off working on *situations*: bunkers, roughs, strong winds . . . What he failed to understand was that I loved pouring two hundred golf balls onto the practice tee, then hitting them one by one toward some arbitrary target, picking them up and starting all over. At the end of such an afternoon I'd have almost no recollection of having practiced. Instead, I felt the way somebody else might feel if he'd spent the afternoon in transcendental meditation. Hitting a perfect golf shot was my own weird version of nirvana. For that split second when the ball was flattened against the clubface, predestined for its target, the shaft of the iron transmitted a current of electricity that invaded my brain like a euphoriant drug.

Because the terrain in that region of the state is almost completely flat, the wind frequently barrels down unimpeded from Lake Michigan, gains steam as it whistles across the Indiana plains, then charges through Ohio so powerfully that most trees have a slight easterly tilt. Working into the teeth of a gale keeps a player honest, because the flight characteristics of a bad shot are exaggerated. A fade becomes a slice, a draw becomes a hook. The premium is on a shot hit arrow straight. I was driving shag balls that afternoon, as usual, but nothing felt right; maybe I was influenced by the new preoccupations weighing inside me

147

like ballast. The immediate pleasure of golf had been muddled by a tangible future.

Jimmy came out to sit on the green bench for a while. I dropped my club and sat next to him. The wind caused his eyes to water and the wisp of gray hair atop his otherwise bald head to stand straight up.

"How're you doing, Teddy boy? Are you keeping your grip relaxed?"

"I'm trying."

"If you want to add some distance to your wood shots, you need to stop strangling the club. You can't draw the club back sufficiently without a very limber set of wrists."

He was so persistent with this bit of advice that at times I wanted to pinch his big Scottish nose with my limber fingers until he squealed. I sat next to him on the bench. "Jimmy, I've inherited some money. Can you believe that? My mom left it to me when she died. Stan thinks I ought to take a whack at the pro tour. Any opinion?"

"Well, that's fine news about the money," he said, and patted my knee. "It's very tough to succeed, but I've never heard yet of anybody who succeeded without giving it a try. I know well enough you'd be one sorry fellow for not taking a crack at it."

The wind was bothering Jimmy's eyes, so he returned to the clubhouse. Meanwhile, I tried to maintain a solid stance despite the gale whistling through the box elder trees behind me. It was only July, but the air felt dry and cool, as if fall were riding in from the west. I took in a deep breath and tried to forget all about the money and the tour. When I drew the club back, I could feel that my hands were too tight around the rubber grip. I made good contact with the ball, but my follow-through was unnaturally stiff. I hit a high fade that drifted well off line. "Damn," I muttered, pounding the turf with the sole of my driver.

A few weeks later I returned to school, wondering what life would be like now that Trayn and Janice were split. Ginny was in Upper Arlington for her student teaching, so I wasn't going to see much of her for a while. And the only times I had managed to see Janice after her breakup with Trayn were at the bookstore and the library. My social outlook was very gloomy. Twice I called Janice's number. "Hello," she'd say. "Hello? Who *is* this?" Then, with my heart clubbing away inside my chest, I'd hang up. I was pitiful.

Meanwhile, Trayn would unbutton his shirt down to his navel so that hair exploded from his chest, and he'd go on the prowl. His gold neck chain was a lure that seemed to attract a strange variety of female. He brought home nurses (Malaysians, Tunisians, Californians and Africans), cheerleaders, budding computer scientists . . . A coffee-colored South American beauty named María Angélica Constantina Valero spent an entire weekend at our apartment, during which time she wore only a T-shirt belonging to Trayn. I would lie in bed at night with my eyes wide open, listening to the cavorting taking place in the adjoining bedroom. Sometimes I'd smell marijuana smoke, then I'd hear giggling, springs popping, toilets flushing, shower faucets chirping. I felt pathetic for resorting to the only thing that gave me solace. But I did it anyway.

I knew that Trayn's relentless sexual pursuits had something to do with Janice, although he hadn't mentioned her name in the four weeks since our return to school. If he was refilling his ego, he was doing a bang-up job of it. And I couldn't even ask Janice for a harmless study date. After all, I had to live with Trayn, and there was no sense stirring up bad blood.

On a Saturday afternoon when the Buckeye football team was on the road, I drove down to German Village, where I could waste my money on draft Bavarian beer. The Hofbrau Haus was a *Bierstube* where somebody with money to burn could find Dortmunder on tap. The beer was served in large clay mugs.

During an hour of dedicated drinking, I'd fed no fewer than ten quarters into the jukebox. Polkas were irresistible to me, sucker that I was for a German atmosphere. A cuckoo clock, a waiter in leather shorts, a row of silver-topped steins, a painting of the Alps . . . and I was deep in the heart of Germany, drunk as the drunkest *Oktoberfest* sot. Some guy at the bar was making up words to the polkas, and I was singing along. I could order my beers in a foreign language. *"Bitte, ein Bier Ja! Dortmunder. Guten Bier, ja?"* Classic sophomore-level *Deutsch*. College was great. The waiter shrugged and went away.

I foresaw only a very distant end to my beer-and-polka afternoon. When the time came, I'd leave my Pacer in the parking lot and walk the twenty blocks back to the apartment. It seemed wise not to slalom through downtown Columbus in broad daylight. I was so drunk I was logical.

The jukebox was quiet and needed feeding. I'd just made my selection and planted my hide at an empty table when I saw her. It was Janice and two of her sorority sisters. She'd let her hair grow out during the summer, and she looked wonderful, framed in light from the opened double doors of the Hofbrau Haus. After having gazed at myself in the mirror over the bar all afternoon, I knew I looked fairly crazed, so I turned toward the painting of the Alps, but it was too late. She'd spotted me.

She came over, placed her cool palms on my sweaty cheeks and turned my head so she could look me in the eye.

"Deutschland über alles," I said, lifting my mug in a cockeyed toast.

"My God. You're *drunk*, aren't you?"

"Very," I said. "Very extremely drunk."

"Are you with Trayn? Is he here with you?"

"Nope. Just me, drowning my sorrows in two-dollar beers."

"Are you sorrowful?" she asked, gliding into the empty chair across from me. "I haven't seen you in so long."

I grinned, shrugged, stifled an untimely belch. "It's been a while," I said. I wanted to flash some of that famous Kendall wit, but it was like climbing the Matterhorn in Keds. "Whew. I really am sloshed." I shook my head as if this were some new realization.

"Come on," she said.

"Where are we going?" I asked.

"We're going to sober you up, Teddy." I didn't want to be sober, and told her so. "Come on," she insisted. She guided me out of the dim confines of the Hofbrau Haus into the fading afternoon sunlight. I gave her the keys to my Pacer and got in on the passenger side. She started the car, then steered it out of the nearly empty parking lot. "Nice car," she said. "Big."

"Where are you taking me?" I asked. Janice was wearing Chanel No. 5, my favorite. At that moment my absolute favorite.

"Keep quiet and roll down your window," she said. We drove all the way up High Street until we got to Worthington, a northern suburb. After that we traveled west for a dozen miles until we came to the Olentangy River Road. She wasn't saying much, but I could tell that something big was on her mind because of the way she clutched the steering wheel and bit her lower lip. We stopped at a McDonald's just outside of Upper Arlington, where I used the rest room and bought myself a cup of coffee. Janice and I went outside, where we sat at a table and watched kids play on the hamburger swings and soda-straw slides. The sky was purple above the Zayres department store across the street. A bank clock half a block away said 7:07.

"Am I your prisoner? You going to rape and plunder me?" I looked at her face. She was studying mine, maybe trying to determine if I was fit for conversation.

"I've missed you, that's all," she almost whispered, as if there were a six-year-old spy hanging from the monkey bars. "A lot."

I said that I'd missed her, too. Then neither of us could think of anything to say, or else we knew what we wanted to say and couldn't make the words come out. "Let's go somewhere," I suggested.

"We've just been somewhere," Janice replied.

"I want to go somewhere. Somewhere else. You drive and I'll give directions."

At the Tremont Road traffic light we turned left and headed back toward campus. "I know where we're going," she said. "I told her she was mistaken. I directed her through a small subdivision bordering the Scarlet Course. One of the streets dead-ended at a chain link fence that protected the golf course from trespassers. During a practice round a few weeks before, I'd duck-hooked a drive into the rough near the fence, and noticed that someone had used an upended cement block to wedge an opening to the forbidden links. After grabbing my blanket (stowed in the trunk for just such an occasion) I led Janice to the spot and she slithered through. Then it was my turn. Although she may have thought otherwise, there was nothing symbolic in my taking her to the golf course. It was simply a private, untrameled place at this time of night.

"We're home free," I said. "There's one old security guard, but he sits in his car all night long, playing with his nightstick."

Janice held my hand and we cut across number eleven fairway, ducked beneath some low-hanging sycamore branches and trotted toward the largest green on the course. I sat down on the barely damp grass, and she sat beside me, so close that our thighs were touching. Everything we wanted to say to each other didn't really need saying.

I put my arm around her shoulder and pulled her tight. She leaned her head against my cheek in such a way that I was breathing in the smell of her perfume. "This is all just remarkable as hell, isn't it?"

"What do you mean?" she said, lying back against the newly mowed grass slope, pretending to look at Orion or Jupiter, something out there on the horizon above the lights of downtown Columbus.

"This is real as hell, that's all." I was incredibly nervous, and wished I smoked cigarettes so I could have one right at that moment. I drew in some warm evening air, and leaned back alongside Janice. There was almost nothing I could do to prevent myself from kissing her. That was why I had brought her there in the first place, after all; this was exactly what I wanted. No. I wanted everything. All at once. Only the vague thought that I was still drunk and possibly too careless held me back. And then even that small reservation disappeared. I undressed her with all the nervous grace I could muster.

I always wondered how I'd feel, how she'd feel, totally exposed, physically and emotionally, as we were right then. I touched her breasts carefully, trying to memorize the mysterious, soft contours of her body.

A shudder moved through her when I went inside. She pushed her chin so hard against my shoulder that I could tell she was scared. I said that everything was okay, although I wasn't sure of that, and I kissed her as reassuringly as I could. I wanted her to drift easily with me into that strange free-fall where sensation is everything and there is no thinking. Something was stopping her, and I wanted it to go away. It was as if Trayn were standing on the green looking down on us.

I wished that I hadn't brought her there; in the middle of making love I was thinking that. I wanted to end it in the middle, apologize for taking advantage of her weakness, but I was unable to do either. Force was building inside me, slowly at first, and then uncontrollably until everything gave way and I was holding Janice tight to protect her. I felt her heart beating against my chest. She was crying. I held her until the evening chill closed in on us.

A little while later we were retracing our steps. She walked quietly beside me, looking down at the black grass. I think she knew then what I had probably known months ago, but was afraid to admit. "I love you," she said. But she said the words wistfully, almost with a sigh.

I watched her crawl through the opening beneath the fence.

Eighteen

The channel across number one fairway is complete, and we're more than halfway in our progress down the rough toward number two green and our crescent pond. All this in a couple of weeks, thanks mainly to Grayson, who works like a diesel-driven machine. He almost resents our ten-minute breaks; he gulps water as if it were nothing but fuel for his labor, then returns to the trench. Meanwhile, Drago, shirtless and hairy-chested, spread-eagles on a bed of moss under the live oak behind number one green. And of course Chapman, beneath the shade of his straw hat, sits like a pudgy sultan in the soft Bermuda grass.

During one of these breaks, a few weeks before he's scheduled for release, I walk over to where Grayson is standing in the trench with only his black head visible above the bank. "How're you doing?" I ask.

"Gettin' by," he says, and granulates a dirt clod with his fingers.

"Can I ask you a question, Grayson?" He studies me with a slightly amused look on his face, but says nothing. "Why are you busting your tail out here every day when you could just as easily do nothing?"

"What difference zat to you?"

"I don't know," I tell him. "Maybe I'm just curious."

"We bes' get started, wouldn't you say?"

"Right," I say, and holler over at Drago and Chapman to get a move on. I don't suppose I'll ever know why Grayson is so fixed on getting the creeks and the pond dug before his release, but that's obviously what's on his mind.

One day every week we have to put away the shovels and get out the mowers; otherwise the Bermuda grass will grow out of control. Mowing has become extremely difficult because of the elongated heaps of soil with which we've contoured the fairways. These mounds are tinged with green from the newly germinated seeds. Only Drago has the skills necessary for maneuvering the reels through the labyrinth.

On Saturday morning, in the midst of my weekly letter to Stan, Ames knocks on my open door. I know before he has a chance to tell me that Maples wants to see me in his office. My stomach tightens at the possibilities that line up in the doubtful side of my brain. "It's the golf course, isn't it, Ames?"

"I'm afraid so," he says. "He was just out there a few minutes ago. I could hear him cussing three hundred yards away. I sort of expected he wouldn't like what you done."

"You knew about it . . . and you didn't say anything to him?"

"Why should I? He never tells *me* nothing."

Maples is twisting pipe cleaners into knots when I walk into his office. I can tell he's furious, but he's going to pretend he isn't. "Sit down, Kendall." I scoot out the Naugahyde chair and sit in front of his desk. He stands for a moment, as if he's going to stretch, but instead he steps toward his bookcase and removes a framed picture of his wife and two kids. He hands the picture to me and returns to his chair. "Have a look," he says. The wife is neither ugly nor particularly attractive. Her hair appears teased and heavily sprayed. The children, a girl no more than ten years of age, and a boy, possibly a year or two younger, are stridently redheaded. "Kendall, I make thirty-six thousand dollars per year. Betty is what you might call a housewife. So we live on my salary. We have a nice house and a new car."

"I'm glad for you," I say.

"Shut up, Kendall," he shouts angrily, then regains control. "If somebody like, for instance, the attorney general were to drop by for a little visit to Moss Point, and if by chance he happened to see the grounds torn up, he'd probably want to know why. Wouldn't you think?"

I tell him, "Sure."

"I said, shut up! Just listen, will you? What would happen to me if I found myself explaining to the A.G. that some of the inmates had taken it upon themselves to create waterways and ponds on state-owned property? Right under my nose. How long do you suppose it would take before he got on the phone and called the governor? Then I'd be out on my ass. Understand?" This time I say nothing. "Well . . . ?"

"Yes, I understand." I'm waiting for the hatchet to fall. I see myself refilling the ditch, with Drago, Chapman and Grayson standing mutinously by.

"Kendall, I'm not going to stop you from finishing the job. Not when you've come this far . . . although I ought to send the lot of you to the state pen to finish out your terms. Instead, all I'm asking is that you either get this job done on your *own* time or fill the son of a bitch in. You can take your pick."

I place the photograph on his desk, tell him thanks and leave the office, knowing that in effect he's killed the project. But I see that the poor guy has no real choice. He's just a bureaucrat trying to get by. I almost feel sorry for him.

For a while, I actually consider finishing the job alone in my spare time, but in a month or so the fall rains will move in and digging will be impossible. The days are getting shorter now, and I would have only a couple of hours in which to work after supper, although there are still Saturdays and Sundays. Drago and Chapman and Grayson certainly aren't going to give up their weekends to grovel in the dirt. I wouldn't even presume to ask them. I've just about decided to do the best I can between evening mess and nightfall, Monday through Friday, and all day on weekends . . . by myself.

My writing will have to wait until nighttime. I get on my blue jeans and khaki Moss Point-issue shirt and my dirty Adidas. Ten minutes later I'm tossing soil like a mole from the leading edge of the ditch and onto the bank.

After an hour, I've made approximately one foot of headway. By my calculations, I'll be in my early thirties by the time the pond and the feeder channel are excavated. It's an utterly hopeless task, so futile that I can't help laughing at myself, dirt-covered, sweaty . . . minuscule beneath the voluminous Mississippi sky. I'm almost ready to climb out when a shadow falls over me. At first I believe it's just a stray cloud floating by, but this shadow doesn't move. I turn around in my muddy hole and stare up at Grayson, who, with the sun behind him, looks like either a UFO or a saint. He tosses his shovel into the trench, then jumps in himself. "Cain't *stand* to see a man working alone," he says, and comes very close to smiling.

"How did you know I was here?"

"Ames. He tole Drago and me and that fat fucker, too."

"Chapman's not so bad when you get used to him."

"I hope that day never comes," says Grayson, heaving a shovelful of dirt skyward.

By late afternoon, Drago has joined us. He's tractoring loads of soil from where we deposit it to the beginnings of an elevated tee over by the fence. "Know what I want to be when I get out of this place, boss?" Drago asks between trips. "A golf architect."

I don't have the heart to let him down, so I feed him a cliché: "Everybody's got to have a dream," I tell him.

Chapman, who attends early morning worship, is up before I am on Sunday. He's plowing through his bureau for a clean shirt or maybe a fresh pair of boxer shorts when my alarm rings and I sit up in bed. He comes over to my side of the room, stands silently above me for a moment and says, "Alas, Sunday is a day of rest. But if you insist on defiling the Lord's day, that's *your* peril. Now, as for next *Saturday,* I'm at your service."

"Do you mean it, Chapman?"

"Call me a fool. But yes, I'm willing."

"I appreciate that. I'd really like to finish digging before Grayson leaves."

"Yes. And perhaps with my help we can achieve that," he says on his way to the shower.

Nineteen

Two days after I returned to Bowling Green for the holidays, Ginny's Christmas card arrived in the mail, the classic reindeer-soaking-his-feet. I was embarrassed not to have mailed one to her, when I could easily have pilfered one of those cards Stan sent to his clients: SEE ME FOR ALL YOUR INSURANCE NEEDS. In the aftermath of my fiasco with Janice, I really missed Ginny and her levelheaded predictability. Throughout that fall I'd reinvented sloth and dissipation. Sleeping through my Western Regionalism midterm was embarrassing only because I'd drooled on my blue book. Willa Cather was irrelevant to my life.

Sometimes I'd lie awake at night, wondering why I didn't love *Ginny*, not that she loved me. More likely, she just enjoyed the weird twists of my personality. I tried projecting a hypothetical relationship with her against the blank wall of my bedroom. I saw us together as newlyweds planning a family, middle-aged with kids, sixtyish without kids, geriatrics with nurses spoon-feeding us applesauce. It was a grim tableau. But Ginny was always smiling. That was worth something.

There was a short note at the bottom of her Christmas card. "I'm only an hour away. Why don't you drive down for New Year's. My folks will be in Bermuda! Luv ya, Ginny."

"That was it! I *luvved* Ginny, and she *luvved* me.

If I didn't take Ginny up on her offer I was doomed to sing "Auld Lang Syne" with Bobby Summiteer and Ned Skaffington and their girlfriends; however, I didn't want to wreck the symmetry of that quartet, and I certainly didn't fancy eating crown roast pork at Lucille's house. Anyway, I wanted Stan to have every opportunity to pursue his secret interests.

I promised myself that if I drove down to Upper Sandusky I'd spend a platonic evening in front of the fire. Maybe we'd catch a televised football game or an old movie, have a few beers or smoke a joint if there was one handy. I was curious to see her on her own turf anyway, eager to see how she decorated her room, anxious to take a gander at old pictures of her sitting on her grandpa's knee. I wondered if her toilet was blue or white. Maybe I could find *some* key to loving her. I was determined that we would *not* have sex.

My grade card arrived a few days after Ginny's Yuletide greeting. Two professors had taken pity on me and had given me perfunctory C's. My Western Regionalism grade was a charitable D. I shouldn't have majored in English.

Stan was shocked. "You'd better hope you make it as a golfer, because if you don't, you're likely to wind up like me, selling damned insurance for a living."

I told him I was going through a tough time and he said the tough time came when I flunked out. He had every right to be angry, and I was ashamed of myself.

At least I had some good material for New Year's resolutions: work hard in school; stay clear of Janice; add fifteen yards to my drives; find a way to love Ginny if at all possible.

On New Year's Eve I gassed up the Pacer at around five o'clock, just as the sun was ducking below the horizon. For Christmas, Stan had bought me a cassette tape deck for my car and a gift certificate at the Record Bar. I bought a few blues tapes, Big Walter Horton and Jimmy Reed, and I played them during the trip to Upper Sandusky.

My headlights caught the thin layer of snow between the rows of corn stubble. Some of the farmhouses were decorated with red and green holiday lights. I could smell smoke from their chimneys. For the first time in months I was actually happy—confused, maybe, but happy. I was singing along to "Big Boss Man," by Jimmy Reed, banging on the steering wheel, feeling black and rhythmic. Then in my rearview mirror I saw the blue twirling light of a patrol car. I was doing seventy miles per hour in a fifty-five zone. He bumped his siren once and flashed his turn signal. I pulled over on the berm of the highway and rolled my window down. It took him ten minutes to write out the ticket.

"Be careful, son," the officer said, handing me back my license. "There are some drunk people on the road tonight."

I said, "Yup," and soft-pedaled it for the remaining twenty-five miles, forty dollars poorer than when I left home.

On Park Boulevard, not too far from the main street of town, was Ginny's house, a big turn-of-the-century beast squatting at the crest of a hill. Christmas-tree lights flickered in the beveled glass of the front door.

I parked next to the curb and walked up the sidewalk to the front porch. Ginny opened the door just as I was getting ready to ring the bell. She was wearing gray pleated corduroys and a Radcliffe sweatshirt. "Teddy, how are you?" She threw her arms around me and patted me on the back. "You're a sight for sore eyes."

"You don't look so bad yourself." I was afraid we might go on trading clichés for an indefinite span of time. "Your house is gargantuan," I said. "A frigging mansion."

"It was my grandmother's house for years. When she died, my father inherited it."

"Beats the hell out of a double-wide," I said. Ginny took my jacket and led me into the dining room where she'd lighted some candles at either end of a long oak table. There were some chips

161

and dip set out, a plate of carrot sticks and some sandwiches from which she had carefully removed the crusts.

"What do you hear from Trayn? Is he having a vacation?"

"Frankly, I haven't heard from him since final exams. He's going to hang around Cincinnati during the break, I guess."

"You know he and Janice are back together, don't you? I can't believe that. But I got her letter yesterday."

"Oh, really?" I said, trying to camouflage the fact I felt sick to my stomach. In the mirror hanging on the far wall was a guy who looked like me, except that the color was gone from his face. My hands were shaking when I lifted a carrot stick to my lips.

"Are you okay?" Ginny asked, touching my cheek with her fingertips.

I told her I was fine, but I wasn't fine at all. For weeks Janice had grown smaller and smaller in my field of vision. I was reconciled to a future in which she played no part whatsoever. And that would no longer be the case. "Sorry, Ginny, I'm just not feeling too well at the moment."

"I know why," she said.

"You do?"

"It's the liverwurst. My dad hates the smell of it, too. But I love it." When I didn't reply, she looked me straight in the eye. "It's not the liverwurst . . . is it?"

"No, but what the heck. They're jerks. Jerks mate for life, just like coyotes." She started laughing until she was sort of hooting really . . . a strange laugh. We were sitting there on the floor of the carpeted dining room, laughing like a couple of crazies. Ginny put her head on my shoulder.

"You're a funny person," she said, and kissed me on the lips. I kissed her back and we sat that way on the dining-room floor, making out for a good half hour.

"I love you," she said.

"Is that l-u-v or l-o-v-e-?"

"L-o-v-e! The real McCoy."

I knew she wanted me to tell her the same thing; I was afraid she'd make me spell it. It was a sad situation if she really did love me, because as much as I wanted to love her in return, the emotion just wasn't there. I wished I was in Greenland or Tierra del Fuego, someplace far away and uncomplicated.

"Do you want to go in the bedroom?" Ginny asked.

I considered jumping out the window, plowing through the bushes, racing to my car and spinning off into the aimless night. "Let me think about that for a minute," I said. I inhaled smoke from an imaginary cigarette, pondered the flame of the green candle before me. "Ginny . . . ?"

"What is it, Teddy."

"It's not right, my making love with you."

"What are you talking about?"

"I luv you very much. I really do. But it's l-u-v."

Without saying a word, she walked out of the dining room, returned with my jacket and tossed it to me. "You'd better go. Please," she said. She was trying not to cry, but I could see the candlelight reflected in her eyes.

"I will," I said, and put my jacket on. "I really am sorry."

"It's okay, but I need you to leave." She walked me to the front door and opened it. She told me goodbye.

I sat in the parked car for a few minutes, watching the plumes of fog that came with each breath I took. My chest hurt from the inhalation of frigid air. I started the car and pulled away from the curb.

The traffic lights were a blur as I rounded the block and headed north toward Bowling Green.

Twenty

What little spare time I have is spent writing things down on the pages of legal pads. Sometimes when I read what I've recorded, I don't recognize Kendall as myself. But there he is, bumbling from page to page, eyes closed to the realities that stare him in the face. And then I'm forced to accept that the twenty-three-year-old man holding the tablet and this foolish protagonist are one and the same.

Every night I add something to my account, often something so painful I can barely cross the *t*'s and dot the *i*'s. But I'm moving toward a truth that this Kendall seemed always to be escaping. I just haven't put my finger on what that is yet.

I did manage a quick letter to Ginny last week. I sent it in care of her folks in Upper Sandusky (I didn't have her OSU address). I told her as little as I could about the crime that sent me here, since I figured Janice had probably given her a sympathetic account of my actions. Mostly I told her about life at Moss Point, about Drago and Chapman and Grayson.

And this morning I received her reply, although I've saved reading it until now, while Chapman is at the movie and I have the room to myself. The envelope is purple, lavender actually, and unscented. My hands shake as I tear open the flap and remove the letter. Janice's handwriting was always full of wild flourishes, circles instead of dots above the *i*'s, sometimes with microscopic smiley faces painstakingly drawn inside these tiny circles. Ginny's script is primitive by comparison, although totally legible. When I finally sit down on my bed to read her letter, I'm almost afraid of what she will say.

Dear Ted,

As you can imagine, I was shocked to hear that you're in jail. I still can't quite believe it, and I have an even harder time understanding the circumstances that put you there. But I know you, and I also know Trayn and Janice. You probably had a good reason for attacking him. Unless I'm totally mistaken, I'm sure that Janice was at the center of it. She was the damsel in distress and you were the gallant knight. Is that about the size of it?

Anyway, it sounds like you're getting along as well as can be expected, and I hope the time goes quickly for you. I think it's uncivilized not to let you serve your sentence closer to home, where at least your dad could visit you once in a while. Sorry I'm so busy, or I'd come down to see you myself.

I guess what I'm about to tell you will make you happy. I hope so, anyway. I'm dating a graduate student in the Sociology Department. His name is Ned (rhymes with Ted anyway) Davidson. He's 6'5" tall and he's got a nice big cute nose. I think we're going to get engaged in the next week or so, depending on whether he's hired at the University of Kentucky, where he interviewed a month ago. If he doesn't get the job, we'll postpone our plans for a while.

I'm sorry things have gone so badly for you, Ted. Janice is a sweet girl, who just happens to be the most confused person I've ever known. She manages to draw others into her confusion, you and Trayn in particular, although she doesn't necessarily intend to. Maybe a year in Moss

Point will allow you to sift all of that out of your system. I hope so, because I care what happens to you. See? I really do love *you.*

Take care,
GINNY

A sincere, perfunctory Dear John letter to Ted Kendall, white knight and dog in the manger. Why did I want her to feel sorry for me? And why would I expect her to carry a torch I'd extinguished so thoroughly on that New Year's Eve back when . . . a year ago? Two years ago?

I go to bed early on Saturday night, depressed by the realization that I'm still the same Kendall.

Twenty-one

For a solid week I spent at least one hour every day grunting in the basement weight room of Ferris Auditorium. Linebackers and offensive guards, big and hairy as yetis, were down there with me, hoisting barbells, straining against weighted pulleys, grinding out sit-ups on the slant board. While they were generally bench-pressing around 350 pounds, I was stuck at 210, at which point I would begin to vibrate. I passed gas, my carotid artery ballooned, my field of vision swam with tiny arrows of light, my nostrils filled with the smell of sweat, mine and everybody else's. There had to be a better way.

Then one evening, when I was reading *Golf* magazine in the periodicals room of the library, I came across an article on Johnny Miller, who had ruined a wonderfully effective golf stroke by spending a winter chopping wood on his Utah ranch. He'd upset the delicate geometry of his original swing and he was still trying to find a new equation, without much luck.

I spent all of a Friday night dreaming up a method of developing *only* my golf muscles. At four o'clock in the morning I was still sitting at the kitchen table drawing a diagram for a specially weighted practice club, a ten-pounder. When the sun came up I drove crosstown to Malone's Ironworks and presented my diagram to the machine-shop foreman. "Give me 'bout five or six days," he said. "I can do her for you."

A week later I stopped back to pick up my brainchild, whose head, an iron sphere the size of an orange, was connected to a solid-steel shaft. The handle was beveled to accommodate a standard rubber golf grip. "Is that about what you had in mind?" the foreman asked.

I told him it looked perfect and paid him fifty dollars in cash. Although I hadn't even fitted the grip over the steel handle, I carried this beast out to the parking lot, where I assumed a solid stance, positioned my hands on the shaft and took a hulking swing. The inertia of the follow-through ripped the club from my clutches and sent it skidding across the pavement. It ricocheted off the tire of a Dodge pickup. "Holy Christ," I muttered.

Routinely slugging his ball 280 yards or more, Trayn devoured par fives, often getting home with a drive and a long iron; yours truly, even with a wicked tail wind, required three shots to make the green. In other words, I was losing strokes every time I played a round of golf. So for exactly half an hour every afternoon, I stood on a secluded knoll at the fringe of the arboretum. There, under the high blue shatterproof sky, I did my practicing. For Ted Kendall, modern-day caveman, snow and freezing rain were mere nuisances. I grunted on the uptake and growled on the downswing. My fingers were red talons by the end of my practice session.

For the first few days of my workouts, I'd wake up in the morning feeling like I'd been starched and pressed. My shoulders throbbed, my pectoral muscles were swollen to the size of small breasts and I was barely able to grasp a pencil to take notes in my morning classes. But I gradually acclimated to the daily workouts, and almost looked forward to them. There was no evidence in the mirror of any permanent body transformation, but that was okay. I would live with "wiry." I *felt* much stronger, especially in the shoulders and triceps. And my spine was more flexible by far, which meant I could take a bigger turn on my backswing. I was hungry to get out on the links, but there were ten inches of snow on the ground. Unless there was an unforeseen thaw, I'd have to wait for the Florida trip to flex my muscles.

I saw very little of Ginny during the month of January. We bumped into each other once at the candy counter in the union. She smiled and said hello. I smiled back, and that was that. New Year's Eve had been painful for both of us, but maybe worse for her than for me. I hated the all-or-nothing philosophy of male-female relationships, and the crazy, disproportionate influence of lovemaking on friendship. Stan and Lucille seemed to have the right idea: share a ham loaf, then go to a movie. Anyway, I wished there was some way I could have prevented Ginny from being hurt by the way things had turned out. She was a nice girl and it bothered me that she was taking things so badly.

I'd adapted fairly well to once again having Janice as a regular presence in the apartment; we were good at pretending that the evening on the golf course had never taken place. But it *had* happened, and I could tell, in the subtle way she looked at me from time to time, that the delicate molecular structure of our relationship had transformed into something maybe more dura-ble. I wanted to think that, anyway. The three of us often played Hearts or Scrabble at night. Janice could now pinch my cheek or slap me on the shoulder without my worrying over implica-tions. Then, one Saturday night, she shuffled out of the bath-room, her robe not quite properly cinched, and I caught a quick glimpse of her before she could cover up. "Oops, sorry," she said. I almost wondered if she had done it intentionally to stoke my coals a little bit for old times' sake.

Sometimes they would argue, and I'd hear Trayn say, "Oh, Janice, you can be such a bitch . . ." And the next morning she'd be holding his hand across the breakfast table.

On the night before our Florida Trip, Trayn and Janice and I watched the Super Bowl together. Janice drank only one or two beers from the case with which we'd stocked our refrigerator for the occasion. By halftime, Trayn was passed out on the sofa, his size-twelve feet resting on the coffee table.

Janice waved me into the kitchen, and I got up to see what she wanted. She was pretending to wash out a few pans in a sinkful of sudsy water. "What's going on with you and Ginny?" she asked breezily.

"Not much these days. I guess you could say we've decided to go our separate ways."

"She seems really crushed, Teddy. I've never seen her so down."

"I'm sorry to hear that," I said. "Maybe I'll send her some flowers or something." What a ridiculous idea! I thought.

"That would be nice," she said. We stood there for a while, each waiting for the other to stop talking in code. She carefully placed a newly rinsed saucepan in the drain rack and dried her hands on a towel. "Does it have anything to do with *us*, with that night we spent together?"

"No, it really doesn't," I said. "Two different things."

"Are you sorry that happened?"

"Are you?"

"No," she said. "I'm glad it happened. I think it gave me a little . . . *perspective* I didn't have before."

"Glad to have been of use," I said. "Another chapter in the book of love, right?"

"Oh, Teddy . . . ," she said, and started to walk out of the kitchen, then stopped in mid-trek. "Did Trayn tell you we're getting married in June?"

"I'm glad for you," I said, trying to sound magnanimous. "That's great. Congratulations."

A few minutes later she'd put on her rabbit fur coat and was gone. Trayn was snoring now, obliterated by a dozen beers. Meanwhile, I felt totally cold sober. I snapped off the TV, grabbed my practice club from behind the door to my bedroom and left the apartment.

The golf team traveled all night through the heart of the Confederacy. Unless the van had a blowout or engine trouble, we'd arrive in Gainesville at about noon. While everyone else managed to get some sleep, I stared out the window at the black pine trees pinned against the blue night sky. Somewhere north of Valdosta, Georgia, I fell asleep against the cold window.

I awakened to the onslaught of illuminated billboards advertising Bob's Alligator Farm, and Citrus Village, and Palm Vista Properties.

We arrived in Gainesville at midday, weary but happy to have made it okay. Our motel was one of those adobe-colored fake Mediterranean monstrosities whose identity came from Alamo arches over every room and logs protruding for no particular reason from beneath the eaves of the red tiled roof. Trayn and I parked our belongings in the room, with its Day-Glo matador on black velvet. To my surprise, the mattresses were excellent.

Within the hour we were at Cherokee Creek Country Club, a 7,000-yard beauty, adorned with sinister plant life, strategically placed ponds and creeks, and greens much smaller than what one usually expected from a Florida course. It was too late for us to play a round, even if we'd been fit to do so. Trayn and I walked the roughs of the front side; we ignored the shouts of the members, who held their fire while we traversed the fairways. "This course has your name on it," Trayn said. "All the OBs are on the right, and the greens are slick. I bet those fat fuckers can't break a hundred on this beast, not even from the *pink* tees." He was right; it *was* my kind of course, except that the par fives were ogres. Looming in the back of my brain was a growing fear that I had only corrupted my touch and timing by swinging that weighted club for six weeks.

Most of us went with Coach Forbes to a public driving range a few blocks from the motel. Garibaldi and Evans went back to their room to catch up on some sleep. "They're just in a hurry to bugger each other," Trayn said as they crossed the boulevard. Although we had the next day to practice, I was anxious to see what all those cold-weather workouts had done for my drives. Coach paid the man in the range booth for two hundred balls each, and the three of us, including a superb freshman named Bill Twyman, started out by hitting some easy wedges toward the 100-yard marker. I was working through my irons as quickly as possible, so I could get to my number one wood, the big question mark.

The club felt flyweight in my hands. A balloon stick. A strand of vermicelli. "Oh God," I said out loud when my first drive migrated stage right like a wayward goose toward a junkyard. "Don't let this happen."

"What's wrong?" Trayn asked. He was still hitting five irons.

"This damned driver feels strange, that's all."

He leaned on his club and watched my swing. I parked another range ball among the wrecked cars. "Take it back more to the inside. The angle of attack is too upright. Flatten your swing, pal."

I tried drawing the club back on a slightly flatter plane. The result was a bizarre hook that whizzed across the horizon. "Now split the difference," Trayn said. I took his advice and drilled a magnificent white bullet directly over the 250-yard marker. In that fraction of a second, as the ball hung in midflight like a small moon, I felt the synapses of my brain sparking. "Amazing!" I yelled. "Will you look at that?"

"Son of a bitch!" Trayn said. "The Incredible Hulk!"

Twelve teams were invited to play in the tournament, including Houston, Duke, Florida, Miami and a few of the other perennial powers. OSU was expected to finish somewhere in the middle of the pack. If we wanted to scare anybody, though, Bill Twyman and Gary Evans, our three and four men, would have to play over their heads. Trayn and I would need to hold our own. Jim Garibaldi, the number five man, wasn't going to contribute much to the cause, but since only the top four scores counted, that was no loss.

On Wednesday, the course was closed except for those of us who would be competing in Thursday's tournament. Trayn and

I played thirty-six holes, trying to get our games back into shape, and also to learn the mysteries of this course with its alligators and foraging armadillos and spooky egrets. I was nailing my tee shots 260 yards, slightly less than I'd hoped for, but taking into account the spongy fairways and humid air, not bad. Trayn's drives were now only fifteen yards beyond mine.

Trayn wasted a beautiful 67 on Wednesday, a score we'd need later on. His second round was a decent 71. I carded 72 and 70, although I had putted poorly throughout the day. The big surprise was Garibaldi, who shot a nice pair of 73s. Trayn and I concluded that he was probably keeping his own score.

As usual, I was an insomniac before the big day. I worried that if I didn't sleep well I wouldn't be sharp for the tournament. Thinking about that kept me awake. I slugged the pillow, pinched my eyelids together and commanded sleep to come. I rolled onto my back and studied a slim, almost invisible strand of intermittent light projected onto a wall by the blinking motel sign. A flag stick? A one iron? I rolled around on the bed for a few hours until I finally drifted into a thin and nonsensical dream in which I was required by some unspecified decree to play a golf hole that began in Columbus and finished in Bowling Green. It was a doglegged hole that turned precisely at Janice's bedroom in Cincinnati. I had driven, pitched and putted my golf ball halfway across the state, through car washes, cow pastures, old folks' homes, fast-food restaurants and high school gymnasiums. It was nighttime and my ball was lying in a yard across the street from Janice's house (which in reality I had never seen); I was obliged to pop a wedge shot through her opened bedroom window, a task I achieved with ease. I went inside her front door, up some steps, down a hallway and into her bedroom. She was standing naked in front of her bed, clutching a biography of Woody Hayes to her small breasts. I realized at that moment that I was also naked. She took the wedge from my hands, before I could chip my ball down the stairs, tossed the club and the book aside and embraced me.

There I was in an alien motel in alligator land with Trayn

sleeping a few feet away, and I was captured inside a goofy sex dream about his fiancée. Unfortunately, I woke up about ten seconds too late.

With mist hovering above the slow-moving water, Cherokee Creek looked like a gray anaconda sprawled across the fairways. Before long the sun's rays would be leaning through the feathery cypress trees, evaporating the mist and the dew from the course. I was standing near the putting green, listening to the rasp of cigarette lighters, the click of practice putts, the clatter of irons knocking together. Trayn was already at the first tee. He was unlucky to have drawn such an early starting time, since his power would be offset by the wet fairway grass and heavy air. His warm-up swings at the first tee were stiff and perfunctory, as if he were angry about the situation. He wasn't even talking to his playing partners. His first drive of the day never got more than a foot off the ground. The ball landed about 180 yards down the right side of the fairway and kicked into the short rough, heavy with moisture. He slammed his driver into his bag, lit a cigarette and let it hang between his lips while he waited for the other members of his threesome to tee off.

By eleven-thirty I was feeling surprisingly sharp, considering my fitful night in the motel room. We were waiting for the group ahead of us to clear the fairway so we could tee off at number two. I was paired with a bandy-legged Cajun kid from LSU and a tight-lipper from Penn State. The two of them weren't exactly hitting it off. Their dialogue went this way: "Would you prefer that I mark my ball?" and "Yeah, why doan you go head an' do dat." I'd already parred number one after hitting a cautious three wood from the tee. (Trayn would have clucked like a chicken if he'd seen me.) However, the second hole was an opportunity to let out shaft. Ordinarily, the creek which crept across the fairway 230 yards out would have forced me to lay up short with a two iron, a concession to my subaverage drives. This time, though, the creek was just part of the scenery between where my ball was perched on a yellow tee and the green, 550 yards out, framed by a pair of white sand traps that resembled elephant ears. I waggled my club behind the ball, imagining its perfectly parabolic flight and my follow-through, a study in balance and amplitude. My playing partners would be full of awe and admiration. Beneath an umbrella of live oaks I stood, thinking of the first bar of Beethoven's Fifth, the trio of preparatory notes and the final explosive chord, at which point the clubhead smacks into the ball. This long-awaited tee shot, which was to measure the value of my training theory, turned out to be a disappointing fade that blooped into a row of Formosan palm trees in the right-hand rough, twenty yards short of the creek. "You got some trouble, my fren," said Maury Thibodaux. I wondered how a guy from Bayou Lafourche ever learned to play golf.

Ten minutes later I was scratching a fat six onto my score-card. I shook my head and tried to put that one behind me.

My redemption came at the next hole, a par three, where I poked a mid-iron to within seven feet of the cup. But birdieing a short hole doesn't carry the same heroic weight as nailing a par five green in two. With some luck, actually an incredible amount of luck, even Stan could birdie a par three hole; but he could never reach a 540-yarder with a drive and a three wood, which I intended to do at number eight on that Thursday morning.

This time there was no creek to clear, no battalions of imma-ture palm trees left and right. Instead, number eight was a broad, inviting green runway. I hauled in my backswing a few degrees this time, thrust my weight into the ball and let fly with a beautiful soaring 275-yard drive dead in the belly of the fair-way. "That's a very nice drive," said the Penn State member of our threesome. It didn't matter that I pulled my four wood ap-proach shot into a deep greenside bunker, then blasted out and two-putted for a seemingly ho-hum five; what mattered was that I was hole-high in two shots with a par in my hip pocket. I felt the rumble of testosterone in my blood. The new, aggressive Ted Kendall had just rolled onto the showroom floor.

Despite his bogey at number one, Trayn had matched my 70 by birdieing the last hole. "I heard you kicked ass," he said to me before he lined up his six-footer. "Would you believe that if I make this we tie for the lead with Houston? Twyman shot even par and goddamn Garibaldi shot—get this!—a sixty-fucking-nine!" In spite of myself, I was almost wishing he'd miss his putt. It was a mean-spirited way to feel, but I'd just shot a great round of golf, and he was ambling back and forth across the green like Bob Hope. The putt was as good as in.

We ate dinner as a team at the Sombrero Cafe, a garish, perpendicular wing of the motel. Amidst the looming Mexican miscellany, I ate my burritos and refried beans. My mind was on golf, specifically an improvement over one of the best days of my life as a golfer. Trayn was across the table from me, laughing and drinking beer, toasting Garibaldi, toasting me, toasting everything he could think of. After dinner Trayn and I lay around the motel room, recounting oddities of our day on the links and half watching some of the Thursday-night TV shows. Then, out of the clear blue, he asked me a question so strange I had to ask him to repeat it. "Have you ever gone all the way with Janice?"

"God, Trayn, what a damned stupid thing to ask."

"Well . . . I know she was leaning on you pretty heavy when we were on the outs. And I was just wondering if you and she had . . . you know, fucked, that's all."

"What difference would it make? She's crazy about you."

"Hey, don't get mad. I don't care if you did or didn't. I was just wondering."

"Well, I *didn't*," I said. "so let's change the subject."

There was a period of silence when we both focused on the TV screen. Finally, he sat on the edge of his bed and looked at me. "Hey, Teddy. Did you see that little Oriental guy I was paired with this morning? The guy from Texas? Would you believe he's Vietnamese. Learned to play golf three years ago." He lit a cigarette and blew a billow of smoke toward a moth-filled light fixture on the ceiling. "All he could say was 'Hello' and

'You up' and 'Not so fine swim in water.' I guess he was talking about the gators. Want to know what he shot? A damned sixty-eight. Shit."

At about eleven o'clock Trayn placed a long-distance phone call to Janice, who was staying at our apartment for the week. "Hey, babe," he said, "what's new?" He listened for a minute or so to what she was saying at the other end of the line. "Hell, Teddy was a *hero*. We needed a seventy from him, and he delivered. The wop shot a sixty-nine. Can you feature that?" Apparently, Janice scolded him for using the term "wop," because he told her to "lighten up."

I went outside to get some air when the conversation got to the "I love you, too," stage. I leaned against the front grille of the OSU van and tried to find the Big Dipper in the night sky, but it was lost in the haze of the city. The air was washed with a fragrance of something in bloom. It was a balmy night like this one when Janice and I had made love on the golf course.

Trayn was probably finished with his phone call, and I was about to go back inside when a homely woman wearing a black dress opened the door of a Bonneville parked next to the van. She must have been sitting in the car for a while, maybe having a smoke while her husband watched the tail end of a basketball game on TV. When she walked past me I smelled orange blossoms.

On Friday I birdied the first of the par fives and was actually putting for an eagle at number eight. If my putting stroke had been more secure, I might have clipped an extra three or four strokes off my score. Even so, my 68 tied me with Trayn for the individual lead in the tournament. Garibaldi had returned to form with a robust 78, while Evans had whipped his ducks back into line. He'd carded a 72. For the sake of Twyman's family and friends, the outcome of his round will be a secret forever.

On Friday night, Trayn and I went to see *King of Hearts* at one of those dollar cinemas located in an obsolete shopping center not far from our motel. Ginny and I had seen the movie in

Columbus a year or so earlier, and I thought Trayn might like it. Of course, he didn't like it at all. His objection? "No plot."

"Better than hashing away the time with golf talk," I said.

After the movie we were walking past a row of peeling bungalows when Trayn said something curious. "Tell you what, Teddy. If you can play over your head for one more day, we might just walk away with this tournament."

"Do you think I'm playing over my head?" I asked.

"You *are,* aren't you?"

I said, "Yeah, I guess I am," and that was the end of dialogue for the rest of the night.

At midnight I was lying in the dark room, staring at the luminous dial of my travel alarm, trying to convince myself that it wasn't so important to outplay Trayn. He was a great golfer, a tough competitor, and he didn't like sharing the limelight with anybody, not even me. For all I knew, Janice was just another trophy for him. He'd played that game hard, too, and he'd won his victory. But that was his business, and not mine anymore, and hardly worth losing sleep over. I tried to make myself believe that, but I hadn't persuaded myself of anything except that I wanted to beat him for once. I wanted Trayn to play the golf of his life, and I wanted to come in one stroke better. Exactly one stroke.

On Saturday I was off early, two groups ahead of Trayn. I'd hoped to be playing behind him, so I'd know what I had to shoot for. But once again, his strength from the tee would be neutralized by the dampness of the morning. He was there at the first tee, patting me on the back, telling me to "go get 'em," things like that. I wished him luck and teed up a virgin golf ball. My jaw muscles felt tense, and my grip on the club was too tight. I backed off for a few seconds, stared down the fairway at a couple of mockingbirds squabbling at the crest of a small rise, then resumed my stance over the ball. My drive was a scorcher that sailed out over the right-hand rough as if it would land in trouble, but near the end of its flight it drew back toward the fairway, where it rolled a good fifty yards. I blew out a stream of air and picked up my tee. "Hell of a hit, Teddy boy," Trayn said.

There were only three holes left to play on Saturday, the final round of the tournament. I had been marching through a green tunnel all day, seeing only the ball and the flag stick. Trayn didn't exist anymore, and numbers were nothing to me. Every shot was self-evident and foregone, each swing as natural as breathing. Sweat glistened on my eyebrows; I could see it there high in my field of vision. As Trayn would say, I was playing over my head. Literally over my head. I wondered if he knew I was five under par.

I'd kept the driving honors all day, and I was standing at number sixteen surveying the contours of the fairway. It had a pair of breasts at just the right part of its anatomy, and an oval face illuminated by the late afternoon sun. I planted my shoes in the soft turf of the elevated tee and took a practice swing. When I finally drove my ball, it was a low-flying beauty, just right of center. I was sure it would be in an ideal position, but at the last second it kicked off the side of one of the two distant hillocks and into a cluster of small evergreens. The outcome seemed impossible to me. It had been a perfect drive.

After several minutes of searching, I found my ball in a nest of brown deadfall beneath a squat arborvitae shrub. I had only two choices. One was to take a penalty stroke and drop the ball two club lengths from where the thing had come to rest. If I took the drop, I'd be stymied by a small battalion of shrubs, with no real opportunity to make a backswing. The alternative was getting on my knees and taking a horizontal swipe at the ball with a choked-down putter. That way I might be able to knock the ball sideways a few feet and into a clear zone. From there, a six iron onto the green, one putt and par.

Sweat dripped down my spine as I knelt next to the bush. My task was to somehow punch a one-inch-diameter ball from underneath a Christmas tree whose lowest tier of branches was only six inches from the bare earth. I hunched over time and time again to fix the ball in my mind's eye. I happened to look over my shoulder in the midst of all this preparation, hoping for some consolation from my playing partners. What I saw instead, in the rough across the fairway, was Trayn, in his canary-yellow slacks, leaning on his golf club like the ultimate spectator. I couldn't read the expression on his face because he was too far away, but I imagined a barely detectable smile creeping across his face.

I took one more peek at the dimpled white egg in its brown nest, waggled the club momentarily and took a vicious swing that sent forth a small storm of needles and dirt. The ball was bound to have emerged from its hiding place. I looked to my left, certain it was lying only inches from the fairway. But there was no sign of it. I lifted a low branch of the arborvitae and took a peek. The ball was still there, slightly dirtier, and even closer to the trunk of the tree. Without thinking, I slashed again at the underbranches and actually dismembered one of them. *Nothing.* I looked over at Trayn, who now had the club over his shoulder like a rifle. His visor was cockeyed on his scalp. A sudden breeze rustled the foliage that surrounded me. It was howling through the green tunnel I'd occupied all day long. It swooped me up and carried me high overhead where I could look down at the guy in the red shirt, kneeling beside a wounded bush somewhere in Florida. Suddenly, I was laughing at myself. I took another halfhearted poke at the ball. "Come out of there, you silly bastard," I said. I was lying four already, and I was having a hilarious good time.

From across the fairway I heard Trayn's voice. "Take the penalty and drop the damn thing."

Just for the heck of it, I took one more swing, making just enough contact to pop the ball into daylight.

Twenty-two

Tomorrow Grayson will be gone from Moss Point and into a world whose mysteries I can only imagine. But now his feet are planted firmly in the deep grass along the fence, where we four stand in amazement at what we've accomplished over the past months. At the moment, the creeks and the pond are merely trenches and a deep pit, but when the clay barrier is shoveled away, the water will rush through and the transformation will take place before our eyes. The pond, while slightly smaller than I'd imagined it (a concession to Grayson's deadline), seems to complement the modest proportions of number two green. Drago, using railroad ties and salt-treated timbers, has built two substantial bridges over the creek. Chapman has played his part, too, manning the tractor in the twilight hours when he would normally be in the prison library probing Old Testament enigmas with his born-again companions. But Grayson himself deserves most of the credit. He would set a pace of one enormous shovelful of damp soil every five seconds, a rhythm he'd maintain until his thick arms got tired, at which point he'd mop sweat from his scalp, flex his fingers, take a deep breath and begin again.

But now it's Saturday afternoon, and the basketball players have quit their game at the sight of us leaning on our shovels, negligent gravediggers. Curiosity gets the best of them, and they juke and jive across the roughs and fairways, passing the ball behind their backs, taking graceful hook shots at imaginary baskets. "Hey, bro', what's happening out here?" one of them says to Grayson.

"Stick 'round, you might find out," he growls.

At this point the guards must suspect a potential jailbreak, because two of them race out of the quadrangle like over-the-hill Olympians. Fortunately, it doesn't take long for them to figure out that the mood is festive. After all, Drago is singing "Oop Boop Diddim Daddim Waddim . . . Chew . . . and they swam and they swam all over the dam . . ." He's also doing a strange dance that could only have been passed down to him from some Yugoslavian ancestor.

"Hey, Drago," I say. "Shouldn't Ames be here when we open up the waterway?"

"I'll get him," he chirps, then cavorts all the way to the warden's office, arms twirling, head rocking from side to side.

Soon almost half the prison population has gathered for the groundbreaking, including Maples himself, who from time to time shakes his head in disbelief.

"Cecil B. De Mille would blush at this spectacle," Chapman grouses.

The time has finally come. One or two shovelfuls from the earthen barricade and the force of onrushing water should do the rest. "Grayson, I think you should do the honors," I say. He steps forward, jabs halfheartedly at the dirt, looks at me balefully, then backs away. To my surprise, he hands the shovel to Chapman and walks toward the quadrangle. I call after him, but he keeps walking.

"I'm honored, but profoundly confused," his stand-in announces. However, when Chapman's clumsy digging finally allows the first slim ribbon of water to trickle over the crest of the dam, there's an enormous cheer. I watch Grayson pause momentarily, exactly where the trench makes a right-hand turn and travels the length of the rough. Within a few seconds, the dam seems to disintegrate, giving way to a torrent of muddy water that sloshes through this channel. I see him nodding almost imperceptibly. Then he resumes his slow trek back to the quadrangle.

Drago has cannonballed into less than a foot of swiftly moving water. He stands up, becomes rigid, then falls backward with a splash. "Aqua Vita," he yells. "Aqua Velva. Aqua *Duck!*"

Before heading back to his office, Maples says to one of his guards, "Get that man out of there. The water is probably polluted." But the guard is too fascinated by these aquatics to respond.

While the rest of the prisoners return to their various Saturday diversions, I follow the creek across number one fairway and down the rough to where it hooks into the pond, which is slowly filling with water. Every so often a confused catfish thrashes the surface with its tail, an action I can identify with, although I know the catfish can swim under the fence anytime he chooses. I feel elated and immensely sad at the same time, standing here on one of the first cool days of September. Maybe the fact that the growing season is over dilutes my happiness, or maybe it's Grayson's departure that brings me slightly down.

Whatever the source of that curious dull ache, it's escaped Chapman and waterlogged Drago, who look like cartoon characters pressed against a green background. They are walking jubilantly in my direction.

"Whaddya think, boss? Is this great or what?"

"I wouldn't have believed it," I say.

"Praise God, from whom all blessings flow," Chapman chimes in.

"Amen. Gimme five!" says Drago, offering his open palm to Chapman, who chooses not to participate.

That evening I stop by Grayson's room to say goodbye. He'll be gone with the sunrise, if I've understood Ames correctly. When I knock on his door, he opens it and tells me to come in. On his bed are two bundles of clothing and a cardboard box filled with toiletries, shoe polish, a small transistor radio and various other personal items. "Here . . . you wan' sit down?" he asks, tossing a pair of shoes off the only chair in the room.

"How does it feel to be clearing out, Grayson?"

"Feel pretty good. I get to see my boy. He only six. Can you 'magine not seein' your boy but once or twice in a year?"

"You missed him . . ."

"Damn right I missed him. He livin' with my sister for now."

"What's his name?"

"Name?" Grayson smiles so fully that for the first time I see he's minus several teeth on one side of his jaw. "Named him Campy after Roy Campanella."

"Campy. I like that. Good names make good people."

"You b'lieve that shit?"

I have to confess to him that I don't. "Listen, I just wanted to say goodbye, and thank you for helping out on the golf course." I stand up and offer my hand, which he grasps firmly in his own. "I'll see you."

"So long," he tells me.

It's a long walk down the corridor. One of the country-clubbers is speaking along with his Learn Spanish at Home record. "*Y ahora si el mundo es chico!*" Somebody else is clipping his toenails over a wastebasket.

184

Twenty-three

On a drizzling Friday afternoon in mid-June I drove my Pacer down I-75 to Cincinnati, where Trayn and Janice were to be married by an Episcopal priest who, according to them, wore a black eye patch and a prosthetic ear. I was supposed to be best man at the wedding, with Gary Evans and Janice's twelve-year-old brother ushering. Ginny was maid of honor, which meant we'd be rubbing elbows at the inevitable punch bowl.

My first stop, once I'd arrived at Fairfield Heights, a wealthy suburb on the north side of the city, was King's Formal Apparel, where I coughed up fifty dollars for a fairly soulful-looking tuxedo. (Trayn picked out the usher costumery.) I tried the thing on and it was a terrible fit, especially the pants, which stopped three inches above my shoes. The German guy who took care of me loosened the suspenders. "Zat should vix you up," he said. The cuff moved one inch closer to my Adidas. "*Now* vee cookink!" he said. "Very nice." The clerk put the ruffled shirt in a box and the tux on a hanger. I paid him the money and raced through a downpour to my car.

From King's it was only five or six blocks to the Econo Lodge, where I and possibly a few of the out-of-town guests would be staying. Someone had paid in advance for my room. That meant I could be a little more generous with my wedding present, which I hadn't yet purchased. It seemed extravagant not to have put Gary Evans and me together in a room, since we were teammates at OSU. But that was somebody else's business and not mine.

Inside my suitcase were a change of underwear, a clean pair of Levi's, a few cotton shirts, my dop kit and a bottle of Jim Beam. With all the lamps lighted against the gloom seeping through the curtains, I poured a glass of whiskey on ice, hoping things might appear a little bit less bleak. It was already three-thirty in the afternoon. I opened the curtains to see what the rain was doing. Tall skinny pillars of water were falling from the roof onto the sidewalk in front of my window. I was about to draw the curtains shut when out on the parking lot I saw Ginny hopscotching puddles between the motel and her red Toyota. From her angle of attack, she had to be staying in the room next door. Maybe there had been a conspiracy to throw us together. I'd thought all along that she'd stay at Janice's house, but there she was, dressed in a green running suit, holding a folded newspaper over her head to shield herself from the rain. There are a few women in this world who look sensational in sports clothes but who don't belong in a formal dress. Ginny was one of these. I downed my glass of whiskey before braving the torrents in search of a wedding gift.

An hour later I was in a small gift shop on Colerain Highway, picking up, then replacing on the shelf a handsome pair of nicely painted his and hers mallard duck decoys, forty-five dollars apiece, but more original than crystal salt shakers or salad spinners. So I bought them. In a matter of two hours I'd dropped $140, and there was still Friday night and all day Saturday to go.

The rehearsal dinner was to be held at the clubhouse dining room of the River Trail Golf Course, where Trayn's bank executive father was a member. Fortunately, the rain had subsided by seven-thirty, when I arrived, more or less drunk, at the club. I carried my wrapped package up the brick walkway to the door, held open for me by a black man in a white sports coat. He showed me where to deposit the gift and guided me to a green-carpeted lobby where wedding guests milled around with plastic cups of booze in their hands. I spotted Trayn leaning against the wall beneath a portrait of William Howard Taft, a charter member of River Trail. "Hey, buddy. Damn, it's good to see you," Trayn said. "Did you find the tuxedo place okay?"

"Sure did," I said. "And a *fine* tuxedo it is. The pedal pusher trousers were a nice touch."

"It doesn't fit?" Trayn actually seemed astonished. "I gave them your measurements. Thirty-two inseam, right?"

"Don't worry about it, Trayn. Everybody's going to be looking at Janice. Where is she anyhow?"

"She and Ginny had to pee."

I plucked a plastic champagne glass from a tray offered me by yet another black man. Mrs. Thompson, who looked nothing like her daughter, tiptoed through the smoke to join us. "I think you must be Ted Kendall," she said, her voice gravelly from cigarettes like the one whose ashes she was blithely flicking onto the green carpet. "Janice says you're something special." I tried to think what this woman must have looked like thirty years before, and whether I would have considered her attractive.

I told her it was nice meeting her, and that Janice was a wonderful person, too. My conversational skills floated in a pool of alcohol at the back of my brain. The champagne and whiskey were rioting in my system. Instead of loosening me up, as I'd hoped, the alcohol had turned me into a stiff, with a permanently stupid grin that I couldn't bring under control. I wished the girls would hurry up with whatever they were doing. Right on cue, the two girls emerged from the rest room. Janice was dressed in an iridescent red knee-length shift that made her look like a flapper. Poor Ginny had painted her eyelids a pastel blue, and her eyelashes were thick with mascara. When she saw me, Janice sprinted across the room and threw her arms around my neck. "God, I feel so much better now that you're here," she said, and kissed me. I shook hands with Ginny, whose roseate lips formed a Betty Boop smile. I told her it was nice to see her.

That awkward moment was saved by the announcement that the dining room was ready for us. The crowd formed a train that shuffled through the double doors and dispersed to the chairs around the circled tables. I was supposed to sit between Janice's little brother Joseph and Trayn's dad, so conversation with Gary Evans, what there was of it, took place only when Mr. Traynham leaned forward over his chicken Las Vegas; then Gary and I would tilt back against our chairs and talk through the briefly empty space. Mr. Traynham didn't seem especially interested in chatting with me, except for a few perfunctory questions, enough to avoid seeming totally rude. I flashed my inebriated grin and said things like "You bet" and "Absolutely." Joseph was drawing futuristic cars on the palm of his hand with a ballpoint pen. The groom-to-be was busy shaking hands with uncles and his father's cronies, who throughout the meal came to our table long enough to stuff his pockets with bills. I looked over toward Janice, who hadn't eaten a bite. Small talk was rampant. And Ginny looked uncomfortable, seated next to Mr. Thompson, who regaled her with some of his favorite jokes, at which she laughed politely. Once, when he'd briefly abandoned her in favor of the food on his plate, I saw her roll her eyes and blow air up toward her stiff bangs. I borrowed Joseph's pen and scratched a note on my napkin, "That man needs a pie in the face," and signed my name. I gave the message to my little buddy and told him to deliver it to Ginny. She read what I'd written, and smiled.

When dessert had been removed from the tables, a quartet of waiters circulated throughout the dining room with bottles of champagne. The time had come for toasts all around, beginning with yours truly. Only when Trayn reached behind Joseph's back, flicked me on the shoulder and said, "Go for it!" did I realize that I was expected to hoist my glass and make an off-the-cuff speech; so I wiped my mouth on a napkin and stood up. Except for an isolated cough emanating from my right, the dining room was dead silent. I searched the tentacles of the chandelier for something to say. Seconds were coming and going, and the wedding guests were getting impatient. When I opened my mouth to speak I wasn't sure at all what was going to come out. "Marriage is a little bit like golf," I began, a total *goner*. Maybe UPS was going to hand-deliver my next phrase. *How was marriage like golf?* "Well . . . uh . . . let's see . . . you've got to play by the rules, first of all. And . . . uh . . . you've got to be courteous to your partner . . . and you've got to sink your putts . . . and . . . and you can't quit before the round is over." Sweat was hanging from the tip of my nose. "So I hope Janice and Trayn play the game as it was meant to be played, and that they have a nice life together." *What a pile of grunt*, I said to myself as I tilted my glass first toward Janice, then toward Trayn, who looked like he might be smashed. People said, "Hear! Hear!" and clapped, as if I'd really pulled it off. Next, Ginny, whose new hairdo had been all but wrecked by the humidity, stood up. Her hands shook so badly that champagne was spilling from her glass. "To long life and happiness!" she said, and sat down. Everybody cheered. At last somebody who could get straight to the point. There were a few more toasts before the dinner ended, mostly clichés. When Mr. Thompson stood up to thank the Traynhams for footing the bill for the rehearsal dinner, everyone filed out of the dining room and headed out the front door.

Trayn caught up with me in the lobby, just before I made my escape. "Wait up," he said, fishing a cigarette from the pocket of his sports coat. "That was one hell of a toast back there. You make that up?"

"Pretty poetic, wasn't it?"

"Brave as hell, I'd say. Anyway, thanks. You were the star of the show."

"No problem," I said, "My pleasure." I was anxious to get back to my motel, where I would run a tubful of hot water, dissolve my humiliation. "Listen, I'll see you tomorrow at noon. Take care of yourself, okay?"

"Yeah, I'll see you."

Ginny's Toyota was just pulling out of the country club parking lot when I got to my Pacer. I jabbed my key into the ignition, started the engine and roared off in pursuit. I followed the red taillights of her car to the motel.

Before she could unlock the door to her room I hollered at her through my rolled-down window. "Did you have a good time?"

"How did you get so *drunk?*" she asked as I trotted across the parking lot. "I was jealous."

"Head start. Brought along some Jim Beam." We stood there in the glow of the motel sign, looking at each other. "I'm glad to see you, Ginny. Really, I mean that. I've missed you."

"God," she said, "you really *are* smashed."

"No, I'm not. I'm seriously glad to see you. You want to come in and watch some TV? I promise I'll be a good boy."

"I will if you'll let me get out of these church clothes," she said.

A half hour later, after I'd put on some jeans and a pullover shirt, there was a knock on my door. When I opened up, Ginny was standing there in her green running suit. She'd obviously taken a shower, because the makeup was gone from her face and her hair was slightly damp. She looked much better. "I hate motels," she said, stepping into the room. "I used to travel with my parents sometimes, and we'd stay in these places you wouldn't believe . . . flypaper hanging down from the ceiling, truckers making noise in the next rooms . . . awful." She sat down on the queen-sized bed, then plucked some rug lint off her white Pumas.

"Want to watch an old movie?" I asked, and strode across the room and snapped the set on. I fiddled with the tuner until a black-and-white picture filled the screen, then settled into a blue upholstered chair against the wall opposite the bed where

Ginny lay, propped on her elbow. We stared wordlessly at the TV screen for about twenty minutes. Colbert and Gable drove away together, happily married, at which point she got up and snapped the set off.

"What do you want to do now?" she asked.

I went over to the ice bucket resting on top of the air-conditioning unit, dropped a few cubes into my plastic cup, poured in about two fingers of Jim Beam and leaned against the door, wondering if my doing so was intended to prevent her escape or facilitate my own. I swirled the whiskey and looked at Ginny, who sat upright at the end of the bed. "That's up to you," I said. "But I was really hoping we might talk. I wasn't too pleased with how things went on New Year's Eve."

"Neither was I. I guess I wanted more from you than I had any right to expect."

"I wouldn't say that."

"Well, I wasn't playing fair. I've always known where your heart is." I chomped some ice and looked at the blank television screen. I wondered how she'd known my feelings toward Janice. "Would you mind answering a question for me?"

I said, "Sure."

"Are you still in love with Janice?"

"I don't think so. I tried to be, once. It didn't work."

"Oh," she said. "Did you and she ever . . . ?"

"Once. That didn't work either." Then, for a minute or two, our conversation stalled.

I'd never seen Ginny really cry in the three years since we'd met. But now, despite her struggling against them, tears were welling up in her eyes. "Sorry," she said. I handed her a few sheets of Kleenex from the complimentary box on the night table and sat on the bed next to her. I put my arm around her and told her I'd give anything to love her the way she deserved to be loved. "I know," she said. "I know that. And I know you feel sorry that you *can't*. But you shouldn't feel sorry. It's just one of those things."

"Would you like to stay here tonight? In my room? There are two beds."

"Actually, I was hoping we might share the *same* bed. I could stand some affection, even if it's just l-u-v."

After the wedding reception on Saturday, Ginny and I stood in front of the Thompsons' house with everybody else and fired rice at Trayn and Janice. I opened the door to Trayn's new BMW so they could make their getaway. Trayn shook my hand and Janice kissed me full on the mouth. "I *love* you, Teddy," she said, patting my cheek with her white-gloved hand. "Thanks for everything."

"My pleasure," I said. Trayn peeled away from the curb and steered the car around a curve. I could hear his horn honking half a mile away.

Twenty-four

The Bermuda grass has surrendered its color to the raw November cold; in its dormant state, the golf course turf is the color of harvest wheat. We've been intending to plug and top-dress the greens for several weeks, but the unmitigated rains have kept us inside. Chapman has already been transferred to the library, whose paltry shelves have grown thinner after weeks of his arbitrary censorship—"the purgation of filth," he calls it. Without sunshine, Drago and I are also doomed to reassignment, possibly in the laundry or the kitchen. Until the weather breaks there's nothing for me to do on the golf course, except straddle a bench in the dimly illuminated equipment shed while he rebuilds a Briggs and Stratton motor or repacks the wheel bearings on the Jake tractor. We'd make a perfect subject for one of those Vermeer paintings: "Mechanic and Idler in Frail Light." Once, when he couldn't find a pair of misplaced pliers, Drago used his teeth to remove a cotter pin from a lawn-mower axle; these are desperate times whose desperate hours we fill with aimless talk and numb speculations. (Do dogs fear death? Is sex worth the price of admission?) Drago tells me jokes. Where they come from is anybody's guess, but his supply is endless. "Okay, boss . . . there's a bear and a rabbit taking a shit together in the woods, right?"

"Right," I say. "Bear and rabbit . . . shitting . . ."

"Well," he continues, "the bear says to the rabbit, 'Tell me, does shit stick to your fur?' and the rabbit says, 'Why, yes, as a matter of fact it *does*,' so the bear says, 'Great!' and wipes himself with the rabbit." Drago laughs so hard at his own joke that he knocks over a can of 10-W-30 oil, which he feverishly mops up with a grimy beach towel.

When I'm inevitably summoned to the warden's office I'm so sure he's reassigned me to the kitchen that I can almost feel greasy suds rising above my elbows. It's Sunday morning, and the warden's face casts a mellow glow. Maybe he's observed the Sabbath by copulating with Gladden's sister. "Kendall, have a seat," he says. I sit down across the desk from him. "Well, how're you getting along out there on the golf course? A little too wet to get much done, huh?"

"We're hoping for a break in the weather."

"Are you worried about being shifted to a new job?"

"Worried? No. I've been expecting it to happen any day."

"Well, you can stay put. Drago, too. That's your baby out there, and anyway, we've got more men than there are jobs this time of year. You may as well waste time out there as anywhere."

"Thanks very much," I say, and for once I mean it. I get up to leave and the warden stops me. "Hold on," he says. "I've got something I want to talk to you about."

"What's that?" I ask.

"You know, most of the men at Moss Point are local, more or less, and we send them home for a few days at Christmas. Since you're from Indiana . . ."

"No, Ohio," I say.

"Okay, *Ohio*. So going home is out of the question for you. But if your parents want to come down here for a few days, I don't see why I couldn't release you to their custody, so long as you stay within a two-hundred-mile radius of Moss Point."

"All I've got is my dad. Is that okay?"

"Unless he's got a prison record, that'll be fine."

"You mean I get some time on the outside?"

"Three or four days. That's it, Kendall."

"Thanks, Warden," I say, trying to contain my exuberance until I'm out the door. From there I race full tilt to the soggy golf course and do a lap around its perimeter, vaulting the swollen creek where it meets the fence. I've tried incredibly hard for months *not* to think of the outside; I've employed every diversion imaginable . . . but now the prospect of freedom, even for a few days with Stan, makes me want to do something crazy, grip the fence, maybe, and yelp like a happy beagle.

At first I decide to phone Stan with the news, but I know that in his excitement he'll hear the details bass-ackward, and I'll have to follow up with a letter anyway, so I skip the phone call and write the letter, which at least he can reread three or four times, then stash in his wallet.

At eight in the evening, a few days later, Harvey Cooke leans in my doorway to tell me that Stan is on the pay phone. I haul down the corridor and pick up the receiver.

"Hello, Teddy. Got your note," he says, so loudly I have to hold the phone away from my ear.

"Can you make it down?" Ridiculous as it is, for a split second I worry that he won't be able to make it.

"Of course I'm going to make it. Did you think I wouldn't?"

I spend the last five minutes of our chat repeating the details I've already mentioned in the letter. I tell him I love him, then say goodbye.

Since that conversation with Stan a few weeks ago I've been unfit for any task requiring either common sense or concentration. The weather has finally broken to the point where Drago and I can get out on the course, but instead of attending to the job of spiking the greens, I find myself standing near the fence and gazing into the depths of the swamp, where on occasion I'll see a blue heron weaving through the dangling Spanish moss. Other times I watch the cars go by on their way to somewhere . . . the hardware store, the post office, the shipyard in Pascagoula. My favorite is the daily school bus. If the weather isn't too cold, the kids slide their windows down and hoot at me, the lonely convict. I'd do the same thing if I were a kid, so I wave as pleasantly as I know how.

On the morning of December 23, one full day before Stan will take me away, I receive two Christmas cards, which bring my holiday total to three, counting the one from Lucille. There's no doubt about who this pair of cards is from. I hold the envelopes side by side, eyeing the spartan script of Ginny and the baroque flourishes of Janice. I carry my mail back to the room, where I debate which I should open first. I decide to go with Janice. Her card is a simple one, a Christmas tree with wrapped packages beneath. I open the card, expecting to see a letter folded inside. Instead, there's a simple message. "Stay warm. Much love, Janice." She must have considered that phrase, "stay warm" very carefully, because for the briefest moment I feel a surge of longing so sudden and so strong that I have a hard time swallowing. The only way I can quell what I'm feeling is to open the envelope from Ginny. She's also capable of breaking my heart, but at least it will be a different sort of wound. Her card this year has a religious theme, which makes me think it's a leftover from her mother's stockpile, but I'm not really disappointed. Inside the front leaf of the card is a short note: "Ned got the job at Kentucky. Getting married in May. Can you come? I'd be very happy if you could. You'll like Ned. He's funny, just like you." Instead of feeling jealous, as I did upon receiving her last letter, I'm actually glad for her. I don't know what's changed to make me feel the way I do now. What I do know is that she deserves to find a solid, affectionate companion, even a pituitary giant like this Ned, whom she obviously loves. On the other hand, I'm not sure that Janice will ever have similar luck; it's almost as if she's programmed to make decisions that will wreak havoc with her life, and I feel sorry for her.

At 7 A.M. on Christmas Eve I'm packed and ready to go. Last night, Stan phoned from his motel and said he'd be here no later than eight. To kill time, I try drinking a cup of prison brew in the mess hall, but knowing that within an hour I'll be able to buy a cup at McDonald's makes that impossible. Drago's mom, a portly woman in a babushka, has already escorted her son through the front gate. Chapman will have to cool his heels until this afternoon, when an aunt from Slidell is scheduled to pick him up. ("She's ardent in her faith, Kendall . . . but *sooo* musty!") Apparently, his brother, from whom he embezzled funds, hasn't yet forgiven him.

I see Ames standing beneath the red EXIT sign, waving for me to come on. "Your dad's here," he tells me. "Go get your stuff." I take the stairs two at a time, trot down the corridor, grab my suitcase and reverse the process.

"Merry Christmas, Ames," I say, and hustle into the visiting room, where Stan is waiting.

When he sees me he stands up and takes a few halting steps in my direction, as if he isn't quite sure it's me. I drop my luggage and give him a bear hug. I haven't kissed Stan since I was four, but now, anybody who sees us would swear we're a couple of reunited Russians. "Son, you look terrible," he says.

"You look great," I tell him. "How are you?"

"Can't complain," he says. But when he picks up my suitcase and walks with me toward the door, I notice he's limping.

"What's wrong with your leg?" I ask.

"Touch of phlebitis. Nothing to worry about." He surrenders the suitcase when I insist on carrying it to the car, parked in the lot outside the front gate.

Stan fishes in his pocket for the keys to the station wagon. "Here, you might like to drive," he says.

"Where are we going?" I ask.

"Wherever you want."

With the window rolled down, I turn left onto Highway 447 and head for Pensacola, exactly 196 miles away, and the source for the innards of my Moss Point sand traps. "Well . . . how does it feel to be out?"

"I wish I could tell you," I say. The swamp gives way to scrubby pig farms and trailer parks and roadside cafes, which look beautiful to me. The fact that I'm behind the wheel, hurtling eastward at sixty miles per hour, makes me feel so euphoric that I can barely keep the car in the right-hand lane. "Stan, I'm not sure I can go back there."

"Is it a terrible place?"

"No. Not so terrible, really. But it's not like this either." I honk and wave at an onrushing semi. "It sure is good to see you."

After we've hooked up with I-10 at Gulfport and we're rolling down the open road, Stan, who's been ruminating for a good while, finally asks me about what happened with Trayn.

"If I tell you now, can we leave that subject alone for the rest of our time together?"

"You don't necessarily have to tell me anything, son. I just thought you might *want* to." He's on the verge of getting his feelings hurt, so I try my best to be honest with him, although I can't bring myself to explain about Janice. Instead, I make myself into something like an unlucky hero.

"I *thought* that was the case," he says. "Not that you should have done what you did. A man should always keep his wits about him."

"Are you embarrassed that your son is doing time?"

"I don't give a damn what the world thinks. Never have. You're my son and I'm proud of you."

Just inside the city limits of Mobile I spot a K mart, in front of which I park Stan's car. "Can you find something to do for a few minutes?" I ask.

"Why? What are you going to do?"

I tell him, "Never mind," and leave him sitting in the front seat.

When I return I have a plastic Christmas tree, a box of ornaments, a string of miniature lights and an important addition to the present I intend to give Stan. "Why did you buy all that crap?" he wants to know.

"For the motel. Deck the halls and all that . . ."

"Oh," he says. "Good idea."

We book ourselves a room in the Holiday Inn at Navarre Beach on the eastern tip of Santa Rosa Island. I adorn our ersatz tannenbaum with the cheap decorations and put the presents (his to me and mine to him) on the floor beneath it. Ever since Mom died, Stan has never quite gotten into celebrating Christmas with the same enthusiasm as before, so it's curious that I'm such a hopeless sucker for all the festoonery and hoopla. I'm extremely pleased with the way the little tree looks, winking away next to the bureau. "You know, your mom always liked a nice Douglas fir," he says wistfully.

"I'm into plastic," I say.

"No, you're not," he says.

That afternoon we sit fully clothed in rented folding chairs on the beach, only a few yards from where green waves roll onto the shore. With our identical black hornrim sunglasses, purchased at a Texaco station down the road, we must look like Mafia refugees, but I really don't mind. Being able to see an endless vista is a far cry from the daily confrontation with the omnipresent swamp. "How're you doing, Teddy?" Stan asks every so often.

"Nirvana," I say.

That night Stan and I watch a football game on TV. "It's a crime they make those boys play on Christmas Eve," he says.

I'm well into my third Budweiser, which tastes magnificent after almost eight months of drought. "This is the first game I've seen since last fall," I tell him.

"Well . . . in that case, the hell with 'em," he says, laughing.

On Christmas morning my eyes feel as if they're approximately one fourth of an inch apart and my frontal lobes are made of concrete. A piddling five beers have given me a classic hangover. I know Stan will give me one of his you-reap-what-you-sow speeches if I tell him, so I down a couple of aspirins and smile over my coffee and doughnuts. "What do you say we open presents," I suggest.

"You open first," he says. The first gift is a beautiful golf calendar with color photographs of the world's most famous fairways and greens. Next, I unwrap an imported Irish woolen cap a little bit like the one that became Hogan's trademark. The present he insists I open last turns out to be a large, framed photograph of my mom when she was in her twenties. She looks a little bit mischievous in the picture, kind of like Ginny, and very pretty. Stan's eyes glass over when he sees how pleased I am. Fearing that I might get choked up myself, I suggest he open the one present I have for him.

Ironically, it's also a photograph, which I've put in the frame I bought at K mart. Drago caught me standing on the apron in front of number one at Moss Point when he took the picture. I'm leaning on a shovel in sort of a cavalier way. The Bermuda grass was at its greenest then. I can remember that I wasn't having a particularly good day when he took the picture, so it's difficult to account for the happy look on my face. The late afternoon sunlight illuminates the swamp cypress in the background. Down in the lower right-hand corner of the picture you can make out the beginning of our excavation project. "This is wonderful, Teddy," he says. I know I've got to do something fast. For eight months, he's probably held back seventy-five gallons of tears, and he's no stronger than the clay dam at Moss Point. I tell him I'm going for a walk down the beach and that I'll be right back.

After sightseeing in Pensacola on Christmas Day, we go to dinner at a Creole restaurant called Roulon's, where Stan and I try crawfish for the first time in our lives. "Give me shrimp any day," Stan says.

Then we drive around the town at night, looking at the Christmas decorations. Unfortunately, I can't get my mind off the fact that I have to return to Moss Point in the morning, and I'm afraid Stan is in the same state of mind.

We check out of our motel at nine in the morning. Again, Stan lets me take the wheel. For a long time neither one of us speaks, nor do we have to. Only a couple of days ago we watched the horizon expand before us, but now, as we travel west, it gradually dwindles into backwater and poverty, the mysterious realm of Grayson. He's inside one of those trailers with the gangly TV antennas. God only knows what he's doing, but he's there. "I wish you didn't have to go back," Stan says.

"Believe me," I tell him, "I'm wishing the same thing."

Twenty-five

Stan seemed genuinely glad to have me around for a few months before I took on the rigors of the professional golf tour. In the morning I'd hear him downstairs, whistling, or softly coaxing Sally to eat the Alpo she had left in her bowl overnight. Through the years, a predawn cup of Sanka had become almost a ritual for him, but he abandoned his habit so he could join me for some Chock Full o' Nuts at eight when I got out of bed. It was fun to watch the caffeine work on him. He accompanied his coffee drinking with an initially calm perusal of the morning paper. However, after one cup he started reading the stories aloud, never getting beyond the first paragraph of any column. When he finished his second cup, he'd fold the newspaper into a tube and chase flies around the kitchen until he was satisfied that he had smacked them all dead.

For the second straight year, I'd failed to break into the top twenty at the NCAA golf championship, although by finishing twenty-eighth I once again made Honorable Mention. That was good enough for Stan, however. He took my certificate to Brophy's Art Shop and paid Mr. Brophy to frame it. The document now hung on the coveted wall space above the TV. Trayn had finished third in the tournament, and had actually held the individual lead until midway through the final round. As a result of our play, we were both eligible to compete in the PGA tournament school held in November at Seminole in Palm Beach. Trayn's dad agreed to back him for one year on the tour, which, as an investment banker, he knew was a pretty safe gamble. And of course I had Mom's inheritance money to keep me afloat for a while.

I decided to stay in Bowling Green for the summer months, primarily to work with Jimmy on refining my short game. Because there were so few traps on the Scottish courses Jimmy had played during his career, he had to admit that they'd never been the strongest part of his game. But that didn't prevent him from barking at me from his folding chair. "Use the flange. Let the club bounce." He'd scramble out of his chair and spread a dollar bill lengthwise next to my ball. "Your cut should be no longer than that dollar bill. Now go ahead and get it right." I'd open my stance, burrow my shoes into the sand, open the clubface slightly and with an easy swing pitch my ball beautifully from the trap.

At around five o'clock I would sit on the front porch, remove my shoes and dump sand into the garden. About that time, Stan would pull into the driveway. "Well, how did it go?" he'd ask. "Any progress?"

"Getting there," I'd tell him. Then we'd throw a tennis ball across the yard and Sally would play fetch. She refused to drop the ball, even to take a crap. "Will you look at that dog?" Stan would say proudly.

Early in August I was standing ankle deep in the shady expanse of rough between number three and number six fairways, only a couple of hundred yards from the clubhouse. The ground was low there, so the grass stayed thick and lush most of the year. Practicing wedge shots from deep rough was one of my favorite things to do. I never fully understood why, but probably it had to do with the fresh dirt and cut-grass smell of the wounds I made with my wedge. There was also something exhilarating about lifting a ball from where it was nested like a quail, and propelling it toward a bank of clouds huddled on the horizon. Anyway, I was working on *flop* shots that afternoon, a softer and more subtle kind of wedge play that can save strokes around the green. I'd just spilled a bag of golf balls onto the grass when I heard a siren howling in the distance. The sound grew louder as the ambulance raced up Fairway Avenue and, to my surprise, tore into the country club parking lot. Attendants dashed into the pro shop with their collapsible cot. *God, it's Jimmy!* I said. I dropped the wedge and ran down number three fairway, through the hissing sprinklers, toward the clubhouse. I arrived soaking wet at the patio in time to see them wheeling him out the double doors. His eyes were wide open, and the hand that poked from underneath the sheet was clenched into a fist. I trotted alongside the attendants, who were hurrying toward the opened tailgate of the ambulance. "What's wrong with him?" I shouted. "What happened?"

One of the attendants collapsed the legs of the portable gurney and together they lifted him into the bay and locked the wheels into position. Only then did the taller of the two men tell me what I already suspected. "Think it was a stroke, but we won't know for a while." Soon they were racing north on Fairway toward the hospital a mile away.

Without bothering to retrieve my club from the rough, I trotted across the street to the house. I changed into some sneakers, called Stan to let him know what had happened and drove to the hospital. Jimmy's wife Katherine, was already in the waiting room when I arrived. She managed a smile when she saw me. "Oh, Teddy, thank you for coming," she said. I sat next to her and held her hand. Within a few minutes, Stan arrived, out of breath and sweaty from chuffing down the hallway. He gave Katherine a kiss on the cheek and sat on the chair beside her.

"How is he, Katherine?" Stan asked.

"He's talking. That's what I've been told. Straightaway they're thinking it's a fairly minor episode. I think he'll be okay."

"Good. That's good," he said, and patted her shoulder. I don't know why I was so surprised at Stan's tenderness with her, but I was quite proud of him at that moment.

I continued to practice through the weeks of Jimmy's hospitalization. When he was finally released to go home, his speech had improved to the point where if I placed my ear up close to his face I could understand exactly what he was saying. Mostly, he wanted to know if I'd finally mastered the sand trap. And of course, I told him I had, which wasn't exactly true.

The country club management was forced to hire a part-time replacement for Jimmy, but I think they knew he would never be fit enough to return to work. Katherine was very patient with him, though. She guided him into their old Chevrolet every afternoon and drove him to the country club so he could sit on the patio bench in the sunshine.

While I stayed out of competition over the summer (actually, I was tired of that aspect of the game), Trayn played in several amateur tournaments, including the National Jaycee, held in Tulsa, an event he won by three strokes. He telephoned me on a Saturday night, mostly to scold me for not entering the tournament myself, but also to crow about his victory. I didn't really begrudge him his half hour of self-congratulation. Who *wouldn't* be excited to win a major amateur title? It seemed a little bit odd, though, that throughout this phone call, our first communication since the wedding, he never once mentioned Janice. It was as if his golfing exploits had crowded her completely out of the picture. I finally asked him if she was doing okay. "Janice? Oh, she's doing fine. If I get my PGA card, she's going to go on tour with me."

"Won't that be kind of expensive?" I asked.

"Teddy, I intend to make lots of money. By the way, Janice suggested I ask you if you'd like to make it a threesome. You know, stay in the same motels, eat together when we feel like it

. . . This is all assuming you get your card, too, which I know you will. Right, buddy?"

His almost aggressive friendliness seemed patronizing this time. Naturally, my decision was made as soon as Janice was thrown into the equation. I was helpless. "Well, Trayn," I said, "you never can tell. I might just win the whole damned qualifying tournament."

He said exactly nothing in reply to that statement. I held the receiver to my ear long enough for him to recount a few more of his exploits at Tulsa, and then I told him goodbye.

Ironically, it was November 4, the tenth anniversary of my mother's death, that I shook hands with Stan and aimed my car toward Florida, where the PGA held its tour qualifying tournament. "Bring home the bacon," Stan shouted. I hated leaving him alone. I hoped that Lucille would spend her Saturday with him. Maybe they could go for a drive along the Maumee River or to a matinee. Even if she did, I knew Stan would suffer through a difficult night.

Twenty-six

"Can I have your hat, Chapman?" Drago asks. (Of course, he's already got the thing on.)

"That horrid chapeau? Indeed you may," Chapman says. "Consider it a token of my esteem."

"What about your plants? Can I have them too?"

Chapman clucks once or twice, places his fingertips on either side of an imaginary migraine. "Those too, if you promise not to maim them."

"*Told* you, boss. He *looks* like a big old fag turkey, but underneath he's got a heart of pure platinum."

Chapman shoos Drago off the bed. "If you *please*," he says. The strain of lifting a heavy box from the floor and onto the mattress provokes a barely perceptible fart.

"I heard that one," Drago says. "We call that a *flirp* where I come from. A little more pitch and you'd have a *twilly*."

"Give me patience, Lord," Chapman whispers.

"About those fish . . . ," Drago says. He's tilted the desk

chair onto one leg and he's spinning it at a rate of about 100 rpms.

"I rather thought Kendall might look after them. Frankly, Drago, it frightens me to think what would become of them in your charge. Perhaps you'd sprinkle psychedelics in the tank, or introduce some predatory leech from the swamp."

"Well, maybe I *wouldn't*. Ever think of that?"

"No," says Chapman, whose lips are turning white. "I'd *like* to keep them, but my Aunt Zola won't allow 'creatures' in her house." I flash a harsh glance at Drago to head off a wisecrack. "Well . . . Kendall, will you take charge of the fish tank?"

"Sure, Chapman," I say, "I'll be glad to look after them. If she softens up in the next few months, you can come back for them."

"I will *never* again set foot inside this hoosegow, not even for evangelical purposes. I've been sufficiently chastened. My penance is complete."

"Jesus walked among the lepers," I remind him.

"Only on a part-time basis." He carefully wraps his beloved statue of the Virgin in toilet paper, three rolls of which he's appropriated from the lavatory, then nestles her alongside his other religious gewgaws in a cardboard box.

"Can I have your pencil sharpener?" Drago asks.

"Are you opening a shop, Drago?"

"Naw, I couldn't sell any of this junk."

"Take it. Take my blotter. Take my bud vase. Here. Here's a nickel. Take that, too."

Drago stops spinning the chair long enough to grab the coin. "Thanks," he says, pockets it and extends his hand for Chapman to shake, which to my surprise he does, albeit grudgingly.

An hour or so after the Yugoslavian has departed with his mementos, Chapman is sitting at the desk, reading his Bible by lamplight. "What're you reading?" I ask.

"Exodus," he says.

"Good choice," I tell him.

"It *is*, isn't it?"

The next morning, a Saturday, Chapman has one last breakfast with the apostles. What a strange bunch they are. Most of them are middle-class family men, futures devastated by their having been caught paw-in-pantry. No wonder they hop aboard the hayride to salvation. But Chapman is in a different category altogether. His humiliation is more private than theirs, and his conversion seems less convenient. His faith is still muddled with ingrained suspicions and biases, but he's come a long way. Now he at least tolerates Drago, a heathen if ever there was one. I consider this a major achievement. But I think it was Grayson, "God's outcast," a *"kneegrow,"* a "member of Ham's race," who seems to have had the deepest effect on Chapman, not that he's going to get hooked on Soul Train or Reverend Ike. If there was a revelation, I think it was when Grayson handed him the shovel that day at the dam-breaking ceremony. I don't think anyone else noticed that but me. And, of course, Chapman.

Immediately to his right at this morning's mess table is a new black member of the born-again squadron, on whose khaki shoulder my roommate has rested his beefy hand in a seemingly friendly way. This is how I'll try to remember him.

When breakfast is finished, he shakes hands all around, then hulks out of the mess hall. I catch up with him in the middle of the breezeway, which, because of an architectural quirk, is like a wind tunnel. "Chapman, wait up," I say. "When are you leaving?"

"Well, Aunt Zola is very prompt. She said ten o'clock, and I believe she'll be on time."

"Take a walk with me . . . come on."

"Let me get a jacket. Then I'll be glad to," he says.

A few minutes later he meets me next to the statue, and from there we tramp through an archway and onto an asphalt path that leads to the recreation area. Although it's mid-February, the air smells fresh, as if it has swooped up fragrance from the tropics of South America.

"Chapman, I want you to know how much I admire you for working so hard on the golf course." I realize this is the beginning of a farewell eerily similar to the one I gave Grayson, and will no doubt give Drago when I leave in a few months.

"I didn't have much choice, really," he says. "We're all slaves here."

"I wouldn't say so," I tell him. "Anyway, I know that Grayson was grateful for what you did, even though he didn't say anything to you."

"Oh, but he *did*. In fact, he gave me this curiosity." From his pocket, Chapman produces a slate-colored arrowhead. "Claims he found it digging that ditch."

"That's a nice little artifact."

"Yes, Grayson and I became quite good friends. I intend to keep his gift as a sort of talisman, carved though it was by pagans."

Except for this arrowhead gift, which might have been nothing more than an afterthought on Grayson's part, I have no evidence that Grayson and he were ever really *friendly*. However, I'm glad that Chapman can leave Moss Point with this conviction. "You're a good man," I say, patting him on the back. "And a good roommate."

"Your tolerance has been greatly appreciated."

"No problem," I tell him. "Anyway, good luck."

"Will you be certain not to overfeed the fish? The gouramis are extremely vulnerable to tail rot, and I believe there's a correlation . . ."

"Count on me." What a relief it is to know that Chapman's not going to cry, or even come close, for that matter.

"Well . . . take care of yourself, Chapman," I say, and shake his hand.

"I certainly will. You do the same," he replies. From my vantage point beneath the basketball net, I watch him plod toward 2-C for the last few pieces of luggage. When he's inside the building, I wander out to the pond, whose water is so clear I can see big surly catfish, the size of rolling pins, cruising the shallows. Then the wind ruffles the surface and I lose sight of them.

Twenty-seven

The PGA likes its euphemisms. Three times each year it conducts a "school" that isn't a school at all. It's a grueling free-for-all among one hundred golfers who want THE CARD, their ticket to riches and glory. Wherever there are rabbits you hear the word.

In February, Trayn and I were in Palm Beach, sharing a seventy-dollar room for a week at the Ramada Inn. On the night before the qualifying tournament we were sitting next to a potted palm in the downstairs dining room, listening to a man dressed in fairway-green Haggar slacks and white shirt drone on about the rules of the game. He was a corpulent old badger with bird legs that seemed insufficient to support his bulk. He looked like an enormous golf ball teed up and ready to be driven down a gigantic fairway. "It's important," he said, "to know what rule applies for any circumstance. Remember, gentlemen, there won't always be a PGA official handy to provide a ruling."

Trayn rolled his eyes. In fact, a rule exists for every imaginable circumstance: ball swallowed by dog; ball buried in llama poop; ball nestled inside the undies of a Hungarian folk dancer . . . there's always a rule. Next, Mr. Golf gave us a few pointers on golf etiquette. Nix on yelling "Goddamnit!" when your ball rims out of the cup. Instead, gaze photogenically skyward, remove your visor for effect, shake your head and say "Oh, my goodness!" If your caddy misreads a crucial putt, tell him he's "in error," but certainly not that he's "full of shit." If a spectator farts during your backswing, calmly recheck the wind direction. *Don't* lobotomize him with your pitching wedge. A few of the fellows seated across the room were actually taking notes, as if this stuff was brand-new to them. Only when our host began his spiel on earning THE CARD did the rest of us stop twiddling silverware and listen. We wanted to hear about the 72-hole tour qualifier held over the weekend; that was all we cared about. That was why we were there: never mind rules and etiquette. I gazed across the dining room. All those rabbits looked nervous as hell, just the way rabbits are supposed to look.

After the serious talk was over, a comedian took over the mike for a half hour's worth of golf jokes. Trayn made bird noises during the silent lapses between jokes. I played pick up sticks with a handful of tees. Everybody clapped when the comedian trudged away from the podium. I wondered if the poor guy trotted out this dumb routine for every member-guest banquet at every country club from Cocoa Beach to Cucamonga. An elder from the PGA executive committee had the last word. He said, "Men, you represent the best the game has to offer. Be a model for every golfer in the country, especially the younger folks." He coughed once or twice, then said, "Good luck in the qualifier."

On the way out, Trayn grabbed a handful of salted peanuts from a small bowl centered on the table. "The whole *thing* was a joke," he said, tossing a goober into the air and catching it on his tongue.

We spent the rest of the night watching TV in our room. I could gauge Trayn's nervousness by the number of half-smoked

cigarettes in the bedside ashtray. At the pre-tournament banquet, I'd stabbed once or twice at my roast beef, but my stomach
was so knotted I couldn't eat. I made the mistake of drinking a
couple of beers, thinking that would settle me down. Instead, I
felt gaseous and out of whack. "I'm going with a three wood off
the tee, tomorrow," Trayn said. "I want to keep the ball in
bounds." My opinion was that he should rely on his power to
make things happen, but I wasn't going to tell him how to play.
I mentally rehearsed my own golf swing, that wide invisible arc
of the takeaway, the forward thrust of the weight on the down-
stroke, the high follow-through. We kept the TV on until
eleven-thirty, then turned out the lights and tried to sleep. I was
watching a trace of red light leak between a crack in the blinds
when Trayn said, "Hey, Teddy. Know what Bobby Morris told
me today?"

"Who's Bobby Morris?" I asked.

"Just some guy I met at the putting green this morning. Anyway, he said he beats off every night before a tournament. Says
it calms him down so he doesn't get the yips. Can you believe
that?"

"Great concept," I said, and squashed my head between two
pillows.

Trayn was smoking Camel filters in the dark. I could hear the
cigarette paper burning in the quiet of the room. Then he
walked across the carpet. The room brightened for a moment
when he opened the door to walk down the hallway; he was
going to give Janice a call so she could tell him how wonderful
he was.

Despite his nervousness, Trayn obviously had everything necessary to survive on the tour. And if he lacked anything, Janice
provided it for him. I wasn't quite sure what to think of his
suggestion that we travel together: him and her and the odd
man out. I figured that after she gave Trayn everything *he*
needed to make it, there would be something left over for me.
But that was a lot of baloney. I'd have to rely on my own skills
and instincts to survive, and Trayn would, too. Still, for some

selfish reason, I wanted her nearby. It made no sense; it only puffed air into some dormant hopes that would be much better off forgotten.

The shaft of light I'd focused on began to twirl before my eyes. A wave of nausea swept over me so quickly I could barely make it to the bathroom in time. I ran water in the sink, turned on the fan and looked at myself in the mirror. "Kendall, you dumb-ass," I said.

On Saturday morning, Trayn and I showed up at the Seminole Golf Course, ready to boogaloo down the meandering highway to fame and fortune. We were here to compete in the PGA qualifying tournament. A lucky few of us rookies would earn the chance to ramble from one tour site to the next, hoping to play well enough on *Monday* to earn a spot on *Thursday*. That's only the beginning of the battle, however. The golfer must play well enough on Thursday and Friday to make the halfway cut, so he can finish the tournament and earn a check. The only way to get around this misery is to earn the $10,000 minimum for an exemption from qualifying. *Losing* the card means returning to school, the *rabbit track*.

Seminole is a murderous golf course where huge cypress trees stab at the sky and date palms line the fairways. Between the fairways are canals and sand and peculiarly shaped ponds, so that each hole seems isolated from the next. The course looks forgiving, but the trouble is subtle and ever-present.

Trayn had an early tee-off time. We drove to the course at six-thirty in the morning, hired a pair of high school kids to carry our sticks, grabbed some free doughnuts on the clubhouse patio, then headed for the putting green, which had just been whipped dry with long bamboo poles. Trayn and I were making nickel bets on who could roll a thirty-footer closer to the hole. I was a much better putter than Trayn, but he could knock the flag down with his approach shots. With my blazing putter, I'd won fifty cents from him already. "Looks like you've got the stroke this morning, Teddy," Trayn said, flipping a pair of quarters into my outstretched palm. We motioned our caddies to follow us to the driving range, where we each hit a couple of hundred shots. A good golfer usually knows by this time whether he's going to fly or crawl through his round, and every shot I made felt right. If I could just stay inside my game, as Jimmy used to say, I'd play well. Trayn's shots weren't quite as crisp as he would have liked, but he had a knack for patching together some low numbers even on his worst days. I wasn't worried about Trayn.

At seven fifty-five I watched him tee off with two young golfers who, like us, were fresh out of college. Instead of uncoiling a frozen rope off the tee, Trayn looped a nervous three wood that ricocheted against a giant palm tree and took a lucky hop onto the center of the fairway. Trayn closed his eyes and blew out some air. I knew precisely what was going through his mind. I said, "That's safe, Trayn." He patted his chest, as if he were warding off a heart attack.

I watched him tack back and forth across the first several fairways. He was recognizable by his lucky demon-red slacks, the ones Janice had bought him at the OSU golf course.

Now I was glad Janice had chosen to stay in Cincinnati with her folks, rather than fly down to be with Trayn. Neither one of us needed that sort of distraction. Anyway, I still wasn't sure how to act when she was around. I was a good loser, though. There was no taking that away from me. She'd chosen him, and there was nothing I could do about it. Nothing at all.

Both my playing partners smoked cigarettes and spoke in two-word sentences. "You're up." "Nice hit." "Get legs." The taller member of this duet, a prematurely bald Texan built like an oil derrick, hit his tee shot at number one into a drainage ditch paralleling the fairway. "Well, I guess I know what I'll be doing for the next six months," he said. I imagined him selling Chevrolets in Amarillo.

I easily parred the first four holes. In fact, I'd drilled a four-iron approach shot onto the apron of the green of the third hole, a good par five. But I sailed my lag putt eight feet past the cup and rimmed out on my comebacker. I said, "Goddamnit!"

(There was no PGA officials in sight.) Still, I'd managed a decent par, which kept me even.

On the seventh hole, at which point I was one under par, I clobbered my drive into a row of immature date palms. My ball came to rest only a few feet from the base of a tree, so I was forced to assume a tight crouch in order to get some steel on the ball. I forced the clubhead cleanly into the shot, but in following through wrapped my shaft around the trunk of the palm tree. My Titleist skittered toward the green and stopped on the steep apron on the left. I was less interested in the outcome of my shot than I was in the ruined golf club I held like a dead snake. This was the first time I'd broken one of the irons Stan had given me eight years before. My caddy said, "Helluva shot." I pushed the rubber grip into the bag, so the clubhead hung out of the bag like a maimed cobra. For the rest of the day I'd have to play without my two iron.

I saw Trayn twice during the outward eighteen. Once he was hustling into the rest room next to fourteen green, and later I saw him through a row of crotons. He had just knocked in a ten-footer, although I couldn't tell if that was for a birdie or par. Trayn was usually pretty demonstrative when he made a birdie, so I guessed he'd saved par.

The two Texans and I had twenty minutes between rounds to wolf down hot dogs, broiled on a grill in front of the clubhouse by a black man in a chef's hat. Because I'd shot a nice 70, I was hungry enough to down a couple of franks and a diet cola. My playing partners, neither of whom were burning up the course, took a couple of bites from their hot dogs, then pitched them into the trash barrel. You could count the day's casualties by the uneaten wieners nestled in with the smeared napkins and Styrofoam cups.

With Janice back at her folks' house in Cincinnati, I was able to hone my concentration on my game for the first two rounds. She was nice to have around until the first bad shot. Then she'd get that panicky look on her face, and she'd start nibbling on her nails; she transmitted anxiety through mysterious airwaves.

She'd say, "Come on, Teddy," or "Hold it together, Teddy," and my game would more or less flutter away like some disinterested sparrow. She wanted me to belt my drives two-eighty like Trayn did. If she'd had her way, I'd growl at my ball before I knocked it off the tee, scrunch down over it like some hulking beast, flash long angry teeth at the gallery.

If I was going to make the cut at Seminole, I'd need to play my own genteel game. As it was, I almost fell off the track on the third hole, the one I'd hit in two that morning. But that afternoon my four iron had gone haywire and rolled beneath a scrub pine. It was a stupid mistake, and I deserved the trouble I'd bought. My ball was nudging the base of the little tree. As I was sizing up my options, I noticed the ground bubbling like a wet sponge around my shoes. I was ready to take a penalty for an unplayable lie when my caddy pointed out the faint line of chalk that encircled the soggy patch of grass: the area had been zoned "casual water," and I was entitled to a free drop no closer to the hole. No penalty. No hazard. I took a few paces back, and dropped my ball one club length outside the chalk boundary, leaving myself a perfect shot at the flag. Instead of taking a probable double bogey, I scrambled home with a par. "Merry Christmas," said the shorter Texan, whose round had flown out the window hours before.

On the last hole of the day, my five iron to the green was way too stiff, but it bounced miraculously against the flag and stopped dead, two feet from the hole. I tapped in for a birdie. My score for the incoming round was a cool 69, just good enough to put me at the top of the board. I'd played well, but there had been a big green net under me for thirty-six holes. I couldn't expect to be so lucky again. *Nobody* could. I was bound to have some bad holes along the way; the trick was not to let a minor tragedy destroy an entire tournament. I could probably even afford one less that brilliant round, provided it wasn't so thoroughly terrible that the other three rounds became irrelevant.

While I'd dodged bullets all day, Trayn had played consistently. I found him in the clubhouse bar, laughing with a couple of other players who had managed to score well. "Hey, Teddy boy, pull up a chair." Trayn took a ferocious drag on his cigarette. Smoke came out of his mouth when he asked how I'd done.

When I told him, "Three under," he shook my hand.

"You little son of a bitch. Where've you been hiding that stuff?"

I assumed a putting stance and swept an imaginary blade over the green plaid carpet. "I was a god with the wand. Not a single three-putt."

Trayn and I ate dinner at a Chinese restaurant a few blocks from the motel, then decided to get some early sleep. I waited in the lobby while Trayn called Janice to tell her he was one under par and "Teddy boy" was burning up the course. To call Stan at this stage of the tournament would be disastrous for both of us. If I told him I was tied for the lead at the halfway point, he'd be a candidate for an asylum if I didn't succeed.

Neither Trayn nor I slept well that night. I had heartburn that wouldn't surrender to any of Trayn's home remedies. As instructed, I drank a whole quart of soda and bitters, but it only made me feel voluminous and sloshy.

When I shook Trayn's hand at the first tee on Sunday morning, he told me to "hit 'em straight"; there was dark circles under his eyes. He watched me knock a good drive two-fifty, almost dead center, and he walked back to the clubhouse.

Since half the field had been eliminated after the first thirty-six holes, we were playing in twosomes for the last pair of rounds. My golfing partner for the final thirty-six was a blond kid named Lyle Belker from Yuma, Arizona. He wore a white Ben Hogan hat to keep the sun off his fair freckled skin. Lyle hit some of the longest drives of anybody I'd ever seen, including Trayn. His first drive soared well beyond mine, and bounded to within one hundred yards of the first green.

My partner was having the round of his life. His drives were deadly screamers. His putting was radar-controlled. Everything in between was right on the flag. I spent the day hacking my way out of the roughs, dodging skinny palm trees, floating high iron shots over enormous ponds. Coming into number thirty-six, I was four over par, and brittle as glass. I knew that I'd played just poorly enough to be sitting right on the fence between success and failure. I needed to birdie the last hole to be sure of my position on the board. But the finishing hole at Seminole is one of the most difficult anywhere. If someone pulled a dense green carpet over an average-sized junkyard, the result would resemble the putting surface of number eighteen green. Depending on pin placement, a ten-foot birdie putt can, in a matter of seconds, yield a nasty comeback putt for a par. By missing that comebacker, a golfer can be left with a treacherous side-hill two-footer for a bogey. And I needed a birdie.

On that last hole, Lyle punched a brilliant three iron into the brisk wind. His ball landed on the high side of the green and nearly spun back into the hole. Because he was three under for the tournament, he had used an iron off the tee, and for the first time all day, I'd outdriven him. Lyle was a club stronger than I was, so I decided on a two iron into the green. "There isn't any two iron," my caddy said. It dawned on me that I'd been playing all day without it; I'd been unable to get the club repaired. I doubted that the three iron was enough stick. I selected a five wood, knowing that if I got the thing up in the air, the wind would take it God only knows where. I leaned into the shot, meeting the ball squarely with the screwheads of my wood, and drove a low windcheater stiff to the pin. The shot stopped only ten feet shy of the cup, leaving me a reasonably simple uphill putt for a birdie. "Hell of a shot, Ted," Lyle yelled.

As I stood over my last putt of the day there were pinpoints of electricity pinging inside my brain. I was nervous, but I knew before I guided the blade into the ball that I owned the putt. It took a small turn at the end of its run and dove into the cup. I was sure that my one over par score would get me what I wanted. And Lyle was two shots ahead of me. After he canned his four-footer, we shook hands. He had an enormous toothy grin on his face, the grin of an Arizona jackrabbit.

I waited for Trayn on the last hole, searching the fairways for signs of his red slacks and canary-yellow shirt. It was three beers later that I finally saw him marching onto the last tee. There was no way of determining from his posture or deportment how his day had gone. I saw smoke curling up from his cigarette, which he tossed aside before hitting his last drive of the day. He had the honors; that was a good sign. I watched his shot climb high into the wind, which pushed it toward a banana-shaped pond halfway up the fairway. The ball bounded off the shoulder of a huge hummock and caromed into the pond. I saw Trayn bend over at the waist, his driver clutched between his knees. I held a warm swallow of beer in my mouth, wondering if he'd just thrown his round away.

If the school qualifier had been held in, say, Cleveland or Toledo, someplace where the wind is steady and all the trees lean toward the east, I'm sure Trayn wouldn't have been tripped up by a head wind. But in Palm Beach in late winter, the air was thin and feathery. The best courses along Lake Erie are flat and open. They *rely* on tricky winds and dried-out fairways to challenge the golfer. Seminole is tough enough on a calm day. When the wind comes and goes, as it did on the Sunday, it can be almost impossible.

Trayn dejectedly dropped his ball near the point of entry, then nailed a two-iron approach that bored through the wind and dug into the green about twenty feet to the left of the flag stick. He'd need to roll his putt into the hole to save a par. He walked around the green when he saw me. His eyes were glazed with panic. "I need this for two over. Whaddya think, Teddy boy? Will that get me in?"

I told him I thought so, although I wasn't totally sure about my own one over par score. Trayn waited while his partner hit a nice approach putt and tapped in, then took a solid stance over his own ball. I was convinced that he'd miraculously drilled the thing directly into the cup, when at the last second a subtle break took hold and swung it well below the hole. He looked over at me, incredulous. I shrugged, raised my eyebrows, tried to let him know I understood what he was feeling. He carelessly backhanded his two-footer into the cup, leaving the ball there for his caddy to retrieve it.

"I think I'm a dead duck," he said.

"Don't know, Trayn. The wind must have given everybody some trouble. It cost me a few shots."

"Well, we'll see, won't we?" He unsnapped his glove and stuffed it in his back pocket. "At least *you're* in. Congratulations, pal." He shook my hand. I wondered if he'd wait to tell Janice he'd come up empty.

We stood for an hour or so in front of the scoreboard, drinking nervous beers and recounting shots we'd played. Trayn told me he'd taken a nine on number seven, the hole where I'd seen him earlier, lamenting his lousy shot. It was beginning to look as if my 289 would hold up, but Trayn was on the ropes. There were eleven players with scores better than his. "I'm a dying man," he said, and uprooted a handful of Bermuda grass. I felt bad for him, and I really hadn't counted on traveling solo from one tour stop to the next. I'd always planned on having Trayn and Janice around to help kill the long, tedious stretches of time between hours spent at golf. That was the optimistic scenario. The more realistic version found me back in Ohio, with Trayn and his new wife raking in thousands on the tour.

We decided to head back to the motel, where we could get good and soused and not worry about violating some PGA code of decorum that forbids vomiting on a championship green.

Trayn raced his BMW along Shoreline Drive, dodging in and out of traffic until we came to the Ramada. He veered into the parking lot, peeled down a row of cars and screeched to a halt between a Beetle and a Jeep Cherokee. Instead of waiting in the lobby while I phoned Stan, he took the elevator up to the fourth floor.

I let Stan's phone ring a dozen times before I allowed myself to believe that he wasn't home. Maybe he was out at Lucille's orchard, helping her with winter pruning. Or perhaps he was in the yard, throwing the tennis ball for Sally. I was disappointed that he wasn't there to take my call.

In our room Trayn was already drinking scotch from a plastic cup. "Help yourself," he said, hoisting a bottle of Cutty Sark. I poured myself some and took a swallow. "Well, here's to the conquering hero, Ted Kendall," he said, and downed what was in his cup.

We wordlessly watched an Atlanta Hawks game for an hour or so, until Trayn staggered into the bathroom and slammed the door shut behind him. I heard a loud crash, the sound of glass breaking. "Are you okay in there?" I yelled. When there was no answer, I opened the door and saw Trayn standing in front of a shattered mirror, a bloody towel wrapped around his fist. "Come on Trayn," I said. "This is crazy. There's another school in six months."

"Yeah," he muttered. "Yeah, sure." Then he sat down on the toilet seat and stared at the tile floor.

He'd been brooding in the bathroom for fifteen or twenty minutes when the phone rang. The voice at the other end of the line sounded like an old man's, somebody with half of his larynx removed. I had no idea who it might be. "Are you either David Traynham or Ted Kendall?"

"I'm Kendall," I said. About then Trayn stumbled out of the bathroom. He was wearing Band-Aids on his knuckles.

"Well, I'm glad to tell you that you've both qualified for PGA cards. Will you please pass that information along to Mr. Traynham if he's there?"

"Sure will," I said, then looked at Mr. Good Sport. "I'll be damned . . . Trayn, we're *both* in. Phenomenal!"

"Man . . . ," he said, shaking his head. "I can't fucking believe that."

I grabbed his wounded mitt and shook it. "Congratulations," I said.

Twenty-eight

I've been unable to sleep very well for the past several nights. My parole hearing takes place today, exactly sixty days before my earliest possible release date. Although I'm technically a ward of Mississippi, the Louisiana parole board has jurisdiction over my fate; a timely court-ordered freeze on the Louisiana inmate population sent me to Moss Point.

"Don't worry about it, Kendall," Ames says to the windshield of his Ford Granada. "They're bound to let you go."

I notice that my knee is bouncing. "Would you mind turning on the radio?" I ask.

Ames says, "Sure thing," and snaps it on. "Find what you want."

I select a Top 40 station out of New Orleans, but anything will do. I want a cigarette, bubble gum, a rubber band, something . . . "You don't think Maples has it in for me, do you?"

"Maples *likes* you, Kendall. Thinks you're a little crazy, but he likes you."

"Does he say in the report that I'm a little crazy?"

"You need to stop worrying."

"I need to take a whiz," I tell him.

When we cross the Pearl River, which separates Mississippi from Louisiana, Ames pulls into a welcome station, where I dash into the rest room. I unzip my fly and stand at a urinal, but I'm too nervous even to pee.

Ames is still sitting behind the steering wheel when I return. "I'm going to run a lap around the grounds here. Okay?"

"This is no time to make an escape," he says, laughing.

I sprint through the dog-walk zone, where a dachshund like Sally is taking a crap, then loop around a trash can, bolt down the straightaway paralleling a rabbit fence, turn left and jog through some dry water oak leaves to the far corner, at which point I take the hypotenuse back to the car. "Feel better?" Ames asks.

I tell him I guess so.

A couple of hours later we're in Baton Rouge, homing in on the state capitol building, a dwarf skyscraper in front of which stands a statue of Huey Long, frozen in midsentence. Circling the immense capitol grounds are dozens of stone buildings, anonymous and oppressive. I imagine that one of them is our destination. But we pass by them without stopping and come to a more amiable environment, marked by placid clapboard houses, beautifully undisciplined live oaks and carefully sculpted magnolia trees. We pull into a reserved parking space in front of a group of old two-story buildings painted dark red and laid out in a pentagon shape around a central courtyard. There's a brass historical marker a dozen yards away which proclaims this to be the "Pentagon Barracks." I find it hard to envision any military sternness thriving in the midst of the lush vegetation and graceful white porticoes. Leaning against the white columns of the porch are several men in khaki pants and matching sports coats, traditional southern young bloods. They're engaged in jovial conversation with a well-dressed woman who can't be more than twenty. I can see steam rising from their Styrofoam coffee cups, and I get the impression that the three of them just stepped out from a party or reception to get some fresh air or share a private joke. "This is *it?*" I ask.

"That's right," says Ames. "Not what you expected, huh?"

A receptionist directs us down a hallway that squeaks underfoot. The walls are decorated with murals: slaves hacking sugarcane with their machetes, slaves driving mules out of corral, slaves dancing happily on a green lawn in front of a preposterously large mansion. We find the door over which hangs a white shingle with the hand-lettered words PAROLE BOARD. Inside is a cramped antechamber all but filled by an old pine desk. The secretary, young and quite pretty, smells like gardenias. "Is this Mr. Kendall?" she asks.

"This is him," Ames tells her.

She taps on a frosted-glass door and says in a loud voice, "He's here," nothing more specific than that. Then she takes her purse from a desk drawer and hurries out of the room. The clack of her shoes on the hallway's wooden planks causes the knot in my stomach to tighten. Maybe she's read my file and is fleeing in fear. More likely, she's just stepped out for a Coke.

Within a few minutes, the frosted-glass door opens, and a man about Stan's age tells me to come in. He's wearing a pink rose in the buttonhole of his seersucker jacket. He guides me to the head of a long table, around which are seated the parole board. He asks if I'd like a cup of coffee, and I tell him no, thanks. (I'm so nervous I might spill it.) Of the seven board members, three are women. One of them is a dead ringer for Janice's mom, right down to the ruby-red lipstick and the 100 mm cigarette. "Won't you sit down, Mr. Kendall?" says the man who is obviously the master of ceremonies. In sitting down, I bang my knee on the apron of the table. The woman immediately to my right notices, and smiles at me.

For several days, I've been flopping around on my prison mattress, imagining a much more ominous scene, one with glaring lights, glowering bureaucrats wearing gray suits and terrible-looking glasses. The walls of this room are adorned with a mishmash of paintings (mostly swamp scenes), black-and-white photographs, yellowed newspaper articles, stuffed deer heads.

Mr. Landrieu, the parole board chairman, introduces himself and the other six people seated at the table. The lady who looks like Janice's mom gets the ball rolling. "Tell us your reaction to Moss Point, Mr. Kendall," she says. The ash of her cigarette is more than an inch long, but she seems disinclined to flick it into the ashtray within easy reach.

"Much nicer than I imagined it would be. Terrible food. But otherwise pretty nice."

"Good," she says. I wait for the beginning of the real test, the moral evaluation, but it never comes. Instead, a barrage of small talk. Maybe they're just feeling me out, trying to figure whether I'm a psycho. These people are having a good time, laughing among themselves about some secret piece of information in my file.

Finally, Mr. Landrieu places his fingers on the edge of the table as if it were a piano keyboard. "Are you ready to go home?" he asks.

"More than ready, sir," I say.

"We have a letter from Mr. Traynham urging us to grant parole at the earliest possible date. And with corroboration from Warden Maples, we've decided to go along with that opinion." Everybody nods in unison. "How does April fourteenth sound, Mr. Kendall?"

"Fantastic," I say. It's difficult to restrain myself from leaping out of my chair and kissing each and every one of these genteel folks smack on the lips.

"That's it, then," he announces.

"Really?"

"We're finished with you. Just stay out of trouble for a couple months and you can go free. Of course, we'll arrange for a parole officer to take over your case when you get to Ohio."

"Thank you," I say.

As I'm walking down the corridor with Ames, I let loose with a childish whoop that brings half a dozen secretaries out of their offices. I smile at them. What can I say? I'm *happy*.

On the following Monday I spend the last of our greenskeeping allowance on azaleas—whites, pinks, reds and lavenders—which we order from a local nursery. It's important to get them in the ground while the weather is still cold. We horseshoe most of the bushes around the tees; the rest we place in the rough common to the two fairways. We pack the roots with peat moss and loam and 8-8-8, a less than ideal fertilizer for blooming plants, but it will have to do. The buds are very immature, but with care they should blossom within the next month.

In an empty metal drum, we mix together three eighty-pound bags of iron and two one-hundred-pound bags of lime. Drago, with his handkerchief tied over his face, looks like a terrorist; lime dust is hell on the nasal passages. "What's this stuff for, boss?" he asks.

"Tomorrow we fertilize the fairways," I tell him. "We're talking *green* here, Drago."

I'm determined to bring the Moss Point Golf Course to the peak of perfection before I leave. Then I'll drag my clubs from beneath my cot and play these two gorgeously landscaped holes for all they're worth.

Twenty-nine

For Christmas, Stan bought me a voluminous nylon suitcase, more than big enough to hold my entire wardrobe, including a new assortment of golf slacks. (Unlike Trayn with his flamboyant taste, I liked grays and browns; if I was going to fail, I wanted to do it quietly.)

It was a typical Ohio February day, gray clouds floating above the trees of the golf course, fairways and greens smothered in white. Through my window I could see double-lined trails of cross-country skiers who had traversed the fairway of number seventeen, then angled off toward the frozen pond.

Stan was sitting on the edge of my bed while I culled out the shirts and towels and toiletries I would need for the months ahead. "Well, how do you feel about this?" he asked. "Are you excited?"

"Sure," I said. "I'm excited . . . and nervous. I might be getting in over my head. I don't want you to be disappointed if I wash out."

"You won't wash out." He lifted the dog into his lap and stroked her ears.

"The tour is a real dogfight—no offense, Sally," I said. "*Trayn* might not even make it."

He lowered Sally onto the carpet, stood up and said, "You've got to think *positive*. Remember that."

The next morning, I waited in my idling car while Stan, wearing no coat over his flannel shirt, ran through a verbal inventory of things I may of may not have forgotten. "Whoa, wait a minute," he said, and scurried into the house. He returned with a flashlight. "You never know when you might need this."

"Oh yeah, I forgot all about a flashlight," I said, wondering why I'd be needing one. We shook hands through the rolled-down window. I told him that I loved him, and to take care of Lucille and Sally, then pulled out of the driveway before he had a chance to get sentimental.

On my way out of town, I stopped by Jimmy's house to say goodbye. He'd regained enough strength over the preceding few months to take short walks around the block with Katherine. But with the ice now covering the sidewalks, he was confined to his own yard, where I found him that morning, scattering rock salt on his front porch. He had on one of those vinyl hats with the earflaps that old men who don't mind looking like derelicts wear, and a red-and-black-checked woolen coat. I parked at the curb, and he shuffled out to meet me. "Well, I guess this is the start of it for you, eh?"

"That's right, Jimmy. Why don't you hop in. I'll take you with me."

"I'd give a lot to do just that. But my traveling days are over." We chatted a while about the weather, about the new assistant pro at the country club (whom Jimmy seemed to like). He was starting to shiver, and his nose was running, so I patted his gloved hand and told me I'd be going. "You've been a tremendous help to me, Jimmy. I'll always appreciate that, no matter what." He told me goodbye and turned to go inside his house. "Tell Katherine to watch for me on TV." He waved to me from his doorstep as I backed onto Walnut Street. I put the shifter into first gear, let out the clutch and headed toward the grim clouds clinging to the black branches of the golf course elms.

By the time I picked up I-70 at Dayton and turned west, a dry snow was blowing across the highway. The air was so dense with it that silos and barns and skeletal transformers loomed suddenly along the roadside and were just as suddenly gone. There was no horizon in front of me now. I felt as though it was not an expanding geography I was traveling into; instead, it was a dwindling and featureless isolation whose boundary ended at my slightly foggy windshield; I was driving into the blankness of my own fear, but if I only drove long enough and far enough, this impenetrable whiteness would give way to green. I hunched behind the wheel of my late-model car, its trunk filled with the particulars of my existence, and aimed toward good weather where, of all things, I'd try to make my living by stroking a one-and-three-quarter-inch sphere down alien Sunbelt fairways.

Just beyond Indianapolis, the snowstorm abruptly ended, and a cold sun glowed through the clouds. I pulled into a McDonald's and ate the first of what I knew would be an unending cavalcade of burgers. In a nearby booth sat a trio of hardhats, on a break from some job. Their work, unlike mine, could be measured in cubic yards and metric tons. They seemed remarkably happy, and they apparently liked their food.

There was no snow on the ground between Indianapolis and Joplin, Missouri, where at eight o'clock I pulled into the parking lot of a Days Inn. The room was $23.50, a sum I paid in cash. At Stan's suggestion, I'd packed my overnight essentials—toothbrush, underwear, clean socks, shampoo, whiskey—in a small gym bag, the only luggage I carried into the motel room. I turned on all the lights. The TV pulled in nineteen channels. I found an Atlanta Hawks basketball game, turned the volume up slightly and sat on the foot of the bed to watch. Fast food had no allure for me. In fact, the only thing I really wanted in my stomach was some Jim Beam. After filling a container with ice from a machine outside the office, I returned to my room and filled a cup with whiskey and ice. Then I spread my road map on the brown shag carpet and tried to figure mileage from Joplin to Big Spring, Texas.

After the basketball game, I took a twenty-minute hot shower, something I wasn't allowed to do at home. I sang a few bars of "Why Do Fools Fall in Love?" but stalled out after the line about the birds singing so gaily. My voice sounded exceptionally good, amplified as it was by the tile bathroom.

This was my night to break ground. I crawled naked (a novelty for me) between the sheets, took a deep breath of motel air, closed my eyes and lay that way for a while, feeling that I'd at least turned the first page in the old book of life. I sat upright in bed when I heard a voice that sounded exactly like Janice's in the adjacent room. Of course, it wasn't her. I knew that. But I couldn't help listening to the activity next door. The toilet flushed, some hangers chirped on a metal pipe, drawers opened and closed. I imagined Janice, slipping out of her slacks, folding them, gliding into the bathroom, removing her bra and panties, checking herself out in the mirror, plucking a stray eyebrow hair. It was a surprisingly easy thing to imagine. Almost automatically, I reached under the sheet and touched myself, wondering how I might feel if I went through with it. I worried that my mom was watching over me at the end of my first day of independence, and how ridiculous I would look giving in that way. So I crawled out of bed and put on a clean pair of boxer shorts. A few minutes later I was asleep.

I was wide awake at five o'clock in the morning, hungry from not having eaten any supper. One nice thing about waking up with the crows was that limitless supply of hot water in the shower, of which I consumed at least fifty ecstatic gallons before toweling off and getting dressed. There was a run of fast-food places up and down the strip where my motel was located. At least one of them was bound to be open twenty-four hours so somebody like me could get breakfast.

Pancake International was filled with truckers at five-thirty.

They leaned possessively over their flapjacks as if somebody might possibly steal their plate. The coffee smelled good to me, but when I sat at the counter and ordered some, I was poured a cup of the palest brew I'd ever seen. I compensated by drinking four cups with my pancakes and sausages and eggs. The meal came to nearly five dollars, and I felt cheated. The waitress was left a quarter tip.

The Will Rogers Turnpike was under construction all the way from Vinita to Chickasha. I was trapped for a couple of hours behind a Winnebago whose fat posterior was emblazoned with the name of the family inside. The Pipenbrinks from Scranton, PA. If I'd drunk three cups of coffee instead of four, I'd have been ahead of this lumbering vehicle. What a lousy break to be the penultimate entry in a five-mile-long parade of furious motorists. I decided to relax and look at the flat landscape that crawled past my window. Oil derricks like miniature Eiffel Towers, bored cows, house trailers held down with guy wires to prevent their being blown away by the unimpeded Oklahoma winds, sorry-looking scrub oaks. I was glad I lived in Ohio where trees were trees. About fifty miles north of Witchita Falls, Texas, the second traffic lane opened up, and an endless train of automobiles, mine included, hurtled past the Pipenbrink family, horns blasting, drivers with fists clenched in anger.

I had lunch at the Roundup Drive-in just outside of Seymour, which was nothing more than a grain elevator, a Gulf station, a few peeling houses and, of course, the restaurant. Barbecued beef (Texas style) sounded good to me. Pauline, my waitress, took pity on me. She probably thought I was cute, compared to her regular roughneck clientele. Anyway, my sandwich was overflowing with stringy, but surprisingly tasty barbecue. I drank a Coke with it, and had some of the homemade apple pie, which tasted metallic, as if the fruit had spent a few months fermenting in a bucket. This time I left a dollar bill for my waitress, although I was afraid to smile back at her when she wished me a good trip, fearing that there might be some of that beef caught between my teeth. The Gulf station advertised cold beer, so I bought a six-pack of Lone Star and put it next to me on the front seat. I figured that by the time I had quaffed the last swallows from the sixth can, I would be off this little secondary road that connected the turnpike with Interstate 20, the beginning of a long rifle shot to Arizona.

The beer and the bright western sunshine made me almost euphoric. I pulled down the sun flap to shade my eyes. Later, twenty miles shy of Sweetwater, just after dark and right in the middle of my Lou Rawls imitation, the car began to shake so furiously that I needed to pull over onto the berm. It was obvious from the way the Pacer veered right when I turned the steering wheel that I had a flat tire. I got out of the car and walked back to the trunk so I could unload the luggage, beneath which was my spare. Changing the tire was no problem. However, it was split alongside the whitewall, a total loss. A new tire would set me back another fifty dollars.

I'd miscalculated the mileage to Big Spring. It was only five o'clock when I rolled up to the only traffic light, so I decided to push toward Pecos, for no reason except that it was the hometown of Judge Roy Bean. A few hours later I was cruising down a small two-lane road that led to this legendary outpost. There was a passable motel on the eastern fringe of the settlement. One mile down the road was a row of dismal shacks with a sign out front: CABINS. I paused at the city limits to debate the wisdom of driving another hundred miles to Van Horn. Because I was feeling tired and slightly wasted from drinking all that beer, I doubled back to the Parsons Motel, where I parked my car between a pair of Ford Ranger pickups and went into the office. A room with a queen-size bed cost me a mere fifteen dollars, which I forked over to an old woman in blue jeans and a Princeton sweatshirt. On a telephone pole at the far end of the parking lot, a tired-looking basketball hoop hung from a few gray boards. I imagined some good-natured games of Horse among the cowpokes.

The TV, a black-and-white anachronism with a rabbit-ears

antenna, brought in only one snowy El Paso station. I had no choice but to watch *Love Boat.* How weird it was to think of these Pecos people, squat in the middle of useless scrubland and tumbleweed, watching a boatload of beautiful people drink champagne and play shuffleboard out in the Caribbean somewhere.

The grout in the tile bathroom was green from mildew, and the shower head was right out of *Psycho,* but I stood under a stream of tepid water until it gave out, which didn't take long. This place was so depressing that not even an iceless glass of Jim Beam could cheer me up. I decided to waste no time in going to bed. I opened a window, but the onslaught of semis was too much. I flopped onto the saggy bed and watched a rectangle of light fly across the wall and disappear with the passing of each truck. It took me several hours to fall asleep, but when I did I sank into a dreamless well so deep that I didn't wake up until nine the next morning.

When I returned my key at the office, I was offered a free cup of coffee, which, because it was served in a china cup, I had to drink on the premises. "You want another'n?" the friendly old guy at the desk asked. I told him I wouldn't mind that one bit.

It was ten o'clock by the time I cruised past CABINS into the most desolate stretch of territory imaginable. Except for the cars on the interstate, and the road beneath me, there was no sign of human influence. No telephone poles, no signs, trailers, wrecked cars . . . . absolutely nothing but an occasional dead jackrabbit sprawled on the side of the road. It was impossible that two hundred miles ahead was a city, El Paso, gateway to the West, the beginning of the last leg of my trip.

I gassed up at three o'clock in Las Cruces, with its three giant crucifixes planted on a foothill overlooking the town. I was glad to be in the Rockies, because Tucson was couched amidst this same range of mountains, just a few hundred miles westward. I would be there that night, tired out maybe, but among friends and off the road.

Except on calendars and postcards, I'd never seen a saguaro

cactus. Every now and then, when I made a turn on a dark stretch of mountain highway, my headlights caught one of those spooky giants, its arms raised almost in fear. I was at the crest of the last mountain pass outside Tucson. I saw the city lights that filled the basin amidst the surrounding peaks. There it is, I said to myself. As I descended into the city, with my car windows rolled down, the warm desert air smelled of cactus blossoms and orange blossoms and cut grass. I was almost euphoric, delivered as I was from the barrenness of western Texas and southern New Mexico. It was nine-thirty, and I was incredibly hungry, hungry enough to eat about eight barbecue sandwiches. But I was even more anxious to get to the Saddleback Inn, where Janice and Trayn would be waiting for me. I could phone in an order for a large pepperoni with double cheese, and I could eat it while I soaked in a hot tub.

The Broadway Avenue exit was very easy to find. I veered off the highway to the end of the ramp, turned left and started looking for the motel. Within a few minutes I saw a large neon motel sign, a rodeo cowboy riding a bucking horse. This place had a beautiful turquoise pool out front, with tourists swimming in the illuminated water. Instead of pickup trucks, there were cars parked in the spaces in front of the rooms. Trayn's BMW was nosed up to the sidewalk in front of 142. I parked in a slot with the number 143 stenciled in yellow on the asphalt. After stretching my legs for a few seconds, I knocked on their door. It opened, and there was Janice, clad in a bright red bathrobe, a white towel wrapped around her hair, cold cream on her face. "Teddy," she said, "Teddy," and she threw her arms around my neck and kissed me on the cheek. "You made it. Thank God. Oh God, it's so good to see you." I stepped inside the room, which smelled of cigarette smoke. "Trayn's in the shower. He'll be right out. Gosh, Teddy, how *are* you, anyway?"

"I'm a physical wreck. I need a drink, I need food, I need a bath and I need sleep. In that order."

"It really *is* good to see you."

"You said that," I told her.

"Well, I *mean* it. What's it been, eight months? Eight months since the wedding?"

"How's married life, by the way? What you expected?"

She gave me a wistful look, shrugged and said, "It has its moments. You know . . ."

Trayn strode stark naked out of the bathroom, toweling off his armpits. He was halfway to the bureau before he realized I was in the room. "Well, goddamn. Who's this?" He pinched the towel around his waist and came across the room to shake my hand. "I *love* this guy, Janice," he said. "Now we can get down to the business of getting rich, right, big fella?"

I smiled at that one. "Sure. Why not?" I said.

"We've got almost a week to get our games in shape before the qualifier. I've found some wonderful courses, including a real bruiser out by Sentinal Peak."

"That's tomorrow," I said. "Right now I need some painkiller and some grub. Let me get unpacked and settled into my room. Then we party, okay?"

"Whatever you want, pal. I know you're bushed. Hell, driving across Texas damn near did me in, too. What a pisser!"

Trayn got into some jeans and helped me get my things out of my car. We brought in my big suitcase, my golf clubs, my shag balls, my gym bag and my hanging clothes. "There you go," Trayn said when he'd dropped the last of it onto my bed. "Keys over there. Might want to pay up before you get too far along."

"How much is this place anyway?"

"Sixty bucks. Nice, though, wouldn't you say?"

"No kidding . . . sixty bucks?"

"It's all there was, buddy. Wait until next week when Watson and Crenshaw and all those boys roll in. This is where they stay."

"But they're rich," I said.

"We will be, too, Teddy," he said. "We will be, too." His voice was so filled with conviction that I almost believed him.

236

Thirty

I've known Drago for a full year now, and he's never once mentioned why he's here. In the first months I asked him several times, but he either changed the subject or pretended I didn't ask. If I turned the heat up, he'd skip off like a nervous elf to a remote corner of the prison grounds. So I quit asking, and almost stopped wondering. We're all entitled to our secrets, after all.

But yesterday morning Drago went to the state capitol in Jackson for his own parole hearing, where I'm afraid the setting was far different from the one I encountered. I know things didn't go well for him, because he didn't show up for supper last night, and right now he's more than half an hour late for work on the golf course. Since he hasn't shown up by now, the chances are good that I won't see him at all. So I decide to track him down.

I knock on the door to 136, but there's no answer, so I check the lavatory. Again, no luck. My suspicion is that he's locked himself in his room. "Drago, it's me, Kendall. Hey . . . open up the damned door." I allow a minute or two to pass, then I slap the door with my opened palm. "It's Almighty God," I bellow. There's some stirring inside the room. Maybe he's jacking off. Crying and jacking off at the same time. "I know you didn't get paroled," I say. "Let's talk about it."

When he opens up the door, it's easy to see he hasn't been crying. At least his eyes show no sign of it. On the other hand, his complexion is roughly the color of a prison spud. "How did you know, boss?" he asks.

"Just a guess. I'm really sorry, Drago. What happened?" He rolls onto his bunk and rests his stockinged feet on the metal frame. I decide to remain standing, but open a window, hoping that some fresh early spring air will cheer him up. "What in the hell did you do to earn a stint at Moss Point, anyway?"

"I don't think you really want to know," he tells me.

"You think I'm going to judge you, Drago? Somebody else obviously beat me to the punch. But you don't have to tell me if you don't want to."

"If you got to know, I killed a old lady name a Fraunfelter," he says. "She was crossing the street and I ran a red light and knocked her flat down dead. I was so scared I didn't even stop. And then the cops came to my mom's house, where I was living at the time, and asked me was I the guy driving the car that killed her. The old lady, I mean. I told 'em that it wasn't me, but my knees were shaking. Then one of the cops tells me to come with him, and shows me where the feather from the old lady's hat is poking through the radiator grille. So anyway, the judge throws the book at me because I wasn't such a hot driver even before that."

"Gosh, that's a shame. You must have felt terrible about what happened."

"Well, she was a old lady, and old ladies tend to die sooner or later, but still, I was the one that killed her."

"What happened at parole yesterday?"

"There was about twenty Fraunfelters there, all mad as hell, and they asked the parole board would they please keep me the whole two years, or longer if that was possible. And of course the parole board hasn't got any balls, so they say, 'Sure, let's let old Drago cook a while longer.' "

"So you have another year?"

"Well, I get another parole hearing in six months, but you can bet they'll all turn up like it was a family reunion. It was *them* I should've run over."

I coax Drago into getting dressed, which he does, but very slowly. Afterward, we head out to the golf course together, where we have to begin mowing the newly greened-up fairways. One sunny week in the seventies has made a remarkable difference in the appearance of the turf. If we wait too long before cranking up the machinery, we'll have to retrain the roots to stay underground.

He's done a remarkable job, Drago has, of tuning the Yazoo's engine. It hums effortlessly through the rough, and burns less than half the fuel it did before the tune-up. Meanwhile, even in his preoccupied state, he is a sight to behold jockeying the Jake tractor back and forth from tee to green, gliding over the adolescent crop of Bermuda grass that has taken hold on the hummocks swelling the contours of the fairway. I manage to keep the sadness I feel for Drago on one side of my brain, leaving room on the other for an absolute euphoria at the way the course appears now. The iron-and-lime combination has made the grass almost greener than green, and the azalea buds are pushing forth little pointed gems of color. We're only a week away from perfection. It was at that absolute pinnacle of verdancy that I always intended to play my first and last round of golf at Moss Point. But I think Drago needs a lift, so that plan might have to go by the boards.

We've put the equipment away at five o'clock, and Drago gives me a paper-thin smile. "The course looks pretty nice, boss."

"Nice? Did you say nice, Drago? That baby is magnificent." I turn him around where he stands and make him look. The late March sun is at the perfect angle for showing off the beautiful subtleties of the greens and fairways. "Tomorrow is Saturday. Tomorrow I get out the sticks. I'm going to play some golf. And you know what, buddy boy?"

"What?" he asks, eyebrows bouncing up and down.

"I need a caddy. Damned if I'm going to carry my own clubs. I'm a *pro*fessional, and *pro*fessionals don't carry their own clubs."

"I'd like that, boss," he says, taking a swipe at an invisible ball.

"By ten o'clock in the morning the grass should be dry. Can you meet me here at ten?"

"Sure thing," he says. I'm glad to see him smiling. I believe I even detect a slight wiggling of his jug ears.

Drago has obviously spread the word through the prison population that Kendall is going to baptize the Moss Point Golf and Country Club. A sizable crowd has already gathered near the first tee as my spikes click on the asphalt path toward the links. The two remainders from the original mess-hall quartet are there with a pair of white stand-ins. I can hear them singing "Baby, I Need your Lovin' " three hundred yards away. Drago's mom has sewn yellow-and-black-checkered triangular pennants for the painted bamboo flag sticks, odd, but strangely apropos. They flutter handsomely when the breeze rises. As I get closer, I see that Maples and Ames and Cooke and possibly the entire prison population have assembled for the occasion. Somewhere in their midst is my Sancho Panza, but I don't see him right now.

When I set foot on the first soft grass of number two rough, I hear applause, first a smattering, then a clamor, and ultimately something resembling an uproar. I know Drago has choreographed this scene. I pause for a moment next to a brilliant red azalea bush, not yet in full bloom, but trying. I just can't bring myself to keep walking. My jaws begin to hurt, and for the next few minutes the throng before me is a blur of moving color. I think of tear-prone Janice and Stan at their absolute worst. I'm

240

overwhelmed by how I feel, lost almost, not lost in sadness exactly, but in a totally unexpected bittersweet joy. Only after I've inhaled and exhaled heavily once, then twice, am I able to go on.

Drago dashes from the midst of the other inmates and takes my golf bag from me. He hands me the driver almost instinctively. "Go ahead, boss. Take some practice swings." I make sure some of the novice fans are clear of my backswing, and I loosen up with all of them looking on. After every follow-through they cheer me like a bullfighter who, from a kneeling position, his just drawn his cape over the horns of a charging bull. Ames receives a fairly inventive tribal handshake from one of the bloods. This is prison entertainment at its finest, and their appreciation is grandiose and totally uncalled for, but I'm actually enjoying myself. "You ready now, boss?"

"I think so, Drago," I say. He reaches inside the utility pocket of my bag and hands me a tee and a Titleist.

I push the white tee into the virgin turf and gaze toward the green, and beyond that the bank of white and pink azaleas. The creek (I prefer to call it a "burn," after the Swilcan Burn of St. Andrews) bellies into the fairway about two hundred yards out, then crawls along the rough for a little ways before traversing the fairway at a point calculated to tempt a good golfer to risk a brave shot, a full-muscled drive. So a fade or even a slightly mishit drive is carp food. On the other hand, a hook will fly the fence and sail into the swamp. I'm pleased by the careful thought this hole demands, and I relish the feeling of terror in my gut.

This is a once-in-a-lifetime situation. I decide to rip a big drive over the burn. A lay-up short of the hazard has no allure for me, and it would surely disappoint the gallery. By clearing the water I will have only a seven or eight iron to the small green, thereby reducing the peril of Drago's elephant-ear bunkers.

I take a few practice swings, check the distant flag for wind direction and finally nestle the clubface behind the ball. I'm on the verge of taking my backswing when a bee interrupts my concentration. He finally zooms off toward the pond guarding the second green, and I retake my stance.

When I finally meet the ball, a powerful current races through my veins. The ball is sailing in slow motion, high, like a tiny satellite, toward the green. It bounds once on the opposite side of the creek, bites into the perfectly firm fairway, takes a beautiful hop and settles dead center, two hundred and seventy yards away. My fellow inmates applaud wildly, whistle, howl with appreciation; except from the bench seat of a fast-moving pickup truck, some of them have never seen a man hit a golf ball. Single file, they follow Drago (who can't help skipping) and me across the hazard, and reassemble in a horseshoe around my ball.

"Well, caddy? What club?" Drago hands me the three iron, a preposterous choice considering my need to fling the ball over the pachyderm's right ear and hold the shot on the small green. "How about an eight iron?" I ask.

"I was going to suggest that—either a three of a eight." He pulls the proper club from the bag, huffs on the blade and wipes off his fingerprints with a towel. He's not a half-bad caddy . . . a bit on the groveling side, but not bad.

One of the prisoners, I can't tell which one, says, "Kill the son of a bitch, Kendall." I presume he's talking about the ball and not Drago.

After a few practice swings, I take a comfortable stance and rest the blade behind the Titleist, then draw the club slowly back until the shaft is nearly horizontal and finally pull the forged head down and into the ball. Unfortunately, the one-year layoff has corrupted my timing, and I push the ball into the maliciously conceived bunker to the right. "Damn," I say.

"Shit," says my caddy. There is good reason to believe that Drago has already lost money on me, because he does one of those palms-up shrugs toward Cooke.

To the great relief of the gallery, I manage a competent blast from my plugged lie in the Pensacola-sand-filled bunker and drop the ball only a few feet from the cup.

The Bermuda grass greens are as nearly immaculate as I can imagine, and the ball is so close to the hole that I'd be a fool not to smack it firmly into the cup. It's no surprise that the putt rolls beautifully into the center of the cup, and the round is halfway over.

Number two is a fiendish hole, very Scottish in character. The fairway is fuddled with mounds and moguls, and at the end of this narrow green carpet is an elevated kidney-shaped green in whose embrace is a sand trap, also shaped like a kidney. It is an especially hungry trap, owing to the wicked slope of the green, which treats a fade far more kindly that a draw, the latter of which is the heart and soul of my game. To hit a big drive is pointless here. The intelligent shot is a well-placed three iron to the oasis of level ground in the left center of a fairway tortured by undulations. From this haven, it's possible to throw a faded five iron into the slope of the green. Of course, if my second shot is struck too well or too thinly, I'll be dunked in the pond that licks the back portion of the green.

My gallery looks disappointed when I reject the driver thrust toward me by Drago. I wink at them. "Strategy," I say, and point to my left temporal lobe.

My three-iron shot is a misshapen missile that curves left into the rough and disappears. So much for strategy. So much for a chance at a dramatic backspinning approach shot faded dead on the stick. "What happened, boss?"

"I screwed up, Drago." He glares toward Cooke, who's smirking pretty boldly.

My ball is nestled in a particularly dense snag of Bermuda, so thick I can barely see the white dimpled skull. "We've got heap big trouble, my friend."

"What're you going to do, boss?"

I shake my head and grab the same accursed three iron from the bag. I take my stance in such a way that the ball is positioned farther back, so I can sock it out of the rough with a descending blow, the result of which could be almost anything. Naturally, I'd love to land it somewhere short of the green and let it run onto the putting surface. But it's an ugly patch of spinach I'm dealing with.

Oddly, my misery is almost fun. I'm frankly glad to be punished by this demonically conceived golf hole. I've hit a lousy shot, and now I'm paying the price: quid pro quo, as Stan would say. Bobby Jones would be pleased by a hole such as this one, a nice little metaphor for life. Quid pro quo. Ram your touring buddy with your car: spend thirteen months in jail.

The cushiony grass nearly swallows my shoes, not to mention the object of my bemusement. After a taking a very upright backswing, I hurl the blade into the ball, which leaps from its nest like a quail and floats in a parabola toward the apron of the green. It takes a disappointing short little hop and runs only about five feet onto the cuff around the putting surface. Although the spectators clap and hoot and roar, none of them knows how good my shot really was. Not even Drago.

Together, Drago and I line up my forty-foot putt. I crouch behind the ball, plumb-bobbing with my Schenectady. My caddy leans over my shoulder and says, "This way and then this way." To my surprise, he's right. Maybe he's an idiot savant with two talents: mowers and putts. I stride across the green and look over my line from the opposite side of the hole. My target will be a point a few inches above the cup.

After reading the putt one last time from the apron, I take a solid, slightly open stance, trying to fix an image in my brain—the ball following its destiny, a meandering pilgrimage toward a metallic cup guarded, black and white stick in hand, by Drago.

When I'm ready to stroke my putt, however, my hands begin to shake. Sweat beads in my eyebrows. My lips tremble. Emotion wells up in my throat. I'm actually afraid I'll make the ball go into the hole; the moment which has held me in its greenness will evaporate. Drago senses my hesitation and clutches the flag more tightly in his fingers.

Finally, I regain myself enough to draw the putter smoothly back, and with a firm forward stroke knock the ball toward its fate. The little critter goes where I've sent it, taking the right-hand break Drago so shrewdly predicted, then arriving at the swelling of the green that guides the ball back to the left, toward the hole. The putt will go in. The certainty is immutable as death, if its aftermath is somewhat less sublime. "Take the pin out, Drago," I yell as the ball approaches the cup.

He jerks the bamboo pole out and stares at the alabaster orb creeping toward him. The ball gradually loses its speed when it arrives on the level terrain where the cup is situated. With almost no velocity left, the Titleist makes one last revolution and rattles into the cup.

My caddy, Drago the Club Lugger, dances a buck-and-wing across the green, the flag stick now a banner of triumph. I sit down in the lush grass and listen to the cheers.

Thirty-one

There are few things worse than waking up with a mean hangover in a strange motel, with no Alka-Seltzer or tomato juice handy to chase the misery. Trayn and Janice and I had stayed up late drinking Coors and playing Scrabble with the TV droning in the background. But at one in the morning I said good night to them and stumbled to my room. After gulping a few aspirins, I stripped off my clothes, filled the tub with steaming water, slid in and lay back with my head all but submerged and my feet pressed against the fiberglass wall of the tub enclosure. I relaxed my muscles, closed my eyes and tried to focus on the vague noises swimming through the water. But when I woke up the next morning an anvil sat where my head had once been.

I hadn't had time to scout out a secluded place near the motel where I could swing my weighted club, but I knew that kind of workout was bound to get out a few of the kinks. My watch said 8:45. Trayn was a habitually late sleeper, so I wouldn't be seeing him before midmorning. I thought I'd heard Janice moving around their room, though. I closed my door firmly behind me, and stepped into the bright Arizona sunshine. The mountains were different here . . . greener, higher, more beautiful than those eerie treeless peaks I'd driven through the day before. The motel had a lush St. Augustine lawn which surrounded the swimming pool. I walked down Broadway Avenue a few blocks to a 7-Eleven, where I bought a copy of *Inside Sports* and a large cup of coffee. I carried my purchases back to the motel, where I sat at a poolside table beneath a large canvas umbrella. Now, with the sun warming the back of my neck and Mount Lemon looming in the north, I was glad Trayn had chosen this place. Leafing through my magazine, I came across an article on sports suicides, not exactly a complement to my relief at having arrived in this pleasant, sun-baked climate. I was about to flip the page when, in the bottom left-hand corner, I saw a picture that made me stop; it was a photograph of a smiling young man sitting on the steps of a mobile home, his baby girl balanced on his knee. It was Gary Triplett, medalist at the NCAA championship in Dallas a couple of years back. I'd played with him during the second round, when he'd shot his 65, a course record. He was a powerfully built kid, with a strange looping follow-through reminiscent of Arnie Palmer's. Triplett jabbered to himself during the entire round. "Thataboy, Trip," he'd say. Or "Get smart. You're not *thinking*, Trip." Some great golfers come out of nowhere; they just show up on the tour and people say, "Where in the hell did *he* come from?" But Triplett was a sure bet if ever there was one. And now I was reading about this Georgia farm boy who won a lot of money on the tour, only to waste it on gold watches and German cars and twenty-dollar scotch. His golf had won him so much; the game was only a machine that manufactured money that bought *things*. His last gesture, before driving his Porsche into a concrete bridge abutment, was to watch a solar eclipse with his daughter. His wife said that only fifteen minutes before his death, Triplett was sitting in the back yard of their new house, staring through a square of smoked glass at the moon as it slid between the sun and the earth. To him, it must have seemed like a bright eye closing. The article said he was traveling at 130 miles per hour when his car hit the bridge.

I hadn't even touched my coffee. I was sitting at the white iron table, watching the blue cloudless sky above the rim of the Catalinas, when Janice snuck up behind me and said, "Boo." I shaded my eyes to look at her. "Hi, how are you doing this morning?" she asked. "Rested up?"

"I'm a little groggy," I said. "Don't much feel like playing golf this afternoon. I guess I'd better, though. Has Trayn been practicing much?"

"All the time. But I wouldn't call it practicing. He's played forty-five holes every day since we got here on Friday."

"I guess that gives *you* time to see the sights."

"Sure . . ." She picked up my coffee cup and set it back down.

"But you'd have more fun with some company, right?"

"That's about the size of it, Teddy."

"Are you sorry you came along? Do you wish you'd stayed in Cincinnati?"

"I did yesterday. I don't today."

I steered the conversation toward coffee, especially the lukewarm paper cup of brew in front of me. We walked together to the carry-out, where I bought us each a fresh cup. "Trayn's convinced he's going to make it on the tour," Janice said as we walked across the parking lot to the pool. "Do you think he's being realistic?"

"You want my honest opinion?"

"Yes . . . I do."

"Trayn's going to be a star. A TV idol. He's got something most of those *flat cookies* don't have, and that's charisma."

She smiled at this bit of news. "What about you?"

"I'm purely comic relief."

"Come on, Teddy. Be serious."

"I probably won't make it. I might if I improve. Realistically . . . I'm a real long shot."

"You'll make it," she said. I laughed and told her she sounded like Stan, whistling in the dark.

Trayn gave Janice a twenty-dollar bill before he climbed into the Pacer with me that afternoon. "Try the Sonora Desert Museum," he said. "I heard it's great. Have fun."

Janice was leaning in my car window, a wistful look on her face. "When will you be back?"

"Around seven. When it gets dark."

She gave us a weak smile and turned to go inside the motel room. "Believe me, Teddy," Trayn said. "She's much happier here than she would be sitting at home in Ohio. I mean, this is my job, right?"

"I guess so," I said. "By the way, where am I taking you?"

"I thought we might try Randolph. They close the course tomorrow to groom it for the tournament, so everybody and his mother will probably be out there today. But I think we should get a jump on the competition. Let's go ahead and play the damned thing."

Sun Desert, the perennial site of the Tucson Open, was closed for major renovations. Instead, the tournament would be held on the Randolph Municipal Golf Course, a fairly nice track, considering it was public and played to death.

Trayn paid our greens fees and rented an electric cart for the afternoon. In all my years of golf, I'd *always* carried my clubs. It was as much a matter of principle as it was habit. I told Trayn and he said, "You're kidding. This is the only way to fly, pal. Especially when you're playing behind dudes like that." He pointed toward a foursome of elderly men who were waiting for the first fairway to clear. "Watch this," Trayn said. He got out of the cart and walked up to a man who looked to be in his eighties. "Mind if we play through? We're professionals, and we need to get in a practice round today."

"I'm an old man. I might die before the round is over."

"What's that mean?" Trayn asked.

"It means wait your turn."

Trayn stomped back toward our cart. "Old coot," he muttered.

Randolph was in good condition, considering the beating it took from hackers like the group in front of us. The greens were soft and true, except for some barely detectable ruckles from the rotation of a dull mower blade. The odd thing about the course was the total absence of large trees. Instead, there were dwarf olives, some sizable oleanders and every now and then a desert oak. But mostly it was scaped with yucca and saguaro and prickly pear and scraggly date palms.

Trayn insisted that I hit first off the tee. Maybe he'd substituted a trick ball when I wasn't looking. "Go ahead, let her rip," he said.

After taking a few practice swings, I stepped up to my Titleist and took a healthy cut at the thing. To my amazement the ball sailed at least 280 yards down the right side of the fairway and trickled up to where one of the Gerontions had stopped to analyze his fourth shot. "What the hell happened? That's the longest drive I've ever hit in my life."

"Combination of low humidity and high altitude. Makes heroes of us all. Figure fifteen yards extra."

"God, it'll take twenty under par to win the tournament."

"That's right. And I'd guess minus two just to qualify."

Trayn stood over his own ball, took an enormous swing and burned his Maxfli 320 yards into the shallow rough at the left side of the fairway. "By the way, the roughs are fucking kikuyu. A total whore to get out of."

He got out just fine, made his par and continued to play well for the rest of the afternoon. I was even par, three behind him. I'd sunk two long putts, or things might have been worse. It had taken us well over four hours to get the round in. Not my style. My timing had been slightly off all day, particularly with my short irons, which on a course like Randolph, where the longest approach shot would be about one-fifty, was unforgivable. Still, it felt good to be out on the course, with the late afternoon sun hurling shadows across the fairways and outlining the whiskery saguaros in gold. I could almost forgive the old guys in front of us for taking their time.

That night we ate dinner at a Mexican restaurant that looked suspiciously like a Taco Bell under new management. Trayn and Janice were tossing down margaritas while I nursed a pitcher of Carta Blanca draft, although I didn't really need another hangover like the one I'd awakened with that morning. "Teddy, I want to hear that wedding toast again. Wasn't that great, Janice?" he teased. "Tell us again how marriage is like golf."

"Look," I said, "I was crazed at the time."

"Play by the rules, wasn't that part of it?"

"I've forgotten."

"And sink your putts, right. Sink your *putz!* Get it?"

"What's going on, Trayn?" I asked.

"Heck, Teddy. I'm just pulling your chain. Look at him, Janice, he's red in the face. I guess I won't ask him about Ginny. Should I ask him about Ginny? Poor old horny-as-a-goat-Ginny . . ."

"You're a little smashed Trayn. Why don't you shut your trap and give me a cigarette," she said. I felt sure the cigarette was just a diversionary tactic; I'd only seen her smoke once or twice before, both times when she herself was drunk. But I could tell from the deft way she handled the lighter that she'd been at it a while.

"You smoke now," I said.

"Only after an affair," she replied, at which Trayn laughed.

He said, "You *wish!*" and pulled a Winston from the gold pack she'd laid on the table. She rolled her eyes toward the faded crepe-paper piñata hanging overhead.

That was the kind of wonderful time we were having in celebration of my arrival in Arizona. Trayn wanted to take a drive up the side of Oracle Mountain for a view of the city lights, but Janice told him he was too drunk for that, so we went back to the motel. I had my fingers on the doorknob of my room when Trayn gently grabbed my shoulder. "Hey," he said, offering me his hand. "I really am glad you're here. And I hope you do well on the tour. I didn't mean anything . . . you know . . . about Ginny."

We shook hands. I told him thanks, and said it was okay. I felt a little bit sorry for him, because Janice was in their room lying in wait; she was furious with him for getting drunk and pushing things as far as he had. But it really was okay. Trayn was being Trayn and he really didn't mean it, or at least later, when he sobered up, he would know he hadn't meant it. He wanted me to succeed. He needed a chum who could tolerate his nature. Never mind that his chum was in love with his wife.

His *wife*, Janice. That was a strange thing to imagine. But at close range I could feel the strong current that alternately attracted them to each other and then, on other occasions, drove them apart. Things seemed almost the same now as they had been in Columbus before their marriage. Only the setting had changed.

Trayn and I played hundreds of holes of golf over the next few days, while Janice sat around the pool in her white OSU visor and her pastel green tank top and her white gym shorts, writing letters to Ginny or her folks or Trayn's folks. I was finally getting my touch back after a ten-week layoff, but I was always two or three shots behind Trayn. My putter had to be blazing for me to stay even, a rarity for me.

Randolph opened on Sunday morning so the rabbits could get in a practice round before the Monday qualifier. Janice talked Trayn into letting her walk around with us for eighteen holes, which was all we were allowed to play, according to PGA rules. We were preparing to tee off when a middle-aged man with a clipboard raced out to the tee and informed us that we'd need a third player. "No twosome, fellas," he said.

"Does she count?" Trayn joked.

The man's visor bounced up and down as he checked her out. "Oh, she counts all right. But not as part of your threesome." He waved over a redheaded kid named Freddie McVee. He had a thick Oklahoma accent, which he exhibited at the first tee

("Hair yew"), and a habit of knocking himself in the forehead with the butt of his hand and saying, "You didn't *do* that. You didn't *do* that." He laughed at everything Trayn said. "I can spit farther than that," Trayn would say, and McVee would have a convulsion. Freddie had a beautiful, natural swing, but around the greens he seemed to lose interest. He'd flick a three-foot putt toward the hole, and if it didn't fall he'd say, "You didn't *do* that," and he'd laugh.

Janice clapped if one of us, including Freddie, did something exceptional. I was sure that she believed Trayn to be one of the greatest golfers ever to lace up a pair of spikes; and he was having a rare day, bisecting the fairways with drives like frozen ropes, floating high spinning wedge shots that backtracked to within a foot or two of the flag, canning meandering cross-country putts dead center. I shot a decent 69, a score that might at least qualify. McVee guffawed his way to an acceptable 70, while Trayn fired a sizzling 65 that, even on a forgiving track like Randolph, was fearsome.

When I woke up at dawn on Monday morning, my bedsheet and blanket were in a knot on the floor. The squinting face reflected in the bathroom mirror a few minutes later belonged not to me but to Lon Chaney; hair riled, left cheek imprinted with the folds of an empty pillowcase, eyes crusted over. I ran hot water from the tub faucet, tested it briefly to be sure it wasn't going to scald or freeze me, flipped the shower valve and climbed in.

I'd already dried off and blasted my underarms with Right Guard when I heard Janice and Trayn moving around next door. Trayn had probably slept like a saint. My stomach felt no bigger than a golf ball, and my hands were shaking. The weighted practice club stood in the corner. Maybe a good workout with that monster would burn off some of the panic. On the other hand, swinging ten pound object of any description, especially this close to tee-off time, would spell adios to any semblance of touch and timing. I settled on jumping jacks, one hundred quick ones.

The fronds of the palm trees outside the motel were perfectly still at six o'clock in the morning. The sun hadn't yet appeared from behind the eastern range, a charcoal-gray silhouette on the horizon. If I hurried, I could down a large cup of coffee before the newlyweds emerged from the motel. Midway in my stroll to the 7-Eleven, I was almost blinded by spokes of light angling down from the summit of Rincon Park.

In a surge of generosity, I bought coffees for Janice and Trayn, which I carefully placed at the bottom of a white paper sack. I carried the third cup in my free hand, pausing every few steps to swill a few milliliters.

They were waiting for me at a poolside table. "I brought you a present," I said, and placed the sack between them. Janice, who looked as if she might have slept an hour or two, was wearing her hair in ponytails, a style that made her look approximately thirteen, a very beautiful thirteen.

"You look like hell, Teddy boy," Trayn said. "Couldn't sleep, huh?"

"Ignore him," Janice said. She had already pried the plastic lid from her coffee and was blowing air across its surface. "*None* of us slept very well last night."

"Is that true, Trayn? I thought you could sleep through a Samurai invasion."

"I didn't sleep worth a turkey's assbone," he said.

"Nervous about the qualifier?"

"Yeah . . . ," he said. "Maybe that was it." But I could tell there was another reason. "By the way, did you know you spilled coffee on your new britches?"

Sure enough, my pristine khakis had a pair of conspicuous brown stains just above the knee. "Shit," I said.

It seemed that all the high school golfers in the city of Tucson had been recruited to serve as caddies for the qualifying tournament. While Janice attempted to make friends with some of the players' wives (an opportunity she'd eagerly anticipated), Trayn and I checked in at the officials' tent, verified our starting times and pairings and paid the balance of our entry fee, another hundred dollars out of my billfold. Trayn asked the tournament director how many slots of the 144 remained for the rabbits to fill. The fellow shuffled through some papers, dragged his fingers down a column and said, "Looks like nine."

"You're joking," Trayn said, and looked at me. "He's joking, Teddy."

"I wish I were," the man said, "but we had a hundred thirty-five exempt players pay their entry fee. Now, there may be a cancellation or two . . ."

"Looks like we've got our work cut out for us," I said.

The caddies were dressed in their high school colors, including one enormous boy dressed in yellow pants (just like Trayn's) and a brilliant purple shirt. I hired a green-clad kid who looked like Lee Trevino must have looked when he was fifteen years old. His name was Tommy Romero. Trayn hired a black kid, whose name I never learned.

We were lucky, Trayn and I, because our tee-off times were fairly early; and since wet fairways and morning humidity weren't factors in this climate, it was best that we get away before the nerves got too frayed. The driving range was crowded with players. A number of them looked like veterans who'd just regained their tour cards after a run of bad luck. I found an open slip between two of these rabbits, one of whom looked familiar to me. I was sure he'd been in the qualifying school with me. "Did I see you at Palm Beach in November?" I asked.

"Yeah, we were paired together in the second round. Remember?"

"Were we? God, I don't remember that. But I was probably focused on getting through the round."

"I know what you mean," he said.

My swing felt slightly strained for the first few minutes on the range, but as I got deeper into the process, my muscles relaxed. After we'd hit several buckets of shag balls each, Trayn and I walked together to the practice green, where we spent a half hour on uphillers, side-hillers, downhillers, left-to-rights, right-to-lefts, lags and knee-knockers. A man with a bullhorn called my group to the tee. Trayn patted me on the back and wished me luck. "Good luck yourself," I said.

Janice looked happy to survey the action from the terrace, where she'd befriended a pair of young women dressed in designer T-shirts and loud shorts. That was fine with me. Unfortunately, she noticed me standing out on the tee, waiting for a middle-aged player named Talbot to hit his drive. When he finally made his swing I wondered if he'd learned it from a lieutenant colonel at some military base in Guam. It was a hacking blow, truncated on the follow-through. I would have laughed out loud if his ball hadn't landed on the imaginary dotted line that runs down the center of the fairway. Since Whaley, the other member of our trio, had already parked his long drive in the rough, I was next up. My ball fell off the tee twice before I could steady my hand to balance it properly. I couldn't help looking over at Janice, who was biting her thumbnails. I stood behind my gleaming Titleist and gazed down the fairway. My palms were sweating so profusely that I had to wipe them on my coffee-stained pants. My practice swings felt stiff, but there was no time to walk away for a five-minute warm-up session. I finally took a stance, riveted my focus on the ball and hauled my driver back through its imaginary plane, until I was suddenly thrusting my weight forward. It was then that I felt the clubhead make solid contact with the ball. Only when my swing was complete did I search the sky for my ball, which had sailed wide right, over a row of prickly pears. Miraculously, the ball began to bow inward toward the fairway. It landed once in the dense kikuyu grass and hopped onto the fairway, short but in play. "Nice going, Teddy," Janice said. I blew out a lungful of air and followed my caddy toward the ball.

I was one over par through the fifth hole, and I hadn't even come close to making a birdie. My approach shots were only adequate, and my putting was getting me by. The first par five of the day was number six, a hole presenting eagle possibilities to even an average driver. I said a silent prayer to Our Lady of Perpetual Birdies. Almost everyone would pick up at least one stroke here. Trayn could probably get home with a driver and a seven iron if he creamed his tee shot. The one possible obstacle to a birdie was a concrete-lined irrigation canal that skirted the left-hand rough; but only a wild duck hook would bring it into play. I had won the honors on the previous hole, when both my playing partners had three-putted from long range. I was thinking about the iron practice club I'd been wielding for the past several months, and how the strength I'd gained would pay off here. Without benefit of a practice swing, I belted a low screamer off the tee; it curled left into the stump of a newly felled palm tree and caromed directly into the dreaded canal. "That's too bad," said Talbot. "A bad kick."

Qualifying for the tournament was now completely out of the question. I might have survived a mistake like that if it occurred during a four-day event, but this was an eighteen hole crapshoot with no margin for error. Randolph was one of the two or three easiest courses on the tour. Level-par golf wasn't going to get me anywhere, let alone one or two *over* par.

I played like a robot for the rest of my round. Maybe apathy was the secret to this game. Without really trying I'd shot one under par through the final dozen holes. And old Talbot, who was totally without emotion for three solid hours, had come in at minus four, a shoe-in to qualify. I sat on a bench outside the clubhouse with Janice, who'd brought me a consolation Budweiser. "You *tried*. That's what counts," she said. She fluffed my hair and kissed me on the cheek. "There's always next Monday."

"Right," I said.

I'd finished that beer *and* a second one when I saw Trayn striding up the last fairway. It was obvious from his buoyant stride that he'd chewed up the course. His laugh carried the two hundred yards that separated us. There he was, standing in the rough fifty paces ahead of his partners, waiting for them to hit their approach shots; he'd outdriven them by that much. He was puffing on a cigarette, explaining some subtlety of the game to his caddy.

Janice and I stood behind the eighteenth green while he read his fifteen-footer. She had her hands pressed together beneath her chin, in an attitude of prayer. For extra luck her fingers were crossed. Trayn glanced back and forth from his ball to the cup, took a smooth stroke and watched the ball roll toward its target. Instead of dropping immediately into the cup, the ball looped 180 degrees around the rim, then fell. The perfect dramatic touch. Only then did Trayn dash across the green, kiss Janice and shake my hand. "Six under," he said. "We're in like Flynn." He looked me in the eye for a minute, as if he knew the answer to the question he was duty bound to ask. "What about you?"

"One over," I said. "I'm out like Snout."

"Aw, Jesus, Teddy. That's too bad." I knew he meant it, but that didn't prevent me from wishing I could burrow my way to Bowling Green, where I could live in anonymity forever.

I played a few practice rounds with Trayn during the two days before the tournament, but I was still reeling from Monday's ordeal. With his nose for flaws in technique, he discovered a bad habit I'd acquired sometime in the last year, one I hadn't noticed. Whenever I hit a short iron I was opening the clubface at the top of the follow-through. "That means you're cutting everything, pal. You're stiff-wristing your short irons. Roll into them."

Once again, he was right on the money, and I noted some improvement in that phase of my game during those several days.

On Thursday morning I was part of the large gallery that had turned out to watch the big-name players devour the Randolph Municipal Golf Course. Although I had paid my hundred-dollar qualifying fee, I wasn't even allowed to use the toilet in the locker room. I was directed to use the Port-o-Let like all the other fans. Janice and I stood behind the ropes at the first tee while Trayn and his playing partners, Chip Beck and Morris Hatalsky, warmed up. I listened to the introductions. Trayn's sounded pretty impressive: twice All-American, winner of the National Jaycee, winner of the United States Interscholastic Championship, Ohio's Amateur Golfer of the Year. Trayn gave a boyish wave to the gallery when the introduction was complete.

His drive off number one was a high arcing beauty, pounded in the general direction of Mount Lemon. For a moment it appeared his ball might actually fly over the peak and disappear. Instead, it landed just left of center, an easy 325 yards out. I heard Hatalsky and Beck laughing. They dropped their drivers and pretended they were giving up. Janice was hopping up and down. "Wow!" she said. "Wow!"

I'd already decided to head crosstown while Trayn was playing his Thursday, Friday and Saturday rounds. It would be suicide to play only on Monday of every week, then be a spectator for the other six days. I needed to work on my iron play, and hiking around Randolph was good for neither my psyche nor my golf game. "I've got to hit the hills, Janice. I need to practice, and I'm afraid I can't do it here," I said.

"You're not *leaving!*" she said.

"Don't worry. I'll be right here if he survives until Sunday, which I know he will."

"This must be tough for you, huh?"

"No. It's not, really," I said, laughing. "I'm glad for Trayn. I just can't afford to take a four-day layoff every time *he* qualifies and *I* don't. That's all."

I don't know why I was surprised when her eyes filled with tears, but I was caught off guard. "I'm sorry," she said.

"I wish you wouldn't feel sorry for me. This is one tournament. I think there are some more down the road."

"Okay," she said. "See you tonight."

The fact was, I felt so sorry for myself that I didn't need any help from her or anybody else. My competitive drive had atrophied to where I could barely drag my clubs from the trunk when I arrived at the Mission Trail Country Club, a beautifully kept semi-private golf course at the foot of Mission Ridge. I explained my circumstances to a bald-headed club pro, who refused to take my green fee. "You're my guest," he said. "I tried the tour about twenty years ago," he told me. "Couldn't cut it. And you want to know what? I'm glad I didn't make it. But if that's what you want . . . then more power to you."

I dropped a couple of golf balls at the first tee, warmed up for a few minutes, then drove both balls down the fairway. This is so damned strange, I said to myself as I walked through the shade cast by date palms poised like Greek columns in the right-hand rough. I stood over the ball that was nudging the long grass. I told myself to roll into the ball, to keep the clubhead closed at the top of the follow-through. I fixed the position of the flag in my mind, took my swing and punched the ball beautifully onto the green, where it bit into the soft turf and spun backward toward the hole. What a simple game golf was.

As expected, Trayn played a spectacular brand of golf. He breezed through Friday's round as if there was nothing at stake, when actually there was everything to lose. Only the top half of the field could go on to Saturday's round, and Trayn was on the leader board all day Friday, where he remained until he double-bogeyed number seventeen on Saturday. Of course, I wasn't around to see the show, but I got a detailed play-by-play in the evenings, over beer and pizza, or beer and hoagies, or beer and beer. During one of these long and extravagant accounts, Janice was busying herself with a piece of needlework. Finally, she tossed it aside and said, "Can't we talk about something else? How about houses, or food, or something? Mountains? Could we talk about mountains? We're in Arizona. We haven't even seen any of it."

"Goddamnit, Janice. Go back to your knitting." Suddenly she threw it at him, yarn and all, then stormed into the bathroom. Trayn laughed so hard he spilled beer on the carpet. "Isn't she wonderful?" I tried to imagine what my mom would have done to Stan if he'd treated her the way Trayn had just treated Janice. He would have been selling his whole life policies from a wheel-chair.

On Sunday, Trayn was in one of the final groups because of his low score. We had time to kill, so we donned our swimsuits at nine in the morning and plunged into the frigid motel swimming pool. Afterward, Janice, wearing a yellow bikini, lay on the diving board to let the sun dry her off. I sat with Trayn on the edge of the pool with my feet submerged in the water.

"She's terrific, isn't she?" He puffed on a Winston and gazed at her in a peculiar way. He sounded as if he needed to be reassured that she really *was* terrific.

I couldn't help staring at her over there. If someone had asked me at that moment whether it was *because of* her or *in spite of* her that I was enduring all this humiliation, I probably would have lied. Trayn was lucky to have her. She had her problems, I was all too aware of that, but as the poet said, *we like because, and we love although.*

At eleven-thirty we arrived at the golf course. Trayn was his usual resplendent self: lucky red shirt, yellow slacks, black-and-white wing tips. He'd been using a professional caddy during the actual tournament, a young man who looked to be at least part Indian.

While Janice chatted with one of her new friends, I watched Tom Watson's group tee off. Only Gene Littler had a simpler swing than Watson's. He looked as if he could take a ten-year layoff, then come back to the game and slaughter par.

One hour later, when it was Trayn's turn to tee off, he pulled his shot behind a clump of oleanders. When he flung the driver angrily toward his caddy, an official immediately strolled over and whispered something to him. Trayn nodded his head.

"What was that all about?" asked Janice, who had joined me for the pilgrimage.

"He was a naughty boy," I said.

It was obvious from the way Trayn played the first hole that his concentration had collapsed. He was taking very little time with his shots, and the result of that impatience was inconsistency. He birdied the easy par-five sixth hole, but instead of riding that momentum, he knocked his next drive into a cactus wilderness from which there was no escape.

He rallied briefly on the back side, but cratered completely on number sixteen, when he hit an easy approach shot into the omnipresent drainage canal. From the drop zone, he flew a nine iron into a greenside bunker, blasted thirty feet past the hole and three-putted. Once again he threw his club toward the caddy; this time the wedge took a funny hop and bounced off the fellow's hip.

Trayn plodded up number eighteen fairway as if he were wearing leaded boots. Here was somebody who would earn five or six thousand dollars his first time out, yet he looked like a man who'd just had his pocket picked.

When he stepped wearily onto the last green, Janice clapped and cheered. I felt a little bit foolish doing it, but I joined in. Trayn gave us one of those tight-lipped smiles that suggest something like "What a damned day." He waited for one of his playing partners to hole out. Then he lined up his own ten-footer, set his putter blade behind the ball and pushed it two feet past the hole. He leaned on his club and shook his head.

But I knew he'd feel much better when he put his check in the bank.

Thirty-two

Moss Point, even with its twenty-seven azalea bushes in full bloom, isn't going to stack up well against Augusta National. However, Bobby Jones himself would be hard-pressed to build a better two-hole golf course using only the wiles of a blackmailing kleptomaniac Yugoslavian and the sweat of four complete novices. I can't bear to think that it will all disintegrate when I leave. I've even sworn Drago to the task of maintaining the links until my return in one year, at which time I intend to grade his performance, assuming the Fraunfelters have failed to relent.

In exchange for his oath ("On my grandmother's grave, boss!"), he wangles golf lessons. He wants to learn to play the game, although he has no clubs and nowhere to play but inside the gates of this prison. I think he just wants to please me, but I go along. "Okay, Drago," I tell him after supper on Friday night. "I'll try to teach you. But golf is a tough sport to learn."

"I'm a good learner," he says. "Look what I did out on the links." If he had a tail he'd be wagging it right now.

On a Saturday morning, one week before my release, we're standing at number one tee. On the ground in front of us are two hundred range balls, oranges, yellows, stripes and solid whites—multi-hued, hybrid mushrooms. Ames has liberated them from the trunk of my impounded car. With the varying temperatures they've withstood over the past year, they're probably defunct, deader than those cheap Orbit golf balls Stan used when we played our memorable round together.

Drago's stance is a thing to behold. His legs are stiff as drainpipes, and he's bent over at a ninety-degree angle. (I've asked him to get comfortable over the ball.) It's very hard for me to believe that only one week ago he watched another man play golf. "Bend your knees slightly," I say, "and keep your ass in."

"Like this, boss?" Now he's taking a crap, or looks like he is. I show him exactly how I want him to stand. He studies my posture very carefully and makes another crude attempt. He looks grotesque. Is this how Jimmy felt teaching those cotton-candy-haired ladies the rudiments of hitting a driver? "Your shoulders, Drago. You look like a nude in a hailstorm. Relax." Impossible. Rigor mortis.

I hand him a five iron and tell him to hit a few balls. He sends his first shot whizzing toward the basketball court. One of the Afro hoopsters curtsies and the ball trickles between his legs. The next one is alligator food. He flails angrily at the third one, misses it completely and comes amazingly close to falling down. "Swing easy. Easy does it." I toe one more ball into position for him. Miraculously, the thing flies perfectly straight, long and clean, down the middle of the fairway. His grin is like nothing I've ever seen before. "There you go, Drago," I say. "A piece of cake if you do it right." But this lovely specimen proves to be an anomaly. What follows is the entire spectrum of horrendous golf shots: quackers, chili dips, bloops, fungos, dribblers, whiffs, worm burners and shanks. "You're versatile, I'll say that for you," I tell him.

Out of all those golf balls, maybe five are on the fairway.

Many of them will never again be seen by mankind. But Drago is a good sport. He's as happy picking the balls up as he is hitting them. "I got a blister, boss. But it doesn't hurt me a bit."

"You're gripping the club too tight," I tell him.

"Oh," he says. "That's bad, isn't it?"

"Heap bad," I say.

I had a dream last night, possibly a nightmare; sometimes it's hard to tell. Drago was head greenskeeper of a magnificent eighteen-hole golf course, not unlike Pebble Beach, where I happened to be club pro. And of course Chapman and Grayson were among the faithful employees who currycombed the fairways and massaged the greens to perfection. I woke up at the point where Drago had speared Chapman with the butt end of a flag stick, its black-and-yellow-checkered pennant still attached. Where Grayson was during all this is uncertain, but he may well have wandered away in disgust. In the dream I fired them both on the spot, told them I never wanted to see them again, especially Drago, the aggressor.

In the morning I woke up feeling guilty. I didn't really want to be rid of him, like the nuisance relative who drops in for the rest of your life. In fact, Drago is a far better friend than any I've had before. I like him. His personality is totally knowable, which isn't to suggest that he's shallow, any more than the pond we dug, side by side, is shallow. The pond is actually twelve feet deep, but if the wind is calm you can see clear to the bottom.

Later in the morning, after I've diluted my guilt with some of the notorious Moss Point java, I feel better.

Because I received my biweekly note from Stan on Friday, I didn't even bother swinging by the mail room yesterday. So for lack of anything better to do, I wander over to 3-A to see if any pigeons have roosted in my mailbox during the weekend. I flick the dial according to the combination I've committed to memory and open the little door. I'm surprised to find a thick white envelope waiting for me. Janice would never stoop to a white envelope. Ginny might, however. To my surprise, the letter is from Trayn. My first impulse is to backhand it into the nearby wastebasket, but for some reason I carry it unopened to the golf course, the only private place to be found on a Sunday morning.

I tear open the envelope and discover my personal scorecard from the New Orleans Open. Of course, I had to surrender the *official* card at the scorer's tent. But here's an indelible record of my triumph over the Lakewood Country Club. This is a weird thing to receive in the mail, and I can't help wondering why Trayn would send it to me. I decide to read the enclosed letter to find out.

Dear Ted,

The people at the parole board told me you'll be getting out of the slam in a couple of weeks. I'm glad to hear that, I really am. I've worried about you and wondered how you're doing. Janice said you looked well, but that was six months ago. I want you to know that if I had the whole thing to do over again, I probably wouldn't have pressed charges. You gave me what I had coming. It was probably what you used to call quid pro quo.

I want you to know that my wheels are almost back to normal. I've been off crutches for a couple of months, and I spend an hour or two every day at physical therapy. But the doctors say I should be 100 percent in another six months. I plan to go back on the tour when I'm healthy. To tell you the absolute truth, I could play golf right now, but I'm not going to risk it. Don't want to develop bad habits while I'm on the disabled list.

As for Janice, I thought we might be able to patch things up. When I saw her last summer, she was willing to give it another shot. I think it's impossible to "start over." You can only pick up where you left off, and I'm afraid I'm not cut out to be married. Not right now anyway. Probably I'm too committed to golf to share my time with anybody, whether I love that person or not. And I did love Janice.

Well, pal, I hope to see you out on the links someday. Wouldn't it be great if we wound up in a sudden-death play-off for a humongous prize.

Hell, we could play for Janice. Take care of yourself, Teddy boy. Good luck.

TRAYN

P.S. Thought you might like to have your scoreboard from N.O. You left it in our room on the night of the mishap. So I enclosed it.

Did Janice really ask him for another try at married life? Or did he make that up just to drive me crazy? I'm determined to believe that Janice told him to go straight to hell. But who knows . . .

What a poor smug son of a bitch Trayn is. I really do feel sorry for him. I have no desire to see him again, let alone play golf with him. He'd recontaminate a game whose geometry and beauty have only recently come back to me. And while Drago is a little bit wilder off the tee than my old golfing buddy, when it comes time to share a beer at the nineteenth hole, give me the Yugoslavian hands down. I almost savor the image of Drago looping balls into the swamp, laughing in a good-natured way at his incompetence, then repeating it . . . Anyway, I've decided to buy him a decent set of golf clubs before I leave this place. Moss Point should be played, and it should be played with reckless abandon by Drago himself.

Thirty-three

Life after golf. I was considering that possibility as I drove past Picacho Peak, sixty miles shy of Phoenix, at twilight on Sunday. While my car droned beautifully down the highway, I imagined myself at age thirty, seated next to Ken Venturi in the TV tower overlooking number eighteen at Augusta, and Trayn down below, lining up a tricky eight-footer on the slick bent-grass green.

"Well, Teddy, you played college golf with Dave Traynham at Ohio State. Didn't you even room with him at one point? Tell us what he's really like."

"Sure, Ken. Trayn and I go way back. In fact, I had sexual intercourse with his wife on a golf course in Columbus. Nice girl. Very nice girl. If you want to know about Trayn, though, well . . . what can I say. He's got that magic, hasn't he?"

A luminous haze hung over Phoenix, where in a matter of a few minutes we'd check into another motel, maybe pick up some carry-out Chinese food (we'd somehow overlooked the Orient in our culinary trip around the world) and eat it with plastic forks while we watched Trapper John, M.D. Then we'd hit the hay. Trayn would sleep like a hound and I would roll around for about six hours. Then off to the links.

Shortly after paying for our rooms at the Granada Court Motel, we tracked down a very economical Greek eatery in the University District. With only one exception, we habitually brought food back to our motel at night or had another human being deliver it to our door. I was surprised when Trayn suggested he buy us all dinner at the Kritikos Restaurant, where we indulged the lonely waiter's penchant for idle conversation. I'd almost forgotten how pleasant it was to eat at a table set with glass and stainless steel and linen.

Trayn did his G. Gordon Liddy imitation with the candle in the middle of the table while we waited for our salads to arrive. Janice and I were playing Name That Tune. She was too young to remember "It's My Party" by Leslie Gore. And technically I was too, except that I'd heard it on the radio as I was coming through El Paso a week earlier.

"Gosh," she said. "Isn't it nice to talk about something other than golf?"

"Speaking of golf . . . ," Trayn began, at which point Janice, with her hands pressed tight over her ears, shook her head slowly from side to side.

"*Please*, Trayn," she said.

"You're the one who brought it up."

"No, I wasn't."

"You decide, Teddy. Did I bring it up, or did she?"

I told them I was starved.

"Let me just tell Teddy one thing, okay, honey? And then we can talk about herpes or Tibet or Tupperware." Janice glared across the table at him. He leaned toward me, and in a conspiratorial tone said he'd phoned the Rio Verde Country Club that afternoon, before we'd left Tucson. "Looks like there will be *fifteen* openings tomorrow. That's more like it, wouldn't you say?"

Janice was stabbing her fork into the moussaka. "Thanks for ruining the first enjoyable night of this entire trip."

"Maybe you'd like to go back to Cincinnati and live with your folks," he said.

For a solid week I'd tried to shrug off their constant sniping, but I'd finally arrived at the end point. I stood up and said, "I've had it with this crap." I wadded my napkin and flung it onto my still full plate. "From now on, I'm traveling alone," I shouted. Janice gently laid her fork on the edge of the plate. Trayn glared at her over the waning candle flame. This was the perfect moment for me to do my dramatic exit, but like a character in a bad play, I just had to get in my parting shot. "You should both be ashamed of yourselves!" I said, before stalking out of the restaurant. I stood on the front sidewalk for a few minutes, half expecting one or the other of them to race out after me. It was good knowing that from then on I wouldn't have to referee their private wars.

Pennants in front of a used-car dealership waved in the dry evening breeze. I walked another mile or so to the college campus, where I sat under a tree in front of the library for a while. I felt much older than the students who entered and exited the enormous Mediterranean-style building. How nice it would have been if Ginny had stepped out of the library at that moment. I almost wished I could try OSU again without golf and everything that went with it.

I took a quick shower when I got to my room, and after setting the travel alarm for 5:45, crawled into bed. Exhausted from a week of disappointment, I was melting into unconsciousness when I heard them open and close the door of 123. The lovebirds knocked wordlessly about the room for fifteen or twenty minutes before it began. "I won't do it, Trayn," Janice screamed. "I *refuse* to do that." By sandwiching my head between pillows I hoped to obliterate the details of their argument. But that proved impossible.

"Like hell you won't."

"What do you think I *am?*"

"You're a little *bitch.*" That was when I heard what sounded like a slap. That was good. I was glad she'd let him have it. I sat up in bed and listened for a few minutes. Nothing. Then she was sobbing. It was muffled, but I knew she was. Or maybe in my exhausted state I'd imagined the whole thing. Whatever it was, it was over now, and anyway, there was nothing I could do. I lay back on my pillow and stared into the darkness. I think I'd been asleep for a minute or so when I was awakened by the knocking of their headboard against the wall. There was a period of silence, followed by another sound filtering through the plasterboard, a faraway sound like wind blowing through tree branches. Then Trayn's voice, and then the sound again. Was she crying? I tried to believe that she wasn't.

Trayn was alone in the parking lot when I stepped out of my room at six-fifteen on Monday morning. "Well, Teddy, what say we do some damage today?" he said, but his joviality seemed strained. His eyes were focused on something over my shoulder, maybe a line of early traffic stalled at a light down the block. "Janice is sleeping in this morning," he said. "She said she'd come out to the course a little bit later."

"Oh," I said, "Is she okay?"

"She's fine," he said. "Listen, about last night . . ."

"You meant at the *restaurant,*" I said, hoping he would read the emphasis as knowledge of what may or may not have happened in their room that night.

He gave me a funny look, as if he didn't have the faintest idea of what I was talking about. "Of course."

"Well . . . what?"

"I want to apologize. We don't want to chase you away. Would you reconsider your plan to part company?"

"I don't think so. The whole thing is dragging me down right now. I don't need it."

"Teddy, I promise things will straighten out. We haven't gotten untracked yet, that's all."

"Let me think about it. That's all I can say."

Trayn threw his clubs and golf shoes into the back of my car, and we drove westward toward Rio Verde. I was telling him about the time Bobby Jones had hit an approach shot into an anomalous shoe abandoned in a sand-filled wheelbarrow during the Masters. (There were other versions of the story, but I liked this one.)

"What the hell did he do. Did he get a free drop?" Trayn asked.

"Nah," I said. He took a wedge and knocked ball and shoe onto the green. The ball popped out and rolled to within a few feet of the cup. Pretty amazing, huh?"

Once we'd registered and paid our fees, we decided to explore the course before the first group teed off. We'd been lucky enough to draw midmorning starting times, which gave us an opportunity to pace off distances and note the peculiarities of this beautifully manicured layout. The fairways were well watered, but very closely cropped. In other words, they were superb. Trayn poked a tee into the putting surface at number one. "These buggers are soft. We can go right at the hole. Hot damn!" An ominous bone-shaped lake would come into play on both number seven and the adjacent number sixteen, a par three. I hoped the trace of wind now ruffling the pond's surface would pick up. For years, I'd been playing windblown Ohio courses, which would give me a big advantage if things got breezy later on.

We still needed to hire somebody to carry our clubs up and down the fairways for a few hours, so we headed for the caddy shack, which wasn't a shack at all, but an isolated wing of the clubhouse. It smelled of shoe polish, linseed oil, grass, sweat or spilled Coca-Cola, depending on where we were standing. The caddy master was a bald-headed guy with a few missing fingers. He took intermittent swigs from a bottle of Dr Pepper. On his desk was a half-eaten dill pickle wrapped in waxed paper. "Nice breakfast," Trayn whispered.

"Excuse me," I said. "We need caddies for the qualifier." The man's eyes barely moved from the sports section of the paper. Without answering me, he picked up a swatter and nonchalantly nailed a fly that had come too close to his pickle. He slowly removed a clipboard from a nail driven into the pine paneling. "Vonsell, Quonsey, Ira, Tuffy, Lawrence, Bobby . . . take your pick. They're yonder." He tilted his bald head toward the long green bench in front of a row of lockers. Prone on the bench was one white-clad black man with a towel spread over his face. I could hear him snoring under there. "That one's Lawrence. I don't know where the other ones is. Check out front."

"Go ahead, you take that one," Trayn said. "I'll look outside."

I wished I could carry my own clubs. But the PGA frowned on that sort of thing. When I tapped the sole of the sleeping man's shoe, he bolted upright, his towel falling onto the floor. Lawrence rolled his eyes wildly, as if he were looking for some reference point. He finally fixed his gaze on me, smiled and made a sound like a hissing radiator cap.

I shook hands with him. "I'm Ted Kendall. I guess you're going to caddy for me this morning." Lawrence seemed to study the look on my face.

"He can't *talk* neither," the caddy master shouted. "Deaf and dumb."

I backed politely toward the desk. "Why in the hell didn't you tell me that?" I said without moving my lips.

" 'Cause he's the best damned caddy we got. You want another'n, I'll get you one . . ." The man was fingering the clipboard again.

"He's really that good?" I asked.

"Take him out to the driving range and show him what you can do. After that, you can decide if he's going to work out."

Lawrence had obviously been through this before. He was once again asleep on the bench, this time with legs right-angled so his feet were flat on the cork floor. I tapped his leg, and he was on his feet, quick as a cat, thrusting his leathery hand into mine. He then slapped his thigh and moved his hand in a high arc, like he was signaling first down and ten to go.

"Let's get the clubs," I said, and led the way to the parking lot.

I fished my keys from the top of the right front tire. No sooner had I done so than Lawrence took them from me and opened the trunk. This was *his* responsibility, not mine. He leaned my clubs gently against the rear fender, carefully so as not to scratch the yellow finish. He then removed the shoe trees from my new white spikes and handed the shoes to me. There was something about the way he handled the various little tasks that inspired confidence. If nothing else, the day's round of golf was bound to be interesting.

There were several golfers hitting shag balls at the range. The caddies sat on the heels of the golf bags, smoking cigarettes and watching. Garth Bailey, the runner-up to Gary Triplett in the NCAA tournament two years in a row, was hitting from the slot nearest the clubhouse. Like Trayn, Bailey had been on Friday's leader board at Tucson, but his wheels had come off on Saturday. He was at the very bottom of the money list by Sunday afternoon. His swing looked extremely rigid, as if he were at gunpoint.

Lawrence placed my bag at one of the empty docks, between two players I didn't know. Neither of them had been at Palm Beach with Trayn and me. My caddy thrust a wedge in my hands before I could ask for it. One of the golf balls from the pool of shags appeared miraculously at my feet. He held up five fingers of his left hand and made a long sweeping gesture with his right, guiding his palm out over the range. (What did this mean?)

Some of the golfers stopped their practicing to watch Lawrence and me play charades. I felt a little foolish flapping my arms, making loops with my index finger, squinting at Lawrence . . . sometimes I just shrugged in confusion. When my last wood shot caromed off the two-fifty post, he patted me on the back and gave me a thumbs-up. He pointed to the spot on his wrist where a watch would have been, had he owned one, and held up nine fingers. Time to get in some last-minute putting practice before tee-off.

I ran into Trayn a while later, as I was walking with my two playing partners toward the first tee. "He's what?"

"You know, deaf . . . and dumb."

"God, Teddy. What are you going to do?"

"Shoot about a sixty-five," I told him.

I was paired with Bailey and a human stump named Wrightson. For once, I'd won the coin flip, which meant I was entitled to hit first. I decided to tee my ball up slightly to take advantage of the freshening tail wind. Lawrence smiled in such a way that I knew he approved. My Titleist was programmed to sail well out onto the fairway, beyond the threatening trap, onto a plateau one hundred twenty yards from the flag. There was no doubt in my mind. A few blades of grass clung to the face of my driver. Without my asking for one, a towel appeared, courtesy of my caddy. I wiped down the clubhead and tossed the towel back to Lawrence.

My swing felt easy and symmetrical. The shaft of my club made a whistling sound as it accelerated downward toward the ball, which, when I made contact, exploded off the face of the driver and climbed high above a hedgerow of ligustrum. At the tail end of its fight the ball curled perfectly toward the center of the fairway, where it landed softly on the turf. There wasn't much of a gallery, just a few tournament officials and some rabbits. But they applauded my shot. Kendall's Caravan.

At the clubhouse turn I knew without a doubt that I would qualify. I'd birdied both the par fives on the front side and had managed to snake in a thirty-foot putt for a deuce on the ninth hole, a par three.

It's easy to love a golf course that loves you back. I was walking through the dappled sunlight of number thirteen fairway. Lawrence's shadow and mine were side by side, his slightly taller and wider. I liked the sound of the clubs knocking together with every step we took. I could close my eyes and count the clicks from the tee box to my ball. Three hundred clicks equaled two hundred and fifty yards. I could close my eyes and let the sound guide me down the fairway. That was very relaxing. By the time I got to my ball I was feeling loose and confident. It was only a matter of following the invisible diagram imprinted deep in the brain, hearing the rhythm of the swing. In the specific sense golf was like a strange sort of dance.

All day I'd barely considered the notion of competition. I was in love with the game, and I was inside it so deeply that keeping score was nothing more than a periodic interruption. Lawrence would hold up however many fingers, and I would write that number down, and then I would record Bailey's score beneath mine. My hands were getting tan; I noticed that when I wrote the numbers down. And I read the name of the pencil manufacturer printed in silver on the yellow paint: PARCO.

On the green, I could squat behind my ball, touch the grass to determine the flow of the grain, plumb-bob the surface to determine the topography, then lean over my ball, oblivious to everything but the subtle geometry that would guide my putt.

The seventeenth hole presented the first problem of the day. My drive had fallen into a boggy swale that would surely be chalked off for the tournament on Thursday. But somehow it had been overlooked. And there was my ball, with mud bearded onto its lower half, the portion I intended to hit. Water seeped up through the grass beneath my feet. When I hit the shot, mud splattered onto my khakis and my shoe tops while the ball scuttled onto the steep slope short of the green. I wasn't bothered. I knew absolutely that I would pitch the ball to within a few feet of the hole, can the putt and salvage par.

At eighteen I was standing over a fifty-foot putt. I smelled my caddy's warm liquor breath as he leaned in to help me read it. He rubbed his hands over the grass to feel its texture and dampness. It was late morning and all the surface moisture had evaporated. The ball would climb one slope to gain momentum for a quick roll through the basin, followed by a slightly slower trek up the opposing rise to the cup. Lawrence punched the air between us and the flag. He wanted me to hit the putt boldly.

I could feel blood pulsing in my fingertips. If I birdied the hole I would probably be the low qualifier, ahead of Trayn, ahead of Bailey and everybody else. I could call Stan on the phone and tell him the news. Maybe I could wind up making some money. Lawrence nodded toward the hole. *Don't wait over it,* he was saying, almost as if he could talk. I anchored my white shoes exactly so. My weight was shifted onto my left foot and I was solid as stone.

He was up there, Lawrence was, with the red flag gathered in his hand. It was then that I made my stroke. A shiver ran up my arms and into my brain. I could read the print on the ball as it moved with the rise and fall of the green, arcing slightly toward the hole and stuttering at the rim. At last it fell, like a slow-motion boulder falls, into the cup.

My putter flew out of my hands. I was dancing across the green, high-fiving Lawrence, whooping like a lunatic bird.

We had to wait on Bailey to sink his tap-in for a useless 74, but he smiled when it was over and patted me on the back. "Nice going," he said. I watched him walk toward the clubhouse with his caddy. He wasn't going to make the cut. But I let myself be happy in spite of his bad luck. My own fortunes were changing. The ball was finally rolling right.

I was feeling jubilant on Monday night, not only because I'd qualified for the Phoenix Open but also because I'd outscored Trayn by two strokes. Even before I made my call to Stan from a pay phone in Scottsdale, I'd contacted the tournament officials at Rio Verde to find out what had happened to him. For his sake, and especially for Janice's, it was fortunate that he'd qualified, too, but my own psyche was lifted by the news that I was the top scorer.

Stan was in rare form when I talked with him. (Did I actually hear him relaying information to Sally?) "Son, that's wonderful news. Just great. I'll call Jimmy tonight and let him know."

"How is he?" I asked. "Still making progress?"

"I think the cold weather's got him down, Teddy. Damned if we didn't get seven more inches of snow last night. I couldn't even start the car this morning."

"It'll be spring before you know it," I said.

"That's right, Teddy. By the way, somebody named Ginny called here the other day. Isn't that the girl from school? Anyway, she wanted to know how to get in touch with you."

"If she calls again, tell her I'll be in New Orleans in a couple weeks. I don't know where I'll be staying, but she can call the Lakewood Country Club on that Monday. They'll have the information."

Stan wanted to put the receiver to Sally's ear so I could say a word or two, but I said I wouldn't cooperate. "I guess that *is* a little silly, isn't it?"

I told him to take care, then waited while he ticked off five or ten synonyms for proud and happy.

Here I was, in one of the most beautiful parts of the country, and I'd barely strayed off the narrow pike connecting my motel to the golf course. That Tuesday afternoon I was in Scottsdale, window-shopping on Pima Drive, when I bumped into Jerry Pate and his wife. He'd won the Open a few years before, but everybody remembered him for diving fully clothed into an alligator-infested pond after winning the Tournament Players Championship in Florida. He noticed me staring at him, but instead of telling me to get lost, he jokingly asked if I wouldn't mind purchasing a $10,000 ranch mink for his wife.

"Sure," I said. "No problem."

They both smiled at me, then walked hand in hand down the block. What a nice life. Jet into town on a Tuesday, take in the sights, buy a few trinkets to please the family, play a few days of golf, win thousands of dollars . . . I was sure I could get accustomed to that mode of existence.

My mind was made up. I'd steer clear of Janice and Trayn for the next couple of days so I could purify my system.

At ten o'clock that night there was a frosted mug of Coors in front of me. The jukebox at the Wagon Wheel Saloon was playing unbroken Waylon Jennings. By eleven-thirty I had drunk at least seven or eight beers. I was just drunk enough to make a decision. I'd get up early and drive all the way to Grand Canyon and back.

I cruised the motel parking lot every ten minutes until the light went out in Trayn's room. When his window was dark, I pulled into a parking space and quietly unlocked my door. Without removing my clothes, I flopped onto the mattress, punched the pillow a few times and went almost immediately to sleep.

The drive from Phoenix to Flagstaff was exhilarating. I rolled the windows down so I could feel the temperature change that accompanied my abandonment of the desert for the next ecological stratum. Saguaro gave way to scrub juniper, which grew denser and healthier as I drove northward. At Rimrock, the jack pines took over. I could see them crawling up the distant mountain peaks. At a certain altitude, the soft green of the jack pines was replaced by the veinlike limbs of leafless aspen and birch. When I finally entered the high mountains just south of Flagstaff, the gigantic dark green Douglas firs took over. Their brown trunks emerged from a dense sheet of snow. I couldn't help wishing Stan were with me. His idea of a vacation was a quick jaunt to Traverse City to see the remnants of his family. I was feeling so guilty at one point that I stopped at a Navajo Indian trading post and bought him a beautifully tooled leather wallet.

At noon I picked up U.S. 40 in Flagstaff and jogged west for another thirty ecstatic miles until I came to the Grand Canyon turnoff. Twice it was necessary to pull onto the roadside to let the Pacer cool down. My hands were shaking as I followed the signs to Yavapai Point.

Because it was February, there weren't nearly as many tourists as I'd expected. I parked between a Winnebago and a VW camper in a huge lot four or five hundred yards from the rim of the canyon. (Did I actually believe that a V-neck sweater was going to keep me warm on a freezing-cold day when the wind was blowing forty miles per hour?) I followed the pine-needle path through a stand of fir trees to where it elbowed around an outcropping of bare granite, and suddenly ended at a broad overlook poised on the threshold of a vista so astonishingly unexpected that I was almost afraid. I tentatively approached the green-painted chest-high fence and leaned against it. Clouds skirted the northern rim, miles in the distance. Their shadows swam back and forth against the variegations of the canyon wall, painting and repainting them with dappled sunlight. Although I didn't know why it was happening, I felt on the brink of crying. I didn't feel sad, exactly, nor was I thinking of the canyon so much, how beautiful it was; instead, I was thinking of Stan back with his dog in Ohio, and Ginny, plodding through her graduate courses, and of course Janice, who would probably never get a chance to see what I was seeing.

By nine o'clock that night I was back in my room, eating a submarine sandwich I'd picked up at a roadside place just outside of New River. Just then I heard a soft knock on my door. It was Janice, who looked quite pretty in the sidelighting cast by the table lamp. She gave me a wistful smile. "We missed you today," she said. "Were you out golfing somewhere?"

"To tell you the truth, I drove up to Grand Canyon. Five hundred miles round trip. Fairly crazy, huh?" I took a sip of Coke from a paper cup.

"You did? Wow." The expression on her face was a strange one, a cross between jealousy and admiration. "I wish I'd known," she said.

"Why, were you worried?."

"No. I would have gone with you."

"How would Trayn feel about that?"

"Who knows. Probably glad to get rid of me." I saw her lower lip begin to quiver, but for once she seemed determined not to cry.

I told her I doubted that.

"Do you?" I didn't have an appropriate answer to a question so obviously rhetorical, so I took another bite from my sandwich. "Well, I'm glad you had a good time," she said. "I guess I'll say good night, then." Was she waiting for me to ask her not to?

It sounded that way to me. Reluctantly, I opened the door for her. "Bye," she said.

Obviously she'd wanted to talk about something . . . and I purposely hadn't given her the chance. In the wake of her visit, I was washed over by a wave of depression. How was it possible for me to experience such total happiness and such utter misery within the confines of one day? I certainly couldn't figure out how. I went to bed feeling equally sorry for her and for myself. I decided to skip the Pro-Am on Wednesday, in favor of a couple of practice rounds at the Papago Municipal Golf Course. If Trayn hadn't decided to play in the preliminary event, I might have chosen to participate myself, since doing so would give me a chance to acclimate to playing with the likes of Trevino and Strange and Pate. But I was in a mood to go my own way, so I practiced alone in the hot sun on a public course ten miles from the motel.

Trayn wasn't scheduled to begin his Thursday round until one-thirty in the afternoon, while I was to tee off at eight-forty with Chip Beck and Bobby Clampett, who as an amateur had once been reprimanded by the USGA for playing a fairway wedge shot from his knees in the Open championship.

Lawrence was waiting for me at the parking lot shortly after seven o'clock. He refused my offer of a doughnut, although I'd purposely bought a few extra on the way to the course. About that time, Greg Norman's Mercedes glided into the parking space adjacent to mine. He nodded in my direction and said, "Hello, mate, how're you doing?" in a perfect tie-me-kangaroo-down Australian accent. "Don't believe we've met."

I shook hands with him and told him my name. He seemed to be searching a mental roster for some particular, something that would ring a bell. "I'm pleased to meet you," I said.

We'd just rounded the clubhouse when my nerves got me. I made a gesture that in any other circumstance would be regarded as obscene, then dashed into the player's locker room, where there was a row of urinals, none of which was in use.

However, Hale Irwin, clad only in his jockey shorts, was standing in front of a locker, while Andy Bean was wearing his trousers but was minus a shirt. God, this is weird, I said to myself. I hurried to finish before the Golden Bear himself decided to use the facilities.

The atmosphere of a professional tournament is completely different from a Monday qualifier. A rabbit like me could sense immediately that there was an easygoing clubbishness among the PGA regulars. Success for most of them was a matter of degree, rather than the all-or-nothing situation that confronted a non-exempt player.

It was precisely in the middle of my follow-through on the fifty-third practice shot on the driving range that my nerves began to settle. To my right was Ben Crenshaw, his eyebrows bleached white from countless hours striding up and down the nation's fairways. And to my left, although we were separated by one empty slot, was Jerry Pate. I'd calmed down to the point where I asked if he remembered me from Scottsdale. He wondered if I was the guy who had stolen his wife's purse, and then started laughing so hard at that little nugget of humor that he had to walk away from the practice balls for a minute to compose himself. These were my pals, Ben and Jerry. I was a pro golfer, after all, about to launch into the world of low scores and big dollars.

Then I saw him. I hadn't even realized he was entered in the tournament, and then I remembered reading somewhere that this year Jack Nicklaus intended to play in five or six events before the Masters. His son was carrying the clubs toward the driving range, and Jack was making some hand gestures that rivaled anything Lawrence had come up with so far. Once, when I was a little kid, Neil Armstrong had come to Bowling Green for some event, the nature of which was, at my tender age, a mystery. During the weeks before his arrival, I had meticulously crafted a paper replica of an Apollo spaceship, which Stan insisted would be of untold value in future years if I could only get Commander Armstrong to autograph it after his address to the citizens of Bowling Green. At the conclusion of his speech concerning the future of space travel, I lined up on the courthouse steps with hundreds of other autograph seekers, but when I was within a few feet of him, I lost my courage and dashed back to Stan, who was very disappointed in me. I had the same mixture of awe and admiration now, as this legendary figure, who had unknowingly guided me onto the path that led to Phoenix, strode toward the vacant practice slot next to mine. This time there was no Stan for me to run to, only Lawrence, who had snapped to attention like a member of the King's Guard. Anyway, Jack Nicklaus smiled when he saw that I was nervous. "How are you?" he asked. He probably guessed that if I couldn't answer that one, I was hopeless. He patiently waited out my stammering reply, and laughed when I called him *Mr. Nicklaus*. Probably he was used to people falling apart that way. I finally managed to tell him my name and say that I was very pleased to meet him. "Where are you from?" he asked.

"Well, I played college golf at Ohio State."

"Oh, come on!" he said. "Did you really? What was your name again?"

"You wouldn't have heard of me," I said. "I was extremely underrated."

"When do you tee off?" he asked. I told him eight-forty, and he scowled at me. "Don't slow me up. I'll be right on your tail." Then he had one last hearty laugh before wandering over to chat with Pate and Crenshaw. Every so often I found myself watching the way he went about his practicing. He was actually aiming his practice shots at an imaginary target no bigger than a pancake. Whenever his ball didn't land precisely where he intended it to, he would pause to examine his grip for any subtle flaw.

To grace the subsequent hours of misery with even a brief summary would be a crime. Suffice it to say that Jack Nicklaus, who was never more than three hundred yards behind me, and sometimes as close as five feet, witnessed one of the worst days of my golfing career. On the second hole, I plugged my seven-iron approach shot into the nearly vertical bank of an enormous greenside bunker, right below its grassy lip. Only a shovel could extricate me from my predicament. With Nicklaus watching me from the fairway, I slashed at the ball, heaving a great wet glob of sand skyward. The object of my assault dribbled meekly into the basin of the trap. My forehead began to sweat, as it always did when I was in dire trouble on the links. But I was only lying three. A nice blast shot would get me close enough to salvage a bogey. Instead, when I swung again the flange of my sand wedge bounced three inches behind the ball, caught the thing at its equator and coughed it halfway up the wall of the trap, where it hesitated, then rolled backward into the divot I had just created. My next attempt was a burning line drive that scattered the gallery clustered around the green, waiting in anticipation of the Golden Bear. I heard them groan sympathetically for the young pro from Bowling Green who was making a shambles of the beautiful game of golf, and incidentally delaying the arrival of Jack Nicklaus by a good ten minutes.

In golf talk, an eight is called a snowman. I carded a very fat snowman while my childhood hero looked on. After that there was no saving myself. Although Beck and Clampett were extremely sympathetic ("Don't worry about it, Ted. It happens to all of us"), it was a humiliating trek up the eighteenth fairway, with the throng gathered there. I amused them with a three-putt green on the last hole. My total was 79, which meant that even if I bettered the course record by ten strokes on Friday, I'd miss the cut.

I raced off the golf course after that, drove to my country-and-western bar and got ferociously drunk. In my stupefied state, I wandered the Arizona State University campus for a few hours, until darkness and dull sobriety drove me to a dollar cinema a few blocks away, where I paid to see two showings of *Key Largo*. At midnight, I returned to my motel, collapsed onto my bed and went to sleep.

The next morning, Trayn banged on my door at about seven o'clock. I wondered what I must look like, dressed in wrinkled brown tones, my hair undoubtedly crested from the pillow. "Hey, pal. Are you sick?"

"No," I said. "I'm going for a new look. What do you think?"

"I guess you had one of those days yesterday."

"You might say that."

"Well, you're initiated now. It can only get better."

Trayn talked me out of withdrawing from the tournament, and waited in my room while I showered and got on some fresh clothes. I wasn't surprised in the least when he told me he'd shot 68 on Thursday, a mere eleven strokes better than yours truly. I was lacing up my shoes when he asked me if I'd thought about hanging in there with him and Janice. "Well," I said, "I'm not going to make this cut, so I guess I'll try to get to Houston by Sunday so I can play in the qualifier. At least there's that small advantage to screwing up here."

"That's right," he said.

"So I guess I'll meet you at the Houston Open. Who knows, maybe I'll qualify again. Even if I don't, I'll meet you there at the eighteenth hole on Thursday afternoon at four o'clock."

"That sounds great," he said. "It's right on the way to New Orleans, anyway."

Then I informed him of the decision I'd arrived at sometime between the two showings of *Key Largo* the night before. "After New Orleans I'm quitting the tour. I'm in over my head."

"You're crazy," Trayn shouted. "Two damned tournaments and you decide that you're over your fucking head?"

"That's not my only reason, but it's the main one."

"What if you win a big chunk of change at Houston or New Orleans?"

"Then I'll play forever," I said.

Janice came out of the motel room to see us off. She was wearing pink sunglasses and a pastel blue terry-cloth visor. "You guys bring home the bacon, okay?" she said, her elbows resting on the frame of my opened car window. While Trayn was fiddling with the cigarette lighter, she brushed my cheek with her fingertips.

Thirty-four

It's almost always on Sundays that inmates are released. I don't know why. Tuesdays are just as good as Sundays. But tomorrow I'll climb into my yellow Pacer and retrace part of the route that Stan and I followed at Christmas. During the final round of the Masters golf championship, while Jack Nicklaus is shuffling through Augusta's fairways, I'll be driving through Grayson's ramshackle town, through Diamondhead and D'Iberville and Escatawpa . . . all the way to Mobile, then north on I-65 into that part of the country where the soil is red instead of black.

Before the sun goes down, I want to make one last tour of Moss Point's queer little golf course so I can etch its contours onto my brain, freeze its colors there forever. After supper, with my Schenectady putter as a walking stick, I wander out toward the chain link fence and discover that doves have once again taken over the top strand of barbed wire. If I were Grayson I'd sneak close enough to snatch one off the fence, then spook them into a frenzy. Instead, I just stand on number one fairway and watch the way the sun plays on their feathers.

The sod at the rear downslope of this green has knit so perfectly that the seams are no longer visible. I stand on the brink of the deepest of the four traps on the course, then jump in. My feet leave prints I don't intend to rake. They'll just have to stay there until wind or rain or, more likely, Drago erases them. When I sit down in the soft sand of the bunker, my entire body is shaded by the steep wall, which feels cool against my back. It's pleasant sitting here this way, with only my shoes in sunlight.

Out on the highway, a gawker almost swerves her station wagon into the swamp. She's seen yours truly, a corpse possibly, another victim of a prison murder just like the one she's read about in the *Daily Herald Tribune Gazette*. Her brake lights gleam in the corner of my eye. She's at a dead standstill now. When the corpse comes to life, leaps from the sand trap and hotfoots it toward the fence, wheeling the putter over his head like a martial-arts lunatic, she peels away. It's fun being a prisoner with one day left to serve.

I walk the length of number two fairway to the pond, which has recently been invaded by the first of what will soon be an army of water hyacinths with their lavender plumes. I hope Drago has the good sense to leave them alone. The cattails he's transplanted from the swamp aren't going to make it, I'm afraid.

There's only one Titleist in my pocket, and after removing the flag stick from the hole at number one green, I place this gleaming orb at the fringe, thirty feet away from my target. I plant my shoes just so, weight squarely on the balls of my feet. My firm putt skitters past a sere leaf, curls down the incline of a small swale and rims the cup. I've misread the break. Do I hear a groan rising from the gallery? I give them an Arnold Palmer grimace and backhand my short putt. Applause. I tip an imaginary hat in their direction. Jimmy waves to me from the crowd and I wave back.

For thirteen months I've thought of Moss Point's golf course this way, a 3-D movie set, almost too vivid to compete with reality. But at the eleventh hour, Moss Point is part of me.

The mosquitoes are coming out of the swamp now, and they want blood, my blood. Insect vampires that rule the links by night. I'm almost ready to head back to my room when a curious thing happens. Two mallards, a male and a female, glide in from the west, straight up Highway 447, like they've just flown in from New Orleans. They bank over the barbed-wire fence and backflap just above the pond, settling softly on the water. The neck of the male is iridescent green. The female scolds him away from the hyacinths, as if that's her private garden, and they quack back and forth for at least a couple of minutes. I think they've decided to spend the night on our pond.

I run to fetch Drago from his room. "Let's go," I tell him. "You've got to see this." We hurry back to the pond, where the ducks, swimming as a pair, create two luminous V-shaped wakes. "If you feed them, they might stay."

"I got a cupcake in my room," he says.

"A cupcake will do just fine. Go get it," I tell him. He runs hunched over, like an Indian, toward the quadrangle.

At seven-thirty on Sunday morning, my car is idling just inside the prison gates. The engine knocks so terribly that I wonder if all the oil has leaked out of the crankcase. I load the last of my belongings into the trunk, with the exception of my golf clubs. Drago is sitting on the hub of my bag with his chin in his palms. "Hey . . . ," I tell him. "I've got something for you. Come on."

I put my arm around his shoulder and we walk together to the office building. Ames is pouring himself a cup of coffee when I open the door. "I guess you're free as a bird, today, eh, Kendall?" Ames says. "Want a cup of coffee for the road?"

"Well, actually, I just stopped in to say goodbye. Incidentally, you've got something that belongs to Drago here, haven't you?"

"Oh, right," he says. "I sure do." He fumbles inside a closet for a minute and produces a golf bag filled with woods and irons. "Here you go."

"You buy these for me, boss?" Drago asks.

"They're your payment for all that work on the links. Works out to about three cents per hour."

"They're really beautiful," he says, touching the blades. "Really beautiful. I got something for you, too," he tells me, pulling some wads of tissue and a bottle cap and a few coins from his pocket. Finally, he fishes out Grayson's arrowhead, the one Chapman was presumably going to keep as a momento of Moss Point.

"Did you filch that from Chapman?" I ask.

He gets a hurt look on his face. "Chapman *gave* it to me, last thing before he left." Somehow, I believe he's telling the truth.

I shake his hand and thank him as profusely as I know how until I've erased the accusation of theft. "I think it's time," I say.

The three of us walk to the car, which is running more quietly now, and load my sticks in the trunk. "Well . . . goodbye," I say, and slide in behind the wheel. I roll the window down to let some fresh air into the musty interior. "I'll be back in one year to pick you up," I shout above the clank of the engine.

Drago, with his new golf clubs slung over his shoulder, nods and waves goodbye.

Thirty-five

Ken Venturi told the folks out there in TV-land that Trayn had a swing like pure poetry. Here was a rookie you could bank on, a superstar burning on the horizon. Already, Trayn's car trunk overflowed with neon shirts and color-coordinated slacks; his bank account was fat and getting fatter; he was on a first-name basis with Watson and Strange and Trevino and Kite. And he'd tied for third place in the Phoenix Open.

While he was winking into cameras and flirting with potential groupies, I was getting washed under by numbers: too many bogeys, too little money in the bank, too many miles from where I belonged. By the time the New Orleans Open rolled around I had about two-thirds of my mom's inheritance left. By eating Campbell's beans and traveling light, I could probably make it through the entire year; but after that I was destined to limp home to teach geriatrics the glories of the pitching wedge.

I was lying in my Gretna, Louisiana, motel room with a sliver of light coming through a crack in the curtains. On the other side of the wall, Trayn and Janice were in bed together. I was calculating the cost of my devotion to the wrong woman at the wrong time in the wrong place. It was a classically hopeless situation, not even a complete triangle.

The three of us had cruised into New Orleans at about 11 P.M. Janice, who'd developed a fine nose for cheap motels, had no trouble spotting the Riverby Inn sprawled beneath the overpass of the General De Gaulle Highway. As usual, we booked adjacent rooms, paid thirty-two dollars to a fat lady with a chihuahua in her lap, got our keys and carried in our gear. A brown spiral of flypaper, an insect Gettysburg, hung just inside my doorway. My bedspread was a flamboyant orange and green paisley thing, and above my simulated-wood headboard hung a Day-Glo portrait of an ill-looking horse, its gaunt face superimposed on black velvet, subtle as an atomic bomb. What the heck, the room was bargain basement, and the TV picked up fifteen channels. I figured this would be the last budget weekend for Trayn and Janice, who were destined for the Ramada Inns of this world.

"Life's a piece of pie," I said to Trayn. We were standing just outside my door. I drew in a breath of river funk.

Trayn pointed his unlighted cigar toward a brick building with paint peeling off its sides. "Fish-processing plant."

"Did we pay extra for that?"

"It's included," he told me. We were a couple of fun-loving guys standing under a big vapor light while moths collided overhead. Janice finally came out into the night, wearing her terry-cloth bathrobe, a matching yellow towel wrapped around her head.

"Shouldn't you both get some rest? Ted has to play golf tomorrow, Trayn, and you're keeping him up." (By earning $22,000 in Phoenix, Trayn was now exempt from the Monday qualifying rut.)

"Am I keeping you up, old buddy?"

"I play better in a coma," I said.

Janice said she liked my winning attitude. "If you qualify tomorrow, Trayn and I will buy you dinner at Antoine's. Right, Trayn?"

"Sure thing."

After good-nights, we went to our separate rooms. I took a hot shower, toweled off, then flopped belly down on the bed, whose mattress nearly swallowed me. I bunched a pillow under my chin and lay that way for a while. Then I turned on a lamp and reread the letter Janice had given me just before I left Phoenix. I'd been keeping it folded inside my dop kit.

Dear Ted,

I really shouldn't be writing this letter, but here I am writing one. Can you believe it, a love letter? Maybe I'm taking advantage of you, but I feel so helpless right now. I just don't know how to interpret the things that are going on in my life, so I guess I'm turning to you. To get right to the point, I feel rotten without you. Seeing you every day makes me happy in a way, but it's also very frustrating. Do I have to tell you why that is?

Trayn is doing exactly what everybody expected him to do, but every time he cashes a paycheck we get farther apart. I really just don't love him, and right now I can't convince myself that I ever did. Something I've discovered too late, right? Anyway, I wish I'd done some things differently a few years ago. Trayn doesn't need me at all. He just needs somebody, anybody, who will tell him how great he is, and be less than he is. Well, that's me. All those things that keep you from winning are the things I love about you. But then I know you want to win . . . so in spite of myself I keep hoping you will.

As I said, the situation seems unsolvable. I just want you to listen to me say what you've known all along. I do love you, and to make matters worse, you love me. (You see, I know something, too!)

I'll probably act strange for the next few days. It's awkward to write a letter like this one, and then pretend I didn't. So ignore me. Okay?

Love,
JANICE

I turned off the lamp, tried to erase her words from my mind and, for once, actually *slept*, sprawled and naked until four in the morning, when an ambulance siren gouged me out of my dream. I was leading the Masters with two holes to play. Number seventeen was a bombed-out stretch of battlefield with skunks prowling the traps and black caddies eating picnic lunches on the green. I was partnered with Nicklaus and Trevino, who told Jack that golf was dead. While they discussed the matter, I angrily drilled a three wood off the tee, and the shot crashed broadside into an Igloo cooler, followed by an explosion of hog jowls and Hellman's mayonnaise and egg salad and caddies running in angry circles. But my ball was only ten feet from the pin. Lee followed with a five wood that bored a hole through one of the rioters, who wasn't black at all but was Mr. Grunzig, my old geometry teacher from high school. He was screeching, "Parabola! Parabola!" His head was a whole-wheat doughnut. Then, the Merry Mex, the Golden Bear and yours truly were slaloming up the fairway when that siren wailed outside the motel room. *"Amigos!* Clear the course . . . lightning!"* That was Trevino.

"Once struck, forever wise," I said.

"My putting has gone to hell," grumbled the Golden Bear.

Lee said, *"Qué?"* and then I woke up.

I took a shower at four-fifteen, made myself a pot of coffee, ate two granola bars while it perked and opened my door to see what the world was like. The sky overhead was black as tar. A bloated cloud engulfed the city beyond the river. I snapped on the television and watched an all-night news station until six or so, when the mattress creaked next door. A toilet flushed, some drawers opened and closed, and I heard what sounded like a conversation, and not a particularly happy one. Soon Trayn knocked on our common wall to be sure I was up. "Been up for hours," I yelled.

At exactly six-fifteen I was sitting in the driver's seat of my Pacer. Janice and Trayn came outside when I started the engine, and we talked through my car window. They agreed to meet me at the ninth hole in order to witness my demise. As I eased out of the parking slot, I saw Janice in the rearview. She looked worried, as if she thought I shouldn't chase after something I couldn't catch. How could she possibly understand that golf, like love, is a game of odd shapes and peculiar motions? Nothing you can throw a rope around—unless you're Trayn. On any given day, the worm can make a U-turn. Why did I always feel so optimistic in the morning?

Lakewood is one of the easier tracks on the pro circuit. The winner would probably come in at around minus twenty. The course is wide open and its enormous greens are soft and slow. There are palm trees and willows and cypress trees lining the fairways—not to mention some impenetrable live oaks. I parked my Pacer under one of these sprawling specimens with its awesome limbs bigger than most of the trees back home. I recognized the Pinto wagon belonging to Freddie McVee; our combined earnings couldn't buy a stick of gum. I was to be paired with him and somebody named Henry Waller, a grump who appeared and disappeared at the various stops like a migratory bird. The first thing a rabbit does on Monday morning, qualifying day, is find a caddy who can count from two to nine. Even at 7 A.M., the caddies were sitting in a cluster beneath a canvas awning near the clubhouse. The scene resembled a slave auction, with golfers circling the perimeter. I focused on a tall, lean fellow, mostly because he wore glasses. I caught his eye and motioned for him to come over. He hopped to his feet. "What's the going rate nowadays?" I asked him.

"Forty," he said. "Fifty if'n you make the cut." His official caddy's badge said MICKEY JACKSON.

"Sold," I said, and handed him my car keys. While he ambled out to the parking lot, I went in to register and pay my hundred dollar entry fee.

Freddie was already on the range when Mickey and I arrived. "What do you say we cut it loose today," I said to my fellow rabbit.

"Like to," he said, and punched a range ball out toward the

one-fifty sign. "This is it for me, unless I make some serious cash."

I told him I was in the same boat. "If there's a God I'll go down the dumpster now and put an end to all this crap."

"I know what you mean." His red shirt was already soaked from the early morning humidity, and nerves.

After hitting a couple of hundred balls each, we picked up our scorecards and joined Waller at the tee, where he was watching threesomes hit their drives down the wet first fairway. Since we weren't scheduled to begin play for another forty-five minutes, we headed for the practice green. Waller was more than welcome to stand out there by himself and let his nerves get frayed, not that we didn't look up every so often, the way rabbits do, to watch players hit their first drives. Our caddies sat on the wet grass just outside the yellow rope, smoked cigarettes and whispered back and forth.

My putter, the only club I could rely on, felt alien in my hands. Sweat dripped down my face and hung from the end of my nose. I was working on ten-footers, but nothing was going in the hole. When your nerves are twisted, you tend to decelerate the clubhead before it meets the ball. I had the dreaded yips.

Waller was over chatting with a PGA official who carried a walkie-talkie. They stopped talking when we approached, and shook hands with us. The official flipped the coin for honors, and I won both tosses. He aimed the rubberized antenna at me. "It's you."

I'd already grabbed my driver from Mickey when Freddie told me to hold on a minute. "Before you tee off, let me introduce you to somebody." He waved over a timid-looking young woman with her brown hair pulled back into a ponytail. I knew instantly that Freddie's goose was cooked. "This is my wife, Suzie." (Half the tour wives were named Suzie.)

"You didn't tell me you had a gallery," I said, and smiled at her. She smiled back, a crooked little row of teeth appearing between her lips.

"Yeah. Flew her in from Tulsa yesterday. We did Bourbon Street last night. Suzie got drunk, didn't you, kiddo?"

I said I was happy to meet her.

The first hole was an average par four with a long narrow trap paralleling the fairway on the left. Since the pin was cut dead center on the green, the optimum drive would be a rifle shot directly over the threatening mid-fairway trap. But my arms were limp pieces of garden hose. I took a deep breath, looked down the fairway, then at the ball. I hit the thing solidly with the screwheads of my driver and burned it well over the trap. "That's a hell of a drive," said Waller, scouting out a nice patch of turf on which to tee his ball. Mickey tossed me a towel so I could mop off.

Waller the gorilla blistered a perfect drive that split the fairway. He'd left himself a soft wedge to the green.

Freddie was so nervous he could barely get his tee in the ground. It was a bad idea to have invited his wife to the party. There was enough pressure on a rabbit without that. He finally jerked the club back and whipped it down into the ball. The thing curled wickedly onto the adjoining fairway. "It's okay, Freddie," I said, "you've still got a shot from over there." When I looked into his eyes, though, I saw he was baked like a flounder. If he were smart, he would hotfoot it with Suzie to his Pinto and drive nonstop to Oklahoma. Instead, he shrugged and said, "Fart."

Waller and I waited near our golf balls while Freddie punched a weak five iron over a row of adolescent oak trees. He dejectedly tossed his club toward his caddy. Since I was farthest from the pin, I had to hit next. " 'Fize you, I'd hit a strong eight," said Mickey. I glanced at the yardage booklet. The sprinkler head to my left was 162 yards from the center of the green; I pulled a seven iron halfway out of the bag, then shoved it back in and fingered the eight.

My goal was to land the ball twenty or so feet past the pin and spin it backward toward the hole. What the hell, I told myself. I took the club back, conscious of nothing but the familiar motion of the swing, pulled the iron down and through the ball and hurled it in a high arc toward the flag. I knew instinctively that I'd hit a perfect shot. The ball landed only two feet from the pin. Freddie shook a congratulatory fist in my direction.

Regrettably, he missed his fifteen-footer for a bogey, and yours truly tapped in for a birdie. (Suzie clapped for me.)

Number two was a doglegged par five. Waller was on the green with his second shot. Meanwhile, my three-iron approach shot had settled on the grassy plateau between two guardian bunkers. Poor Freddie had already dunked his tee shot into the shallows of a pond. He actually intended to splash the ball out with a wedge. He was standing with one bare foot in the water and his other foot on the bank. A miraculous recovery shot might just get him close to the green, but the chances were microscopic. He hurled his wedge into the partially submerged ball, spewing algae and water and mud in all directions. In the aftermath, his pale blue pants were dappled with sludge. The ball had vanished. "Where did it go?" he yelled. "Anybody see where it went?"

Miserable as he looked, I hated to tell him what I knew: the ball had settled into the murk. We made a polite search of the general vicinity, Mickey and I, but we knew it was a lost cause.

Suzie realized he was finished. Her eyes had filmed over, and she stood frozen at greenside, casting the dark shadow of a mourner. Every terrible shot had a label for her: this month's car payment, next month's groceries, money for the baby's vaccination, money for the flight home. But this was the clincher. The exclamation point. I saw everything written on her face, even though I'd heard her promise Freddie she'd be invisible, "a quiet little mouse." It was no use now. His game had come undone, his swing had turned rigid as a mathematical calculation.

I had more than sixty feet to the flag stick. I tried to put Freddie out of my mind so I could focus on the task before me. I touched the damp grass, analyzing its grain. My putt would drift down into a valley and up a rise to a plateau, dying a little in its climb so it could roll evenly across the straightaway until its final left-hand turn near the hole. I finally got around to stroking the ball, but too firmly. It scrambled well past the cup, leaving me a precarious downhiller for my birdie.

Waller wasted no time in lagging close enough for a tap-in. Then we watched Freddie McVee carelessly run his putt five feet by. He marked his ball with a dime and trudged over toward Suzie to wait while I finished out.

A chickenhearted putt on my part would surely yield a foot of break, yet if I hit the ball firmly I risked running the thing past where Freddie's marker gleamed in the sun. But I had exactly nothing to lose, so I placed the blade behind the ball and spanked the thing toward its destination: it scurried like a rat directly into the hole. I was two under! Freddie accidentally sank his five-footer, but he'd let an easy birdie opportunity slip through his fingers.

I was a hero on the front side. I gave every putt a chance at the hole, and I was clobbering my drives. When I ran into Janice and Trayn, he was drinking Budweiser from a can. "Minus four," I said.

"You're four under? Goddamn, save some of that for Thursday."

"I knew you could do it," Janice said.

Trayn gave me a sip of Budweiser, a violation of tournament rules, but I didn't much care. I was too happy.

I bogeyed number ten, but birdied twelve to make up for it, then parred in for a 68, tying me with Waller. Old tight-lipped "Fats" had matched me stroke for stroke, although I wasn't really aware of that until I tallied his score at the end of the round. Freddie had been done in by a 76. Poor guy was Oklahoma bound. It's not easy to smile when the road you've mapped out for yourself dead-ends in a duck pond. But he smiled gamely and shook my hand. "I wish you luck," he said.

"Same to you and Suzie." Janice walked over to where she was standing next to a Pepsi cart and said something to her.

Suzie started to cry, and Janice gave her a hug. "That's the worst part," said Freddie, glancing over his shoulder.

"It's tough," I said.

Trayn wasn't saying much but he was taking it all in like someone who's just stumbled onto the scene of a natural disaster. "I think you'll be back, Freddie," he said.

"Nah, this is it for me. I'm tossing it all in." He went over to his wife, grabbed her hand and guided her toward the parking lot, where his caddy was already loading golf clubs into the Pinto for the hasty getaway.

"See you," I said. Maybe Freddie could lead something like a normal life now. He could make decent, predictable money, maybe sell his double-wide and move into a real house with geraniums on the porch. But of course he didn't want that. He was infected by competition and crazy enough to take on the pro tour. Unless he put his adrenaline in a bottle and airmailed it to Timbuktu, he'd never be happy.

Trayn and Janice and I stood in front of the big scoreboard near the putting green. A blond woman was posting scores, hole by hole, with a Magic Marker. "No need to stick around here, slugger," said Trayn. "You're in like Flynn." He gave me a high five, then with his opened palm swatted me on the butt. "Let's go into the French Quarters and grab some lunch."

I paid Mickey three twenty-dollar bills and arranged to meet him on Wednesday for the practice round.

I got into my car and followed Trayn's BMW, watching the ends of Janice's hair whip at the edge of her rolled-down window. We crossed the Mississippi River bridge, cruised past the Vieux Carré exit, got off the highway, couldn't get back on, meandered through some rutted back streets, got misinformed three times, drank some Cokes at a gas station, aimed the cars toward the river again and by some miracle found our way to Camp Street, which fed us into the Quarter. I could provide a postcard description of what I saw: iron balustrades, little black kids tap-dancing in front of an opened violin case at Jackson Square, Oriental tourists wearing identical Pat O'Brien's

T-shirts . . . No sooner had we parked the cars on Chartres Street than we witnessed a howling good tiff between a duet of angry queens, each convinced the other had done the dirty deed with somebody named Alex. We hiked six blocks to the Café Lafitte, where we could eat lunch. We dodged dog poop and gobs of phlegm and empty Dixie bottles along the way.

The bar was dark and cool, black fans hanging down like vampire bats. "I want a Pimm's Cup," said Janice.

"A what?"

"I read about it my guidebook. You're supposed to have a Pimm's Cup and a muffaletta at the Café Lafitte. It says so right here." She held a red paperback in front of Trayn's nose.

A lispy giant came to take our order. "Three muffalettas and three Pimm's Cups, please," she said.

The sandwich was about the size of a Frisbee, and stuffed with cheeses, meats, and olive salad. We downed four or five Pimms each until we were thoroughly pickled and ate our enormous sandwiches.

The three of us wandered through the Quarter that afternoon, then drove in tandem back across the Mississippi to our motel. I started to feel sick just as we crossed over to the Gretna side of the river.

While they sat in folding chairs at the pool, I shared time between the toilet and the bed, where I lay staring at bugs collected in the light fixture until a gray wave would sweep over me and I'd race to the bathroom. Trayn and Janice bought me some Lomotil at a K & B, and after taking two tablets I went to sleep almost immediately. On Tuesday morning I awoke nauseated, and so feeble I could barely crawl to the toilet. Janice, wearing her bikini, came in several times that day. "How are you feeling?" she'd ask. The room was filled with my embarrassing stink, but she dutifully ran hot water in the lavatory, soaked washcloths and placed them on my forehead. "Think it's food poisoning?"

"It's bad, whatever it is. I'd be better off dead."

"Can you survive if Trayn and I go into the French Quarter?"

The mere image of the French Quarter provoked another wave of nausea.

"Maybe I should stay here," she said to the closed bathroom door, behind which I now hid, trying to do what had to be done as quietly as possible.

"Go on, have a ball," I said.

On Wednesday morning I was much better, but still too weak to play the practice round. However, fearing that I'd lose the services of my caddy, I handed Trayn fifty dollars to give Mickey so I could claim him for Thursday's opening round.

By midmorning I was feeling so well that I drove out to the golf course, but decided to do nothing more strenuous than sit on a mound of grass next to number nine green. A cool breeze blew in from the Gulf, rattling palm fronds, ruffling the triangular flags strung across the patio in front of the clubhouse. Trayn was a dew sweeper that morning, so I felt sure he'd be hiking up the fairway in a matter of minutes. I watched Lietzke, Eastwood and Connors hit their approach shots onto the green, all of them within twenty feet of the pin. Back on the tee I could make out Trayn's group, waiting for the threesome to get out of range.

Lietzke was away, and I was watching him line up his putt from the fringe. When he'd taken his cross-handed grip and gotten comfortable over his ball, I felt a shadow fall over me. I turned around and saw Mickey standing there. He squatted on the grass, so close I could smell his perspiration. We shook hands. "You watch this putt, Ted. You watch if he don't miss it on the high side." Sure enough, when Lietzke finally stroked his putt, it refused to come down to the hole. "Everybody miss that one to the right."

"Damn, you know what you're talking about, don't you?"

"Some says I do."

About the time Trayn came marching up the fairway, Mickey was gone. I walked over to a soft-drink stand, bought a Coke to help settle my stomach and returned to my grassy hummock.

Trayn hit a nice high approach shot to number nine green.

The ball landed near where Lietzke had hit his a few minutes before.

"How you feeling?" Trayn asked when he saw me, poking at a cigarette butt with the sole of his putter.

"Better."

"Good to hear. We're going to kick ass tomorrow. I'm three under right here." He gestured toward his ball, as if it were destined to roll into the hole for him. He lined up the putt very carefully, stood over it for ten or fifteen seconds, took a nice smooth stroke and watched the ball refuse to take the break. "Son of a bitch," he said.

Since Janice wasn't on the course, I wondered if maybe she'd gone back to their room. I decided to drive back to the motel to make some hot-plate soup, then take a nap.

Janice was sitting in an aluminum folding chair alongside the pool, reading a paperback. I rested my elbows on the chain link fence and said, "Hey."

She set the book aside. "How're you feeling?"

"Pretty fine," I said. "Better by the minute."

"You look better," she said. She came over and placed her hand on top of mine. Neither one of us said anything for a few seconds. I watched a bead of water trickle from her throat to her breasts. "Teddy . . . did you ever wish you could start all over again?" She looked beautiful in the sunlight mottled by the branches of a willow. We could very easily have been standing alongside the reflecting pond on a Saturday afternoon. If I'd said the right words then, maybe things *would* be different now. Maybe not. "Teddy . . . ?" She flicked a ladybug off my arm.

"Sometimes I feel that way, too."

Her eyes filled with tears. She wiped them away with the back of her wrists, smiled a crooked smile and shrugged. "I don't know what I'm doing anymore. If I knew where to go, I'd just drive away." We watched a pair of sea gulls roosting on the hood of a pickup truck. "Trayn's more involved with golf then he is with me. We haven't made love in more than a month, at least not what *I* call making love. He makes me do things I really don't want to do, Teddy, things I can't even talk about. Things that hurt."

All of this was coming out of her so quickly, as if she were opening a pent-up vein of frustration. "And you don't love him anymore . . ." I prompted her, wanting her to go on and say it.

"I thought I did once. Now I wonder even about that. Pretty stupid of me, huh?"

"Jesus," I said. There was a row of semis parked behind a distant warehouse. A man climbed into the cab of one with red lettering on the door. Lafourche Seafood. "I don't know what to say, Janice. Would you have married me if Trayn hadn't come along?"

"What would it help if I said yes?"

"Nothing, I suppose."

"Well, for what it's worth, I would have."

Then she covered her face with her hands and sobbed until I reached across the fence and pulled her close. She put her head against my neck and I could smell her hair and feel her shoulders moving under my embrace.

When she shifted her head from my shoulder and looked at my face, mascara was tracking down her cheeks. "You ought to see yourself," I said. With my thumb I wiped some of the smudge from beneath her eyes.

"I'm going to get cleaned up," she said. She fetched her towel from the deck chair and walked toward her room. My plan for the morning had been to buy a Pepsi from a machine and drink it with a can of chicken soup, then take a nap after my lunch. But suddenly I was overcome with an urge to strip off my clothes and jump naked into the pool, swim to the bottom and stay there. When Janice had walked halfway to her room, she turned around and said, "Why don't you come in out of the hot sun. Talk to me while I get dressed."

I knew the dangers of accepting her invitation, but I followed her into the half-darkness of the motel room and sat at the foot of the bed, expecting her to vanish into the bathroom to change out of her swimsuit. She was very nervous having me there; I could tell that from the way she fiddled with brushes and cosmetics on her dresser, and the way she kept glancing over her shoulder at me with a sort of frightened expression on her face. Then she turned away from me and unfastened the top to her swimsuit, revealing a horizontal band of pale skin where the strap had been. I could see her breasts in the mirror, and she saw me watching. It was a curious game: the mirror made everything okay, since I wasn't looking directly at her. Then she removed the bikini bottom and stood in front of the mirror looking at me, not trying to cover herself at all. I could see my own dumbfounded face, her in the foreground, me in the background, a wonderful variation on a scene from a French movie. Pinpoints of electricity were coursing through my bloodstream.

When she turned around to look at me I was helpless to do much more than turn back the covers so she could glide under the sheets. I took off my clothes in the dimness of the room, folded them over the back of a chair and slid in next to her, snuggling against her nakedness.

"We shouldn't do this," I said, but I didn't mean it. She put her finger on my lips to silence me, and then she pressed her mouth warmly over mine. I knew this would be the last time we would ever make love, and knowing it, I wanted to forget that there were such things as a past and a future. Only a present tense.

We made love as if we owned the patent on it, wordlessly, since whatever we might say would disrupt something that needed, for once, to be simple and clean and uncomplicated. Right then, we were alone on a kind of floating oasis. Afterward, she cried for a while, although it didn't seem like she was sad. Maybe it was wistfulness she was feeling. Or maybe it was that isolated moment of happiness that made her cry. "I love you, Ted," she whispered. I told her I loved her, too. And, of course, I did.

I held Janice for a long time, glad not to feel guilty, as I thought I would. I was only concerned that between us we'd formulated a difficult new equation that would prove to be all but unsolvable.

When Trayn came in that afternoon he found Janice at poolside, I suppose. I was in my own motel room, staring at the ceiling, wishing for all the world that I could go to sleep.

The New Orleans Country Club provided a breakfast buffet for all the golfers, tournament sponsors and officials. The bald-headed man who stood at the door of the dining room was showing everybody in, shaking hands, laughing. When I approached him he put a beefy hand on my sternum. "Sorry," he said. "This is for golfers and officials only."

"I tee off at eleven. I'm Ted Kendall."

"Ted who?" he asked, and started leafing through several pages trapped on a clipboard.

"Kendall. K-e-n-d-a-l-l."

"You have some identification?"

"Sure," I said. "In my golf bag."

I spotted Waller over in a corner, munching on a ham biscuit. "Ask that guy over there. He knows who I am."

"You know Hank Waller? Okay, then. Go on in."

I filled up on scrambled eggs, bacon, sausage, grits and blueberry muffins. I sat alone and swilled coffee until my blood pressure climbed to tournament level. When I'd eaten everything except the dark green rim around my plate, I was ready to get my sticks and my caddy and get down to business.

I was about to check the grassy area beneath the infamous live oak where caddies sprawled in the wet shade and smoked cigarettes when I saw him standing in the parking lot.

"Well . . . ," he said, "how're you feeling this morning?"

"Not bad, Mickey. Ready to hit the driving range?"

He hoisted my clubs out of the Pacer trunk, checked twice to see that they were all there and nodded toward the practice range, which by now was crowded with players. I hit a total of two hundred practice shots and was pleased with the way I was swinging the clubs. "You're going to do good today, Ted. You're swinging nice," said Mickey.

I was fifteen minutes away from tee-off time, so I needed to get out to number one. But as usual I had to relieve my bladder so I wouldn't wet my pants if I hit a bad drive on the first hole. I dashed into the clubhouse. A stuccoed partition separated me from the golfers who sat between the walls of lockers. Watson was straddling the bench, chatting with Billy Kratzert and Greg Norman. I stepped up to a urinal and realized that Lee Trevino was standing next to me. I grinned at him and said, "Hi." My wits had fluttered up through the acoustical ceiling. "Had to take a leak," I said.

"You always wear your golf glove when you do that?" he asked.

"Helps me keep a grip on the little bugger," I said. He grinned and dropped some spit into the cigarette butts that twirled in the water when he pulled the handle to flush.

"Well . . . good luck," he said.

I wasn't convinced that he was referring to my golf game, but I told him thanks.

Mickey followed me to the first tee. I was greeted there by a tournament official who introduced me to my playing partners, Tom Kite and David Graham. Although Nicklaus wasn't entered in the New Orleans Open, I'd drawn two of the best players on the tour. I shook hands with Kite. His glasses looked thick, as if he might be blind without them. He looked younger in person that I'd supposed he would. "So you're from Bowling Green," he said. "Spent a night there once. Bought an Ace bandage at a drugstore."

"A lot of people do that," I said. He guffawed politely. There was an attractive-looking woman standing just outside the ropes, stage left. She was biting little chunks from her Styrofoam coffee cup, which she held in both hands. I supposed she was Kite's wife.

Graham shook my hand, too, but he wasn't in a conversational mood yet. Kite said, "Keep your eye on Graham. He'll

306

kick your ball OB if you give him a chance." Graham smiled and snapped on his golf glove. He'd won driving honors.

A man with a bullhorn introduced him to the gallery gathered around the hitting area. The litany of championships and awards took a full minute to complete. The gallery clapped and Graham waved at them. He wasn't wearing a hat, and I wondered if the Louisiana sun wouldn't get to him before the round was over.

I was pretty sure my biography would consist of my name and hometown, followed by snickering from the fans. But somebody, maybe Trayn, had given the man a long list of accomplishments, many of which I'd never heard of. I came across as somebody to be reckoned with. Unfortunately, I was introduced as Ted *Kendale*. I touched the bill of my cap in acknowledgment of the generous applause and my new name. My testicles began to hurt the way they always did when I was scared.

After Kite's introduction, Graham stepped up to the tee. He poked a drive that climbed like a hawk until it reached apogee, high above a distant range of cedars, and fell onto the fairway. Dead center. Everybody clapped and howled like they'd never seen anything like it. "Nice hit," I said.

I decided to tee my own ball just inside the right-hand marker. Fear made me feel weightless; when I drew in a huge breath I thought I might float up into the humid Louisiana sky. I took a few practice swings with my driver, which felt alien and peculiar. Kite smiled at me and nodded as if to say, *Don't worry, just hit the thing.* Somehow I managed to bring the club down and through, making reasonable contact with the ball. It nicked an oleander switch a couple of hundred yards out, and stayed in the right-hand rough. The clapping was very polite.

"That'll play," Graham said. "That'll play," freely translated, means you've hit a sub-average shot and you're damned lucky the outcome wasn't disastrous.

While Graham and Kite made routine pars at number one, I took a miserable bogey. My tap-in putt curled completely around the hole before it decided to hang on the edge. "A little tight, aren't you?" Kite said. He pointed toward a pint-sized golfer marching up number two fairway. "You ought to play with Chi Chi sometime. He'd loosen you up."

"Rodriguez? Hell, you'd kill him before the round was finished, mate," said Graham.

That bogey was still reverberating inside me when I stepped up to the tee at number two, the first of four par fives. Kite and Graham had already knocked their drives well down the fairway. I disregarded Mickey's suggestion that I hit a three wood. One nice thing about being a lame duck is that there is absolutely nothing to lose. "Give me the driver," I said, and held out my hand for it.

"Ain't no point to it."

"You want to get paid?" I asked. He quickly handed over my number one wood. After taking a pair of hefty practice cuts, I stepped up to my ball, placed the clubhead on the turf behind it, drew smoothly back, almost to parallel, then let fly. My drive, a crunching 285 yards, divided the fairway into perfect halves, which meant I could reach the green in two if I creamed a three iron. I'd actually outdriven Kite and Graham, both of whom seemed as surprised as I was. "You can get arrested for that," Graham said.

It gave me a lot of pleasure to step aside while my partners hit their second shots. I was usually the one standing back on the fairway. They both laid up well short of the green, in nice shape but with no hope of making an eagle. Mickey and I walked out of the shade to my ball, a beautiful white orb on a green carpet. This time I got no argument from my caddy when I asked for a four iron. The wind was slightly behind me, which meant I could take a little bit off my swing and still get home. In my eagerness to get the club cleanly beneath the ball, I hit a fat shot that looked as if it might stop well short of the green, but it landed on a patch of hardpan and took a monstrous leap forward onto the front apron, leaving me with a seventy-footer up an undulating slope. Mickey rolled his eyes in an I-told-you-so way.

That green was one of three on the course that had been attacked by a brown fungus, so my ball would have a bumpy ride.

Kite nestled a soft wedge shot to within five feet of the hole. Graham wasn't so lucky. His ball spun backward from slightly beyond the flag stick, to a small rise just left of the hole, where it hovered momentarily before rolling to within three feet of my own ball.

Mickey leaned over my shoulder to help me line up the putt. I smelled Dentyne on his breath. "Shoot for the middle of that hump yonder," he said.

I touched the grass to gauge the flow of the grain. "Hit the sumbitch a good poke, 'cause the green is slow, mighty slow."

My white shoes were almost blinding, and the sun glinted off the putter shaft as I stood over the ball. My ears felt hot and my legs were rubbery. The brass putter blade barely brushed the fringe on the forward stroke and the Titleist skittered across the green, bouncing on the mottled grass, rolling past Kite's gleaming dime, until at the last moment it veered toward the plateau, where it sat momentarily like a nipple on a breast. I was almost ready to tap it in when Kite told me to wait a second. The breeze rocked the ball very subtly from its perch. It trickled sideways down the incline, directly into the hole. A supernatural phenomenon. *Kendale* carded an eagle to go one under par.

Instead of crumbling like a desiccated tortilla, as I had in Phoenix and again in Houston, I was gaining strength. It was simply a matter of attitude. The equation was simple: success was inversely proportional to testosterone level. The scorer's sign, carried by a young kid at the head of our parade, showed the world that I was a very respectable two under par after nine. It wasn't what anybody would call an *extraordinary* half-round of golf, but at least I wasn't longing for a ski mask to wear for the rest of the round. After the first hole, I'd overheard Mickey humming Negro spirituals. Now he'd changed his tune. He was adding up his potential earnings.

Janice and Trayn met me at the turn. He was to be among the very last players to tee off. He gave me a thumbs-up sign and made a question mark with his eyebrows: *How are you doing? Is everything okay?*

I raised a clenched fist and smiled. Janice's worried look transformed itself into an expression of pure joy. She'd feared that this round would be the end of the road for me. Now she had reason to believe otherwise, although nine holes of decent golf hadn't fully convinced me that I'd last on the PGA tour.

When my seven iron at number eleven caromed off a rake handle and kicked due east into the center of the cup, I knew that all I had to do from that point on was to keep hitting the ball until the round was over, grin amiably, toss out a compliment every now and then, shake hands on the eighteenth green, pay off my caddy, evacuate the course as quickly as possible, drive at a high rate of speed back to the motel and start partying. Trayn and Janice clapped like a pair of fools when that little miracle occurred. "Rub against him," Kite said to Graham. "See if you can get some of that stuff on *you.*"

Kite was burning up the course, too, snaking in putts from every angle, knocking approach shots stiff to the pin, wearing out the bill of his visor in acknowledgment of the frequent applause. I sank a rainbow ten-footer on the last hole for a mind-boggling 68. Kite shot a 67 for the day, and Graham made 71. They were in position for a move on Friday, but *my* feet were in the blocks, too. "Go get them tomorrow, Teddy," said Kite as we shook hands. "You play a nice game."

"We're gonna make some money, Ted," said Mickey. "Yes sir-ree!"

He said he would meet me the next day at noon. I promised him I'd shoot a 63. He took off his glasses, wiped them on a towel and grinned. "I hope you do jus' that!"

I bought myself a Budweiser from a vendor and sucked cold beer for a while. I polished that one off and bought another to carry with me on my trek across the course to where Trayn was having his day in the sun.

Janice was standing next to number six green, where Trayn was leaning over a tricky downhiller that resembled the one I'd three-putted a few hours earlier. He was wearing his lucky canary-yellow pants and his macho neck chain with the gold dragon's-tooth pendant. "How's he doing?" I asked.

"Not so good," she said, and pointed toward the scorer's placard.

"Plus three? Are you kidding?"

"He's playing pretty well, but he kicked out of bounds on number one. Hit a tree root with his drive and the ball went straight out like this." She made a fish out of her hand and showed me how it darted stage right. "That pretty much unscrewed him."

"Maybe he'll snap back."

"I don't think so. This putt's for par." We watched him dink the putt and leave it two feet short. He backhanded that ball into the hole, then stomped over to his caddy. I could read Trayn's lips as he slammed the putter into the bag. "Fuck!" Or maybe it was "I'm fucked."

"It's going to be a long night, Ted." I shrugged my shoulders and then looked over at the scorer's placard.

"I guess his playing partners aren't exactly setting the world on fire either." I downed the rest of my beer and chucked the can into a wire trash container. "Kite shot a damned sixty-seven just to make me look bad."

Trayn barked at his caddy every now and then. He even paid a grudging compliment to his playing partners when they did something half decent. But he was just playing in. I knew the feeling. We stayed clear of him until he emerged scowling from the scorer's tent, baked and fried. "What a bunch of shit," he said.

"It's okay, honey," she said. "Everybody has days like this."

"I don't need that," he said. "Let's just get the hell out of here." Janice looked over at me like I might be able to throw her a rope. I shrugged and walked toward my car. I turned toward them one last time. "See you at the motel," I said. "We'll down a few beers and forget about it."

I waited for half an hour at the motel, imagining they'd be

pulling in any minute. The shadow from the warehouse had nearly engulfed the parking lot and the first stars were appearing overhead. I went inside 116, got out of my golfer's costume, slipped on my swimming trunks and padded barefoot toward the heated pool. I did a deep dive and swam a lap underwater. I touched one of the submerged lights and glided in the opposite direction as far as I could. I surfaced near the edge where my towel was wadded up, and Janice was standing there with the last rays of sun behind her.

Trayn was off somewhere boozing it, his tradition after a bad round. He figured alcohol could kill the germ that had infected his play, and he always consumed a prophylactic quantity, so that when he returned from one of his binges Janice would have to undress him and roll him onto his side of the bed.

At eight-thirty, when we were convinced he was still at a tavern getting his snoot full, we ordered a pepperoni with double cheese from some pizza place around the corner. I wasn't too hungry, but I forced down a few slices, knowing I'd need some fuel to endure Friday's round.

"So . . . ," I said. "Looks like I've reached a high point in my short but illustrious career." I'd decided that if we were going to talk about what had happened between us, it would be Janice who would bring it up. I took a slug of Gallo Hearty Burgundy from my plastic cup. "Maybe I'll stay with the tour for a while longer. You know, to see how it works out."

"I'm glad to hear that, Teddy."

"I'll give it another shot next week, but I'll tell you something, Janice. This isn't the way I want to make a living. I only want to go out in a blaze of glory," I said.

"I don't care what the reason is. I'm glad you're staying," she said. "You're the only thing that makes me happy right now."

"It's good to hear that," I said. "But the whole thing is mighty damned confusing."

We managed to let that conversation dwindle into a parade of trivialities. I poured her some wine and for the next hour or two we played imaginary strip poker, a game Janice invented for the occasion. She was down to her imaginary panties and bra when I drew an inside straight and demanded that she take them off. Slowly.

At about nine-thirty I heard a car door slam in the parking lot. Then there was the sound of keys jangling against the door of room 117, where Janice and I were taking in a detective show. I got up from the bed where I was sprawled to let Trayn in.

His face was pale and sweaty, the way you get after you've been sick in the bushes somewhere. He smelled like scotch. "Well, greetings," he said. "Glad to see you've been taking care of things in my absence." He stood there at the threshold with the swimming pool illuminated behind him. "Yeah, you've got everything under control here." He tossed his car keys onto the bureau five feet away. They ricocheted off the mirror and fell onto the orange shag carpet.

"Where've you been?" Janice asked. "We were starting to worry."

"Sure. I bet you were worried sick." He strode past us and disappeared into the bathroom.

"I'd better get back to my room," I said.

"I wish you wouldn't," Janice said. "I don't like to be alone with him when he gets like this."

From behind the closed bathroom door he said, "Careful. I can hear every word." The toilet flushed and he reemerged, toweling off his face. He raked a piece of cold pizza from the cardboard box and took a careless bite from it. He chewed with his mouth open. "Hell of a day, wasn't it, old Ted? I guess *you're* happy. Won't be calling it quits *now*, will you?"

"Maybe. Maybe not. What's it to you?"

"What's it to you? Listen to him, Janice. What's it to you? Why, that's impolite."

"Trayn, come on," she said. "Don't be this way."

"Don't be what way? Oh . . . I see. You mean stop picking on Teddy." He sat on the end of the bed and put on a pair of Adidas over his bare feet. "Well, just for the record, I know

313

exactly what you two have been up to lately. Nobody had to tell me, either."

"Trayn," I said. "You're way off base. Nothing's happened between Janice and me. We're friends. Like you and I are friends."

"Look," he said, standing over me. "Stay the hell away from my wife or I'll kick your damned ass from here to China."

By now, of course, Janice was crying—sobbing, really. When I stood up to leave, he pushed me back into the chair. Janice grabbed him by the arm and he let her pull him away. Without saying a word, I got up and left them alone there.

In my room, I snapped on the TV and turned the volume up so I wouldn't have to listen to what was going on next door. But I could hear them anyway, or at least I could hear *him*, screaming at her. And then things went unexpectedly quiet.

I stood under a hot shower for a half hour or so, trying to sober up, trying to patch together some coherent rationale for what had just taken place. I'd just about decided it was *their* problem to solve when the phone rang. I wrapped a towel around my waist and walked over to the night table. I fully expected to hear Janice begging for sanctuary from Trayn. However, it wasn't Janice; it was Stan at the other end of the line. For two weeks we hadn't spoken, because there was nothing I could say to make him proud or happy, the function of every phone call I'd ever made to him. And now he was calling me. "Hello, Teddy?"

"Stan, hi. How in the world did you ever track me down?" I was already trying to decide whether to summarize my ups and downs or merely to dodge the truth in some clever way.

"I called the Lakewood Country Club this afternoon. They had the information, and I thought I'd better get in touch . . . but you've been tough to get ahold of."

"Something must be wrong. This is an ungodly hour," I said. "Are you okay?"

"I'm afraid I've got some bad news for you. Jimmy died last night in his sleep. I knew you'd want to hear about it."

I sank down onto the mattress and said something like "Oh no," or "God, no," and then I just sat there half listening to Stan as he told me how Jimmy had been failing for more than a month, in and out of the hospital, once to the Cleveland Clinic for tests. He'd worked up to the last day, had asked about me, sent his best, expected big things from me . . . It was just phrases strung together.

"Teddy, are you all right?"

I told Stan to hold the phone while I took some deep breaths, then lay on my back with the receiver cradled next to my cheek. "I'm coming home," I said.

"No, don't do that. Jimmy would be furious with you if he knew you'd quit a tournament to come to his funeral."

"I'm playing lousy, Stan, and I'm not making money. The tour's eating me alive, and I'm coming home."

"Son. Come on, I don't want you to quit. At least not on account of Jimmy. Now I wish I hadn't called."

"Don't worry about that. I'll be home tomorrow."

"I can't stop you, but I wish you wouldn't."

"Bye, Stan."

With the air conditioner moaning in the background, I began tossing things into my suitcase: clean clothes, sweaty shirts, wet towels, all of it unfolded. I called the front desk for an outside line and phoned for a plane reservation. A clerk told me that the first flight was leaving in slightly less than an hour. "Fine," I said. "Save me a seat."

For a few minutes I sat immobilized on the edge of the bed, my eyes closed. When I opened them, I saw particles of air vibrating inside the room. Jimmy was dead . . . in a coffin, and somehow I never thought he would die. He was old when I first knew him . . . had always been old except in photographs . . . would always be old. He never changed. Not like Stan, who got older every year. And now Jimmy was only an image standing at a window looking out at big trees and green fairways.

I felt strange and disembodied sitting in an alien motel room at the base of the continent where everything flowed out of it into the Gulf. Stan was up in Ohio with Sally and occasionally Lucille for company, Jimmy dead, my mom dead, Janice within my grasp but out of reach—that dream and the golf dream corrupted by a wash of numbers—fives and sixes. And anyway, what exactly did I want to do about that lovely problem of Janice, whom I loved? There wasn't any point in denying I *was* crazy about her. I'd only managed to complicate that problem beyond repair: a wonderful moment of pure insanity *that* was.

Maybe I should have laid everything on the line for Trayn right then. "Sorry, old buddy, but she thinks you're the wrong ticket. If you want to know the truth, she's in love with *me*, Kendall the Bogey Shooter." And then, of course, he'd laugh, damn him, and say something like "Come on, Teddy boy. The bitch isn't worth the trouble." He'd probably want to go somewhere and get a beer so he could tell me how he'd screwed her standing up in the shower. And the hell of it was that I'd probably have joined him.

Feeling shaky, I walked to the big window of my room, pulled open the acetate curtains. Lightning flung itself down from a distant bank of clouds, black above the warehouses. There was a pause, then thunder rolled in like an enormous breaker above the rooftops. Big drops of rain splashed on the windshields of the cars nosed up to the sidewalk.

The one-thirty flight would take me directly to Ohio. Ohio. The name was like an exhalation of breath, a breeze blowing in off Lake Erie. Better than this rainy, dark, depressing hole in the earth. To get there, simply drive breakneck out of this city with its Superdome and oyster bars and gritty French Quarter horse turds, then hammer up I-12 alongside Lake Pontchartrain. Leave the Pacer in the long-term lot forever . . . I'd be on that plane when it flew toward the heart of the country.

I carried my luggage across the motel parking lot to the car, opened the trunk and tossed the suitcase in with my golf clubs. Rain pelted down on me and pinged against the tin roof of the warehouse. The thunder was closer, more aggressive than before.

Janice deserved some sort of explanation for my sudden decision to bug out, so I knocked on her door. Wearing only her nightgown, she opened up enough for me to see that there were welts on her cheek from where Trayn had obviously slapped her. "Goddamn! He *hit* you, didn't he?" I said. I pushed past her into the room, hoping I'd find him so I could land one good punch before he ground me into talcum. I expected him to gambol out of the bathroom, naked except for his gold neck chain. At which point I'd march straight across the room and give him a good sock in the jaw, followed by a kick in the nuts. For Janice. And then while he was crouched in the corner, gathering strength to kill me, I'd give him the true picture. That I was in love with his wife, and that if he really wanted to know, we *had* made love before, and would make love whenever we damned well felt like it because she was out of his life forever and if he ever wanted to *fuck* somebody he could go and fuck himself. But

Trayn was gone. "Where is he, Janice?" I asked.

"I don't know. He just drove off."

"Are you okay?" I asked, and touched the welt Trayn's hand had made on her cheek.

"Teddy, I don't want you to get in the middle of this," she said, placing her hand on my shoulder. I think she knew how ridiculous that sounded, since I'd been in the middle of *everything* for five years. She even managed a sort of whimsical smile before she started to cry, her shoulders trembling.

"You've got to leave him, Janice. Now."

"I know . . . ," she said in a barely audible voice. "I will."

"*Now,*" I said.

"Tomorrow. I will. I promise."

"I've got to fly home tonight," I told her. "Stan just called me a few minutes ago. Jimmy died last night, and I'm going home to his funeral. It's important to me, and I have to go. Can you call me at home tomorrow . . . to let me know how things are?"

"Oh, Teddy, I'm really sorry," she said. "But you're not leaving in the middle of a tournament . . . not when you're playing so well," she said.

"That doesn't matter, believe me. It's nothing. Golf. Hitting a golf ball for money. Or no money. What the hell difference does it make if I do that or something else equally ridiculous," I said, not sure if I believed any of it. "Listen to me. You call the police right away. You tell them to get over here *now* so Trayn doesn't come back and hurt you again. Understand?" She nodded, and I told her I had to hurry to catch my flight. I gave her a handkerchief and she wiped her eyes. And then I kissed her. She kissed me back, hard, and held me tight, as if she didn't want me to leave her. Ever.

"You love me, don't you?" she asked.

I brushed a strand of hair away from her eyebrow and pressed my lips against her forehead. "Sure," I said.

Abandoning her to those circumstances made me feel numb with depression. If my brain had been functioning right, I'd have stayed with her until the police came, but, as they say, I had a plane to catch. We kissed one more time, and then I told her goodbye. "Lock the door and call the police. You understand?"

She nodded, and then softly shut the door.

I'd barely backed my car out of its parking slot when Trayn's BMW squealed in the motel driveway and skidded to a halt in the glare of my headlights, all but blocking the exit. He got out of his car, staggered over to my driver's side window and tapped the glass with his finger. He had a big grin on his face, a big arrogant drunken grin. I cranked the window down. "Where in the hell are you going, Teddy boy?" he said. His breath smelled like whiskey. "It's way past your bedtime."

"I'm going back to Ohio. That's all you need to know, you bastard. I just saw Janice, by the way. You hit her, didn't you?"

"Listen, Teddy boy," he said. "You don't know what happened in there."

"Like *hell* I don't. You'd better goddamn well leave her alone tonight. The police will be here any minute to make sure you do."

"I'm not going to bother her," he said, and spat on the wet pavement. "Besides, I'm surprised you're not holed up with her yourself. She's a damned good piece of ass, isn't she, Teddy boy?" He reached in and biffed me on the shoulder. A good joke. "Yeah, you go ahead and seize the opportunity . . . fuck her just like you did last Wednesday. Honest. Be my guest. I'm through with the bitch." Then Trayn straightened up and began to laugh, his head tilted back so far I could see rain splashing off his face.

He was still laughing when I shoved the car door open and got out. Then, without hesitating, I hit him square in the mouth as hard as I could. He stumbled backward a few steps and, with blood trickling from his mouth like a movie cowboy, looked at me in disbelief. Of all things, he tried to shake my hand, and again I punched him as hard as I could. He staggered for an instant, then lunged for me and wrapped his arms around my midsection, after which he wrestled me to the ground. He sat on my chest and pressed his knees on my biceps. "You're a fool, Teddy! Listen to me, goddamnit." I freed one of my arms and tried to punch him, but he grabbed my wrist and held it against the pavement. "But I forgive you because you're my buddy and I love you."

"You're a psycho queer," I yelled. "Who but a goddamned psycho queer would go around hitting women, treating them like dirt. I bet you were in the French Quarter just now . . . getting a blow job in an alley from some poor sap."

Trayn immediately got to his feet and pulled me up. His eyes were glazed, making him look more sad than angry. "Don't go away," he said. "You're my pal." He tried again to shake my hand, but I refused. There was blood on the front of his white shirt, and in the glow of the vapor lights I could see tears glisten in his eyes.

"You're a damned sicko. That's exactly what you are. You want some advice? You ought to get some goddamned *help*." He gave me a gentle slap on the cheek and started to walk away.

I'd gotten back in my car, started the engine and put the car into gear when Trayn materialized in the glare of my headlights, hands on hips like a cartoon he-man. "Better get out of my way," I shouted. "I'm warning you!"

"Hey, Teddy boy," he yelled back, "you'd be a damn sight better screwing Janice every day and playing golf than running back to your old man. Don't be a jerk."

I suppose he was going to put his foot on my front bumper when something ignited in my brain. I hated him, I was jealous of him and I wanted to hurt him so badly his career would be over. He'd hurt Janice, humiliated her time and time again, and now my brain was just an angry cave. I stepped on the gas pedal, knowing *exactly* what would happen. He had no chance to move, and I wanted it that way. I felt the impact of my front bumper against his shins, heard his hands slap the hood as I drove him backward and pinned him against the side of his BMW. I let my back tires spin on the wet pavement when I pressed on the accelerator. He was bawling. I could see that eerie, agonized look on his face. I'd broken his legs. I knew that, and I was *glad*. It was what he deserved. I put my gearshift into reverse, eased back a few feet and got out. He was writhing on the wet asphalt. "That's for Janice!" I said, my heart beating fast inside my chest.

What happened next I can only recall in fragments. Janice ran out of the motel room. I remember her screaming at the sight of him. He was moaning, trying to get up, maybe to come after me. "Did *you* do this? Did *you* do this?" she screamed.

I guess I told her to call an ambulance. Or was it the fat woman who did that? Someone put a blanket on Trayn to keep him warm. Janice knelt next to him, lifted his head against her breast, stroked his hair. I'll never forget her stroking his hair. I felt betrayed. And I stood off to the side, waiting for the police to arrive, wondering what it *was* with Trayn and Janice.

Thirty-six

For soul-searching it's hard to beat the midnight highway when the only signs of life are semitrailer headlights bearing down on you from the oncoming lane. In the background there is the radio evangelist hungry for the souls of spiritual defectives and lonely insomniacs and night-shifters and people like me who thread their way along the Dixie interstates. Near the Kentucky border I tune in an all-night country station. Merle Haggard and "It's Not Love, But It's Not Bad." Realities swarm more fiercely in the Pacer's high beams. The music does me no good, so I snap off the radio and let my mind unravel like the road before me. I'm thinking of Frost's poem "The Road Not Taken," and how the poet seems to have lucked onto the right path in life by choosing the one that was "grassy and wanted wear." Old Mrs. McCutcheon made us memorize that poem in the eighth grade . . . "two roads diverged in a yellow wood, And sorry I could not travel both and be one traveler." I don't know why, exactly, but that poem becomes a kind of mantra as I roll northward through the dark.

Realities. Number one: I'm either a loner or simply lonely. I haven't come to any firm conclusions on that score. However, except for Drago, I don't have a true friend. Why is that? Number two: I'm in love with someone who is poison, but who can't help it and doesn't deserve to be held accountable. Three . . . four . . . five . . . all have something to do with golf, which I also love and which is *not* poison but a kind of mysterious balm capable of delivering me from grief and fear and boredom. (A waxy and poetical thought, probably due to Frost's infection of my brain.) Another reality I've shoved to the back of the list has to do with liabilities of the soul—just the sort of thing those radio preachers excavate so fervently. Traynham has his own spiritual deformities, but are they any worse than mine? And if he can't fill his life with golf, what will he do? If he were a horse they'd have to destroy him, as he's fit only for the green turf of the fairway.

Highway 71 cuts through the rocky outcrops whose scarred innards flare in the headlights. Eventually, Louisville's soft glow hovers between two distant foothills. The highway passes through the business district, where mercury lamps cast an eerie light over the buildings; the concrete roadway appears almost purple. A mileage sign for Cincinnati greets me just beyond the Redbirds' baseball stadium: 101 miles.

For the next two hours I listen to a call-in show. The subject is ostensibly gun control, but the forlorn callers fill the airwaves with rummage-sale topics ranging from homosexual concentration camps to premenstrual syndrome. The host is very patient with these people.

My stomach tightens when at last my tires roll onto the pavement of the Ohio River bridge. I'm happy as a man can be to arrive at the last real milestone of the trip, but my brain is derailed by the proximity of Janice, who now lives with her parents in Fairfield Heights. My intention has always been to cruise blithely through the city as if it didn't exist; however, when the exit sign shows bright green in my headlamps, the Pacer veers into the turn lane, glides onto the semicircular ramp and sails beneath the black tree branches that hover over Foster Boulevard. Three stoplights, a right-hand turn onto Gardenside Road, half a mile, left at the 7-Eleven, seven blocks to Bear Hollow Trail, third house on the right. Her house. A two-story colonial on a street whose trees heave up the sidewalks with their roots.

Why am I parked in front of Janice's house at 2:38 in the morning? Am I going to credit-card the front door open, neutralize the alarm system with a stream of urine, cha-cha up the padded stairs to her bedroom? Then what? A good question. I sit behind the wheel of the car for ten minutes, listening to my heart beat, knowing damned well I love her. And then, almost on cue, a light goes on in a room I think must be hers. I'm a moth, suddenly, floating on dusty wings from the door of my yellow conveyance . . . across her lawn to the shrubs below the light. The garden is covered with white gravel, a few pebbles of which I hold in the palm of my hand. Will I toss them against her window . . . like Romeo? Yes, I say, completely oblivious to what I might do if the sash is thrown open and I'm looking up into the face of Janice. Just then, a silhouette passes by the luminous window shade, but it's only her father, probably on his way to take a pee. I drop the pebbles onto the lawn and retrace my steps to the car, suddenly aware that I'm just a prowler and fair game for the local constabulary. With my criminal record, I'd be doomed to a couple of years in the slammer. I start the engine and drive away, toward my final destination.

It's five-thirty in the morning when I ease up to the curb outside the cedar barricade of Fort Stan. I'm going to have to work on him about that; thirteen months of living behind a fence is just about my limit. So as not to rouse Sally and provoke a barking frenzy, I gently close my car door just enough so that the dome light goes out. Stan will be awake soon enough. For now I'll let him sleep.

I'm a little sore from sitting behind the wheel for more than eighteen hours, but I'm not tired. The cool April air smells like ketchup, although the tomato season is months away. This familiar aroma is borne by a slight breeze that drifts between the Aldridge and Ferringer houses, beyond which looms the Heinz smokestack, black against the lavender horizon.

I know I must look pretty crazy standing in the center of the road doing jumping jacks in the fragile morning light, but there's no traffic on Fairway Avenue at this hour, so I can afford to be foolish. I flap my wings like a stork, feeling light enough to lift off into the atmosphere. I touch my toes, rotate my trunk, twirl my arms . . . When the knots have finally loosened, I unlatch the front gate as quietly as possible and step inside the fence. The yard looks exactly as it has always looked, except that at this hour the colors are washed in gray; even the folded vertical leaves of the tulips are gray. I've just about decided to go for a walk around the block when I notice a small mound of earth in one corner of the fence. Instinctively, I know what lies under the fresh, black soil, and my chest aches with sadness for Stan, who's obviously withheld the news of Sally's death, not wanting to dilute the joy of my homecoming. I find one of her soiled tennis balls at the base of the leafless buckeye tree, toss it over the roof of our house and walk through the open gate toward the golf course.

Number seventeen fairway is glazed with a silvery dew. When the moisture lifts in a few hours, it will reveal grass still in transition from straw brown to emerald green. According to the radio weather report, the temperature should climb into the high sixties, and if this trend continues, green will triumph. The forsythias flanking the tee are in full yellow bloom now, vivid in the semi-darkness.

Undaunted by my presence, crows squabble up and down number fifteen, feasting on the renegade dandelion shoots Ernsthausen will soon exterminate with a dose of Weed 'n Feed. In the high branches of the pin oaks along the rough, the first rays of sunlight outline the soft tinge of early leaves. I feel lucky to experience the arrival of spring twice in one season.

All these fairways . . . so much acreage . . . I feel as though I'm rediscovering forgotten terrain. At the border between the golf course and city park property, the prevailing westerly wind has blown trash onto the rough: deflated balloons, a hairnet, candy-bar wrappers, paper bags, Dixie cups, a tattered kite, newspapers and things that defy classification. The refuse of winter washing onto the first traces of spring. In the rising light, almost drunk on freedom, I patrol the rough, searching out even the smallest shred of paper. I put each piece of trash in a grocery bag, still greasy from somebody's fried chicken. Whenever the bag is full, I empty it into the huge black dumpster near the swimming-pool bathhouse. With a red sun poised above the distant rooftops, I return again and again, until the grass is beautiful and uncorrupted and almost green.